PARADISE BROKEN

Eco Action Adventure Novel

Empowering love

ROB MARSHALL

Paradise Broken
Copyright © 2026 by Rob Marshall

LCCN: to follow

ISBN
978-1-96665-214-4 (Hardcover)
978-1-96665-213-7 (Paperback)
978-1-972618-17-2 (eBook)

*Thank you to dearest Maree for all her support and encouragement
to help craft this novel into what it is today.*

TABLE OF CONTENTS

PROLOGUE

B rent stared out at the ocean. The sun beamed down causing the waves to sparkle as they rolled onto shore, gently lapping at his feet. He turned to his friends, excited to get the boat out into the bay so they could drop their lines.

"Ready to catch us some tea, Stevo?" Brent called as the two men worked on getting the boat into the water.

"You bet mate!" Stevo smiled.

Soon after they launched from the beach, water started to gush into the boat and they realised no one had put the bung into place. Moving quickly to rectify the situation, Brent jumped overboard and retrieved the bung which was hanging near the hole. He swiftly screwed it into place and Stevo turned on the bilge pump. Thankfully the bailers, that Brent had leapt to help his wife Janey with, were not necessary as the bilge pump did its job at quickly forcing the rogue water back into the ocean. Roger, who had sat back to keep out of the way, laughed as he captured what he found to be the more amusing parts on his camera. For nearly 20 years, the three couples; Brent and his wife Janey, Stevo and Sue, and Roger and Heather had escaped away for some quality time together on their annual summer holiday. They had already been camping for a few days, yet this was their first opportunity to get out in the boat because they hadn't been having the best weather. Roger was right in his element when he was around the camp; a day spent with his feet up and a good book in hand suited him perfectly. However, Brent knew he couldn't have endured another day stuck at camp, walking the beach and playing cards - or whatever other time fillers the women put forward. He was looking forward to a bin full of snapper - evidence of a successful day out at sea.

As they headed out across the bay the group searched to find the perfect spot to cast the lines. Brent sat at the helm while Janey poured sunscreen into the tanned skin on Brent's neck and back, kissing him as she rubbed it in.

"Cut that out you two!" Stevo exclaimed with a knowing smile, "There are other people around you know!"

Brent scoffed cheekily at Stevo's comment. "We know how much you love us Stevo."

After 25 years of marriage, Brent and Janey remained as deeply in love as the day they had married. Their many years together had seen their relationship grow from strength to strength and raising their family had filled them with great joy. Janey, Brent, and Stevo each knew they would always see themselves as the Kaimai Kids, no matter where life took them they would always be loyal to the area of New Zealand where they grew up. They stopped in a potentially good fishing spot and Brent cast his line into the ocean. With one smooth movement nylon peeled off his reel and it wasn't long before the snapper began to bite. Stevo hauled in a decent sized fish while Janey struggled with the weight of whatever it was she had managed to snag. Her slim body was bent over the line, and Brent admired how her regular physical activity on the farm which kept her fit. There wasn't a single cloud in the sky which meant the pictures Roger was taking were set to be gorgeous.

CHAPTER ONE

As the rickety old school bus turned the corner, it shuddered over corrugations and pot holes formed in the metal road due to only seeing a grader once in a blue moon. Huge plumes of dust billowed from behind the bus.

Brent was nervous as he saw it approaching his driveway. His mother had been taking him to school for his first four weeks, leading him into his classroom with his little hand encased by hers, but now he had get used to the bus he would be required to catch for the rest of his school life.

"You'll be fine, Brent," reassured his mum as she hugged him tight. "Janey is catching the bus today as well and it is only her first day at school."

Sniffling but trying to be brave Brent replied, "Ok, see you this afternoon."

Brent knew that Bill Webber, the bus driver who had overseen this run for longer than anyone could remember, was proud to know every kid on the road—and all the ones who were about to start school too.

"Good morning, young fellow. You must be Brent," said Bill.

Brent, a timid five-year-old, just nodded while looking up the steps in amazement at the man who had spoken.

"You can sit here, Brent," Bill directed, grinning at Brent as he pointed to a single seat next to him. "You are first on the bus, so you get the best seat. There's another youngster starting today, just up the road a bit," Bill said.

Brent smiled. "Yes, sir. That's Janey. Her parents are friends with my Mum and Dad. Janey and me, we always ride our ponies together, and we get to go eeling when Dad takes us. She is going to go to my school too, but I've been there longer 'cos I'm bigger than her."

Janey was waiting patiently by her gate. As soon as the doors were fully open, she clambered her way onto the bus quickly.

"Hello, Janey," Brent piped up.

"Hi, Brent" came Janey's soft voiced reply.

Bill intercepted. "You must be Janey. Brent just told me how you were starting on the bus today."

"Yes, that's right, Mr. Webber. Our mums wanted us to catch the bus together."

"I am looking forward to getting to know you. I try to learn about all the kids who take this big old bus every day. You sit right here, pet, near the front, just behind Brent," Bill kindly offered. "We will be doing lots of travelling together."

It took roughly an hour and a half for the bus to arrive at school after picking up all the other children. As the bus pulled up outside the school gate, Bill warned the older children, "When you get off the bus, please make sure you don't knock Brent and Janey over as you get down."

Bill looked warmly at Brent and Janey, "I will see you here at ten minutes past three, you two. Enjoy your day, kids!"

A teacher was waiting at the gate to greet the new bus children, making sure each had managed to get to school safely. She had promised both children's mothers that she would help for the first few days by seeing that the two children made their way from the front gate to their classrooms.

The loud school bell rang at ten minutes past three, indicating the end of the school day. Children began running in every direction towards waiting parents or the waiting buses.

Bill Webber saw Janey approaching the bus with a worried look on her face. As she struggled to get up the large steps, Bill looked up and down the long line of kids ready to board. Brent was not in the line.

"Have you seen young Brent, Janey?" he asked the small girl.

She was on the verge of tears. "No, Mr. Webber. I don't know where he went when we left the classroom."

"Don't worry, sweetheart. I won't go without him."

"Maybe he went to play with his friend on the field," Janey offered. "They were late to class after lunch because they were playing a game out there. He might have forgotten all about catching the bus."

"I'll go and see if I can find him," Bill reassured her as he swiftly jumped off the bus in a movement only one who has done so a thousand times could manage.

"Thanks, Mr Webber," called Janey.

Bill wandered through the school grounds to the field where, sure enough, Brent and his friend were passing a ball around. Brent was so engrossed in his next big kick that when Bill tapped him sharply on the shoulder, the young boy jumped.

"Hey, Brent, you are meant to be on the bus!"

Brent turned around to face Bill with a mingled look of shock and regret. "Oh, I'm sorry, Mr. Webber. I forgot Mum wasn't picking me up today. I just really wanted to play with Stevo!"

Bill smiled. "That's OK, but tomorrow you must wait at the front gate for the bus—as soon as the bell rings! The bus can't wait for you everyday."

"Yes, Mr. Webber."

Brent turned to his friend. "See ya tomorrow, Stevo. I've got to go and catch my bus!"

Stevo shouted back to Brent, "I gotta run too, or Mum will growl at me. We only live down the road and I am supposed to go straight home!"

Stevo's voice was cut off by the wind as he ran farther across the freshly mowed grass. Stevo had started school just two days after Brent yet the pair had already become inseparable. They both loved being outside, and their teacher sure had her work cut out in keeping them on task in the classroom. Stevo wasn't at all keen on reading and writing, but he absolutely loved sport. Brent put his heart and soul into whatever he was doing and it wasn't unusual for him to become so engrossed in whatever he was doing that he often forgot the other things happening around him.

The bus with the two five-year olds arrived at Janey's gate just before 4.35pm - first on in the morning and last off each evening made for a very long day. Brent and Janey's mothers were waiting for them.

"Thank you, Mr. Webber," the children called together.

"Home for us, I think Brent. I know two children who will be in bed very early tonight," laughed his mother.

"See you tomorrow, Janey," called Brent as he climbed into his Mum's car.

"Yeah, see you in the morning Brent!" replied Janey with a happy wave.

CHAPTER TWO

Stevo's family lived and worked in town where they ran the one and only auto workshop. He loved coming out to the country to stay with Brent. His parents were grateful to Brent's family who had him to stay so often - even though Brent's parents felt they hardly ever saw the boys. The minute Stevo arrived at the farm, the boys would tear out of the house and head for the great outdoors. The boys loved to be out climbing trees, building forts, running races, swimming in the creek, making mudslides, or eeling and catching kouras - which they then would boil up in the little billy Brent had received for his previous birthday, alongside his camping set. They loved damming little creeks with rocks, riding horses or bikes – anything to do with the outdoors and always with little Janey in tow. Stevo was happiest out at Brent's farm, his parents were always busy with the auto shop, and the highway near his house meant there were no safe places for Stevo to ride his bike or play. Stevo became like another son to Brent's parents.

Brent's father and mother loved horses, trekking as often as they could. Brent's mother's passion for horses had rubbed onto Brent who learned horse care and riding skills at an early age. Stevo and Brent would spend hours in the stables helping her and riding the horses. Brent's family had bought their horses, broken in, from friends living near the East Cape. These horses were renowned for their sure- footedness, excellent temperaments, and responsiveness. They were friendly horses and a pleasure to catch and handle. The piebald mare was their prized horse; a very red, chestnut mare standing 16 hands high; quite big for a coasty mare.

When the three children weren't exploring Brent's farm, they could often be found over on Janey's property. Janey's parents were share milking on a dairy farm. They had worked hard and saved up to buy their own cows. This was the herd that they milked on the boss's farm, meaning they could then share the profits. The kids did their best to help in the busiest times, especially during calving season. The children would mix the milk powder for the weaned calves and fill the bottles with the colostrum for the newborns. The boys always laughed at Janey because she would sing and talk while she fed the young calves, thinking they could understand her.

The three children also loved going over to Quade Daniel's farm, situated right next to Brent's family's lifestyle block. There was a stream running through the bottom of Quade's farm and the kids had spent hours damming it up to create a water hole that soon became popular with all the kids in the community during the long hot summer holidays. Wild flowers grew along the banks of the stream, flourishing when the weather conditions were right.

Janey and Brent continued to catch the bus to school throughout their primary school years and in many ways, they became like brother and sister; always looking out for each other.

As Janey climbed onto the bus one day, she whispered to old Bill Webber who was close to retiring, "Today is Brentie's birthday."

Brent got annoyed when she called him Brentie so she often did it to get a rise out of him.

Bill smiled as he turned to Brent, "Happy birthday, young Brent, you must be thirteen now? I thought it was your special day today. It seems like only yesterday that you first rode to school on my bus."

"Thanks Mr. Webber. Yep, I am thirteen now!"

Bill who wood carved as a hobby, had carved a little horse especially for Brent. He handed it to the birthday boy, who was both surprised and genuinely touched by the gift, "Thanks very much, Mr. Webber! It's really cool."

"That's okay, young Brent, enjoy your day!" nodded Mr. Webber. "Wow, that's cool," exclaimed Janey.

She turned and gave Brent a wee hug, whispering, "Happy birthday, Brentie," as she climbed into the seat next to him.

The following day, Brent took one look at Janey as she boarded the bus and knew there was something seriously wrong. He could see her eyes were red rimmed and her usual smile wasn't there. He had only seen her look this sad once before, and that was when her grandfather had died a few years earlier.

"What's wrong?" he asked worriedly, as he moved over, pointing to the empty seat next to him for her to sit on.

"We are moving to a farm quite a way away from here," squeaked Janey, close to tears.

"What?!" exclaimed Brent. "When was that decided? When are you going? You can't leave!"

"Well," Janey replied meekly. "Mum and Dad have been talking about moving for a while, but I thought we would still be in the area. But they got a really good deal on a farm - so we are moving on the first of June. They have wanted to buy their own farm for so long and finally they're able to."

"We will still be able to see each other, won't we?" Brent begged, not believing the depth of his despair at Janey's news.

She had been his best friend for most of his life. He didn't want Janey to see how he was feeling - he could see she was already feeling bad enough.

"I guess we will just have to make the most of these next few months," Janey decided.

"Wait until I tell Stevo. He'll be gutted," laughed Brent in a desperate attempt to cover his own feelings.

"Yeah, whatever," Janey grimaced with a half smile.

Bill had overheard their conversation. "That is exciting for your family. But you will all be missed in our community."

"Aww thanks, Mr. Webber," Janey blushed. "Right now I don't even want to *think* about going away."

"Me either," whispered Brent sadly.

"Mum says I will start at a new school for a few months, then change to high school," Brent heard her say.

"It will be so strange finishing school without you," Brent finally managed to say as he turned to stare out the window.

The months slipped by, one adventure seemed to just melt into the next. By the end of May, when most mornings meant a thick layer of fog stretched across the farmland like a crisp blanket, Janey and her family moved to their new farm.

The morning of her departure, Brent sped over to the farm with a little bunch of wildflowers he had picked for her from the banks of Quade's farm. Janey threw herself at Brent, sobbing as she begged him to promise to always keep in touch.

Brent promised they would be friends forever, but he just couldn't grasp the magnitude of his feelings for Janey McIntyre. He had always imagined her to be nothing more than a friend, but that afternoon as the truck pulled away with the last of their belongings and Janey waving sadly out the back window of her father's car, Brent realised he had never been so devastated in all his life.

Some stroke of fate meant the McIntyre's new farm was right next to that of a couple who had been friends with Brent's parents for years. The couple had a daughter who was one year older than Brent and Janey. One weekend, not long after Janey and the rest of her family had moved, Brent went with his parents to visit their friends and the McIntyre's new farm. Brent raced over to see Janey the minute his parents pulled up at their friend's place. He knocked loudly on the door and was immediately greeted with a warm hug from Janey. She grabbed his hand and they ran outside to explore the new farm.

"It's just not the same at home without you – on the bus, at school and hanging out at the weekend," Brent sighed, kicking at the grass as he walked.

"Yeah, I know what you mean," Janey sighed. "The girl next door is okay - but she's not you, Brent."

Brent looked up into Janey's eyes and the two friends shared a thoughtful moment, broken only when one of the farm dogs started barking loudly.

"I guess we will have to write letters, and call each other whenever we can," decided Janey.

"Yeah, and you can come stay during the holidays," Brent thought aloud to which Janey nodded enthusiastically. "Good idea, let's go and ask our parents."

Brent and Janey were able to keep in regular contact through their letters, and the occasional phone call throughout their teenage years. Their parents approved of the holiday stays, as they knew how close the children had become over the years. Most school holidays, Janey would catch a bus to Brent's house and they would spend their time outdoors either on the farm, out fishing, swimming in the creek, or surfing at the ocean beach. Stevo often came to stay at Brent's during the holidays too as the trio loved helping on the farm and meeting up with friends up the road after a long day. They would often go down to the stream where they would light a fire, have a barbecue, and spend hours laughing with each other. Each day they would squeeze in as many outdoor adventures as they possibly could, always wishing for just one extra hour before the sun slipped behind the hills, leaving the valleys cloaked in a thick blanket of stars.

When the three found themselves in the 6th form, Janey wanted to go to her school ball. She approached Brent with the idea of being her partner.

"Absolutely not," scoffed Brent. "I won't know anyone there!" "Well, I had thought of that actually…" Janey paused to see if she had caught Brent's attention. "You see, my friend really needs a date too. So I was thinking, you could be my partner and Stevo could go with my friend!"

"You really want to go to this ball?"

"Oh yes Brent, it's all everyone at school is talking about. Just think, we never get dressed up for an adventure outside the gates of the farm!"

Brent smiled at the idea. "Sure Janey, let's do it!"

On the night of the school ball, Brent's parents took the boys over to the McIntyre's farm. Janey was in her room when Brent and Stevo arrived. When she finally came out of her room, Brent's jaw dropped to the floor. Her blonde hair framed her doll like face, while the pale blue dress made her skin glow. Her adolescent years being nearly over had left her with breasts and hips that filled the dress to perfection.

Brent held his breath as he handed her a pale-yellow flower corsage, and he was struck with the realization of how lucky he was to have this beautiful girl as his very best friend.

Throughout their final school years, Brent and Stevo spent a lot of their spare time hunting pigs and deer. Brent liked to say they were freelancing, purely because he didn't want his father to think they were poaching. Fences and boundaries meant little to them as they always wanted to see what was over the next ridge. Brent's father received a couple of phone calls from neighbours - each suspecting the boys had been in places where they shouldn't have been, but nobody could ever pin anything on them. Brent and Stevo knew their local area like the back of their hands and were avid night hunters as they loved spotlighting deer, pigs, and possums. They made good money by selling possum skins, as well as cashing in on the occasional deer or pig. They walked for miles up hill and down dale just to get to their favourite hunting spots. At night it was a different world, due to the vast number of nocturnal animals that aren't seen during daylight. They often stopped for a rest after climbing a steep hill, lying flat on their backs to gaze up at the stars.

"Millions of stars," Brent would always say.

Stevo would stare up at the Milky Way to find Venus, Orion's belt, the Devil's Pot, and the Southern Cross, while searching for any other visible planets or constellations. Often shooting stars sped across the night sky, and while enjoying a moment to relax after a long night of hunting, Brent would always make some remark to Stevo about how amazing it all was. It never ceased to amaze him. The two friends were true outdoorsmen, happiest when they were out amongst nature. During their teenage years, they had to set themselves a time limit when they ventured out spotlighting, trying not to stay out later than midnight. They knew they couldn't perform at school if they were too tired. If they got any game on a late hunt, Brent would sort out the dressing of it before school the next morning. They got great pleasure from filling the freezers of their families and friends.

The boys also enjoyed going fishing and hunting down the Coast. They had part time work while in their last two years of high school. Stevo had saved up enough money to buy himself an old Toyota Hilux.

They clocked up the kilometres by driving out to their favourite fishing and hunting spots. Always looking for an adventure, they would take their dogs up the rivers to hunt pigs and deer, and when not at school they spent many days fishing the coast. Their local area had lots of hunting and fishing areas, perfect for the two outdoor-loving young men to be living near. They worked hard and they played hard, finding they had burnt the candle at both ends most weekends.

Upon leaving school, Brent got a full-time job working for Quade Daniels on the farm next door to his parent's block. It wasn't long before Brent moved in to live with him. Quade was generously helping him to get his own herd together, by giving him 20 calves a year as a bonus, if Brent worked hard and raised Quade's calves well. Brent's parents had bred a beautiful mare from their own chestnut mare, which they had kindly given to Brent when he began his full-time employment for Quade. Years earlier they had wanted to give him a horse of his own, and their advertising led them to find a stallion in their area with all the qualities they were looking for to mate their chestnut red mare with. The stallion's mother had been bred down the East Coast, and its father was an American quarter horse, thorough bred cross. The stallion had a good temperament and was a very sure-footed horse. Brent's Mum mated her mare with the stallion. The mare had a filly, which Brent's mother lovingly reared and broke in.

Brent was hoping Quade would take him on as a share-milker when the time was right.

Stevo found himself a job with the contractors building a dam for a Hydro Scheme. Stevo loved this physical work and enjoyed being able to drive all sorts of large machines. He especially enjoyed the team environment, making great mates with some of the other hard- working men. Stevo and Brent both enjoyed the social aspects involved as Brent would often join Stevo and the men he worked with for a few drinks together after a hard day's work.

Janey had decided to train as a nurse and found herself with very little time to socialize. She tried to spend as much time with the boys on the weekend as she could. They all led very busy lives - working and socialising. The friendship between Brent and Janey grew from strength to strength.

The boys never went out looking for trouble, however, it often managed to find them. Brent and Stevo ended up in quite a few fights - none of their own doing. They weren't keen on starting fights, but they refused to back off when they were challenged. Brent knew that as soon as he or Stevo became involved, there was no way they would stand down. He didn't know why he had a deep desire for revenge after something was started - it could have been due to being dealt an overdose of pride when he was born, or from frustration caused by too much testosterone. Despite the reason, Brent and Stevo had their own rules about what was right, and they would always stand up for their beliefs. If the situation led to a fight, then so be it.

Brent had developed into a young man who chose to spend his time hunting and fishing rather than chasing girls. The only girl he had ever found himself able to relax with was Janey. Stevo was a bit of a lady's man who had never held onto a steady girlfriend for long, choosing to play the field instead. Stevo found himself wondering if he too loved Janey, conscious he could never say anything because of the strong love he could see Brent and Janey had for each other. However, there were times he felt jealous pangs rip through his body, worsened by the knowledge that he could never let those feelings affect their friendship. Their late teenage years were spent hanging out in their local pub, where they made some good friends amongst the many new people they met. Brent and Janey continued to have a strong friendship, which soon blossomed into a mature relationship. Stevo was always good company, and his quick wit certainly kept every one of his companions entertained. He used to invite girls he knew to go out with them but found no one sparked his interest to the extent where he wanted to take the relationship further. One night they went to a dance at the hospital nurse's home where Janey lived. There were a great number of lovely girls there, but no matter how many Janey introduced Stevo to, he remained uninterested. He resigned himself to the fact that when the time was right, he would know if it was meant to be. He and Brent still managed to go hunting and fishing often, but Stevo secretly felt that it wasn't quite the same now that Janey came along whenever she could.

Janey rang Brent one evening.

"Hi, I've been invited to the 21st of one of the girls who was in my class at high school. Do you and Stevo want to come? I asked the birthday girl if Stevo would be able to come so he could be our sober driver."

"Sounds great," Brent replied. "Will be good to meet some of the people you went to school with."

During the evening, Brent glanced up as a group of people came in the door. Big Sam, whom Janey had also been at high school with, was amongst the group of newcomers. He came over to Janey and they talked for ages. Big Sam wrapped an arm around Janey's shoulder. Brent tried his best to ignore the attention Big Sam was giving Janey, until he saw him try to kiss her on the cheek. Big Sam had already sunk a few drinks, leaving Brent concerned about what might happen next as Janey hadn't seemed to mind the attention she was getting until Big Sam kissed her. A worried look flashed her face, and Brent heard her tell him to stop. Big Sam kept his arm around her, oblivious to what she was saying.

Brent thought he had better intervene.

"Take your hands off her, right now … Did you not hear what Janey just said?" Brent spoke quietly, not wanting to make a scene.

Big Sam pushed Brent on the shoulder, jarring him back into the wall directly behind him. Brent didn't retaliate, until Big Sam taunted, "Oh, are you gutless mate?"

Brent laughed. "Step outside and we'll see who's gutless."

Brent was eyeing up the end of Big Sam's chin. Brent glanced at Stevo with a look that said all hell was about to break loose. Brent took a big swing, landing the punch directly on Sam's chin and sending him flying. It was one of the biggest punches Stevo had ever seen Brent throw, and as Sam spiraled backwards, Stevo watched as Big Sam's head hit the concrete. Sam lay still. He was no match for Brent, due to both Brent's natural ability and his extreme fitness from years of farm work.

Janey screamed at Brent. "Stop it! Stop!! Brent, stop! We don't want any fighting. One punch is one too many."

Brent was watching to see what Big Sam would do next. Stevo went over to where Big Sam was lying to check he wasn't too badly injured, "Janey, you stay with Brent, I'll help this other guy." He held out an arm to Big Sam.

"Sorry about my mate. I don't know what came over him. Let's go and have a few beers and put this all behind us."

Not sure what would happen next Brent watched carefully as Stevo helped Sam up. Brent felt Big Sam deserved the punch due to slinging so many insults but he was wary of retaliation.

"Sorry mate," Big Sam held out a strong hand to Brent. "I just wanted to catch up with her. I haven't seen her since we left school. My mouth ran away on me."

"It didn't look like Janey wanted your attention. You were really insulting," replied Brent with a fake smile.

"Yeah, I guess I got a bit carried away. Sorry, mate."

They shook hands and did their best to put the fight behind them - in the way only men are ever able to do. As the evening continued, Brent eventually lightened up on Big Sam and they all thoroughly enjoyed the party as they quickly discovered they shared many common interests.

The 21st had also shown Brent just how much he loved Janey. She was his very best friend and had been ever since that first day of school all those years ago. He knew she was the one he wanted to spend the rest of his life with. Brent decided the day would come soon when he would take Janey down to his special spot, the one by the stream where he, Janey, and Stevo had built the dam that created their swimming hole when they were younger. When Brent was working, he often went and sat there to have his lunch. The birds would be chirping in the tall trees while Brent watched the clear water trickle it's way merrily down the stream. Ducks and swans enjoyed a lazy swim and flew only briefly to get over the makeshift speed bump; the walls of the dam. English oak trees stood proudly along the side of the stream, providing a lovely sense of serenity amidst the busyness of the farm. Across the stream was a backdrop of native bush where the Rimu, Totara, and Kauri reached proudly into the sky. On the nearby bank, Brent enjoyed looking out for the wild flowers that grew. He had developed a sixth sense about them over the years and called them his magic flowers. He always knew that when they started to sprout, with their multi- coloured faces pushing up through the soil as they reached for the sunshine, that the grass too would begin to grow. Brent had observed how if the wild flowers had a good flowering season, the grass would also grow well. And if the flowers didn't bloom particularly well, the grass wouldn't either. Brent wasn't overly superstitious, but he intrinsically believed his time spent down by the creek lunching, swimming, weeding, or looking after the flowers, was very precious time. He often took down dry cow dung so that he could fertilise the wildflowers to keep them healthy. He gave them water to keep the moisture around their roots, as the sandy soil always dried out badly during the summer. He always felt the flowers responded to his care. Over the years he'd felt a sense of not being alone whenever he was down by the stream and he was convinced there was more to these flowers. It was as if they loved having someone around, tending to them, talking to them, and caring for them. Brent often wondered if they got lonely, all the way down by the stream at the back of the farm. He imagined that someone would have once cared for them - back before they were dumped down in loads of topsoil. He swore to himself that no matter what happened, he would always come to look after the wildflowers. He knew Janey would grow to love them too, especially when she returned with him to the stream and remembered the adventures of many years ago.

It was here that he would ask Janey to make him the happiest man in the world; if she would be his wife for the rest of their lives.

CHAPTER THREE

One sunny weekend, when the cloudless blue sky stretched its way across the green grass, Brent packed a picnic basket and took Janey down to the stream. As they sat nestled together amongst Brent's wildflowers, Brent said, "I reckon these flowers are magic. They have amazing colours when things are going well and last for age in a vase. If things are not good, they just die when they are picked. He knew his belief in the magic qualities of the wild flowers expressed his sensitive side, and like most typical kiwi blokes, he didn't want to be mocked by his mates for being a softie. In his heart, he knew the strength of his love and passion for Janey was infinite. He knew it could never be rivaled. He realised the only other thing he felt so passionate about, that came anywhere close to his feelings for Janey, was his trust in the power of the wild flowers. His certainty in their magic was evident as he described their existence to Janey. Brent explained how she was the first person he had ever shared his convictions about the flowers with, to which Janey laughed nervously. He was slightly embarrassed, his checks flushed as he looked down at the grass under his feet, hanging over the edge of the red-and-white-checkered picnic blanket. Janey noticed her oldest friends shift in energy.

"You really are serious, aren't you?"

Brent looked up at his girlfriend with a smile.

"Yes. I have a special feeling about these flowers, and it gets stronger and stronger the more time that passes."

Janey looked around at the wildflowers growing along the riverbank, noticing how rich and deep their colours were.

"Well Brent, the soil here just suits perfectly what these flowers need to flourish. And I can see you have an electric fence along the bank to stop the cattle from getting near the stream or damaging the flowers."

"Yes, I like looking after them."

Janey asked, "Do you know why the flowers grow here?"

"Well, I think that years ago, Quade must have put a few loads of topsoil from an old house site along here, beside the stream, to help stop erosion. I reckon the bulbs would have already been in the soil. The grass was smothering them, so I cleared the grass away, put up the fence, and have been looking after them ever since. They have flourished since I have been looking after them. Oh, and I planted the rose here. It was growing up by the old house site - which only has the concrete chimney still standing now. I thought it would look good amongst the wild flowers and it was struggling to survive where it was growing. It must have been cared for once because it is doing really well now. I prune the rose when it needs it. It is a Rosenfee according to Quade, he knows a lot about flowers, especially roses."

Brent stopped talking, thinking and realizing he was probably boring Janey as she didn't necessarily share his passion for the wildflowers. Janey surprised him by smiling broadly and opening her arms widely, as if to fill her being with as much of the surroundings as she possibly could.

"Oh Brent, it is all just so gorgeous, and the deep red rose blooms are absolutely magnificent. They are quite stunning, and their fragrance is something else. This rose is the essence of scented beauty!"

"Just like you, Janey," whispered Brent as he ran his hand through her soft hair. Janey put her hands on his face pulling him towards her, kissing his lips.

She sighed elatedly as she spoke.

"Oh, this is so wonderful Brent, I am here in this lovely field with you, by this absolutely pristine stream with all of these beautiful magical flowers, and that incredible rose. Everything is just amazing." Brent's commitment to caring for the flowers had genuinely impressed Janey. They lay there together, soaking up the sun and cherishing the moment. Brent thought about the extraordinarily good growth of the magic flowers this year. They had bloomed for months, and with a greater depth to their colours than ever before. He felt as if they were displaying all their majesty for Janey and himself, as if they knew what he was planning to do.

Brent's voice came soft but strong.

"I think these flowers are an omen. When we get married, I would love you to carry a bouquet of them. When we are trying for our first child, we will pick some of them. If they last well in the vase, I know all will be well with the baby."

Brent could see that Janey was taken aback by his seriousness. "You mean, you want to marry me?" she whispered as she stared into his eyes.

"Yes," answered Brent. In one swift movement he managed to both sit up and drop to one knee directly in front of her. "Janey, will you be my wife?"

In his heart, Brent knew Janey was his true love. He had never met anyone who could have him feeling so excited, simply by the thought of seeing her. Nor had he known anyone who made him want to share his innermost thoughts, secrets, fears, and dreams. He had shown his softer side on many occasions but never quite in this way, with the tenderness in his voice as he spoke of the magic flowers. Janey was Brent's first friend, his very best friend, and he could not imagine a life without her by his side.

"I would love to be your wife, darling Brent," Janey answered, as the smiles instantly spread across both of their faces. He reached out towards a beautiful red new rose bud, easily breaking it free from the Rosenfee bush with his strong hands. As he passed the rose to Janey she looked deep into his eyes and whispered, "Brent, these flowers can be our love flowers as well."

Brent kissed Janey softly on her lips before pulling her body towards him and holding her tightly.

"Yes," he murmured into her ear, "this is definitely our flower of love, with its beautiful red-hot colour, exactly how my heart feels for you, Janey."

The beaming smiles stretched from ear to ear on both of their faces.

"Oh, Brent," giggled Janey as her fiancé pulled her down towards the checkered picnic blanket. "You definitely believe in the mysterious - and that is exciting!"

The wildflowers waved gently in the breeze, their colours appearing even more vibrant than they had just moments before.

CHAPTER FOUR

They happily shared the news of their engagement with Quade. "Wow, that is great news," he beamed. "How would you like to share milk on my farm? I know you will make great dairy farmers."

"Are you serious, Quade?" queried Brent.

"Never been more serious, just like you about this wonderful lady," smiled Quade.

"That is an amazing opportunity. We would love to share milk on your farm," exclaimed Brent.

Six months later, they were married. They all worked hard to ensure the continued success of their beloved farm.

Janey and Brent had always adored children, and they decided they would love to have a big family. A few months after their wedding day, Janey suspected she might be pregnant. Because of Brent's strong belief in the magic of the flowers that continued to grow down by the river, she went down to the river to pick a bunch. The flowers lasted in the vase for weeks, blooming brightly.

Eight months later, Daniel, who they named after Quade Daniels, was born. He was a strong, healthy baby boy who blossomed in the country air. While Daniel was young, Brent and Stevo would still go out fishing and hunting together, even though Brent wasn't keen to go away as often. Eugene was born eighteen months later, and Janey had again picked a bunch of wild flowers when she thought she might be pregnant. Like Daniel's bunch, Eugene's also lasted for weeks. If Brent bought flowers in town to give Janey, they would only ever last a week at the most. The length of time the magic flowers bloomed for would vary.

Janey was always quite anxious if the flowers wilted quickly, especially if they had been picked for a family occasion. There was a marriage in the neighbourhood that many were dubious about as the couple didn't seem very well suited. Janey picked some flowers on the couple's wedding day, only to find the flowers had wilted the very next day. The bouquet looked as if the vase had been hit with an overdose of roundup! Brent and Janey were not at all surprised when they discovered that the marriage lasted just six months.

One hot summery day, Brent looked up from working in a paddock nearby the river as Janey walked past.

"Hi, love. Where are you going?"

"I'm going to pick some wild flowers, I think I might be pregnant again," she grinned at Brent. He let out a shout of joy and ran over to Janey. He hugged her tightly and spun her around, "That's awesome news."

They walked the rest of the way to the stream hand in hand. They picked a large bunch of bright coloured flowers. As they were walking back to the house, a large gust of wind came and whipped the flowers right out of Janey's hand. Brent rushed around picking them up, ensuring none were left on the grass. He glanced awkwardly at Janey.

'Where did that gust of wind come from on a still day like this?' They took the flowers home and gently put them into a vase. The following morning, Janey woke up with a terrible pain in her stomach. They called Brent's mum and asked her to come and sit with the boys while they rushed to the doctor. Unfortunately, there was nothing the doctor could do; she had already miscarried the baby. Janey was admitted to hospital, and when Brent returned home he was astonished to find that every single one of the wildflowers had died in the vase. Tears began to stream down his face, he couldn't believe that he and Janey had lost their child before it had been given a chance at life. He grabbed the vase holding the dead wildflowers and threw it hard, watching as the pieces smashed all over the ground.

"You are not my magic flowers any more!" he screamed at the shattered mess.

The following day, when Brent collected Janey from the hospital he decided to tell her about the flowers. He explained how he felt they had lost their magic. Janey, with tears pouring from her eyes, turned to Brent and whispered, "Maybe they are magic, Brent. They were trying to tell us something. Remember when they blew out of my hand? That never happened with the other two. Maybe they really did know there was something not right with this baby."

Brent knew how Janey desperately wanted a daughter so he tried to comfort her as best he could.

"We'll try again when you are well. Don't worry Janey, we've got plenty of time. Our boys are young and we have only just begun our married life together. Five years of happiness and lots more to come." The loss of their baby seemed to only strengthen Brent and Janey's relationship. They continued to run the farm successfully, buying the farm from the estate when Quade passed away. They named their new property Rosenfee Farm - after their love flower. Brent felt that Quade would have liked the new name, as he also enjoyed going down to the stream to admire the flowers. He had always been proud of how Brent tended to them, often complimenting Brent with how well the flowers were doing.

Brent and Janey kept trying to increase the size of their family, but for about four years they found their efforts to be unsuccessful. They gradually accepted they would instead be grateful for their two healthy boys who had become the great joy of their lives. Daniel, even as a toddler, had the knack of sorting out problems between his brother and their playmates. He idolised policemen and was determined to be a cop when he grew up. Just when life seemed to have settled into a pattern for them, Janey discovered she was pregnant again. She was very nervous and anxious but couldn't wait to tell Brent.

"I can't believe it, just when we had given up," smiled Brent through happy tears, grabbing Janey by the hand as they rushed down to the stream to pick a large bunch of their wildflowers. Brent put them carefully in a vase where they went on to bloom for weeks, confirming for them that all would be well with their baby.

Eight years after Brent and Janey had Daniel, Janey gave birth to a beautiful, healthy, wee girl who they named Ingrid. Stevo was really pleased for his friends. He was an honorary favourite uncle to the children, as he had always been more like a brother than a friend to Janey and Brent. He loved spending time with the family at the farm, taking the children eeling or fishing and sharing many meals with them all.

CHAPTER FIVE

Brent and Stevo went on a hunting trip during the roar. The roar happens around the beginning of April each year when stags scent out cycling hinds and essentially spend their time marking out their territory, roaring, mating and defending their harem against other stags.

The men had spent a successful week at one of their favourite hunting spots where they retrieved a ten-point stag. On their way home, they had decided to stop in at a bar for a celebratory drink - before Brent knew what was happening, Stevo was chatting up the barmaid. Brent sat quietly at their table, watching him work his magic with the barmaid who was laughing and toying with her long locks of blonde hair. Brent noticed how Stevo had become so entranced by the barmaid he had to drag himself away from her to make his way over to Brent with a huge smile upon his face.

"Hey mate. Sorry for leaving you alone for so long. I think I finally know how you feel about Janey. This lady, Sue, she's amazing! She usually lives in our area, but is down here on a working holiday. She is between jobs, and her parents live here, so she thought she would come and stay with them for a while and work while she decides what to do next. She has applied for a secretary's job with a shipping company and is now just waiting to see if she gets the job." Stevo paused for a breath before launching into more rapidfire talk about Sue. "I really hope she does because then she will come back up north - I want to start dating her. I feel as if I have known her all my life, even though we have just met!"

Brent looked at Stevo, and realised he had never seen this side of Stevo before. He had always scoffed at the idea of love at first sight, but he could tell Stevo was for real - and the look on Sue's face was equally as happy.

"I'm happy for you bro, must be fate that we stopped in here on our way home." Brent realised how close he felt to Stevo, and was honoured his best friend had shared his feelings about Sue so openly and honestly.

"I feel that way too mate, Sue is the real deal!" The men stayed longer than they had planned to so Stevo could spend more time chatting with Sue. When it was finally time to leave, Sue and Stevo embraced as if they couldn't let each other go. Stevo had written down Sue's address and phone number and Brent observed how Stevo held tightly to the piece of paper the entire way home, intent on not letting it go.

Stevo laughed as he exclaimed, "Hey, this is a shock! I guess this hunting trip might have turned out to be more successful than we had originally thought."

CHAPTER SIX

Sue didn't end up getting the job she had applied for but made the move north anyway. Sue had immediately felt the same way for Stevo as he felt for her. She picked up work in bars for a few months, and then Janey, who still had contacts at the hospital even though she had given up nursing, managed to find her a job in the office. Sue and Stevo soon became inseparable and began living together within a very short time. It was obvious to everyone who knew them that they had a genuine connection.

The couple often joined up with Sue's sister, Heather, and her husband, Roger, who also lived in the same area. Heather and Roger had been married for five years and had two children; one girl and one boy. Roger worked as a professional photographer and he owned his own photography business in the city. Heather had trained as a teacher and had taught in primary schools before she and Roger had their family. The three couples, Brent and Janey, Sue and Stevo, Roger and Heather made fast friends. One one occasion, they sat at Rosenfee enjoying a late summer bbq. Heather asked about the horses as she had always been a very capable horsewoman, enjoying both dressage and show jumping.

Brent smiled, "You won't believe it, I bred from a red mare my mother gave me years back The strong chesnut red gene came through the breeding line and the foal was the spitting image of his mother. I named him Big Red and he is the strongest most powerful horse I know – you will all have to come ride him sometime!"

Roger looked around, his eyes wide with fear. "Uh, no thanks Brent. I like to admire horses through a camera lens, not so much of a rider."

Stevo laughed, "You're such a townie Roger, we will make a farm boy out of you yet!"

One night Stevo's phone rang.

"Hi mate, haven't seen you for ages. How are you?" It was Stevo's mate, Ricky. "There's a pig hunting comp this week. Wondered if you want to check it out."

"Hi, Ricky. Yeah, long time, no see," answered Stevo. "I've got work this weekend but might come to see the weigh in."

"Cool, Spider is hunting in the comp. Hopefully he'll get a big poaka! Would be good to see him take home a prize. I'm not able to hunt either but will be going to the weigh in," replied Ricky.

"Awesome, haven't seen Spider in a while. Sue and I will pick you up to go to the weigh in. No point taking two cars. I'll see if Brent wants to come too," said Stevo.

"Sounds great, see you on Saturday," said Ricky.

Ricky's brother, James was known as Spider. He had received the nickname Spider from his freaky ability to climb anything – bluffs, cliffs, trees - you name it and Spider could climb it. Sue had just bought herself a new car. As soon as Stevo mentioned the idea of an afternoon out, Sue had jumped at the chance to take her new car.

"Cool babe," smiled Stevo. "Hopefully Brent will be able to come as well. The cows are dry at the moment so he won't be milking tomorrow. He and Janey have just come home from a few days at the beach, but he might be able to get away."

Stevo called Brent, who also thought it sounded like a great idea. Janey was still busy sorting things out from their holiday, and the kids were enjoying being home so they wouldn't want another day out, but Brent assured Stevo he would come.

"Are you sure you want to take your car, Sue?" asked Stevo when he hung up the phone.

"Sure do! It hasn't had a long run yet, you can test its power!"

At 11am the following day, they arrived at Brent's to pick him up. After picking up Ricky, as they traveled along the highway, Stevo opened the car up, and they could all feel the car's power as he put his foot down.

"It's not bad, Sue. A really good buy, I think," he commented proudly.

Brent and Ricky were also impressed with the power.

"Wow!" cooed Brent. "It's nearly as good as your truck, Stevo!"

It didn't take them long to get to the Pub where the pig hunting competition was being held. They parked next to a large truck with two really nice looking hunting dogs on the back.

"Strange colour for a hunter's truck," Brent commented as he observed the trucks bright pink paintwork.

Inside, they found Spider talking with a few friends whom he quickly introduced to the others. Among them stood a guy named Goat. When Sue looked questioningly at Spider, wondering why he would be called Goat, they all laughed.

"He's had that goatee beard longer than we even care to remember," answered Spider. "Somehow the name just seems to suit him."

"I can see how he got the name," laughed Sue. The others joined in the laughter.

They were admiring the big boars that had been brought in. The pig carrying competition, which was always really fun to watch, was just about to start. The contestants had to carry a pig through and over obstacles, and at the end of their run, they had to down a pint of beer. Many of the contestants had entered solely for the free pint. However, they soon found out this was the hardest part of the task - because they were all puffing so profusely from completing an obstacle course with a 60kg pig on their backs! Some of the contestants were falling down with the weight of the big boar on their back, yet somehow Stevo had still managed to talk Brent into giving it a shot.

Brent managed to hoist the large pig onto his shoulder, and he was off. He raced down the track, over the tire course, around the Kowhai tree, and back towards the sign. The organisers had used an old road sign as one of their obstacles as they were very resourceful, using anything available to make it difficult for the competitors. Brent stumbled slightly as he scrambled under the sign but managed to regain his feet before making it to the finishing line. He dumped the pig on the back of the truck and tried his best to down the beer as quickly as he usually could. He was puffing so hard he couldn't swallow, so he threw it over his shoulder instead. His antics caused more than a few laughs amongst the large crowd gathering for prize giving.

While they had been looking at the pigs, Ricky had taken a fancy to a nice, fat looking boar. Stevo who had noticed Ricky eyeing up the pig asked his friend,

"What are you thinking, Ricky?"

"I'd like to buy this pig off the hunter. It would be pretty tasty. I wonder if he would sell it to me."

"I agree, it would be very tasty. It's pig number 45. We'll have to try and find the hunter who shot it."

After watching the competition, and checking out all of the big boars, they moved into the pub to have a beer and watch prize giving. They wanted to track Spider down to see if he could help find the owner of boar 45. There were lots of raffles being won, and the major hunting prizes all went to well deserving hunters. Spider was rapt with himself, as he managed to win a prize for the average weight of his pig. The drinks were flowing as the winners were happily shouting rounds for everybody. One of the winners was a tall, attractive, brunette woman wearing tight blue jeans and a cowboy hat.

"She could be straight off television," admired Brent.

"Oh yeah, her?" Spider laughed. "That's Miss NZ Pig Hunter." "Does she drive a pink truck?" asked Brent. "Cos' we saw one in

the car park."

"Yeah man, that'd be hers. There are very few weekends when that truck isn't out hunting. She can hunt better than most of the bloody men I know! She's mad keen on hunting aye, she goes out as often as she can!"

"How did she get the name, Miss NZ Pig Hunter?" piped up Ricky "I had no idea there was such a title!"

"Ahh … Well, her father was a pretty well known, local hunter. She used to go hunting with him. Reckon the hunting bug's in her blood. She has a couple of brothers, but they aren't into it the way she is." Spider paused and took a gulp of his beer, grinning as he continued,

"I guess we also call her that because she is such a good looking hunter. Mad keen, and good-looking with it. Can't get much better than that, aye!" laughed Spider.

The rest of the night went really well. Sue, who was the sober driver since she had her new car, enjoyed watching Stevo having a good time. The men indulged in a few beers and relaxed, talking hunting with the other guys. After tracking down the hunter who owned 45, and checking out if he wanted to sell it, Spider invited them back to his place for a steak, a few more beers, and some of his home brewed rum. The hunter of 45 was more than happy to make some money from his boar, and the purchase was made. Spider loaded number 45 onto the back of his short wheel base ute. It was an epic hunting machine. The tires were really wide, with huge grips due to the deep treaded pattern on them, which helped them to drive through any mud hole or rough terrain. It had a short wheel base which Spider had modified so that the axles sat close together and made it easier to negotiate any terrain without getting stuck like a longer wheel based vehicle. It's short wheel base and wide deep treaded tires meant that it could climb up and get itself out of any mud hole. It was painted khaki green to blend with the hunting environment.

The boys and Sue had all settled themselves with drinks in Spiders lounge, chatting and laughing about the events of the day - especially Brent's antics earlier at the pig carrying competition! Spider put the hot plate on to heat up, and when it was at sizzling temperature, he threw on some of his finest tenderloin beef steaks. He brought out a barrel of his home brew rum and convinced the men to each have a glass. Ricky and Brent knocked the rum back before reaching out to quickly refill their glasses, while they eagerly caught up on each other's news. Stevo drank more slowly and Sue didn't sample it as she was the sober driver.

They got stuck into a good feed, happily talking away a few hours. Sue and Stevo had a coffee while Ricky, Spider, and Brent kept enjoying the rum. The conversation eventually turned to Miss NZ Pig Hunter - how good looking she was, and about her cool pink truck. Stevo hinted at what all the men were thinking as he winked.

"I bet everyone wants to go hunting with Miss NZ Pig Hunter."

Ricky and Brent were trying to communicate with each other but as the home brew had taken away their ability to speak clearly, all they were able to do was mumble and move their lips.

"Come on, Brent. Time to go, mate," said Stevo. "Mmm," mumbled Brent.

Spider and Stevo helped him to get onto his feet and they all moved outside to the car. It had gotten really dark, which confused them all, as they seemed to have lost track of the time slipping by. Spider began to search for the switch to the outside light, "It should be here somewhere. I'm sure it was here yesterday."

Stevo laughed as he helped Spider to find the switch, shining some light on the outdoor path. Stevo helped Ricky to get into the car. Ricky was mumbling '45, 45, 45' over the scuffing sounds of their feet on the driveway.

Stevo had hoped the rum would mean Ricky had forgotten about the boar, but his mumblings indicated otherwise. As soon as Ricky had his seat belt on, he was fast asleep. The home brew had taken its toll. Brent called out good-bye to Spider as he climbed in beside Ricky. Spider had heard his brother mutter 45 and he half stumbled/ half rushed off to open his shed. He had locked both his truck and the pig away when they had first got home as he didn't want 45 to be stolen.

Stevo said to Sue, "Looks like we are taking 45 home!!" "Oh, yes. The pig Ricky bought."

She seemed oblivious to the smell, the blood, and the lice. She walked around the car and popped open the boot with a flick of a button on her key chain. Stevo peered in. It was so clean and tidy. He spotted Spider struggling with 45, bringing him to where they stood by the car. Stevo intercepted him, asking him if he had a tarp or something they could lay across the bottom of the boot.

Spider gave him an amused look.

"Oh, yeah mate, sure thing. No worries."

He staggered back to his shed and after a bit of crashing and banging he came out with an old sack which looked even dirtier than 45! Stevo knew that at one o'clock in the morning, and in his drunken state, Spider had done his best to find something to lay 45 on. He gave the sack a shake and laid it in the boot of the car. He moved over to grab a leg of 45, so he could help to heave it into the boot. Spider was hanging onto another leg and with the weight, Stevo felt like he was dragging them both and when they threw 45 in, Spider nearly went with it. 45 landed perfectly on the sack and Stevo quickly closed the boot.

"See ya later, Spider. Thanks for the food and drinks," called Stevo.

Brent and Ricky were already snoring on the back seat.

"Babe, you are amazing. That pig will make your car all smelly but that doesn't worry you. I'll sort it in the morning."

"All good, love," said Sue. "I had a great afternoon. So pleased you had a good time catching up with your mates." Stevo loved her calmness and her total trust in him. He knew she was the woman for him.

"Let's drop Ricky and 45 off as soon as we can," said Stevo. "That smell is something else!!"

Sue laughed.

Stevo was watching her as she drove them home. She had a lovely smile. When she noticed him watching her, he gave her a wink and blew her a kiss. He knew he was going to spend the rest of his life with Sue. When they got to Ricky's place, Stevo managed to wake Ricky and Brent up so they could help drag 45 out of the boot and place it in Ricky's shed for him to sort out in the morning. They waved goodbye as Ricky stumbled inside.

Janey was waiting for Brent as they pulled up at Rosenfee farm.

It was far later than when she had imagined they would be home. "We are all fine," reassured Sue. "But someone might have a bit of a hangover tomorrow!"

They all laughed as Brent staggered towards the door.

"Thanks for bringing him home safely. We will catch up soon," called Janey as she followed Brent, making sure he didn't fall over and hurt himself.

Stevo and Sue headed for home with smiles on their faces, laughing about what a great day it had been.

A few weeks later, Stevo and Sue discovered Sue was pregnant. They decided to get married right away. They went to a registry office one Friday afternoon and, with the Justice of the Peace and his secretary as their witnesses, they got married. They invited all of their friends and family over for dinner that evening, and told them what they had done. Despite feeling they had missed out on celebrating the wedding, everyone was overjoyed for them. Janey and Brent arrived the next day carrying a big bunch of their wild flowers from down by the river. "We just know these will flower for weeks," Janey exclaimed – and sure enough, they did.

Stevo and Sue's eldest son Josh was closely followed by his younger brothers Thomas and Bradley. All three boys had Stevo and Sue's blonde hair, Stevo's charm and athleticism, and Sue's gentle nature.

Brent and Janey, Stevo and Sue, and Heather and Roger spent many happy holidays together during the years that followed. The children all considered themselves as cousins, even though Brent and Janey's children were not blood relations of the other children. They shared many common interests, especially a great love for camping and fishing holidays. Despite Stevo's many attempts, Roger was nowhere near the outdoorsman as Brent or Stevo, yet he was quite happy going along on the annual camping holiday. He would take hundreds of photos, and had carefully crafted many albums, which the kids loved to pull out when they were together, laughing as they remembered the great adventures they had experienced together.

"Remember that time Dad fell off the boat trying not to let that fish run away with his line," laughed Sharon, the eldest daughter of Roger and Heather.

"Yeah, nearly as funny as the time Stevo tried to get you to skin that deer," teased Ingrid. The girls laughed, they had always been especially close and were flatting together at University down in Dunedin.

"Uncle Rog, I always loved that you got this photo of Josh dressed up as some kind of sea monster that time the beach was covered in seaweed. Remember how he scared Thomas so badly he wouldn't go out to pee at night. I thought he was going to wet the bed!" Bradley smiled. He missed his two elder brothers, they had gone off on their OE and were roaming free somewhere in Eastern Europe.

"We sure have had some good times over the years," Sue smiled.

CHAPTER SEVEN

On their annual fishing trip, the sea was calm as Brent steered the boat towards one of their favourite fishing spots. They usually found success there, and over the years had regularly caught enough fish to feed their families during camping trips. Brent turned back to smile at Roger who continued to take photos while Janey soaked up the sun. Stevo appeared to also be enjoying the beautiful weather as they cruised across the water towards their secret spot.

"Looks like it's still our spot," piped up Janey.

"You know it darling, not a boat to be seen anywhere." Brent stopped the motor while Stevo let the anchor down. "Those snappers are ours!"

The snappers were biting well and within just two hours their fish bin was full to the brim, and they had already reached their limit.

"You guys keen to stay out, chase some tuna and marlin?" Brent suggested.

"Oh yes, I'd love to get a photo of a marlin!" chirped Roger. Stevo scoffed, "A photo? I'd like to haul one of those bad boys in, not just see it in a picture!"

The day was perfect to be out at sea. It was warm and the sun was shining. There was just a slight sea breeze, predicted to pick up later in the day, but perfect for keeping the hot sun from making the heat unbearable.

Brent turned to his friends. "Righto then, my mate chases marlin and tuna for a living, and he says that the blue water which marlin liked has come in closer to land this year."

"It all looks pretty blue to me mate." Roger scanned the ocean to try and see what Brent was referring to.

"Actually Roger, blue water is when the temperatures have reached 19-20 degrees Celsius or more. It follows the troughs on the seabed, and the tide brings it closer to land, which then brings the marlin and tuna within reach of fishermen – like us!"

Brent's boat had always been great for excursions well out to sea, when the weather was right, because it was fast and able to easily get home quickly if the weather ever changed for the worst. After checking the fuel levels, and that they had the right lures, they began to head further out to sea, bouncing over the waves as they covered the miles. Seagulls chased the boat in the hope of a free feed. It seemed that every sea bird and fish was as happy as those out fishing, making the most of the beautiful weather after the previously dreary, unproductive days at camp because the sea had been too rough to get out. Stevo suggested trawling for kahawai to use as live bait.

"Sounds like a good plan to me," agreed Brent.

Slowing their speed, Brent noticed how the colour of the water had changed. The murky coastal waters which were discoloured by tidal movements, and rivers and rains on the land washing sediment down into them had been replaced by the most beautiful blue water the ocean could offer.

"Wow, just look at that water! It is amazing!" Stevo grinned,

"Yeah, the marlin reckon it's pretty good too!"

Roger who had thought all water was blue, was utterly amazed at the clarity and colour of the water that surrounded the boat. He reached for his camera, excited at the prospect of further testing his new camera's colour options. Janey took over the wheel while Stevo and Brent cast out their lines. As they gently cruised through schools of fish, many a strike was made - but none were landed. Brent suggested a nice cup of tea might go down well. He leant down and picked up the chilly bin, resting it on the side of the boat while he got out the makings for four cups of tea. No sooner had he started to get the cups out, his line went tight. Racing to his line, he knocked the chilly bin over and the entire contents were tipped into the water.

"First things first. I'll worry about that soon," he yelled, and turned his concentration to landing the kahawai.

Roger was panicking about the contents of the chilly bin, while Janey turned the boat around. However, it was too late and the only item that could be rescued was a single cup. The other items had already sunk their way down to a watery grave.

"Well there's no question about it now. We just have to go back to shore. We can't stay out here with no food or drink," complained Roger.

Brent turned to Janey, raising his eyebrows as if to say, 'here we go again.'

"Well, I can't waste this fish," Brent reasoned with a grin as he held up the fresh kahawai. "That would make losing the chilly bin a total waste of time!"

Stevo turned to face Roger.

"Just look at the colour of this water, Roger. See how blue and clear it is. You can see down in the water for metres. It's perfect for marlin. And perfect for you to test out your new camera."

Roger caved.

"Yeah, I see what you mean. It looks wonderful. Well, I suppose we should try to catch just one then."

"That's the spirit, mate," Brent grinned, patting his friend on the shoulder.

Baiting the big hook with the live kahawai was an easy job for Brent and he cast the line out into the sea. Stevo and Brent knew there were bigger predators underneath these schools of fish, as they had seen the small fish in the schools suddenly leap out of the water. Big fish like marlin and mako sharks often made their way through schools of fish during feasting, making the most of the chance for a larger meal while all of the smaller fish were rounded up. The water was frothing with the feeding frenzy of fish and the seagulls and gannets were diving into the surrounding waters and coming up with a mouthful, each and every time. Roger inserted a new SD card into his camera and sat poised, ready for the big strike to happen. He was looking really enthusiastic, which Brent noticed out of the corner of his eye. His eagerness made Brent feel better for dragging Roger out on yet another outdoorsy adventureLost in his thoughts, as Brent watched Janey's beautiful long hair blowing in the breeze as she stood across from him at the help, he felt a jolt as the Shimano 75 begun screaming.

Brent hollered excitedly,

"I've got one! I'm sure it's something big!"

"No, it's only the North Island," quipped Stevo. Janey laughed and winked at Stevo.

"Yeah Brent, you think you're Maui from the Māori legend!" "Who's Maui?" asked Roger.

Janey, steering the boat and looking back at Roger, yelled over the noise of the engine.

'Maui is the Māori demi God who pulled up Te Ika a Maui, or the fish of Maui out of the ocean while fishing with his brothers. The legend explains how the fish, shaped like a stingray, was so large that his jealous brothers decided to destroy their brother's catch with their knives. They carved away at the fish to create what we know as the valleys and mountains of the North Island of New Zealand, or Te Ika a Maui.

Roger stared blankly at Janey.

"Gee is that right? The North Island is Maui's fish? I've never heard that legend before."

Stevo confirmed Janey's story.

"That's right Rog, and the South Island is considered to have been his waka, or boat in English."

Brent looked over at his friends and smiled as the new reel continued peeling out the nylon. Brent kept his grip on the rod.

"Yo Stevo, can you clip my gimbal belt on for me?" The rod slotted into the holder on the gimbal which strapped around his waist to take the strain leaving arms free to hold the rod and wind the line in - a very useful invention for game fishing. The gimbal was a present from Janey along with the Shimano 75; she had known Brent would need them if he hooked a big fish.

As Brent prepared for a tussle he hoped this would be the big one he had always dreamed about. Stevo reeled in his line and prepared the gaff. He stowed everything they didn't need into the space in the front of the boat. Brent's rod was nearly bent double with the weight of the fish. Stevo sighted the marlin on its tail about 200m behind the boat and screamed.

"We've got a marlin! And it looks like a big blue!"

Janey immediately reduced the speed of the boat until they were just idling.

"Now we just have to land it," grimaced Brent as he fought against the weight of the fish. He knew that landing was never easy with such big fish due to their great power. Blue marlin have always been known as being the most difficult to land as they can go so deep. Getting all of that weight back up to the surface on a 24 kg line would not be an easy task. Brent struggled with the fish for over an hour, while Janey kept the boat on a safe course. Roger wanted to capture every moment of the strike on film. With his seasickness quickly forgotten, all four of them were absolutely buzzing. Stevo encouraged, "Good work Brent, just take it slowly."

Brent was winding furiously so to keep the slack out of the line. The fish appeared to be coming towards the boat as the line was running so freely. His heart sank as he thought the fish must have gotten off because the line was coming in too easily. Suddenly the line went taut again and the marlin leaped out of the water, just 50 metres from the boat. Brent felt an absolute blast of exhilaration as the massive fish splashed back into the water. It moved away and began peeling out line from the 75 Shimano. He screamed in surprise,

"There's smoke coming off the reel!" Stevo, with a wink of his eye, laughed.

"No that's just water spray Brent, concentrate on your job." Brent could see the spool getting low on nylon.

Stevo yelled to Janey, "Start following the fish."

Janey swiftly put the boat into gear and spun it around carefully, keeping the angle perfect between the fish and the boat. In no time at all they were in hot pursuit of the big fish, trying to interpret the movements of the fish and then maneuver the boat to stay on its tail, no matter which way or how fast it turned.

Big ocean swells smacked across the transom, and water was coming into the boat. Janey reached over to turn the bilge pump on without faltering to follow the marlin. They followed the fish for a few hundred metres, until Brent retrieved some line back onto his spool. The fish began to slow and Brent was getting more and more of his line back. Stevo had the gaff ready for when the fish got near the side. He had already given Roger instructions for what they would need him to do. They didn't want the huge fish on the boat and would need to put a rope over the tail of the fish as it approached the boat.

The fight continued with Brent concentrating hard on the line, and Stevo anxiously anticipating the opportunity to land their marlin. The time would come when everything would be up to Stevo and Roger. All of the responsibility would fall upon their crucial role to get hold of the trace and secure the marlin amid the adrenalin charged circumstances. Brent began winding the marlin towards the boat but its power was too great, and again it took the line out at a tremendous speed. Janey immediately put the boat back into hot pursuit as the spool was again getting low. Brent's Shimano 75 was a mid-range reel, not really designed for such a huge fish. He found himself wishing he had a bigger reel. Janey was doing a magnificent job of keeping the boat in the right place, anticipating the marlin's moves and watching the line, about 150 metres from the back of the boat. Janey had them right on the trail of the lively marlin, and they were finally beginning to gain on the fish. Stevo and Roger were holding on at the back of the boat, helping Janey by telling her where the fish was heading. With the ocean swells, the line would become submerged until each swell passed. The marlin had the boat heading further out to sea. They could not afford to make a single wrong move with this big fish. The marlin was putting up a great fight, determined on not giving in, and would repeatedly take the line out. Brent tightened the drag on the reel, knowing it was risky as the line could break, but hoped that it would help to slow the marlin.

Janey gazed at the blue water the motor was churning at the back of the boat.

"Have you ever seen such beautiful water, Roger?" "No, Janey. It is amazing."

Stevo was talking to Brent animatedly, giving him words of encouragement. The fish was continuously trying to go deeper, causing Brent to really struggle to keep it near the surface. They gained metres as the marlin drew closer to the boat. Tightening the drag on the reel had worked and the fish was slowing, even though it had managed to go quite deep. They got their first close look at the enormous marlin as it was about 5-10 metres below the boat and the water was crystal clear. They had been fighting the marlin for about two hours and it still had plenty of fight left. Brent was doing everything to play the marlin correctly, keeping the rod end up high and watching his reel doing its work despite all the pressure on it.

They were more than three hours into the fight when the fish finally begun to show signs of defeat. After its last run, Brent had finally gotten it back to the boat, even though it had gone really deep. He was winding hard, working the rod to inch the fish up, just a small bit at a time.

"We are winning, Brent. Hang in there," exclaimed Stevo, giving Brent some much needed encouragement. The fish was getting nearer to the surface. The end of the trace was just a few metres down. Stevo waited, knowing that he and Roger would need to be in action in just a brief minute or two. Stevo had got some big leather gloves ready, and he told Roger to put them on. He explained how he needed Roger to grab the trace when he told him to, and that he must pull on it as hard as he possibly could to help bring the fish to the boat where Stevo would gaff and secure it.

"Go! Go, Roger! Pull him in!" he yelled.

Roger grabbed hold of the trace, and the huge fish came up towards the boat. Stevo knew if he missed, that the fish would either pull Roger over the side, or tear the hook right out of its mouth and be lost. The marlin was just behind the motor, it just had to come a little bit closer for Stevo to make his move. As the marlin neared the boat, Stevo drove the gaff into the fish and punctured the perfect spot behind the eye. The massive fish began to thrash at the back of the boat and the sea behind the motor turned into a white froth.

"We got it!" Brent shouted ecstatically.

Putting the boat into neutral Janey rushed to give Brent a huge hug, one that was eagerly returned as Brent thanked her for her wonderful job of steering the boat. Brent shook Roger and Stevo's spare hands as they struggled to keep control of the fish. Brent grabbed the rope Stevo had secured to the boat so he and Stevo could make sure the massive fish was secured to the back of the Warrior. Roger had never seen the large spear that poked out from the front of the head of a marlin so close. Roger exclaimed in amazement at its size.

"They use it to stun their prey," explained Stevo who then reached out and grabbed the marlin by the bill to secure the head to the boat.

Janey looked around at the men.

"You are awesome deckies," she offered with a big smile. "That's one thrilling conclusion to a great day."

Stevo and Roger both give her a big hug and a few cheerful thumps on her back.

"You're one hell of a skipper, Janey," exclaimed Stevo.

"You're the best, love. You did amazing work driving the boat."

Jane smiled elatedly. "Thanks, love. It was really exciting. I'm so pleased you have landed the marlin."

Brent began to feel his muscles, stiff and sore after playing the fish for so long - but his smile was stayed put and he looked gratefully round at his best friends.

"That sure was some exciting mayhem for a while there. Lucky we had that harness because I don't think we could have landed this big fish without it - and of course without all your encouragement and hard work. We made a great team. Thanks heaps guys."

The boat had been drifting while they secured the big marlin. Stevo grabbed some cans of beer which luckily had been in the under floor hold, not in the upturned chilly bin.

"Not a bad days fishing aye, a bin full of snapper and a great big bloody marlin!"

He passed everyone a cold beer as they all looked admiringly at the massive haul of fish.

"That's one hell of a big fish, Brent. Reminds me of the big stag we got in our mountain hunting possie, another beautiful specimen."

"Yeah it does Stevo." Brent replied with a twinkle in his eye. "Hey that reminds me. Did I tell you I was talking to a helicopter

mate a while ago? He told me about seeing another big stag up there recently. We should head up and have a go at it."

Janey and Roger looked at each other and feeling a little left out Janey piped up.

"What about us? It's a team effort. We all have to go!"

"Do you think the other girls would like to go too?" Stevo asked. "How would we get there?" Roger asked apprehensively.

"On horseback," Stevo and Brent answered in unison, already envisioning the entire hunt.

"Heather loves riding horses," replied Roger. "I'm sure she would love to go. Not sure if I will make it though."

"You have to come, Roger. We are a team!" cried the others. "Oh!! We will see." Roger replied meekly.

"We'll work on it and just see what happens," Brent reassured Roger.

Brent looked around and noticed the sea was getting a little worked up and that there were clouds building on the horizon. The sun was beginning to sink lower in the sky.

"We had better start heading back. It will be a long slow trip with the marlin on behind."

They turned towards home and back toward the camping ground where the car and boat trailer were waiting and Brent took over steering.

Roger spent much of the return journey losing his lunch over the side as his seasickness returned with a vengeance. Janey had her arm around Brent's shoulder as he steered the boat towards the shore. She had complete faith in his seamanship and knew he would get them all home safe and sound - even with an approximate 265 kilos worth of marlin on the back of the transom!

Stevo was hanging onto the back of Roger's shirt to ensure nothing more than his lunch made its way overboard.

"Fishing for the day is finished," quipped Stevo. "We don't need any more ground bait."

Roger looked up at his friend, a speck of food balanced on the end of his jaw.

"Thanks, Stevo. It's all right for you, but I feel really gross."

They still had a long way to go home and the ocean swells were getting bigger. After two hours battling big swells during increasingly high winds, while towing the massive fish, they finally crossed the bar and entered the safe waters of the bay. It had been a very slow journey with the fish hanging off the back of the boat and the setting sun was casting long shadows over the silent waters of the bay. The boat cruised slowly across the calm waters, and the fish caused a big wave off the transom. They could see people had gathered on the beach, noticing the boat was bringing in something large. Roger pointed towards the crowd.

"Hey! I think that is Heather and Sue!"

He sounded so pleased to be near the shore again that he already appeared less green.

"I can't wait to tell them the story."

The others just looked at each other and smiled.

(22 years earlier)

The two newborns lay side by side in separate hospital bassinets. Slade and Luke were fraternal twins whose mother, Kate Clark, had fallen pregnant when she was only seventeen. Her pregnancy had been difficult, and riddled with many health issues. Their biological father was not around and had not even known she was pregnant. Kate had passed away as a result of complications from their birth when the twins were just one day old. Their grandmother, Julie was suffering from terminal cancer and therefore not in a position to look after them long term. With a heavy heart Julie asked her very best friend Shona if she would care for the boys and raise them as her own. Shona and her husband Hone already had their hands full with their own children as they had three older children and had recently had a fourth child, ten years younger than his closest sibling and just two months older than the twins. Regardless, Shona promised to contact Julie and let her know their decision as soon as possible.

Julie gazed down at her sleeping grandsons and thought of how proud her daughter would have been of her sons if she had made it through. One boy was a large 7 pounds 5 ounces with lots of dark hair, and the other boy was a smaller baby, 6 pounds 4. He had tufts of blonde hair covering his little head.

Following their birth, in her last coherent moment before losing consciousness, Kate Clark had named her twin boys Slade and Luke. Julie kissed each boy on the forehead and promised them both. "I will find you both a good home together, if it is the last thing I do."

Early the next morning Julie's mobile rang.

"Hi Shona, thanks for ringing back so quickly. I have been beside myself with worry. How did you get on talking to Hone?"

"Well, he took a lot of convincing, but after a long discussion he realised, as I did, we have no choice. Māori culture knows this type of caring for non-biological children as whangaii and Hone knows that when we can help, we must. Hone knows the Coast is an awesome place to bring up children and we just can't see a friend in need without helping out. He just wants our kids to have all the great experiences he had as a child growing up, and we would love to have the twins as part of our family. You never know, maybe one of them will follow in Hone's footsteps and learn to play the guitar. When are they able to leave the hospital?"

Julie had begun to cry so hard with relief that she could hardly reply. "They are still getting used to feeding and haven't quite regained their birth weight yet. If all goes well, they should be settled by early next week."

"I will come up with my baby, Jake, and help you with them. The sooner I get to know them and they get to know me, the easier the bonding will be. I am still feeding Jake, but won't have enough milk for three babies. We will keep the twins on the bottle. Have you named them yet?"

Julie explained how her daughter had chosen their names before she died. Shona whispered sadly, "Well, we would never go against her last wishes, their names shall remain as Slade and Luke."

"Shona, thank you so much for coming here. I can't express my gratitude to you enough. You have made a dying woman very happy, knowing that my grandsons will have a stable life surrounded by a loving family. They are my only living relations and will inherit my estate when I go. I will set up a trust which will cover their living expenses and their education." Julie's voice wavered with emotion, knowing she wouldn't be able to watch her grandsons grow.

"You don't have to do that. We don't want any money. We are really looking forward to having the twins as part of our family," Shona offered kindly. "I have no other family, please Shona. Use that money for whatever your family and the boys need."

"You can rest assured that we will treat your grandchildren as if they are our own children. There will be no favouritism. They will have a good life down on the Coast," Shona paused, reaching for her oldest friend's hand. "Thank you for thinking about us, regarding the money. I will talk to Hone and he will know what the right thing to do is."

"There is one other thing. Their mother kept a daily diary for years. There are quite a few books. I haven't read them, but I have put them together in a box and would like you to have them and to share them with the boys when you think the time is right. The diaries might help them to understand their mother."

"No problem," smiled Shona. "We will keep them safe until the boys are old enough, and only then will we share the diaries with them. It is important for them to know about their birth mother and her family."

"Thank you from the bottom of my heart," Julie whispered as she let go of Shona's hand and pulled her friend towards her, smiling as the two women embraced, surrounded by the three sleeping, baby brothers.

CHAPTER EIGHT

Filling the snapper bin, catching a massive marlin, and making the decision to revisit a favourite hunting place from their youth for one last time had made it all very memorable; a trip the four very tired fishermen would never forget.

Sue and Heather were waiting on the beach with a chilled glass of Chardonnay for Janey and a well-deserved beer for the boys.

"What a day we've had," exclaimed Roger.

Heather and Sue were keen to hear about the adventures of the day. The massive fish was a magnificent sight.

"I will back the truck down and we will drag the fish ashore. Then we will load the boat onto the trailer," Stevo called to Brent.

"Your Toyota Hilux will never drag this fish out of the water. Do you think we should use my truck?" Brent teased, with a sly grin on his face anticipating the reaction from Stevo as he knew how much Stevo loved his Hilux.

Stevo scoffed,

"You should know better than that Brent. My Hilux is far more capable than your Mitsubishi."

"Yeah right, I believe you," replied Brent, rolling his eyes.

Brent laughed and offered to cut the marlin in half so Stevo could fulfill his dream of pulling it ashore using his Toyota Hilux.

"Won't be necessary mate," rebuffed Stevo. "You know my truck will do everything a Kiwi can throw at it, Brent."

Brent smiled and shook his head cheekily as he watched his friend climb into the cab of his beloved truck.

A large crowd had gathered near the boat, as word of their catch had spread through the camp like wildfire. They got the fish and the boat up to the tent, amidst much excitement from the other campers. After a few more beers, the guys decided to hang the fish and gut it while the girls put on the barbecue. Brent remembered they had to weigh the fish before they gutted it so Stevo asked the camp manager to bring down his scales, and it wasn't long before he arrived with them sitting on a tractor with a loader. The fish weighed in as a 265 kilo blue marlin and everybody watching was in awe at the size of catch. Somehow it managed to look even bigger hanging up on the loader. Roger laughed, "I know what we will be eating for the next six months. Oh! That reminds me! Heather, guess what I've gone and gotten us into? A hunting trip for all six of us, up to Brent and Stevo's hunting spot in the mountains. After all this marlin is gone, guess what we'll be eating for the six months after that?" Heather absentmindedly replied, "What?"

"Venison and, more than likely, plenty of it. After watching these two in action today I know there won't be a shortage of fresh meat!"

As all of the other campers drifted away, the group found themselves left on their own, discussing their upcoming hunting expedition.

Stevo talked to the others about the ideal spot to take the girls, where they would enjoy swimming and fishing after a three-day horse ride up a river. The girls expressed their apprehension about the horse riding as, apart from Heather, they hadn't ridden much since their youth. Stevo mentioned how Gabe Jackson, a friend living down on the coast, owned a big station and would be more than likely willing to lend them the horses.

Brent, quick to remember Gabe, exclaimed,

"Oh, I know Gabe. He's that mate of yours who I graze my Big Red, with - isn't it?"

"Yeah, that's the guy. He's great," Stevo confirmed.

"He's a great bloke," Brent explained to the others. "Stevo and I spent a lot of time mustering and hunting on Gabe's place and in lots of other places in that area. Ahh, Stevo wouldn't it be great to see him again and introduce him to everybody?"

Janey piped up, "I haven't seen Big Red for ages and I've wanted to. We haven't seen him since you and Stevo took him to Gabe's place."

Gabe's place was only about an hour's drive away from their campsite and Brent suggested they make the journey to visit him the following morning.

"Great idea, Brent," agreed Stevo. "I'm sure he will have enough horses for all of us."

"Yeah, and the right gear too. Hopefully he will have a packhorse we can borrow to help carry our gear. It will be great to ride Big Red again."

Stevo and Brent were grateful that Gabe was such a good guy since it was a huge favour to ask. The 6 friends enjoyed their dinner of fresh snapper, which had been cooking on an open fire while they laid down their plans. After the excitement of the day, and with more in store for them tomorrow, they felt a good night sleep would serve them all well. Their goodnight calls sang out to each other as they entered their separate tents.

CHAPTER NINE

Things had remained unchanged on the ranch since Brent and Stevo had last been there. The old cane chair remained unmoved from its position on the wide veranda that wrapped itself around the grey, weatherboard villa. Stevo noticed that Gabe must still be smoking, as he knew the cane chair was his favourite spot to get his nicotine fix and admire the view. The group made their way up Gabe's driveway and into his big station. Stevo realised how much he was looking forward to seeing Gabe again as it had been a few years since they were last together. He climbed down from the cab of his truck. He saw the front door open and Gabe stride out onto the veranda. Gabe held his hand up to his forehead, shielding the sun from his face and straining his eyes in order to recognise his visitors. A broad smile lit his face when he saw Stevo making his way across his front lawn.

"Hey!" he called out. "Long time, no see mate! How's it been?" "Life's pretty good aye," Stevo smiled as he greeted his friend with a hand shake and a friendly slap on the back.

Stevo introduced Roger and the girls to Gabe. Janey rushed over to the fence leading to the paddock on the other side of the drive way as she noticed Big Red grazing there. Brent had come around the truck and as Gabe saw him, an even larger smile spread across his face.

"You remember Brent, Gabe."

"Of course," hollered Gabe. "How have you been, Brent? Are you still milking the cows?"

"Gidday Gabe, yeah still milking," Brent smiled.

"Big Red's looking really well," Janey called to Brent. She had often spent many hours riding him and brushing him down with love and care; knowing Big Red had the x factor of horses. He was intelligent and could run like the wind. He was brave, taking on any obstacle with ease.

Janey would often remark to Brent about what remarkable things Big Red could do and how quickly he picked up on simple things like opening a latch. He could jump like a deer and had an extraordinary sense of smell. Sometimes she would take him swimming in the river at home because he loved the water and could swim like a fish. He was very powerful and athletic, standing 16.2 hands high. She had always been very kind to him and would often give him sneaky treats from the kitchen.

"Must be the lifestyle on this beautiful farm and all the nice mares he's got, aye?" Gabe chuckled, always one to throw in a joke. "It's good to see you again Brent. Stevo often tells me about your hunting adventures, sings your praises he does! From what I hear, you've developed into a true Kiwi outdoorsman. Stevo's description has ya sounding like a cross between Stony Burke the great rodeo rider, Peter Blake the sailor, and Crocodile Dundee the Australian bushman, at times!"

"I think Stevo is getting confused with himself," Brent replied, touched to hear how highly his best friend had spoken about him. "But we do have some pretty hair-raising moments, Gabe."

Roger handed over the fresh snapper they had brought for him to enjoy as Stevo began to relay their story of how they had managed to catch the big marlin.

"We'll bring round some big marlin steaks for you after it is smoked," promised Stevo.

"Come on in guys, let's have a cup of tea and say hello to Emma." Gabe lead the way into the house. The heart rimu table, which had always been the centre of life in the house, dominated the large dining room. Three huge stag heads, and half a dozen boar heads, lined the wall.

"I see you haven't got any new heads since I was last here," quipped Stevo.

"Too busy farming mate," sighed Gabe, looking slightly disappointed. After a cup of tea and some more small talk, they told Gabe about their plans to go for a hunt up in the mountains. Gabe explained how the course of the river had changed quite a lot due to the heavy rain that had fallen recently, and cautioned them that they may encounter a few problems in accessing certain places due to slips. Gabe leaned in towards Stevo and asked,

"Will you be staying at the big Bullring or will you be going up into the Green River country?"

The Bullring received its name from a time when all of the big cattle stations first started on the coast. The rivers were unfenced meaning a lot of cattle escaped. The Bullring boasts about 30 acres, and is situated on a big sweeping corner of the river, with huge areas of sand. The bulls and other cattle used to go out and fight, congregating in the area because of the large amount of lush grass around the edges. The Green River, high up in the valley, got its name because the deep waterholes have a very green appearance - even though their water is sweet, clean, and pure.

Stevo explained their plans to Gabe,

"No, we don't intend to go up to Green River country this time. We will stay at the Bullring, and head off up our secret creek to hunt." With a wink of his eye he added, "A mate of mine said he saw a big stag in there, from his chopper, a few weeks back. Hopefully he will be roaring his head off when we get there."

Gabe nodded in agreement,

"Yeah mate, should be some good hunting up in there. No-one has been in there for a while. Because of the big storm, you will need to take a good axe and a spade. There could be a lot of slips and fallen trees getting in your way."

Stevo and Brent's eyes had both lit up, the men were keener than ever after hearing the news that no one had been up there since the big storm which had caused havoc across the country - taking roads and power out and causing massive erosion and slipping.

They had decided they would make the trip in late March, when the stags would be starting to roar. Gabe was more than happy to lend them the number of horses they required and he wistfully expressed his desire to go with them, but regretfully had to accept that he would be in the middle of shearing and unable to make it.

"I'll even lend you my old Commer horse truck. It's a dear old girl, but it will get you there safely," Gabe kindly offered. He had a lot of affection for his truck and it had been well looked after. He then exclaimed,

"Hey, would you like to take my pig dogs too? I know there are a lot of good pigs up there! Blue's a great pig dog, a cross between a kelpie and a German short head pointer. I called him Blue cos of his big blue spots, he is such an awesome dog! Buck's a bull mastiff cattle cross. He's big black and tan with a really muscular body. Buck is keen as mustard on pigs and he is naturally fit. He has some serious scars from pig hunting from being on the wrong side of a few big boars!" Gabe chuckled at the memory. He had great pride in his dogs which he had been breeding for years. He certainly wouldn't lend them to just anyone, but he trusted Stevo and Brent implicitly after knowing them for years - and from witnessing the kind and respectful way they treated their own animals. Stevo explained how they were mainly after a big stag, but that they would be happy to take Blue and Buck to give them a run. Brent smiled, saying they would definitely be keen to see if there would be some good pigs around. Blue, who had been lying at Brent's feet began to wag his tail, as if he knew what they had been talking about. Brent reached down to give him a rub behind the ears. "Yes boy, you'll be a great help, mate and we will bring Gabe and Emma back some nice pork, won't we?"

Blue leapt up, expecting to be heading off right away. Brent explained to Blue that he would be back soon and that would be the time to go hunting and everyone laughed as Blue turned full circle and lay down with a huff, even though his tail continued to wag.

The group spent the night at the ranch. They stayed up late drinking far too much rum until the wee hours of the morning.

Next morning Emma cooked a big breakfast which they all enjoyed before getting ready to depart.

"See you again soon. Once we have got everything at home organised, we'll be back for the horses!" Brent exclaimed, the excitement of the impending trip slightly lessened the thumping in his head.

"We'll also need a pack horse … I guess they'll all need shoeing, ay Gabe?" Stevo remembered.

"What will you need a pack horse for?" queried Gabe curiously. "To carry the big stag heads out, of course!" replied Stevo with a wink.

"Ha, yeah right!" Gabe retorted cheekily. "I've got a man who shoes all of my horses for just $60 a horse, d'ya want him to do them? Up to you, 'cos I know you can shoe yourself, Stevo."

"Ah, Gabe I think you had better get your man to shoe the horses so they'll be ready for us. I don't think I'm gonna have the time to do them," replied Stevo.

"I hope you have got a really quiet one for me," Roger asked meekly.

Gabe looked over to where Roger was looking very concerned about the size of the horses.

"There are a couple there who don't buck too much, make sure Stevo and Brent put you on one of them," Gabe cautioned with a wink.

He waved the group of friends off, smiling to himself.

The following day was their final day of camping. After packing up the tent and filling the cars with all of their gear (and all of their fish!) they called their farewells to each other.

"We'll be in touch really soon to sort out things for the hunting trip," confirmed Brent.

"Oh great," Roger responded with a sound of apprehension in his voice.

"Yeah, talk to you soon," added Stevo, enthusiastically.

Brent and Janey had decided to drive home the longer way, so they could call in to see Daniel, their oldest son who had followed his childhood dream and was working as a policeman. They took the marlin in to be smoked in Daniel's town, knowing they could easily pick it up after their big hunting trip. Daniel listened excitedly as his parents spoke of their holiday, the big marlin, and the approaching trip up the coast. Nodding in agreement, Daniel mentioned he had also heard from his friend who flew helicopters,

"Apparently there are some really good pigs up there Dad, and the odd good stag too. Nobody has really been up there since the big storm. No need for the hunters to do all the work to get up there - plenty of pigs and deer lower down."

Daniel mentioned that his younger brother, Eugene, was planning a visit around that time.

"Can we borrow your boat while he is here, Dad?"

"No worries Daniel. But I doubt you will catch a bigger marlin than us! We could take you out and show you how real fishermen catch fish. If you boys want some pointers, just let us know," laughed Brent. "When is he coming?" Janey asked, anxious that she hadn't seen

her youngest son since Christmas.

"Sometime towards the end of March," Daniel replied.

"Oh that's great! It'll be around the time we are heading up the coast. What do you think Brentie, we could drop the boat off and see the boys on our way through?" asked Janey with a wide smile, that Brent could not resist. "Thanks honey, I will find out the date, I was planning on giving Eugene a call when we get back to Rosenfee."

CHAPTER TEN

Julie's decision to ask Shona and Hone to accept Slade and Luke into their family was the best thing that ever could have happened for the twins. Without the love and care of Shona and Hone, the twins would have become wards of the state as there was no-one else in the world who was able to care for them. They became younger siblings to brothers and sisters who accepted them with the same love as those of blood relatives. Shona and Hone went on to parent two more children after the twins' adoption. They made a very happy family of eight children and two loving parents. Slade and Luke had a very happy childhood, growing up on the Coast and enjoying the outdoors in the midst of a large cheerful whanau. The twins and Jake were inseparable while they were growing up, often talking about what they would do when they left school. Slade showed from a very young age, that he was the natural leader of the trio. He was often the one who made the decisions about what they were going to do during weekends and holidays. Their childhood was happy and their parents were kind but firm. The boys always had to ensure their chores were done before they were able to enjoy the wonderful playground of the bush, streams, and sea which were right at their doorstep. There was no shortage of ways for three active boys to keep themselves busy and have lots of fun. Hone would often take them and their older brothers out shooting for possums or rabbits. Many nights were spent around a fire singing while Hone strummed a melody on his guitar. Jake had inherited his father's musical talent and would often accompany him on his ukulele or the guitar Shona had bought him. Like most Kiwi families; Ten Guitars was their favourite campfire tune.

Hone taught the boys how to catch eels and trout in the numerous creeks throughout their neighbourhood. Hone would often take them out when he checked his crayfish pots, and they became quite adept at catching snapper with home-made rods. They soon learned how to tell what they could keep and what they needed to throw back. One of their favourite Christmas presents, when they were ten, was a fishing rod and reel. Jake, Slade, and Luke each received one and they were well treasured and looked after. The boys always took care to clean the rods carefully after each use, in the way that Hone had taught them so as to prevent the sea salt from causing their equipment to rust and fail.

Pig hunting was Hone's favourite recreation, meaning that the freezer was always full of wild pork. When Slade, Luke, and Jake were deemed to be old enough, they would accompany him on his expeditions. Hone taught them gun safety, waiting before they were older before they could take their turns to shoot the gun. Hone always kept the boys safe, he always carried the gun, made sure they stood behind the shooter, and only ever allowed the boys to shoot if they had identified their target with complete certainty. Their safety and care for each other were the most important hunting skills Hone taught them. It became tricky sometimes as they either all had to go or none of them. Hone couldn't find it in his heart to leave one of them at home as he knew how close the three of them were and how much they loved doing things together.

Slade really demonstrated his soft side in the depth of his love for Luke. He would always take Luke's side in an argument, even if he didn't fully agree with him. He was physically bigger than Luke and, if needed, would use his size to his advantage. If there was trouble at school, the siblings stuck together and supported each other. Between Slade and Luke there was a stronger bond than between their other brothers and sisters. But they had their moments - as all families do. Arguing followed by the slamming of a bedroom door and Shona trying to calm the situation wasn't an unusual occurrence in the family home. Hone and Shona always got the children together to apologise to each other after any sort of problem, helping where they could, to patch things up between them.

"There is no greater gift than family" was one of Hone's many, well known sayings. He often shared his wisdom with the family, and his greatest desire was to bring up a family of polite, well-mannered children, who each achieved to the best of their personal ability, cared deeply for one another, and had respect for other people.

The Smith children began their formal education at the local primary school as they didn't attend either a pre-school or kindergarten because of their remote location. Shona did her best to make sure each of her children could at least write their own name and count to ten before they went to school. When the boys first started school, Slade, Luke, and Jake were placed in the same class, enjoying friendly competition to see who would do the best. Luke was a quiet hardworking boy who showed promise even before he started school. He would spend hours drawing and writing on any piece of paper he could find. Luke managed to achieve better results than the other two, mainly due to his hard work and diligence. The other two loved the outdoors, and preferred the idea of being out fishing or catching eels over studying. Slade and Jake both struggled with their schoolwork and would never complete their homework. The minute their schoolbags hit the floor every Friday afternoon, they would be off outdoors, their schoolwork barely crossing their minds again until Monday morning. The boys made lots of new friends at school yet remained very close to each other. They discovered the attraction of girls and this sometimes caused animosity between them - especially Jake and Luke who often liked the same girl.

Their primary education continued with Luke excelling in most subjects. Slade and Jake did only the bare minimum, and instead of going to school they often spent many hours hunting and fishing. The boys each managed to complete their schooling at the local high school, where Luke had continued to remain in the top position of their class. Slade had begun to push the boundaries that Hone and Shona had put in place. He had made his way in with a rough crowd, and soon found himself in trouble. He started bullying some of the other kids, and when he was 14 he seriously beat up a boy who did nothing more than look at Slade in the wrong way and made the mistake of answering back to Slade with a smart comment. His studies were suffering, and the teacher called Hone and Shona so they could discuss his behaviour. The teacher shared her concerns that Slade had the potential to do well yet could not understand why he lacked the desire or motivation to make something of himself. When Hone and Shona returned home they called Slade into their bedroom so they could talk privately about what his teacher had said. Slade got really angry at the fact his teacher and parents had been speaking about him, he could not see the love and concern that was motivating the conversation.

Slade turned to Hone with a jeer,

"You can't tell me what to do. You are not my real father!" Hone, recoiled from this comment and replied,

"I'm the only father you have got, mate. Never think you can talk to me like that, and don't you ever beat up any kid again - or I will sort you out properly."

Slade rolled his eyes at Hone before storming out of the room, slamming the door to every room he passed through on his way to his own. After that conversation, things were never quite the same between Slade and Hone again. Shona told Hone to leave it as she knew Hone would have loved to have given him a thrashing right there on the spot. "You need to be more understanding of the boys, Hone," Shona empathised. "It must be getting harder for them to feel like part of our family, as they grow older the differences are becoming more obvious.

I wonder if we should give them their mother's diaries to read."

"No," Hone disagreed. "They are still too young. We don't want to unsettle them any further. Especially Luke, he is in a really good place. Maybe you are right and this could just be a phase for Slade. Hopefully one he will grow out of."

Hone's thoughts of the diaries that he and Shona had read in order to gain some understanding of the boy's birth mother. Their motivation for reading the diaries lay in their desire to be the best parents they possibly could be for the boys. The diaries held information about the biological father of the boys and about the lives of their mother and their grandmother. They were not going to be particularly easy for the boys to read. Hone and Shona agreed they would wait until they felt the boys were stable and secure enough that they could handle the contents of their mother's deepest thoughts.

CHAPTER ELEVEN

A *month after leaving Gabe's ranch*

The sun had only just risen when Stevo called Gabe to say that he, Sue, Brent, Janey, Roger, and Heather were on their way to pick up the horses and dogs for their hunting trip. Gabe sighed wistfully as he clutched the receiver.

"Sadly I haven't been able to make alternate plans and I just can't join you on this one. Don't worry though, everything is ready to go, and I will see you all soon."

When they arrived at the ranch, Emma was waiting to meet them at the horse paddock. She smiled at their enthusiasm as they cheerfully called out of the truck windows to greet her. It was a lovely day; the sky was a deep blue, it was warm, and the sun was exuding the perfect temperature. The group piled out of the truck and made their way over to where Emma was standing. Roger was wearing his well pressed trousers, a clean white shirt, and resting on his head was his green, wide brimmed hat. The women were wearing denim jeans and various coloured check shirts, without any prior co-ordination they seemed to have created a ladies hunting trip uniform. They all knew the appropriate clothing for the trip into the mountains from the experience they had preparing Brent and Stevo for their many hunting trips. The horses had been led into the paddock for selection, and the girls climbed up onto the rails of the yards.

Brent would of course be riding Big Red, and Stevo had already picked his horse; a piebald stallion called Stormy. Brent and Stevo made their way up to the house, carrying the smoked marlin for the outside chiller Gabe used to cool the fresh meat he killed. They already had their next job lined up, getting the Commer truck ready to cart the horses, so they left the others at the horse paddock to make their selection.

"I'll have the piebald," exclaimed Heather.

"Ah, good choice Heather. This beauty is Misty," Emma smiled. "Gabe names many of his horses after the weather."

A quiet, dark red and white skewbald appealed to Sue. "I'm not a very confident rider but I'm really looking forward to this camping trip," said Sue.

"That's Thunder," Emma paused after noticing Sue flinch. "Don't take any notice of his name, Sue. He's as quiet as a mouse."

Roger, camera flashing, was mumbling quietly about the various ways he could get himself out of the trip at the last minute.

"Oh, you pick one for me, Emma," Roger paused, and then added quietly. "But please make sure it's a quiet one though."

Emma picked out an older grey mare that was still very agile and capable of a trip up the valley.

"Cloudy will look after you," Emma reassured, sensing Roger's reluctance to ride. "Cloudy is very placid and isn't easily strayed."

The group could hear a vehicle making its way up the unsealed driveway quite quickly, and they looked to where they saw a dust cloud making its way closer. It was the farrier.

"Gabe tells me this is an urgent job," called Joe as he climbed out of his truck.

"Sorry guys, the shoeing of the horses slipped our minds," apologised Emma.

"Never you mind Em, I'll sort them out for ya, as always," replied Joe, cigarette smoke billowing out of his mouth as he spoke.

Janey had been quietly watching the horses, sizing them up before being the last to choose hers. She found herself drawn to a beautiful, yellowy/gold palomino mare named Lightning. She came towards the others, leading her horse.

"You had better go and catch your horse or she will be shoeless!" Janey warned Roger, who instantly paled.

Janey laughed as she had already put the lead on Cloudy for Roger, who grumbled his thanks as he took hold of the rope Janey passed to him.

"Is the weather always bad down here?" queried Roger, semi- jokingly. "Of course not, why on earth do you ask?" replied a baffled Emma. "Because your horses are named after bad weather features, none of them are named Sunshine, or Rainbow, or Spring!" Emma laughed,

"I suppose it does seem like that, but only because of the horses you have all chosen. We have an old golden palomino stallion that we've retired from work, his name is Golden Sun. He has some brood mares up there with him – one is even called Rainbow! There is also Brighty, Starlight, Starface and Starbright. They have been the shining stars of our brood mares. I promise we do have beautiful weather here, Roger, and we also have the horses named after them."

With horse shoe nails in his mouth, Joe still managed to call to Brent and Stevo,

"Gabe tells me that you are going for a hunt up the river, I think it looks like the weather is going to be good for another week or so yet. We could do with a bit of rain down here though. It's been very dry lately and Gabe is worried about the grass. Hope the weather holds out for your trip. You could have a bit of a handful with the rest of your group."

He paused before adding,

"What's with the guy with the camera?" Brent just winked.

"Ah, that's Stevo's brother in law, Roger. He's a good guy, but I guess it takes all sorts."

Brent and Stevo loaded the horses onto the old commer truck as the shoeing was completed.

They all strolled their way up to the house for a hearty country meal; bacon and egg pie, sausage rolls, and sandwiches.

They finished eating their lunch, expressed their gratitude, and bid farewell to their friends as they headed for the vehicles. Brent and Stevo each climbed into a driver's seat, Brent in the commer truck and Stevo in his truck.

"I'll travel with you, Stevo," Roger decided, still very wary of the horses.

"Oh, Heather and Sue are coming with me," Stevo replied, much to Roger's dismay. "Brent might need some help with the truck and the horses. So I think you had better travel with him and Janey."

Stevo paused when he saw the look on Roger's face, adding, "We'll follow you though so we won't be too far away should you

need anything. Lead the way, Brent!"

Blue and Buck eagerly jumped up to sit in the cab.

"You dogs had better stay on the floor. Don't even think about sitting on my knee!" warned Roger.

The old pack horse was a bit hesitant to get into the truck but after a bit of coaxing they eventually succeed in getting her on. Gabe had also very generously loaned them the saddles for each horse, including his prized pack horse saddle, which were all loaded onto the back of Stevo's truck.

"Ok, let's hit the road!" called Brent as he slammed home the final bolt to the back of the truck. "It is going to be a long slow trip, 70kms up the windy coast road."

The horses took a while to settle as the old Commer started the journey off by shaking and rattling its way down the road. Brent was a bit worried about the truck but it seemed to right itself after a few kilometres. Roger was, as always, occupied with his camera, clicking away at anything that was interesting to him.

"I hope we are going to pass some shops. I don't want to run out of room on my memory card. I forgot to bring my spare," he mentioned, half to himself and half to the others. Brent and Janey passed a look between each and other and shook their heads.

"I would be more concerned about my backside if I was you Roger; you have three days on the horse ahead of you!" Janey grimaced.

They had left Gabe's ranch at exactly 1 p.m. and were aiming to be at the river by 3.30pm at the latest to give them a couple of hours of daylight to saddle up the horses and begin their journey up the river towards their first campsite.

CHAPTER TWELVE

Arriving at the river, Roger threw open the passenger door of the Commer truck and immediately fell clumsily onto the sand. "Hey, watch your step Roger!" Janey laughed. "You could hurt yourself."

Roger looked up sheepishly.

"That step was further down than I thought!!"

"Hope ya can stay on a horse better than that," chuckled Brent as he held a hand out to Roger, who pulled himself up while mumbling something about checking to see if his beloved camera was ok. Buck and Blue were off, stretching and running up the river, eager to get going. Their noses were high in the air, taking in all the smells from the fresh afternoon breeze wafting down the river. Stevo pulled in and parked right next to the Commer, immediately stepping out and giving the dogs a whistle. They came running straight to him and he gave them an affectionate scratch behind their ears. Brent was busily checking out the banks for a good place to unload the horses. Sue and Heather tumbled out of the car and stretched their legs.

"Brent, what about over here?" Janey asked, pointing to a likely looking bank. "Thanks, Janey, it looks perfect to me! I think there's just enough room to manoeuvre the truck. I'll back it in, then you guys have gotta start unloading. And make sure you tether the horses securely when you get them off - we don't want to have to chase them all over the river as they are very fresh and eager to get to work!"

"I'll just be a minute," Roger called as he made his way into the bushes.

"We all know what you are up to," laughed the others.

Stevo oversaw the unloading of the horses, one at a time, to ensure it all went smoothly. Janey helped by tethering the horses to a nearby Pohutukawa tree, making sure they were unable to wander up the river. They managed to quickly unload the well used leather saddles from Stevo's truck, and identify which saddle belonged to each horse. They smelled strongly of lanolin oil which had been lovingly rubbed into them for preservation.

"Hey Roger," called Heather excitedly. "Give us a hand to get the horses ready for our trip."

"Sure, love. Show me what to do," replied Roger.

They put the girths around the horses and then stretched the horses legs forward to make sure that there was no skin pinching underneath the girth strap and put their breast plates and crops on so the saddles would stay in the right place on the horses. Brent finished loading up the packhorse before joining Stevo and Roger to put their rifles into the scabbards that hung from their saddles. Brent owned a Winchester 270, Roger was content with a 303 that once belonged to his grandfather, and Stevo had his stainless steel Ruger 308 that Sue had bought him for Christmas. Stevo had shown her which rifle to purchase on one of their trips to town, explaining how the stainless steel would prevent rust. Stevo had never been the best at cleaning his hunting gear after using it, unlike Brent who had always cared for his gear really well which always gave him confidence that his shot would go exactly where he wanted.

"Did you know, Brent, that the rifle is the seventh most important

tool of all time, in terms of its impact on civilisation? Humans have always made spears, slings, and bows, but the rifle puts all those tools to shame with its accuracy, power, reliability, and range," said Stevo.

Brent's mouth dropped open in complete astonishment. Stevo laughed at Brent's obvious reaction,

"Don't worry, Brent. I haven't become a scholar overnight. I read all that in the Bugle – the deerstalkers magazine," he smiled while admiring his new gun.

Brent quickly regained his composure.

"Never mind the seventh, Stevo, your gun must be the most important tool of all from the look of it."

Brent too lent over to admire the gun, knowing how proud Stevo was of it, quite rightly, as the Ruger 308 was the best gun Stevo had ever possessed.

"When you are out in the back of beyond you can't compromise on quality, mate. Although, that thing is bloody shiny isn't it Steve? It will scare all the deer away!"

"Yeah, yeah," laughed Stevo. "I've got a reel of tape to put around the stainless steel barrel. Hopefully that will disguise it."

Brent had packed a few bottles of good rum, and Stevo licked his lips and pointed.

"That'll taste good after we bag the big stag."

"Knowing us mate, we'll be having a few drinks before then, Stevo!" replied Brent.

"OK everyone, saddle up, we're off!"

Everybody climbed up onto their horse with ease, except of course Roger, who struggled to make his way up onto his old mare. Janey quickly jumped down and legged Roger up.

"Are you comfortable?" she asked.

"I suppose I am as comfortable and ready as I will ever be, up here sitting on this scrap of leather, on top of this old horse," sighed Roger. Janey just smiled to herself at Roger's observations about the saddle and horse – neither which were as old or as crappy as Roger had made out. She re-mounted her horse in one easy movement. Roger hated how he was always the one who struggled to keep up with the others. Buck and Blue had sensed they were about to get moving, and were spinning around in their excitement to get going. The dogs weren't sure if they were allowed to go, so they ran just a little way up the river. They were constantly looking back to see if the horses had started following them yet. The dogs' excitement to get moving had rubbed off on the horses,

also very eager to begin the trek.

"Okay …" came Brent voice from where he sat proudly and tall upon Big Red. He looked around at his fellow saddled riders and then glanced towards where the trucks were parked up – one last check before they made their way up the river.

"All right, team," Brent called out. "We are now ready to move.

So let's go, let's be out there doing it!"

Roger looked pleased to be acknowledged as one of the team, and felt a twinge of excitement as they headed off with Brent in the lead. Brent noticed the dogs had managed to run a bit further away than he had realised. He whistled them back, and smiled as they swiftly came running back looking like they were wondering what the holdup was. The wide mouth of the river, where it entered the sea, was where they were starting their journey from. The first hour was pretty easy going, as the river was braided and easy for the horses. Everybody seemed to be managing their horses well, even Roger, who had managed to ride while taking some spectacular photos of the scenery. His old mare had got in line and she was following the other horses.

"I am beginning to think I am going to enjoy this trip more than I thought possible," he commented.

After another hour of riding, the river had begun to narrow up. The native bush on both sides of the river was getting thicker. The air was filled with the sounds of birds chirping. The riders had to swat the mosquitoes away which were trying to feast on them.

"There'll be no more cell phone coverage from here on. If you want to ring the kids you had better do it now," Brent warned the others. Janey called Daniel and asked him to ring Eugene and Ingrid to make sure they were all okay - and to tell them they would see them when they returned from their trip. Heather spoke to James, and asked him to ring Sharon, Sue called Bradley and spoke to him briefly. Josh and Thomas were still overseas. The kids all wished their parents well, expressing their hopes for a great trip – and a great hunt. While the ladies talked on their phones, Brent motioned that he wanted to talk to Stevo.

"The river is down quite a bit, and it is dry, just like Joe was saying." "Yes, it's been a long summer. The rains will come soon but not for another week, I hope," Stevo smiled.

As Brent lead the way up the river, he came around a corner to find a big, deep pool that contained large boulders. It was going to be impossible for the horses to get through. After having a good look around, Brent could see that they would have to get their horses to jump a 1.5 metre high bank out of the river, before the pool, and then try to make their way around it through the bush. The rest of the party had caught up while Brent was deciding what would be the best thing to do. He pointed the dilemma out to Stevo.

"Looks like we will have to jump the horses up here to get around. The storm has changed the river quite a lot."

Stevo nodded his head in agreement as he rolled himself a cigarette. Brent backed Big Red up a bit, so he could get a clear jump at the bank. He gave Big Red a dig with the heel of his boot and held on as the horse leapt up the bank. There was plenty of scrub and debris in front of the horse as it reached the top, which then flattened out. Big Red's front feet had hit a big rotten log which was lying in the scrub at the top of the bank. The log, being quite long and heavy, rolled over half way with the impact of the horse's front feet. The big chestnut shied violently sideways, nearly throwing Brent off.

"What on earth could have spooked you? You're the bravest horse in the whole world!" Brent spoke lovingly to Big Red.

Brent looked sideways towards the log, his eye catching a movement. There was the biggest, ugliest weta Brent had ever seen - and it was looking very agitated. It was crawling its way up on to the top of the log, each of its long spiny legs were arched in defence mode. The log, being hollow underneath, was the perfect home for this native New Zealand insect. This particular weta was far larger than usual, nearly the size of a young kitten. It held its heavily armoured head upright, giving a really annoyed appearance at having its home destroyed. Its powerful mandibles were waving around as if to say; come near me and I will tear you to bits! It's large, spiny hind legs had begun flexing its body up and down. Brent could tell this thing was really perplexed. The reddish brown head, and the stripy yellow and brown abdomen, made it look even more heinous.

'God …' Brent thought to himself. 'This is the most repulsive, God awful thing I have ever seen!'

Brent had read about these big wetas, but had no idea just how big they could be. He had learned that they could be cannibalistic but mainly ate insects and leaves. As he backed up his horse, the massive weta began to move forward along the log. He knew that these things could jump so he kept his distance.

Brent looked around to see where the others were. As he turned his head, Janey was just getting her horse ready to jump. Before he had a chance to say anything, she had landed safely and swiftly at the top of the bank. Brent pointed towards the log and Janey looked down at the log as Brent noticed the shocked look on her face. The rest of the horses easily made their way up the bank and everybody, including the horses, looked at the weta. The horses had their ears pricked forward as they too watched the weta which was now standing and eyeballing the intruders of his environment.

The weta had become really agitated with the audience. It had begun to rub its back legs together, making an awful screeching sound while opening and closing its jaws. All along the bottom of the log were heaps of tiny white dots.

"Must be eggs," Stevo spoke, exhaling a lung full of cigarette smoke. "This things got a whole bloody nest in here!"

As they looked, they noticed that there were another pair of large feelers poking out of a second hole. Roger moved his horse forward so he could get a better photo. The giant weta rushed along the log, his long legs waving towards Roger. His horse stepped backwards so quickly that Roger just about dropped his camera.

"Wonder what these things are eating up here that's making them get so huge. That's one oversized weta. It's the ugliest thing I have ever seen. We should check our sleeping bags tonight before we get into them," Stevo observed.

After they watched the massive weta for a while and Roger got some great photos, the group rode along the bank, dropping back into the creek further along. They rode for another hour without too many dramas, making their way around logs and slips. At one point, Stevo motioned to Brent.

"This storm really did some damage in here. I think we could be in for a few problems tomorrow."

"Yeah," sighed Brent. "I'll say. It really looks like it could get bad - and difficult riding."

Brent had noticed a good area on the right-hand side of the river to set up camp.

"What do you think about camping here for the night, Stevo? It's only about an hour or so until dark."

"Looks good to me, there is plenty of wild river grass for the horses, the grass has thrived on the fertile river flats so that will keep them happy. Blue and Buck have been for a few looks up the sides for pigs, but they haven't come across anything yet."

They quickly organised their camp for the night. Brent got the fire going while Janey, Heather, and Sue organised the food for dinner. Roger was looking very bent over as he wandered into camp after tethering his horse securely. Stevo glanced over at Brent and asked how he was feeling after the long ride.

"Got a sore backside, Brent?"

"Not as bad as Roger's by the look of him!"

They managed to put together a nice dinner, after which they shared a few rums under the stars. The stories became more and more exaggerated as the rum began to flow more freely.

"I hope there are more than just those two bottles I saw," Stevo piped up.

"You should know me better than that! There are plenty more on the other side of the horse's saddle bag, all wrapped up in newspaper so they don't break or make a noise. You have to keep the load balanced, you know," laughed Brent.

Stevo smiled at his friend, then turned to the others, "We had better get some sleep. We have got two very long days ahead of us before we reach the Bull Ring, where we will set up our proper camp." "Don't forget to check for wetas!" reminded Heather, to the squeals and protests of the rest of the crew.

They all found their sleeping bags, zipped up their flies to keep the dew off, and settled down for the night. Brent checked on the horses and tied the dogs up for the night.

"We don't want you two going off on adventures while we are not there to share the fun," he said as he threw them some biscuits.

After such a big day of organising the trip, getting the truck and horses ready with all of their gear, saying their goodbyes, and riding this far up the river, they were all very tired.

"Another big day tomorrow," commented Brent. "Sleep well."

Stevo nodded his head in agreement, and they both climbed into their tents ready to hit the sack for the night. Brent and Stevo always kept their guns within easy reach at night. You never know what could happen when you are hunting out in the wilderness.

CHAPTER THIRTEEN

Life on the coast was quiet for the three boys. When Slade turned 15 he told his family of a decision he had made, "That's it, I have had enough! I'm never going back to school again. I'm gonna move away and find a job in the forestry."

Luke tried his hardest to convince his brother to stay at home, but Slade had already made up his mind.

"We've never been apart before, Slade. I really want to stay at school and pass my exams. Why don't you get a job helping Dad with the crayfishing?"

"I'm too dumb to stay at school any longer, Luke. Any way that's your dream, not mine. There's no way I could ever work with Dad," scoffed Slade. "My mind is made up, and I've already talked about it with Dad. He thinks I am better off getting a job too. I want to get away from here."

"Dad has got a mate who will give me a job in a forestry gang and I can stay with Nan until I get a flat of my own."

Slade could see that Luke looked shattered by the idea of being separated from his twin brother. He reluctantly agreed that this would probably be the best thing for Slade.

Hone got in touch with Jazz Jones, an old mate of his who ran things in one of the forrestry businesses. Things were organised quite quickly and, early in March, Slade moved away from home to board with Hone's mum; Nan. He began to work in one of the forestry gangs right away, with Jazz Jones, overseeing him.

In the beginning, Jake and Luke would go up every couple of weeks to visit him on the weekends. Jake would always take his ukulele so Slade could enjoy a touch of home with a sing-along after a few beers.

Slade was making really good money, and he had managed to make some friends. He was enjoying a great social life. He had quickly moved out from Nan's home and gone flatting with some of his work mates. Slade had bought himself a small ute which gave him some freedom on the weekends. Jake and Luke realised that they were both quite envious of their brother's success but they both knew they wanted to stay at school until they passed their exams because they believed their father when he always said they only had one chance at their education. They had goals they were working towards, which included an apprenticeship after they left school. Hone and Shona didn't want them leave school as Hone desired for his boys to have a good education and a trade behind them. Jake and Luke's visits to Slade became less frequent as the pressure mounted at school. Slade was growing like a weed and the forestry work was making him physically stronger. He had made some good friends; with both his flatmates and the other guys at work. They were a very social group and often stopped off at the pub for a few beers on the way home from work. Even though Slade was still under the legal drinking age he looked much older due to being over six foot tall and his long black hair. His workmates always covered for him on the very rare occasions he was ever questioned about his age. Things had been going well for Slade and he had found himself really enjoying working for Jazz Jones.

One night, during the middle of his first year away from home, Slade was down at the pub having a few drinks with his work mates. A gangly bloke who was the friend of one of his work mates approached their group and began talking to them. He kept looking at Slade at every opportunity. Slade had finally had enough of being stared at,

"How come you keep looking at me?"

The air went stiff all around them as everyone drew in a large breath, wondering what was going to go down between the two men. They knew Slade was easily riled, and they had found it hard to get him to back down in the past. The guy turned to Slade finally, looking at him directly,

"Sorry mate, didn't mean anything. Just thought you looked like a bloke I used to know. He looked just like you when he was a teenager."

"Is that so?" questioned Slade calmly, when he realised the guy wasn't looking for trouble.

The bloke asked for Slade's surname at the exact same time Slade was handed the pool cue and told Slade,

"You're up mate."

After sinking both the green and the purple, quickly followed by the white, he returned to find himself unable to answer the man's question as he had disappeared. Instead, Slade turned to his work mate, his interest still captivated by the strange encounter.

"Has your friend gone?"

"Yeah. He reckons you look exactly like an old friend of his. I know the guy he means, and I can definitely see a vague likeness. But then, I didn't know him when he was your age like my mate did."

The pool cue was handed to Slade again, and the conversation changed to other things.

The next day he was sitting with the boys, sharing their lunch after a long morning of work, when the conversation came back around to him and his alleged look alike. He had not been able to put the thought out of his mind. Slade had always known that Hone was not his birth father, yet had never thought about the possibility of having a real Dad, and perhaps finding him. Slade kept wondering if the man he looked so much alike, could possibly be his father.

A few weeks passed and Slade tried to push it from his mind as he had lots of questions but as he hadn't managed to see the guy from the pub again he had not even a single answer.

After a long day of working in the hot summer sun, Slade had gone down to the pub to enjoy a couple of cold beers. He had just cracked the top off his second bottle of Steinlager when he looked up and saw the bloke he had talked to a few weeks earlier, drinking with some of his friends.

Slade decided to wander over and say g'day,

"Hey, you know this guy you reckon I look like, what's his name?"

The elder man looked hard at Slade, again aware of the striking similarity between the two men.

"Joe Sisson. Why's that mate?"

"Well, I was adopted at birth and I have no idea who my birth father is. It's been playing on my mind if I look so much like ..." Slade paused. "Joe, you say? Yeah, um that maybe Joe could be my father. Do you reckon there is a chance he could be my father?"

"Ooh, I don't know anything about that mate. Joe is about my age, so of course it is possible, but I wouldn't have a clue."

"Do you know where Joe is living now?"

"I'm not sure. I think he is still around here somewhere, but I haven't seen him for quite a while. He had a bit of trouble with his lady, and then he lost his drivers license so he couldn't come out into the bush logging. He got a job in the mill and used to get picked up by the work van. I know someone who would know where he is living if you wanted me to try find out?"

"Thanks, mate. I'll let you know if that's ok." The bloke was more than ok with that.

"Yes, I am curious now. Whatever you want, I'm not worried."

Slade turned and walked back to his table, he ran his hand through his hair as he tried to absorb all of this new information. Slade felt that he needed to talk everything through with someone, and he decided that his Nan was a very wise woman so he would seek her advice about what to do. He promised himself that he would go to see her as soon as he got a chance.

Slade could sense that Nan was a bit worried about him wanting to find out about his birth father as she thought it could unsettle him rather than bring him peace. She knew Slade had always had a great life as part of her family living down the coast. After Slade had left, Nan called Shona to tell her that Slade had been asking questions, and to get her advice about what she should do next. Shona thanked Nan for ringing and explained that the boy's birth mother had left diaries for them to read when they were old enough. Shona had read the diaries belonging to the boy's birth mother, and remembered that in one of them it claimed that the birth father's name was indeed Joe Sisson. Shona and Hone decided that because of what Slade had been told they had better tell him about the diaries now. He was already putting two and two together, and they knew it was better if the news came directly from them. They went to see Slade one weekend and stayed with Nan. Slade came to visit, and Shona showed him the diary she had brought up with her. Slade kept very quiet and still as he read every single word his birth mother had written in the diary laying open in his hands. His mouth fell open as he read the passage containing the information about his father several times. The name in the diary was exactly the same as the name of the guy that the bloke at the pub had said he looked like. He was amazed. He hugged Shona and Hone.

"I can't believe that my birth father is living in the same town as me. I think I want to meet him."

Shona began to look worried.

"Do you think that is a good idea? He might not even know about you and Luke."

"I know I won't be able to settle until I have met him, I love you both dearly but this is my birth father. He won't ever be able to replace you in my life, but I just feel that I need to meet him."

"Whatever you think is best, Son," encouraged Hone. "You know we are always here for you."

They hugged each other again. A single tear made its way down Shona's cheek and fell onto the back of her son's shoulder. Shona knew that this day was always going to come, but she could not quite believe it had come so soon.

Slade felt quite excited about the possibility of meeting his birth father, even though he loved Shona and Hone as parents, something made him desperately want to meet Joe Sisson.

He rang Luke one night after work. "Hey Luke, how's it going? Did Mum and Dad tell you what I have found out about our birth fathr?" "Yeah, and I'm not happy. Mum and Dad are our parents. I don't

want to even talk about him," replied Luke angrily.

"Hang on, I just want to meet him to see what he is like. Nothing will change with Mum and Dad," said Slade.

"Yeah right. It won't be the same. I told you I don't want to know or have anything to do with this guy," said Luke.

"Maybe you'll change your mind when you meet him. We'll see," said Slade.

"Whatever!!" Luke slammed the phone down.

Slade decided that they should try to meet Joe the next time Luke came up to stay- but he didn't say anything to Luke because he didn't want to upset him any further. Slade had Joe's address, from the man at the pub. Slade was really excited about the possibility of meeting his biological father.

One Saturday morning, Jake and Luke arrived in the city to stay for the weekend.

"Hi mate, how are things with you? Dad gave me some crays to give to you. They are in the boot, I'll just go and grab them," Jake remembered suddenly.

Slade followed Jake out to the car. Jake popped the boot and pulled out a sugar sack full of crays.

"Man! These are some fat looking crays! Thanks, Jake. I'll give Dad a ring to tell him thanks."

"He would like that. Mum too. They worry about you being up here on your own. You have got them really worried with this stuff about wanting to find your birth father."

"I know, but it's just something that I feel like I have to do. I need to talk to Luke and see what he thinks."

"Yeah, sooner the better, I reckon. He doesn't talk about it at all," Jake lowered his voice as they headed in through the door.

Luke had turned the TV on and was swigging on a beer. Slade and Jake both dropped onto the couch with Luke, and Slade grabbed the remote and immediately switched off the TV.

Luke yelled, "Hey man, what the hell? I was watching that!"

Slade lifted his hand to silence his twin, and stated that they needed to talk.

"I think you know what about, Lukey." "Yeah, I guess I do," sulked Luke.

Jake was looking embarrassed; he had never seen Slade so serious before.

"Are you okay, Slade?"

"Yeah, yeah. We just have to talk about what I have found out. We have always known we are adopted and I have this real need to meet up with our birth father."

Jake and Luke both sat there silently.

Luke eventually looked at his brother,

"Why are you doing this, Slade? Can't you see how hurtful it is to Mum and Dad?"

Jake sat there saying nothing.

"Have you never wanted to know who our birth father is?" Slade asked.

"Never gave it a thought until you brought it up. Hone's my dad and always will be - no matter who this Sisson guy is."

"Hone's my dad too. But I want to know who my birth father is and what he looks like. I have found out where he lives. I've told Mum and Dad."

Slade could see that Jake was now looking really embarrassed.

Luke said, "Okay I can see you are not going to let this go. We might as well find out what you know about our biological father, and then we can all get on with life."

Slade filled them in on the story about how he found out about Joe Sisson, and how similar the bloke at the pub reckons they were.

Jake finally spoke,

"That's cool, Slade. We will go and see him if that is what you want. Is it okay if I come with you when you go to see him? I'll just wait in the car."

"Of course that's okay. We will need your moral support, you're our brother Jake."

"C'mon mate, cheer up," said Slade. There is nothing wrong with wanting to know your family history." Jake reminded his two brothers of the Māori ideology of 'whakapapa.' Māori people have always believed it is your whakapapa, your geneology, which creates who it is that you are. Without your whakapapa, you are nothing.

"Ok," said Luke. "We'll just go there. It will put Slade's mind at rest and hopefully that will be the end of it."

"I hope so. Where is this place, Slade?" asked Jake.

"It's over the other side of town. I've got the address here," Slade held out a scruffy piece of paper.

"Let's go now then, before I chicken out," whispered Luke.

He was upset but that he also wanted to get it over with. Slade had thought that he and Luke would go to meet their father on their own, but he could now see that Jake was having none of that. He was going to be a part of it come hell or high water! As they headed out to the car the emotions were running quite high, so they continued to speak very little.

Luke finally asked Slade,

"What are you gonna say when we walk up to the door?"

"Look, I don't know. I'll think of something," responded Slade, who had also been wondering the very same thing. "I feel as bad as you do about this, but we've got to at least have a look."

"I guess," Luke muttered.

Jake tried to relieve the tension quipping, "Hey, he might be really rich or something!"

Neither of the twins made a comment. They were each engrossed in their own thoughts. As Slade turned the key in the ignition, Luke told the boys,

"I'm going to need a few drinks after this!"

Slade pulled up at the address he'd been given and turned the car off. They all just sat there looking around at the house, the street, and at each other. The house itself looked like an old state house and the lawns clearly had not been mowed for a very long time. There was an old, shabby looking car in the driveway.

"This must be it, the address is right," whispered Slade.

Luke could see Slade was now feeling a bit reluctant and he was wearing a very grim look. Trying to break the tension again Jake scoffed,

"Don't think he's rich!!"

Slade just gave Jake a stare as Luke spoke quietly,

"Well, we're here now so we might as well go up to the door and see what happens."

The twins clambered out of the car. "I'm just going to wait here," called Jake. "Nah, come up with us."

"No, I'm waiting here. You two need to do this together," he reassured them kindly.

"Okay, if that's what you want. We won't be long."

Luke and Slade walked slowly up the broken path to the front door and Slade knocked nervously. Music was coming from inside.

Their first knock wasn't answered so Slade knocked again, a little louder the second time. Just as he did this, the door was opened by a big guy wearing a grubby grey tee shirt, that appeared to have once been white and without the gaping hole near his belly button. He let out a loud belch as he demanded,

"What the hell do you want?"

Slade was a bit taken aback by this and Luke just stared on in silence.

"What do you want?" the man repeated even more impatiently, "Hope you're not debt collectors again," he growled, looking past them and towards the other person Jake, in the car.

"No," Slade finally managed to say. "We are looking for Joe Sisson." "You are looking right at him," boomed the big guy.

Just then, a woman's voice yelled out,

"Who's that, Joe? Close the door, its bloody cold!"

"Well, quick. What do you boys want? I've got a card game going." Slade, thinking quickly, said the first thing that came to his mind, "We heard you had a chainsaw for sale."

"Nah, not me young fella."

The door was given a swift kick by a dirty-socked foot, and their biological father was gone.

Slade and Luke both just stood there. Slade was stunned and unable to move or speak. Eventually he turned, grabbed Luke by the shoulder and they slowly began to walk down the path.

"What the hell did you say that for?" demanded Luke.

"Don't know bro. It just came out. I couldn't ask him straight out if he was our father."

"Well, was it him?" asked Jake.

"Yeah, that was Joe Sisson alright," shuddered Luke. "Well, what did he say?"

"He says that he hasn't got a chainsaw for sale!" laughed Luke. "What did you ask him that for Slade?"

"I don't know. I just couldn't come out and ask him if he was our father. It just didn't seem the right time." Slade repeated, really upset with himself.

"I guess you're right, can't just rock up to a guy's house and tell him we are his long lost twin sons! Actually that was some pretty quick thinking, Slade."

"Shot brother, just didn't have time to think of anything else!" Slade realised that he had seen a resemblance between himself and

Joe Sisson and could easily see how the first connection had been made. "Well, what are we going to do now?"

"What's with all the bloody questions?" snapped Slade.

"This was your stupid plan, got any other great ideas?" Luke threw back at him.

"Hey, both of you! Cut it out. It's okay guys," interrupted Jake. "There is no point in arguing about this. Let's head back and think about what we should do next."

"Joe's a big dude. I reckon he did look a bit like you too Slade. Got himself a big pot belly, though," Luke mentioned, trying to break the tension. "And his missus can sure yell loudly!"

"Yeah, she seemed like a crazy one aye!" replied Slade with a smile on his face.

He had become even more curious about getting to know Joe Sisson – his birth father. He knew he would be going back.

The boys decided to head into the local pub and have a few beers before going home. They weren't particularly in the mood for socialising but Slade thought a change of scenery and a beer may give them a new perspective on the situation.

The boys were hungry as they had not eaten much, and mid afternoon was upon them. Once they got back to Slade's place, they ate some of Hone's delicious crayfish and shared a couple more beers.

"I think we should go back today," said Luke.

Luke knew that now Slade had seen Joe, he wouldn't be able to let it go until he knew more about the man, and whether he knew anything about them.

"I reckon if we leave it for later, we will worry about it all night and probably won't get any sleep."

"I guess you are right," sighed Slade, relieved that Luke seemed to be okay now they had actually met Joe.

"If we are going back today, we had better go because it will be starting to get dark soon."

They pulled up at Joe Sisson's house for the second time that day. This time the sun was lower in the sky, casting shadows across the garden. Slade slammed the door in his hurry to reach the front door; Luke could hardly keep up with him. Slade rapped loudly on the door with his fist. A woman with ratty hair and the deep creases of a heavy smoker appeared, looking the boys up and down as she snarled,

"What do you want?" "We want to talk to Joe."

Slade did not want to waste time now that they were brave enough to have come back. Joe came to the door and eyed them suspiciously as he recognised the twins from earlier in the day.

"What are you back for? I ain't got a chainsaw for sale. I already told you that."

"Well, nah. It's not about that," spluttered Slade. "Spit it out then, boy," growled Joe.

"A bloke down at the pub told me you are Joe Sisson." "Yeah, and I already told you that's me."

"Well, my name is Slade and this is my twin brother Luke. We are looking for some relations of ours with the surname Sisson."

Big Joe put his hand up and rubbed his jaw roughly.

"What, you reckon you might be my cousins or something?" "Something like that," muttered Slade.

"Well I don't know where you got your information but ya never know, we could be related. I would invite you in but as you can see I have got a bit going on right now."

At exactly that moment, a loud cheer came from inside where Joe's mates were still there playing cards and drinking.

"How about you boys come back tomorrow? We can talk some more and try to find out just where you fit in. My sister will be here tomorrow and she knows everyone and everything about the family. See you about 12 o'clock, okay?"

"Sure, thanks. 12pm would work for us," confirmed Slade. He was beaming with excitement. "See you tomorrow."

Luke held up his hand to say farewell as they traipsed back to the car.

"He thinks his sister knows everything about the family - our news might be a bit of a shock for them!" said Slade.

"Ha, yeah I reckon! I hope it goes okay when we come back tomorrow."

"Time will tell, I guess."

When they got to the car Luke laughed as he told Jake, "Well, we have an appointment for lunchtime tomorrow." Slade glared in Luke's direction and snarled,

"I'm pleased you think this is all so funny, Luke."

Jake could see that Slade wasn't seeing the funny side, and that instead both of them were quite unsettled from the day's events.

"I'm sure he didn't mean anything by that comment, Slade. Sounds like you'll know more tomorrow so it wasn't a waste of time coming back this afternoon. It will put your mind at rest."

"Yeah you're right, Jake. It will."

"You know I don't think it is a joke, Slade. I was just trying to lighten the tension. It seemed Joe didn't have the foggiest idea who we were. Thought we might be cousins of his - what a shock he is going to get!" exclaimed Luke as he slapped his twin on the back.

"Yeah, he doesn't know anything about us," echoed Slade sadly. "Maybe he didn't even know our birth mother was pregnant. It

sounds like his sister knows a lot about the family history though." "Doesn't look like he's got much except a big pot belly," sighed Luke. "Shouldn't judge a book by its cover, Luke," warned Jake.

"Oh, so you're a scholar now, are you?" laughed Slade.

"Nah, but you should give him a chance. Don't be so down on him. Let him have his say tomorrow and see where you go from there." "Yeah, I guess you're right," Luke agreed. "I'm starving. Let's go home and eat the rest of Dad's crays."

Just before midday the following morning, the boys headed to Joe's place again. This time Jake came with them as they wandered up to the house where a dark haired large built woman greeted them.

"Hi!" the woman called cheerfully. "I'm Tina, Joe's sister. You must be the boys Joe was talking about. You really think you might be related to us?"

"Yip, that's right. I'm Slade Smith and these are my two brothers Luke and Jake." Joe came up behind Tina.

Pointing to Jake Slade said,

"This is my brother, Jake. He is not related by blood to the Sissons. We think only me and Luke might be. We were fostered at birth when our mother died, and brought up by Jake's family. We have only recently found out our birth father's name."

"Ok, wow!" exclaimed Joe's sister. "Who were your birth parents?" "Our mother was Kate Clark," started Slade.

"Kate Clark, did you say?" interrupted Joe. "Yes," Slade confirmed tentatively.

Joe looked surprised.

"Oh, that's a name from the past. I knew Kate. We were an item once."

"Shona and Hone Smith are our parents," confirmed Luke, all of a sudden very tired and no longer wanting to continue the conversation.

"Well come in and let's sit down," Tina looked deep in thought as they sat down at the table,

"Kate's boys?" she muttered.

Joe led the way to the lounge where a mini beer fridge was sitting right next to what appeared to be his favourite chair. He pulled some cans from the fridge and handed them around.

"Well, Katie and I had a good time for a while. But things turned pretty rough. I was going through a bad time around then."

"What do you mean, a bad time?" questioned Slade. Joe held up his beer can.

"Too much of this, and on top of that I was doing a few drugs back then too. But I got it sorted and I'm better now. After we broke up I went to rehab for a while before heading to Aussie where I got a job. I heard from some mates that Kate had died, and I wanted to come back for her funeral - but I was broke. Life in Aussie wasn't all it was cracked up to be. I didn't know she was pregnant. They didn't tell me that bit."

"Well, she was. And she had twins … Luke and I." Slade held his can up to his twin brother before continuing. "She kept a diary, and in it she named you as the father of her babies."

"What!" exclaimed Joe as he leapt to his feet. "You must be joking."

He had been looking a bit sad remembering Kate, but his look had now changed to one of absolute bewilderment.

"No, couldn't be. I'm sure I would have known."

"Well, that's what she wrote in her diary anyway," Luke mentioned. "Shit mate, I just don't know what to say. So you boys reckon you

are my sons? I can't cope with this. Sorry, but I just have to go. Tina, look after the boys."

"Hey wait, we know it's a big shock," said Slade. "We just needed to see the man our birth mum named as our father."

"Nah, gotta go," muttered Joe.

Shaking his head, he staggered his way down the hallway towards the back of the house. Tina watched as he walked away, then turned to face the twins.

"I'm sorry boys, your news seems to have rocked Joe. He doesn't cope so well with unexpected things. But please, tell me everything you know."

Slade and Luke explained the finer details of the discovery of their birth parents. They had grown up with the knowledge of Kate and their grandmother Julie, who had been at school with Shona, but were of course just as surprised as Tina and Joe with the latest discovery of their paternal heritage.

Tina smiled at the boys, as she realised that they would now on be a part of her life in which whānau had always played a huge part. "This is just amazing. Of course it is the absolute last thing I expected when Joe said you were coming today. Could you give us some time to absorb all this?" Tina paused. "How about you give me

your phone number, and either Joe or I will be in touch?"

Slade took the piece of paper that Tina handed him, writing his details as he spoke.

"I know it is a bit of a shock. We were exactly the same when we first found out that Joe was our father and that we are both living in the same town yet knew nothing of each other. I have felt really unsettled ever since, I just knew I had to try to meet Joe."

"I can definitely understand that," Tina empathized as she took back the piece of paper, patting Slade's hand as she did so. "We just need some time to think. I am sure Joe will be in touch soon."

"I hope so," piped up Luke. "And thanks for letting us come over. And sorry for the shock. We didn't really know how else to tell you." "I can only imagine what it must have been like for you," Tina said.

She gave the boys a brief hug and then they headed back to their ute. "Well, I'm pleased that's over," sighed Luke.

"Over? What? Over? Bro, it is only just the beginning!" "He took the news quite hard, didn't he?"

"It would have been a big shock for him. We have had time to prepare ourselves, it came right out of the blue for him! I hope he contacts us soon. I would like to get to know him better."

Slade was feeling quite let down, he had hoped for something different. He wasn't sure what exactly, but he had thought his biological father might at least want to get to know him, or that he would be slightly more welcoming. Joe didn't impress either Slade or Luke very much and they drove home quietly, each deep in their own thoughts. After Tina waved the boys off, she closed the front door and followed Joe's footsteps down the hallway. She found him, slumped in his favourite dining chair with his head in his hands, leaning against the rustic kitchen table. Tina plonked herself down on the

seat adjacent to her brothers.

"Well, that was the very last thing I expected to hear. But, I do think those boys are yours aye Joe."

"I think they could be, Tina."

"The big one is a dead ringer of you."

"Yeah, he does look a bit like I did at that age. I know Kate wouldn't have written down that I was the father if it wasn't true. She was very honest. I just can't believe she didn't let me know, they're my sons too for fuck sake!"

"Kate would have had her reasons. You were pretty unsettled back then if I remember correctly," Tina offered kindly. She made her way over to the third drawer which held a lot of photos, including some of Joe from when he was younger.

"Hey, look at this, Joe. This is a photo of you when you were about 18, but it could easily be a photo of Slade even though he is a bit younger. He looks just like you did at around that age."

"Yeah. Just hope he doesn't turn out like me, Tina. I've made a real mess of some things in my life and to find out now that I've got two sons that my ex-partner didn't even want me to know anything about, pretty much takes the cake. Ahh, Tina. Maybe she was right to do what she did, they're certainly better off with their family down the coast. I don't want them to know what a loser I have been."

"You are not a loser, Joe. Don't talk like that. You have made some dumb decisions and had some problems, just like we all have, but you have got a lot of good things going on for you too."

"No, Tina. I always took the easy options in life, and I'm still paying for it. No license and having to rely on others to get me to work, bloody useless! I'm not going to encourage the boys to come back and get to know me better. They are much better off without me in their lives. It looks like they are doing okay and I would hate to mess things up for them. It must have been really hard for them to come around here to see me. They are brave boys."

"Give it a bit of time and see what happens, Joe. You owe them that much. You're over the drugs and seem to be coping well. Maybe the boys could be good for you, give you something positive to focus on, and make you really happy. You could be good for them too. They are obviously looking for something that is missing, Joe - and it's you. You have got a lot to offer them and it would be good for you to get to know them and learn about their lives."

Joe was getting very emotional, thinking about how he had never made it to Kate's funeral and about how he had treated her.

"Don't worry. It will all work out one-way or another. We will leave things as they are for now," said Tina.

CHAPTER FOURTEEN

Weeks went by and Slade and Luke had still heard nothing from Joe or his sister. Because of this, Slade had found himself slipping into a never-ending bad mood. He had also begun to drink more and more heavily. He was taking days off work and calling them his 'Me Days.' On these particular days he would just mope around, lie in bed all day, drink whatever he could find, and feel extremely sorry for himself. Luke and Jake had long gone back to the coast, but they called him regularly.

Slade had pinned all of his hopes onto the meeting with Joe, and now had no idea of where things stood. All he knew was that he had managed to meet his biological father, only to find out that Joe had then wanted to know nothing about him and the reality was causing Slade to slink into a deep depression. He was working hard and drinking hard. He was taking more 'Me Days' than he should have been. The alcohol he was consuming always seemed to help him to forget for a while, but as soon as he sobered up he realised that the truth had not changed and this played with his mind. Slade had spent many hours thinking about the situation, and about what type of guy Joe must be. 'This guy must be a gutless wonder, not even able to sit down and talk with Luke and me!' Slade realised. 'Joe didn't even seem to be interested in the fact he had two teenage sons sitting right in front of him, two boys who just wanted to get to know him, to know something, anything, about their birth families. He didn't even acknowledge what it was like for us to get up the courage to go around to his house and meet him! He clearly doesn't care about us or what we might be feeling.'

"Man, this sucks," Slade spoke aloud to the ceiling while lying in bed on one of his Me Days. "I wish that guy in the pub had just left me alone, and then none of this would have happened."

Slade knew that he could not stand this waiting game much longer. After hearing nothing over the following days, he decided he would drive past Joe's place. Slade stopped outside the unkempt section. He felt the rage boil through his blood; he slammed his fist against the steering wheel and decided it was time for them to have a talk. When he got out Slade slammed the door of his ute behind him. He could see a light on inside Joe's house. He marched straight up to the front door and banged on it forcefully. The door shook with the force of his fist, but he didn't stop to care. He was beyond angry at how Joe had completely ignored him, and Slade felt that he needed to tell him how he saw treating people that way as totally unacceptable, especially his two sons. Joe came to the door pretty quickly. When Joe looked out from behind the door, Slade could tell he was shocked to see him standing there. Joe wearily looked past Slade to try and see if anyone else was with him.

"It's just me, I'm on my own. There's no one else here." Joe looked at Slade blankly.

"Can't you even say hello, you prick? I am your son! You can't even greet me? Don't you even want to get to know me and Luke?"

Joe was dumbfounded, he knew he had behaved badly, but he had not expected the young man to have the gall to turn up to his house unannounced and in such an obvious bad mood.

"Sorry, boy," came the defeated reply. "I was not expecting this, you took me by surprise."

Slade, with a deep snarl in his voice, took half a step closer towards Joe and warned,

"Don't you ever call me boy. You *know* my name. Why haven't you even bothered to call me?"

"I have got nothing for you, Slade. And I don't want anything from you. You are far better off without me in your lives."

"I don't want anything from you, Joe. I just wanted to talk to you and get to know something about my family history. I had hoped we could just have a few beers and get to know each other a little bit. But now, I don't ever want to see you again. I wouldn't even go and have a drink with you if you asked, because you couldn't even be bothered to call and explain how you were feeling!"

"I am sorry Slade. I wanted to call you. I wanted to get to know you. Truly I did. But I just couldn't get my mind around what you had told me. I needed to get myself sorted before I contacted you. I can't take any pressure."

This comment made Slade even angrier, his response exploding from his lips.

"Pressure? That's a joke! What do you think I have been under for the past few weeks since I found out about you? Luke and I put ourselves out on a limb to come here and see you, and look at the way you treated us!"

Slade was very close to throwing his right fist in the direction of Joe's nose. He was getting angrier and angrier. Joe knew he should try to say something that would calm Slade down, but the more he thought of what he could say, the more his emotions took over and he found himself unable to form a single word.

Slade looked at the man in front of him, this cowardly man who didn't even have the courage to make a phone call.

"I had thought that getting to know you might be good for us both, but I guess I was wrong."

Slade could feel the anger was about to give way to the lump rising in his throat. He turned so Joe could not see the tears beginning to form in the corners of his eyes, not wanting Joe to know how badly this entire thing had brought him down.

"Now I don't ever want to see you again. You just disappoint me. Thank God I have got a decent father, a real father who actually cares." Joe remained motionless, leaning against the wide-open front door. A couple of tears had already made their way down his cheeks to join the many other stains on his old grey tee shirt. Finally Joe managed to form a sentence.

"I do want to talk with you and Luke, Slade," he whispered softly. Joe had recovered enough to talk, but Slade was through with talking. He spun away from Joe and stalked down the driveway back towards his ute. Turning his head back he yelled,

"Mow your fucking lawns!"

The entire ordeal had left Slade feeling really drained and tired, but he knew he had to call Luke and tell him what had gone down. Luke picked up on the 14th ring, which nearly drove Slade into despair. However, when Luke did finally answer he was really pleased to hear Slade's voice.

"Hey Bro! How's it going?"

"Not that good, Luke. Don't have to worry about Joe any more. I told the prick we don't ever want to see him again."

Luke was shocked.

"Why on earth did you do that?"

"Prick never rang us or nothing. So I went over to see him and told him what I thought of him."

"How did he take that?" Luke asked nervously, knowing just how scary his twin could be when he spoke his mind.

"He said he hadn't got himself sorted and was under a lot of pressure … Pressure? Huh?"

"For real? He obviously doesn't think of anyone but himself. To be honest bro, on first impressions I never liked him anyway. We are both far better off without him."

"Yeah, you're right, Luke. I have to go. I am feeling really tired and I need to get to bed. Say hi to Jake, Mum, and Dad for me. I miss you all."

"Yeah Bro, we all miss you too. I will ring you tomorrow. Take care." "Thanks Luke. See ya."

Slade had always been quite a private person, so he had not told either his flat mates or the other guys at work about what had happened with Joe. The entire experience had really shaken Slade and as the months bled into each other, he felt the distance grow between himself and Shona and Hone. Not because of anything they had done, but because he felt he had disappointed them. They called him frequently, always wanting him to come down to the coast for a weekend but he always told them that he was extremely busy with work.

Slade felt as if he had made a huge mistake by trying to find his birth father, and because of this he didn't deserve to call Shona and Hone his parents. He became really withdrawn. Everyone who knew Slade was worried about him. Slade was still taking plenty of 'Me Days' and barely seemed to register when the boss docked his pay.

Like most towns and cities, the handful of recreational drug users lurked around. Slade had always managed to avoid them, despite quite a few of the boys from work offering him marijuana in the past. He had always said no because he didn't want to let his family down, and he had always been happy enough to stick with his Steinlager. One night at the pub, one of the boys from the forestry gang approached Slade. "Hey bro, I know you've been having a rough time lately. Don't know what has been going down but I can see that you really need to relax. I've got something that will help you to feel real cruisy."

Slade wore a confused look before realising what his mate was referring to.

"You reckon?"

Slade resisted for a while, but his mate was very persuasive, convincing him how just one smoke would make him instantly feel better.

The two men made their way outside and found a secluded area where they could light up a joint. It wasn't too long before Slade felt his problems evaporate as the marijuana elevated his dopamine levels to leave him feeling carefree and super relaxed. When the two men joined the rest of their friends back inside the pub, Slade was back to his old self, laughing and joking with the rest of the boys just like he had been before the Joe Sisson incidents.

The following morning Slade woke up thinking about how great the marijuana had made him feel, and how small his problems had seemed while he was high. He soon realised how marijuana could be exactly what he needed; a way to forget the trouble he had caused with his family, and something to help him through this bad patch in his life. He decided he would get up, and go meet his workmate to talk about getting his own personal supply.

This saw the beginning of Slade's drug use, which for a long time he managed to keep under control. Despite being offered stronger drugs on many occasions, he kept only to marijuana.

Slade had his first brush with the law on an evening when he was high. He found himself in a fight at the pub with a fellow patron, badly beating him up. Slade was dragged away from the fight by his friends who then took him home. After an appearance in court, Slade was given a warning and a community service sentence that he completed, but it did not deter him from continuing his drug usage. In the months that followed the marijuana gave him a time and space to be able to forget about the situation with Joe, and how he felt as if he had upset Hone and Shona deeply.

Slade refused to come home for more visits, and Luke knew his brother's behaviour was breaking their mother's heart. Slade needed to be on the coast, where he belonged, the time near the sea would be good for his spirit. However, Slade wrongly felt as if he had ruined any chance of being part of the family due to his attempts at creating a relationship with his birth father. No matter how hard Luke tried to convince him otherwise, he found himself unable to change Slade's mind about visiting more often. Slade was worried about what irreparable damage he had caused to his relationship with Hone, as he and Hone had fought through some serious disagreements in the past. His respect for Hone was deep and he did not want to get into arguments with Hone or say or do something more to damage their relationship.

After passing their exams, Luke and Jake finished school in December. They wanted to work for a year, so they could get some money behind them before beginning their apprenticeships. They moved to be with Slade, hoping this might help to bring him back into the family. Jazz Jones offered each of his brothers a job in the same forestry gang as Slade's. The three boys found themselves a place to rent, living in the bottom storey of a farmhouse together. Luke and Jake could see what a good time he was having with his pockets full of cash. He had traded his small ute for a bigger one that he could use for hunting – although he also found it gave him no trouble when he went out looking for girls in town! He had always been a very good looking man, with his straight black hair, dark eyes, long eyelashes, and well-toned physique due to his hard labour in the forest. His expressionless face concealed his feelings. He held strong opinions. His brothers learnt at a young age not to argue with him, even if they thought he was wrong. These strong opinions had sometimes led Slade into scraps. He had quickly built himself quite a reputation as a fighter, often ending his nights out the back of the pub with a guy on the receiving end of his strong fist.

Jake and Luke soon discovered the good life that Slade had been enjoying. They too began to do really well in the forestry industry; working long hours and getting paid heaps of overtime. The three boys spent a great portion of their weekly income on alcohol and/or drugs. They often invited their mates over to their flat for a sing-along and beer, which would carry on into the wee hours of the morning. Jake tried marijuana for the first time during one of those nights. He had always been a strong willed and confident man, so he easily managed to control his drug use to the occasional smoke with his workmates. Luke did not particularly like the smell or the taste of the marijuana, or the effect it had on him or his brothers, so never used it in the same way that the others did. Their favourite pub had a couple of pool tables, and Jake quickly proved himself to be a bit of a champion as the boys had always played a lot of pool down the Coast. They soon learnt that they could make quite a bit of money by challenging others to a game. Quite often, fights erupted in the pub over who had won the pool, and whether it had been won fair and squarely.

One night, during a particularly long session of drinking and smoking marijuana, Slade, his girlfriend Laura, and the other boys were at their local. Slade had been wrongly accusing Laura all night of looking at another bloke. Nothing she could say could convince him he was wrong, and that she had eyes only for him, as he was clearly in one of *those* moods.

Slade looked up from his pint and saw a big, mean looking dude sitting across from him at the bar. He had long, shoulder length hair and despite his cleanly shaven jaw he had a real mean look, emphasized by a big scar spanning the length of his forehead. He looked to be at least 10 years older than Slade. He was grinning at the group from across the bar, eyeballing Slade. Slade took an instant hate to the man in the split-second their eyes met. The situation rapidly deteriorated until Slade slammed his glass down on the bar and walked straight over to the big guy who had turned away and was laughing with his friends. Slade stopped in front of him and headbutted him so hard that he flew backwards, smashing into a row of pints that the bartender was pouring. The return punch knocked Slade in the jaw, and as the two spilled outside to continue their scrap the barman called the police. Despite being a foot shorter than his rival, Slade was stronger; he fought the guy until he lay in a puddle of his own unconsciousness. Laura tried her best to break up the fight; she was tugging on Slade's arm as he continued to lay into the guy on the ground.

Slade then turned his attention towards Laura. "You caused this by leading him on, you little slut!"

"No Slade, God!" She screamed at the top of her lungs, with tears running down her face. "You are just drunk, and you have been smoking too much fucking pot, Slade! Get a grip on yourself!"

This made Slade even angrier. He yanked his arm free and instantly used it to backhand her in the face with such force that she flew across the car park. Luke and Jake tried their best to calm their brother down but he was completely out of control. They had never seen him so aggressive before. He had had a few fights but was never like this. He was yelling and swearing with every punch he threw.

Luke and Jake didn't know what to to. They just looked at each other in disbelief. Luke felt his suspicions confirmed in regards to the possibility of their brother abusing heavier substances than marijuana. Sadly, far too many of their friends had already fallen slave to Methamphetamines, commonly known throughout New Zealand as P, due to the widespread epidemic of its abuse. He had guessed Slade had been using for a while, but hadn't said anything as he had not been able to catch him in the act.

The cops roared into the car park, leaping straight out of the car and towards the action. The biggest cop rushed up to Slade who promptly turned on him by throwing a fierce punch which dropped the cop like a stone. Slade looked down at the man in blue and laughed, oblivious to the repercussions of his actions.

He then began to sing obnoxiously,

"I fought the law and I won, I fought the law and I won!"

Luke and Jake pounced on Slade. Luke was on the verge of tears as he yelled for his brother to stop what he was doing. Slade heard the quiver in his brother's voice and immediately calmed down a little.

His change in demeanour gave the police the opportunity to place him under arrest. The handcuffs were slapped on his wrists and were only released once he arrived at the cells to hear he was being charged with assault on a policeman, common assault, and assault on a female. Slade rang Hone in desperation to see if he would be able to help.

The first thing Hone did was arrange a good lawyer for his son. After such a long time without seeing his father, Slade was really pleased to see him. Hone and Slade had a long talk in the cell, as Slade was not released on bail. Hone gave Slade a big hug as he begged,

"What has gone wrong, boy? Why are you behaving like this?

Why are you doing this to your mother and me?" Slade looked at his father remorsefully.

"I don't know, Dad. That stuff with Joe Sisson really played with my head. I felt like I had let you both down. At the pub, God, I just lost it.

I don't know why I got so carried away. I will never do it again." Hone questioned Slade as to why he would want to hit a woman.

"Only gutless pricks hit women, son."

"I just lost it Dad. I didn't want to hit her, it just kinda happened. She had caused me all this trouble …" Slade paused, instantly realising he could never justify his behaviour no matter how hard he tried.

"Well, you know what I think of people who hit women. Do not *ever* do it again." Hone looked at his downtrodden son before continuing. "You've changed mate. You're not into drugs or anything silly like that are you?"

Slade had already decided not to talk to Hone or his brothers about his involvement with P. He had first smoked it with a workmate and quickly found it to be even better than marijuana for helping him to forget. Since his arrest he had realised that if he had not been high on P he would never have acted the way he did. However, Slade also knew that he was getting a real taste for the white powder. He felt himself craving it, thinking about when he could get his next hit, and debating with himself if he still had his use under control – denying what was the beginning of his addiction and instead focussing on the fact that the drug seemed to set him free.

The court hearing sentenced Slade to a 6 month prison sentence on being found guilty of all charges.

CHAPTER FIFTEEN

Dawn broke early the next morning over the meandering river. The surrounding bush twinkled with dew as the early sunlight glistened on the leaves and branches. Stevo was the first to rise, and he noticed the last of the early morning fog drifting off the tops of the hills as he looked up the valley. The broad streaks of sunlight were coming through the trees as the sun made its way up and over the ridge, shining down over the river.

"It's going to be a great day," he greeted Sue with a kiss.

Janey made her way towards the river with her face wash and toothbrush in hand. She glanced up towards the tops of the high peaks far in the distance. She could see they were engulfed in white snowy cloud formations, and she thought to herself how they had the appearance of soft whip ice cream, as it wisped and busily changed shape.

As the sun continued to rise, warming the atmosphere, it caused the clouds to slowly dissipate and fragment, and they spiralled their way higher into the sky. The tops of the peaks had made themselves clearly visible, and a beautiful blue sky exposed the beginning of yet another magnificent day in Aoteoroa.

"Wow, what a fabulous sight. Those people who never go out into the great outdoors have no idea what they are missing!" said Janey.

"You're right, Janey. We are so lucky in New Zealand to have this beautiful scenery right on our doorstep," agreed Stevo, who had moved to crank up the fire and get the breakfast underway for the team.

When Janey arrived at the river; the perfectly still water was sparkling in the early morning light. She stopped for a moment, before she had her wash, and leaned forward over the edge of the river and carefully regarded her reflection. Brent quietly made his way towards his wife and joined her on the sand. Standing beside her and also looking down upon her reflection he sighed,

"That sure is a beautiful sight."

He slid his arm around her waist and she turned her face to give him a gentle kiss. They hugged each other, enjoying the rare private moment away from their friends that meant they could help bathe each other in the river.

"Now I'm awake and ready to face the day!" Brent exclaimed with a sly smile as they joined the others for breakfast. "That cold water really wakes you up!"

After breakfast was finished and cleaned away, the horses were saddled up and readied to get on the move. As they mounted, Brent and Stevo strapped their scabbards onto their saddles. The bullets they had been carrying in their pockets were loaded into the magazines of their rifles; just to be ready in case any game appeared on the river trail. Brent let the dogs off and placed the dog chains on the pack horse.

Heather said, "Are you ok Roger, all settled on your horse?" "Sure am, love," replied Roger.

"Let's go," urged Sue.

"I can't wait to see what today brings," said Janey.

"You will see lots more of nature's paradise," said Brent.

He set off leading the packhorse up the river and everybody followed in single file.

They rode for a few hours, and lunchtime was quickly approaching. It had been a fairly uneventful morning, but very pleasurable riding. Brent put the idea of stopping for a brew to the others, an idea which was enthusiastically agreed to. After sighting a nice corner in the river, with a bit of lush river grass and some driftwood banked up against the edge, Brent headed towards it. Brent got a fire going while the others secured their horses. The driftwood burned easily because it was so dry. It was burning so brightly it was like it had been doused in petrol. They noticed Heather, Sue and Roger were gently rubbing their backsides.

"A spa would be so good," mused Sue. "Don't torment me!" Heather replied.

Without the luxury of a hot spa pool, they had to make do with rubbing Vaseline into their dry, sore skin. Roger used his Deep Heat to help his muscles relax a little.

"Just as well you brought that Deep Heat with you Rog. There's a world of hurt out there for you if you are unprepared," smiled Brent as he got to his feet. He wandered off across the river, still holding his cup of tea, to where he had sighted a nice pool a bit further up the river.

"Where are you going?" asked Janey. Brent replied, "I'm just going to check out this pool for trout." "Wait for me babe, I'll come too!"

They approached the pool, careful to stay back from the edge and not let their shadows fall into the water so as to scare the fish. They watched as the beautifully clear water made its way down the rapids at the entrance to the pool.

'It's an ideal feeding place for fish," whispered Brent to Janey.

He watched the pool for a few minutes longer, noticing that there didn't seem to be as many trout as he had expected to see. As they watched a large rainbow trout made its way out of the rapids and into the main pool.

"Look! There's one, Brent!" exclaimed Janey.

"Now, that is a decent sized trout!" Brent replied. "I'll go and get Roger with his rod."

Janey sat quietly by the pool, watching the trout to make sure it didn't disappear. It was swimming amongst some boulders in the rapids. The thought of a big trout quickly helped Roger to forget about his sore backside. Grabbing his best rod and bag of lures, he and Brent raced back across the river to the pool.

Roger passed Brent his camera with the words, "If I hook anything make sure you get a photo."

After only a few minutes with his line out, Roger hooked the big rainbow. In his excitement at the size of his catch he nearly fell into the water! The trout had put up an impressive fight; doing numerous lengths of the pool, leaping, and peeling the reel out many times as Roger played it skilfully. But it wasn't enough, and Roger skillfully landed the large, 5.5kg rainbow trout.

Brent admired the catch,

"Now that is a beautiful river rainbow, Roger!"

Janey was thrilled for Roger, watching him whistling as he put his scales back into his well-prepared fishing bag. Roger held the fish up and beamed from ear to ear as Brent took a photo.

"I can see why these are called rainbow trout," Janey whistled in admiration.

The sides of the fish's body perfectly displayed the colours of the rainbow and because this fish was in such a spectacular condition; the colours were amplified. The fish was literally gleaming as the sun shone down upon its faintly scaled skin.

"The trout look as if they are thriving in these clear waters." "Yes," Brent agreed with his wife. "But there are not as many as

there should be. I wonder why that is? There wouldn't be any fishing pressure here. Maybe it is because the river is running low and they have gone downstream looking for food. I imagine the next time it rains they will come back up here."

"Yeah, don't know mate. Only hunters come this far up the river," piped up Roger. "And there wouldn't be many of them either, what with the huge effort it takes to get here and all!"

Brent and Janey laughed, they were really happy for Roger. "Looks like you've got us our tea, Roger!" shouted Stevo as the girls congratulated him on the catch.

Stevo pulled out his big bowie knife. This particular knife was one that Stevo was very proud of as he had made it himself from an old saw blade, using a piece of a deer's antler for the handle. He had always enjoyed making knives, but this particular one happened to be the ultimate in bowie knives. He had made an identical one for Brent, but unfortunately, Brent had lost it on one of their hunting trips.

After gutting the fish, they placed it into a plastic bag and stowed it on the pack horse to enjoy for dinner later that evening. Together the group moved off up the river which was really starting to narrow up, making it a bit tougher for the horses. The pace was much slower than it had been before lunch. Buck and Blue were working further up the river in front of the horses, and had begun to look really keen. Brent noticed the change in the dogs' behaviour and realised there must be game nearby. Brent threw the packhorse lead to Janey and nudged his horse forward into a trot so as to keep up with the dogs who were really motoring their way up the river.

Brent pulled his 270 from its scabbard, hoping that the dogs would chase a deer or pig down into the river. As he moved up the river to where the dogs were, he saw where a big boar had just made its way across the river. He heard Blue baling hard, from way up the side of the river. From the barking, Brent could tell there was only one dog there but before he could begin to worry he heard the sound of Buck running through the leaves to join his brother in barking at the pig. The dogs were baling furiously, but were positioned high above on a very steep slip running right down into the river. The big boar broke straight down into the slip and the barking ceased momentarily while the dogs chased the boar back down towards the river. The party had managed to catch up to Brent, and they kept moving slowly up the river.

Brent called to Roger,

"The boar has broken on the dogs and is coming straight towards us. Get your camera ready!"

Roger quickly dug into his saddle bag to retrieve his camera. "If you bring Cloudy up by Big Red, you can get a good photo."

As they sat on their horses, waiting for action, the boar crashed down through the undergrowth at the bottom of the slip and emerged suddenly at the river bank. The boar never slowed for the water and lunged straight into the river at full speed. Water sprayed up into the air like a fountain as the boar's powerful frame propelled it out into the river, heading for a deep part of the river where the dogs wouldn't be able to get near him - if they tried, it would be at their own peril. The dogs also arrived at the river at full speed, two very determined hunters due to their breed. Their excellent noses had tracked the boar along the ground, and when they spotted the boar in the river they began barking continuously. They were wise enough to know not to get into the deeper water as the big pig held the advantage. The boar almost appeared to be smirking at the dogs, its gleaming ivory 4 ½ inch tusks stuck up out of its bottom jaw waiting to tear them to pieces. The ivory grinders were in the top jaw, curled up beside the snout where the tusks ground on them to help keep them razor sharp. They protruded like a pair of daggers, and any self-respecting pig dog would do it's best to keep well clear - as Buck and Blue knew to do. The big boar had its crown jewels submerged just below the water just in case of a surprise attack from behind. Its mouth hung open as he glared at the foe, baring his gleaming mouth of ivory. These big pigs are very intelligent. The boar knew how to keep the advantage and that it must lure its enemies into deep water or dense bush undergrowth with lots of vines and tangled undergrowth. When backed into a corner they would propel themselves forward at speed, leaving their attackers with no escape from the sharp ivory that the big pigs possess.

Dismounting, Brent again called to Roger,

"Sneak up and get a photo while you can. He might break again." As Roger snapped furiously on his camera, capturing some beautiful photos, the dogs were still baling and keeping the big pig's attention. Blood was trickling from Buck's front leg. The boar must have swiped at him with his tusks when they were first baling it. Brent thought how he had better finish the pig in case he managed to hurt the dog some more. He aimed the 270 Winchester at the boar's head and fired. The 150 gram ballistic tipped bullets, Brent's favourite, took the big boar out instantly. It rolled over in the pool and the dogs rushed in to grab an ear each. They had heard the gun go off lots of times before and knew now was their chance for a bit of payback. Massive eels swarmed from nowhere as soon as the boar's blood began to taint the water.

"Wow!" yelled Janey. "Watch out for your toes, Brent. Look at the size of those suckers!"

An eel poked its head out of the water as Brent rushed over and stuck the pig with his favourite Svord, straight bladed, sticking knife. Brent knew he needed to bleed the pig as soon as possible after the kill to prevent the blood from discolouring the meat. This knife came a poor second to the lost knife that Stevo had made. Brent loved this knife because when he sharpened it, it kept its finely honed edge for ages. He loved the excellent shape of the handle, which made it easy for him to hold with his big hands, especially when he had to stick wild game. Another eel latched itself onto the pig's leg. The fresh blood had sent the eels into a desperate struggle for food.

Roger looked very excited,

"I wonder if there are lots of pigs in this area? It might be pig city up here, Brent. Plenty of poaka for keen hunters like us!"

"There will certainly be plenty of them around. Poaka for dinner, yum yum," answered Brent with a grin. "Pig city or eel city? I am not sure because there seem to be lots of them about too!"

"You guys know a lot of Māori words, its great the way you just use them when you are talking. I didn't know poaka meant pig. I have only heard of kunekune," said Janey.

"Kunekune are short legged fat pigs, this poaka will be more tasty than one of them," said Brent. It was a mighty awesome sight, two beautiful pig dogs such as these up against a mighty boar. Stevo had his work cut out, controlling the pack horse with all the commotion, and keeping the other horses under control. Janey took the horses' reins, talking to them and patting them to calm them down as Brent and Stevo dragged the pig onto the sandy river bank.

"That's one, big, boarasaurus, Brent!" exclaimed Stevo.

Roger took a couple of close ups of the big boar, including a photo of its massive ivory tusks. He also captured action shots of the eels raising their heads out of the water. One of the eels was at least a foot across at its widest point. Brent commented on how huge some of the eels had grown since he was last up here. Some looked very different from the native long finned eels he usually saw when he was out in the bush. Everybody stared in disbelief at how ravenous the eels seemed. They appeared to be almost climbing out of the water in order to get themselves closer to the pig. They were biting and attacking each other, spurred on by the blood in the water which was making them go crazy. "Hey Roger, can you please grab my knife? It's over there on the bank," asked Brent.

"Sure," replied Roger. "Pleased to be helpful." He handed it to Brent. "Thanks, mate," said Brent.

Brent and Stevo gave the dogs a big pat and told them what good boys they were. The dogs were also looking quite pleased with themselves. Stevo, checking out Buck's front leg, motioned to Brent, "It doesn't look too bad, just a bit of a skin rip. He'll be fine. I'll put a bit of antibiotic powder on it tonight."

"That's good, I was worried when I saw the blood, it's why I took the shot when I did. I think we should gut the poaka and hang him up in a tree. He will be okay for a few days until we pick him up on our way back through."

Brent and Stevo looked at the surrounding bush, searching for a nice hardy tree. The big boar would easily weigh more than 200 pounds. Brent spied a good branch hanging out over the river. He grabbed a rope and threw it out over the branch, tying it onto the horn of his saddle as Stevo hooked the other end onto the back legs of the big boar. Brent urged Big Red forward by nudging him with the heel of his boot, dragging the big boar up so they could hang it easily over the branch. The horse pulled hard on the rope and the big boar slowly rose up high in the tree. Brent moved his horse around by another tree and Stevo grabbed the end of the rope and tied it off. The two hunters stood back and admired their work and the size of the massive boar. Stevo was whistling his favourite tune as Roger snapped photos of the boar hanging over the water.

Within mere minutes, a buzz filled the air as the blowflies start to arrive.

Roger observed,

"Hey, do they seem like massive blowflies to you guys? If I was hit by one of them when I was riding, it would knock me off my horse!" The blowflies were very persistent, the noise they made was deafening, and no matter how much they were swatted they wouldn't leave.

Stevo agreed,

"Yeah, I can't understand it. Massive poaka attacked by massive eels and now massive blowflies. Brent, we had better hang this boar higher in the tree to keep it safe from the blowflies."

Knowing that they wanted to have some meat left to take home, Brent agreed. He also knew the pig would be safer further up, as it would be cooler, hanging higher in the breeze. The blowflies were obviously intent on eating the pork. They were determined and really hungry, much bigger than any fly they had ever seen at home. The men wrapped muslin cloth around the pig and raised it higher in the tree. Big Red was pawing the sand and pricking his ears forward. Brent reassured his horse with a friendly pat and some calm words, telling him that everything would be okay. Once the boar was removed from just above the river, the eels seemed to calm down, disappearing as the blood dissipated down the river.

After seeing the eels Roger stated, "I'm not sticking my toe in there!"

"No, I wouldn't either," agreed Brent. "Those eels are something else. I've never seen eels so ravenous or massive. There's also something different about some of them that I just can't put my finger on."

Stevo nodded,

"Well let's all just keep an eye out when we are in the water now, aye?"

CHAPTER SIXTEEN

Luke and Jake were there to pick Slade up on the day he was released from prison after he had served his 6 month sentence.

Jake and Luke had held onto their old farmhouse flat while their brother was on the inside, even though the rent was fairly expensive for just the two of them. However, the house had become home. They still spent their days working in the forestry gang, and had been using Slade's ute while he was away. Little did they know, that the time in prison seemed to have only made Slade harder, despite their hopes that he would come out as the brother they dearly loved and missed. When Slade made his way through the doors and out into the sunlight, Luke hardly recognised him as the twin brother he had grown up with and loved all of his life.

During the following weeks Luke came to realise that Slade had come out of jail even leaner and meaner, and with even less respect for women. He made derogatory comments about his ex-girlfriend, Laura. He couldn't see that it was his behaviour, instead choosing to see it as hers, that had landed him the jail sentence in the first place. Judging from the scars on his face, he had obviously been involved in many more fights during his time inside. As a person, Slade had become quieter, talking nowhere near as much as he used to. Slade didn't seem to want to talk about his prison time.

"It must have been quite brutal in there," thought Luke when he realised how Slade had changed drastically from what he was like before he went into prison.

"What do you reckon about saving some money and going on a holiday overseas, Slade?" asked Luke one night when they were relaxing in front of the tv.

"Nah, I'm all good here," said Slade. "I'm not going anywhere." "Thought a change of scenery would be good for all of us," said Luke.

"Yeah, whatever," replied Slade without taking his eyes of the tv. Slade seemed disinterested in the conversation and lacked the desire to think about his future. Luke remained keen on securing an apprenticeship, he was saving his money from the forestry job so that he would have a nest egg for when he was on the lower wage that apprentices received in order to get their free training and education. Slade was very lucky that Jazz had kept his job open for him. Jazz held Hone in the highest respect and he felt that Hone's son would hold a lot of great qualities beneath his tough exterior; including being

a very hard worker.

A few weeks after he had been released Slade wrapped an arm around the shoulders of each brother and proposed an evening out on the town.

"Let's go and get on the turps. It was a long dry six months and I haven't had much to drink since I came out."

The three brothers had a really good night, enjoying each other's company as they were all in a really happy mood. When the pub made the call for final drinks, the boys piled out of the pub and into Slade's ute. Slade insisted on driving, despite the copious amounts of alcohol he had consumed after being dry for 6 months. He turned the stereo up full bore and began to hum,

"I fought the law and I won. I fought the law and I won." "That's an appropriate tune you're humming," laughed Luke.

Slade took a corner too fast, lost control of the wheel, and the ute flew over a ditch and ploughed headfirst into a fence not too far from their flat. The boys climbed out to check for damage to themselves and the vehicle. Thankfully they were all fine, but unfortunately the right front fender of the ute had been pushed back into the wheel causing the axle to bend severely. The ute didn't even require a full inspection; the boys were already aware it would not be capable of driving further that night. They checked their surroundings to find that they did have some luck on their side; the paddock they had crashed into was empty. They knew they wouldn't be able to do anything that night, so after digging the bourbon bottle out from where it had become safely wedged under the backseat during the crash, they made the rest of their journey home on foot.

Next morning, Luke rang their boss Jazz Jones.

"Hey Jazz, we've had an accident and won't be able to get to work today."

"Ow, hope you're all ok," said Jazz. "Yeah, we're fine thankfully," said Luke.

"I could send the van to pick you up for the next couple of days if that would help. It can't be for many days though. You will have to get yourselves another vehicle," said Jazz.

"That would be great, thanks," said Luke. They were grateful for this temporary offer. With their good work ethic they would have walked to meet the van if they had to.

Winter was setting in across New Zealand, and the work was not as plentiful due to the deterioration in the weather. They were very lucky to all have their jobs in the forestry gang, as the workload was becoming more and more erratic leaving them working many half days. As they had done a lot of overtime during the busy season, they had been able to put some of their money into savings. Because there was less work, Luke, Jake, and Slade spent more and more time at the local pub.

CHAPTER SEVENTEEN

During the next few weeks after their accident the work continued to slow. One day about a month later the team was sent home just after lunch time. Slade, Jake, and Luke decided to use the opportunity to stay in town and get some supplies while the shops were open. They were strolling towards the butchery when Slade spotted a sign saying 'TATTOOS.' They had all been talking about whether to get a tattoo or not for quite a while as they felt slightly left out because quite a few of the men they worked with in the forestry gang had them.

Slade turned to his brothers.

"How about we get a tattoo each? Not much else to do this afternoon. You know how neat they look on the guys at work."

Jake nodded and said, "Yeah, that could be cool. What do you think Luke? Let's go in and have a look."

They make their way into the shop, a small buzz sounding as they crossed the threshold to alert the tattooist that he had visitors. They headed towards the bench seats surrounded by little tables covered in books holding pictures of many different tattoos.

"You all right, Luke?" Jake asked his brother. He had noticed the worried look upon his face.

"Yeah, why?"

"You look a bit nervous, that's all."

"This could hurt. I guess I'm still not entirely sure whether I really want one or not."

"You'll be right," interrupted Slade impatiently.

A man came out from the back room and approached the boys. "Can I help you gentlemen?"

Slade's face broke into a full smile at being called a gentleman. "Yes, you definitely can! We would like to get a tattoo each." Luke winced at his brother's words.

"Well, you have some of the books, there are some more under the bench you're sitting on, they all have samples showing you what I can do … Or have you got your own design in mind?"

The boys jumped up to grab the rest of the books from beneath them. Slade nodded his head at the guy.

"Thanks mate. Hey, when do you reckon you could do our tattoos?"

"Well, we are not busy at the moment. You make up your minds about what you want and we will be in business. We can do them today. Just remember, a tattoo is permanent so choose carefully."

Slade turned and looked at Luke and Jake. Flicking his eyes he mocked, "He sounds like Mum!"

"Hey, how much for one like this?" Jake asked, pointing to a beautiful koru pattern.

"It depends how big and where you want it," replied the tattoo artist.

Jake outlined a large area on his upper right forearm. "Okay, that will be about \$250 for a single colour."

"That'll do me!" Jake decided. He had chosen a koru which symbolised growth and new beginnings within the Māori world. He always loved looking out for koru in the bush; a baby silver fern fond that was still spiralled up, waiting to unfurl itself.

Slade, who had been watching and listening intently, held the book up to the artist.

"This one's the one for me," he pointed towards a snake and dagger tattoo. "I want it in the same place as Jake. It says that it signifies strength, so that's definitely the one for me!"

"That one will cost \$350 because of the red in the snake. Is that okay?"

"Sure is," agreed Slade.

Luke smiled at Slade's surmising about his strength.

"What about you, Luke? What tat are you going to get?" encouraged Jake.

"I think I like this eagle. It signifies freedom and nature, so that's me sorted. I'll get it on my upper forearm too, so we all have them in the same place," decided Luke.

"Choice, that's a nice eagle bro," confirmed Slade, making his twin beam.

"Let's do it."

"Who wants to go first?" asked the tattoo artist. "Your idea Slade - so you're up first!" laughed Jake. "Yeah, I reckon," echoed Luke.

"Ok, sweet as … pussies!" Slade scoffed at his brothers as he followed the artist into a seedy little room at the back of the shop.

The tattoo artist popped his head back around to Jake and Luke to say that Slade's tattoo would probably take between two and three hours. He suggested they go and do something while Slade got his tattoo. He explained that he would get his other artist to come in so that when they returned they could both have theirs done at the same time.

"That sounds good, we'll be back in a couple of hours aye Luke?" "Yeah ok. Let's go shoot some pool while we wait. Whoever wins

can pick who goes next - if we don't go in at the same time that is." "Sounds fair enough to me. And I know who will be going next!"

Jake smirked knowing that he was a better pool player than his brother.

The boys headed off to the pool hall. Jake, being a bit of a shark at pool, slapped his brother on the back.

"Best of three, Luke." "Yeah, cool Bro."

Jake set up and then swiftly broke, sending three solids flying home. He had soon won the first game. Luke held a determined look on his face, and had a good break at the start of the second game. He played well, managing to win the second game.

Jake looked over at his brother.

"Lukey, this one settles who gets to feel the pain first."

It was Jake's turn to break, and he soon had most of his balls down. He missed sinking his last ball, leaving him with his solid red and the black 8 ball left. As he passed the cue to his brother he teased, "Looks like you'll have to sink them all on this turn, Luke. I don't think you'll be getting another chance."

"Yeah right, just watch me," quipped Luke.

Luke chalked his cue and sunk each ball one after the other. Soon there was just the black left and Jake's solid red remaining. Jake was very impressed with Luke's pool skills, thinking that it must be the fear of pain that was helping him to play so well.

"Those were some good shots, bro. Let's see if you can finish it. You won't want to miss that black bro, or you'll be leaving me set up," laughed Jake, trying to make Luke more nervous than he already was. Luke tapped the white just hard enough for it to sink the black - but stay against the cushion of the table if he missed. The white stroked the black nicely, cutting it straight to the corner.

Luke was ecstatic! He held his cue high in the air and yelled, "Yes!! Jakey, the pains all yours!"

"Nah, you'll get some too," laughed Jake. "Good shot, bro!" said Luke.

Luke placed his hand on Jake's shoulder.

"I think *you* are going to feel the pain first with that big koru you are getting."

Jake just smiled and said it would be worth it; he wasn't at all nervous about the pain.

"Hope so," whispered Luke.

They headed back to the tattoo shop. Opening the door, they peered into where Slade was sitting in a chair and the tattoo artist was working on his arm. Slade saw their eager faces and gave them a broad smile and a 'thumbs up.'

"Won't be long now," the tattoo artist called, as he lay the gun down briefly so he could spray the skin with disinfectant before wiping the ink and blood away. "Just take a seat, gentlemen."

A further half hour went by before Slade appeared. There was a mirror in the waiting room which he marched straight up to so he could admire his new ink. Luke and Jake jumped up from their seats to get a good look at it.

"Ah, choice!" marvelled Slade.

"Yeah, that looks really cool brother," conceded Jake.

They both had huge smiles on their faces. "What do you think, Lukey?" queried Slade.

"Yeah, that looks mean as, Slade! That red ink in amongst it really makes it stand out!"

The tattoo artist came into the front room, wiping his hands on a grimy hand towel. "We'd better get working on your big koru, Jake."

Jake's brave demeanour had changed to a quiet, serious look. He asked his brother if it hurt much.

"Yeah, it hurts like hell, bro. Be strong," laughed Slade, winding Jake up, as the tattoo artist beckoned Jake into the room.

Slade and Luke smiled to themselves.

"Only time I have seen Jake look like that is when Dad is about to give him the belt."

"Yeah, he looks really worried."

The tattoo artist came back out after he had Jake seated. He began to walk towards Luke, whose smile diminished with every approaching step.

"My partner is going to do yours, Mr Luke, if you would please come right this way."

Luke was taken by surprise, he swallowed deeply, as his twin brother slapped him on the shoulder and wished him luck.

"It doesn't hurt that much Lukey, not like I told Jake anyway. You will be fine."

Luke sighed in relief, grateful for the kind words from his brother. He gave his twin a weak smile as he followed the man into another small room.

"Hi, what tattoo are you having, Luke? My name is Art."

"For real? Cool name for this job," marvelled Luke. "I'm having an eagle."

"Ah, yes. This one?" Art confirmed by pointing to the picture in the magazine that the other artist had given him. "It has some nice detail, we wouldn't want to get it wrong!"

Slade wandered down the street, had a few beers at the pub, and then dropped in at one of his favourite stores before heading back to the tattoo shop two and a half hours after his brothers had first sat in the tattoo chairs. When he re-entered the shop, his brother was just emerging from the back room.

"Man, that's cool as, Jake! Do you like it?"

"Yeah, man. It feels really good aye." Jakes voice was full of pride as he admired his tattoo in the mirror. "It didn't hurt as much as I thought it would."

"Ha, yeah it isn't too bad aye. I suppose it depends on where they are putting it," Slade smiled. "I've been out and bought a really short sleeved muscle shirt so I can show the boys down at the pub. I got you and Lukey one too."

"Oh, cool! Thanks Slade!"

They heard footsteps and eagerly turned their attention to where Luke was striding out of the other room with his shoulder turned towards them.

"What do you guys think of my eagle?"

"Yeah, man! That's really cool, Luke," approved Jake. Slade nodded.

"Yeah, Luke. That's mint, I love it."

They paid the tattoo artist and pulled their muscle shirts over their heads before wandering off down the road. They decided to head straight for the pub so they could show the boys. Slade strode right up to the bar and ordered three beers. Luke and Jake stopped short, just behind Slade who then passed them each a beer. They walked casually over to the table where their mates were. Holding their arms up they looked around at their friends and demanded,

"What do you think, boys?"

"Wow, those are some pretty mean tats!"

Everybody was looking their way, including two young ladies who came over to admire the new tattoos. The brothers revelled in the attention, proudly showing off their works of art.

CHAPTER EIGHTEEN

A few weeks after they got their tattoos, they were walking home from the pub. Jake was holding the half empty whiskey bottle in his hand that had been passing between the three brothers who each took a swig. As they approached the local petrol station they took a shortcut across the forecourt, stopping to admire an XR6 turbo Falcon parked at one of the two pumps closest to the road. They noticed it still had the keys in the ignition.

"Nice car!"

"Why yes indeed, Jake," agreed Slade as he looked over at his brother, an idea forming in his mind. He quickly scanned the area, observing that the owner was right across the forecourt in the shop, paying for his petrol. It looked as if nobody had yet noticed their presence.

"Bugger walking any further. Let's take this car."

"What? Are you for real?" squealed Luke in astonishment. "We can't, it's not ours plus it is too flash for us!" Jake scoffed. "Who cares, let's go guys!"

They were all feeling very brave, and quite tired, after drinking so much at the pub. Maybe Slade's idea wasn't so bad after all, neither one of them could really be bothered walking the rest of the way home.

"You keep an eye on the owner, Luke," ordered Slade. "And you had better drive, Jake. You haven't drunk as much as Lukey and me." "Are you sure this is a good idea?" whispered Jake with a sincere note of concern in his voice.

"Of course it is," laughed Slade. "Best one I have had for days!"

"We had better be quick if we are going to do this," Luke warned, trying to hurry his brothers up. "The dude is just paying for his petrol - hope he filled it up for us!"

They all laughed as they jumped into the Falcon. Jake gunned the throttle and the tyres squealed as he roared out of the petrol station and hooned off down the street.

"Wow! Feel that power. I've never driven anything as flash as this. Beats your ute any day, Slade!"

He glanced down at the clock on the dashboard, 24 hour time; 23:01. Luke leaned across from the passenger side and turned the stereo up to its maximum volume. He dug around the glove compartment and found a Metallica CD which he promptly put into the head deck. He put down the reclining seat, as Slade was sitting behind Jake, and as he lay back he rested his feet up on the dashboard. Slade passed the joint he had sparked to Luke, neither of them particularly interested in anything else now that the car was theirs.

Luke was nursing the whiskey bottle while Slade enjoyed the smoke that had found its way back into his hands. They raced off up the road, rubber burning all the way. The owner had called the police. A patrol car was already in the area and it was not long before it was on their trail.

After seeing the patrol car coming towards them, Jake managed to duck down a side street.

"What the fuck do I do now?" he yelled at Slade and Luke.

"Just relax and keep driving, you're doing a good job. They won't catch us in this," reassured Slade.

"Maybe try to lose them, then we can decide what to do," Luke spoke through a mouthful of whiskey. Jake took a corner at such a speed they completely wiped out a give way sign and narrowly missed a couple of pedestrians.

"Whew that was close!" Jake shouted over the music.

"It will teach them not to walk so near the road, stupid pricks," Slade snorted.

The patrol car slid sideways around the corner behind them. Jake buried his foot into the accelerator and the Falcon pulled away at an even higher speed, and the chase roared its way through the streets.

This Falcon was a powerful automatic. Jake wasn't used to handling automatic gear changes in such a strong machine and as he approached an intersection he hit the brakes too hard. The car spun 360 degrees clockwise, narrowly missing the police car that was in pursuit. Jake again forced his foot down hard, and raced off in the direction they had just come from. In seconds they were reaching 110km in the 50km limit zones of the tight side streets.

"Wow!" Slade laughed. "This is bloody awesome! I didn't know you could drive like this, Jake!"

"I didn't either. And believe me, I am not enjoying it!"

"You are doing well. You'll have us all to safety in no time," encouraged Luke, sounding far more confident than he felt.

Jake gritted his teeth and grasped the steering wheel tightly. The end of the road was rapidly approaching; meaning Jake would need to make a sharp turn at the T intersection. Jake began to turn the wheel towards the right as he had already decided that would be the best way to go. As he began to take the corner, he saw that he had forgotten the road to the right was currently a no exit due to the extensive road works happening further on ahead. Without stopping to panic, Jake reached down and yanked hard on the hand brake, while spinning the wheel to the left. The car easily spun itself 180 degrees, and they headed off down the road in the opposite direction. They had lost some distance from the police car, which was now approaching the T intersection for the first time. As Jake sped past it the police car saw them and hastily turned to the left to make chase. The police car took the corner too close and hit the kerb, becoming airborne before landing on the front lawn of the house opposite the intersection. Jake saw the whole thing happen through the rear view mirror, he smirked as he floored it and the falcon roared off. A second police car was coming towards them at top speed. Somehow it didn't see them until the very last minute. Jake had seen the lights flashing and quickly ducked up a side street. The police car overshot the road, screeched to a halt, and had to back up to turn onto the road that the boys were on. This mere number of seconds was all Jake needed in order to be able to get away. He twisted and turned through a few more side streets, all the while checking behind him for police cars. He sighed when he finally felt that they had lost his trail.

"We need to get out of here. The cops are hot on us now," Luke said, stating the obvious.

"Yeah bro, I didn't think I was going to be able to lose them!" Jake appeared to have relaxed a little. "Give me a swig on that whiskey bottle. My mouth has dried out. It must be nerves."

Slade held out the joint to Jake. "You may need a suck on this."

"No thanks. I need my head clear if we are going to get out of this in one piece. Where do I take us, what are we going to do now?" "We'll get out of here and head for the coast for a few days, just until things cool down. We'll go and chill out up the valley. We'll text Jazz and tell him we're going hunting. He won't mind if we bring him back some meat. There's no work on anyway," Luke said. His brothers smiled over at him, also agreeing that this would be a great way to avoid further trouble with the law.

Jake had lost the police, but knew that they would have put the call out on their radios to keep all of their cars on the lookout for them. He headed in the direction of the main road, knowing that once they were on the highway he could make their way toward one of the forestry roads, cut through the forest where they had been working, and then down through the gorge and out onto the main highway again where they would be well on their way to the coast. They came out onto the highway so fast they crossed the white line where a motorbike coming down the highway had to swerve to miss them. The rider lost control of the bike and slid his way over to where he ended up in the scrub beside the road. Jake looked in the rear vision mirror and was relieved to see him sitting up by his bike.

"Thank God, he's okay guys!"

"Stupid prick, having a bike anyway," slurred Slade. "He could get seriously hurt."

Luke looked over at his twin to see if he was being serious, "You for real, Slade?"

"Well, nothing is going to damage his thick head, is it?" was Slade's reply, his eyes barely open and a smile on his face. He opened one eye a little wider as he reminded his brothers,

"We aren't walking."

Jake lowered the speed as he drove up the highway, remembering the police would have other cars out looking for them. They safely made it up to the top of the hill and turned right onto a forestry road. As they headed along this road, which was potholed from all the logging trucks, Jake almost lost control several times. Luckily he had always been a skilled driver, and each time he almost wrecked the car, he managed to regain control and continue to head for the coast. After they got back onto the highway, they had a fairly uneventful drive towards the coast. The miles flew by as they reached speeds of up to 200 kilometres on the straights. They avoided townships by taking the back roads, the light of the full moon illuminating their path.

Finally, Jake caught the first glimpse of the sea and the mountain ranges in the distance. Seeing those familiar sights was always able to create a settling effect over Jake. To him, it felt as if his soul knew that it was coming home.

'It will all be okay,' Jake thought, trying to calm himself down. 'This is just a bad nightmare and all will be well when we get home. Not long now, thank God.'

Slade and Luke had been in an alcohol and marijuana induced sleep for at least an hour. Jake found it increasingly hard to keep his eyes open. The Bob Marley CD that had been playing was now finished, and everything was quiet except for Slade's snoring and weird mumbling. Jake had noticed how often Slade talked to himself in his sleep, it was as if he was continuously tormented by something. Jake wondered about what his brother may have really gotten up to in prison, aware that he had drastically changed while he was in there.

Jake looked at the dash board clock; 03:03. He thought to himself he could manage to drive for about another half hour before he would need time to stop for a rest. He had already had a short break while his brothers slept; at one point he had pulled over to snap off the bumper since it had dropped down and started to drag along the road. After a few scrapes coming through the bush, and a couple of drunken toilet stops, the trip had taken a bit longer than normal. However, Jake didn't mind too much as he loved the sound of the powerful engine roaring and he hoped that one day he would be successful enough to purchase one of his own. He looked across at Luke who looked so peaceful, despite being curled up against the passenger door. Luke seemed oblivious to what the repercussions of the previous night's activities might be.

'He is just too easy going. He seems almost seems stupid at times,' thought Jake, as he lit a cigarette in yet another attempt to stay awake. 'He just goes with the flow, knowing me or Slade will sort everything out.'

As the alcohol and drugs wore off, Jake had been thinking about what had gone down, concerned with what Hone and Shona would think. He was feeling really annoyed with himself for allowing Slade to get him and Luke involved in this escapade, and just generally involved in doing criminal stuff. He glanced back at his other brother in the rear view mirror, thinking how sad it was that Slade really seemed to have gone bad. Jake had mentioned this to Luke after Slade had come out of prison. Luke had said, "He'll be fine" but now he realised that it looked as if Slade was prepared to drag Luke and himself down with him. A lone tear made its way slowly down Jake's cheek. Jake was pleased they had decided to head up to the coast for a few days and he hoped that it would give them all the well-needed chance to clear their heads and sort this out with Slade. Jake felt that it wouldn't be wise for him and Luke to stay around Slade as it really did seem that he had come out of prison as a hardened criminal. Jake figured it must be due to the influence of the people Slade had met in prison as to why he had turned his mind to think in the ways of a criminal. Jake was disappointed in his brother's choices. They had always been so close, but now it felt like his brother was choosing a different path in life – one that Jake wanted nothing to do with.

"If Slade wants that way of life, he will be on his own. He can have his new mates and forget about his family. I'm sure Luke will think like me, and I know Mum and Dad already do." Jake looked in the mirror and realised he was talking to himself in his frustration.

He glanced again at the clock on the dashboard, 03:37. Jake knew that after a few more corners they would be at an old bush road where there was a good spot for dumping the car and burning it. This was the only way he could think of successfully getting rid of the Ford, and the old bush road was notoriously famous for concealing burned out vehicles. Jake knew it would be very bad if they were seen anywhere near the car. He also feared that the police all over the country would be keeping an eye out for it. He suddenly felt really angry, he was swearing at himself for getting involved in this mess. More tears had begun running down his face as he thought of all the people he loved; the people he had let down – Hone, Shona, Jazz, and his honest workmates.

He pulled the car into the gravel road, deciding to drive a couple of kilometres before turning down the little side track which ran past some native bush. He figured it should be safe to light it there, even with the full moon nobody would see the smoke because it should still be dark for a few more hours. And when the burnt out shell was found, Jake knew it wouldn't look out of the ordinary because of all the other wrecked cars dumped there. The car would take a while to burn so they would need to use that time to get back to the road and hopefully manage to hitch a ride quickly. Plenty of trucks were on the road during the early hours of the morning, Jake didn't think it shouldn't be a problem.

Jake drove until he found a secluded spot on some damp grass, tucked away from trees and shrub - yet also out of view from the little off road. As the car came to a halt, Luke and Slade woke up.

"Where are we, Jake?" Slade yawned. "Up a bush road, not too far from home."

"What do we do now?" Luke wondered aloud.

The boys were all very tired as the alcohol had half worn off without any food or water in their stomachs. Jake was past exhausted and had begun to feel scared too. They talked about whether to take the plates off the car, deciding it would be better to remove them in case the Police found a way to be able to trace the theft to them.

"We are sounding like real crims now, covering our tracks," Jake sighed.

"Yeah bro. It's crazy to think all of the tricks and tips I heard on the inside are gonna help us out now. The best thing to do is to always cover your tracks."

They looked through the rest of the car, searching for cash and anything else they may want to keep. In the boot they found a screwdriver and spanner that proved useful in removing the plates. Luke wandered out into the bush a small distance, dug a hole using a piece of broken road sign, and then buried the plates deep in the earth.

He got back to where his brothers were standing, their raid on the vehicle over.

"Get anything guys? I think we just need to get rid of it. If we are going to burn the car, then let's do it. I'll get something to start a fire." "I reckon we should give ourselves up to the cops," Jake suggested

quietly. "This is just a mess and it is only going to get worse." Luke didn't hear Jake's words, but Slade did,

"No way, Jake! It might be okay for you, but I've got prior convictions. They would come down so hard on me in court; it's just not worth it for me. There's no going back now. We won't get caught if we stick to the same story."

Slade paused, looking at each of his brothers carefully,

"The story is that we have been in the bush cos there isn't much work on at the moment. So we are heading home to catch up with the family."

"I don't know, Slade," Jake pushed the issue, "We did some bad stuff and I reckon we should own up to it."

"All we did was steal a stupid car and drag the cops off. It's not that bad."

"Whatever you say," Jake retorted, with disbelief in his voice.

"If we are going to torch this car, can you guys please stop arguing and get on with it so we can get the hell outta here?" Luke's voice was muffled as he was half inside the car, trying to start a fire by lighting the seat covers with a cigarette lighter.

"Here," Slade grabbed Luke and gently shoved him out of the way. "I'll show you how to burn it bro."

He flicked open the petrol cap and, even though the car was low on fuel, he pushed a stick down into the tank and drew out enough petrol to catch a light.

"Luke, Jake! Get back in case it explodes!"

Seconds later the car burst into flames, sending an explosive fireball at least 10 metres into the air. The force of the explosion lifted the car about two metres off the ground. The boys had managed to get far enough away so that they could stand and watch in amazement at the results of Slade's handiwork.

Luke yelled,

"Far out Bro, that was one good explosion!" Jake now had a really sour look on his face.

"What's biting your ass, Jake? You are looking really annoyed, or are you just tired?"

"Never mind me. But yes, I am tired, Slade. Tired of you getting into trouble, and now Lukey and I have got involved too. We have become criminals!"

"I never made you drive the car, Jake. Besides, you're not a criminal until you get caught."

Jake could not believe what he was hearing. "Yeah right, whatever."

Jake felt sick to his stomach; he knew Slade was right; no one had forced him to drive the falcon. He could have chosen to stop at any time during the chase. He had no idea how he was going to be able to look his father in the eye, knowing what he had done. Now that they were so much closer to home, the reality of their crime was weighing down on Jake's shoulders.

"It was a buzz, boys. We had a good night and we are not going to get caught. I'm not going back to prison, and you boys aren't going to do any time either. Now, let's go home!"

Jake couldn't leave it there.

"Do you like being a criminal, Slade? Haven't you got a conscience? Taking other people's stuff is wrong."

He looked over at his other brother for support, noticing how Luke was standing with his head hung low. Luke didn't say anything.

"It's not about that, Jake. I just like the buzz. Fighting gives me a big buzz. It makes me feel like a warrior!" roared Slade.

Jake felt instantly angered with Slade's lack of remorse,

"God! You are not a warrior, Slade. You are just a big thug with the beginnings of a drug problem. You hit women! You disgust me! You, thinking you're a warrior? Please!"

Luke stared in disbelief at what he was hearing Jake say.

Slade marched right up to Jake and grabbed him by the front collar of his shirt. Luke stepped forward, inches away from both of his brothers,

"Let Jake go, Slade. Please let him go."

Slade was seething. Jake was looking into Slade's eyes, trying to see something he could hold onto, anything that would help to keep all of the good memories alive.

Slade let Jake go, smoothing his shirt down where he had grabbed him,

"Sorry, Bro. I don't know what I was thinking about. Don't you go saying that sort of crap again, aye? I've known you to have a few puffs too, Jake. We are all in this together."

"You really want to be a warrior, Slade? You would be much more of a man if you were more like Dad."

Jake's voice was cracking up; he could feel himself becoming very emotional. Slade sensed that Jake was not prepared to let it go until he retracted what he had said about being a warrior,

"Sorry about saying I feel like a warrior, Jake. Never knew you were so touchy about that. A warrior is a very proud man who only fights for what he believes in, not just for fun. You're right, I am not a warrior."

"A true warrior is one who looks after his family and would never hit a woman."

"You're right bro; I agree Dad is a great warrior. Now we need to get out of here."

Jake felt good that Slade had acknowledged him and as they began to walk away he thought how there seemed to still be some hope left for Slade after all.

By the time they made it back to the highway, it was nearly 5am. The sky was still dark, but they knew it wouldn't be too long before the sun rose over the east coast.

"We should be home by day break if we can hitch a ride," Jake spoke, breaking the post-fight, awkward silence.

A logging truck spotted Luke's high visibility top and decided to pick them up as he thought they must be bushmen.

"Where are you headed boys?"

"We need to get about an hour down the coast."

"Jump in, I'll drop you off. I'm going that way to pick up some logs further on."

The boys climbed up into the cab, it was a squish but they were grateful for the ride. The truck rumbled its way over a large bridge by the river before pulling onto the road that followed the coastline. Jake looked out to sea, watching how the full moon was giving the eerie effect of a moonlit path across the ocean. The sea usually was able to calm him, no matter what was going on in his life. However, this morning it wasn't working. Jake just couldn't shake his concern of explaining their unexpected arrival to Hone and Shona.

CHAPTER NINETEEN

After enjoying the success of their hunt, Brent and Stevo decided to continue everyone moving up the river. The group were looking forward to dining on Roger's fresh trout for dinner.

At least a couple more hours of solid riding remained ahead of them before they could even begin to think about setting up camp for the night.

They rode for about an hour, and their way up the river was starting to get really rough and gorgy. As they made their way around a corner Brent noticed a large slip had made its way into the river just a little further ahead.

He called over to Stevo who had ridden up beside him,

"This must be what Gabe was talking about. Looks like there has been a lot of damage up here with slips, that landslide there, and all of those trees coming down into the river."

As they neared the slip, they could see no way to make it around or over without a lot of digging and cutting. They could see a big rimu log blocking their way up the river. Brent and Stevo dismounted and passed the reins to the girls so they could closely examine the log jam on foot.

"Looks pretty bad Brent," Stevo sighed.

The left hand side of the river appeared to be their best chance, despite the large rimu log lying in the way. It looked as if it was where the main slip had come down. There was a lot of dirt and shingle made from mudstone or papa-rock. The rest of the river was covered by a large smattering of logs and heavy debris which continued to allow the water to run freely underneath.

"Shit mate looks like we are going to have to cut this log Brent.

Then we can try to get the horses up around the sides."

They went back and explained their plan of attack to the others. Roger turned pale.

"There's no way I'm going to ride a horse up around there." Brent grinned as he pulled the axes off the pack horse.

"Long way to walk, Rog! You girls might as well make a fire and brew a cuppa while we hack away at this log. We might be a while."

"Sounds good to me," agreed Janey.

Pointing to a sandy spot by a grassy bank Janey grinned,

"We might as well go over there make the fire, sit down with our cuppa, and enjoy the view of watching the axe men work."

They hitched the horses to some branches overhanging the river. Stevo and Brent began to cut the tough log which was at least a metre through. There was plenty of dry drift wood lying around, making it very easy for Heather and Sue to get the fire going.

Janey waded out into the centre of the river and stood on a small sandy patch. The river flowed gently around on either side of her. She looked in awe far up the sides of the river. "Wow," Janey said. "It is fascinating how the trees manage to hold on; growing at all angles as they run all the way up the sides of the river. The bluffy cliffs of stable rock jutting out and the screes of soft, pebbly, papa rock running hundreds of metres down into the river are amazing."

She gazed further up the river.

"Brent!" she exclaimed, pointing at the rockface. He stopped chopping and looked to where Janey was pointing. A group of wild flowers was blowing in the wind. As they watched a few flowers detached from the bunch and fell to the river below.

"Wow," Brent said. "They are like our magical wild flowers. Hope the ones dying isn't an omen."

"Oh, Brent, how could anything go wrong up here in paradise? It is just a coincidence," replied Janey, smiling. Their belief in the power of the flowers was one of the many things she and Brent had in common. Brent resumed his chopping as Heather also waded out to join Janey, and together they looked upstream as far as they could see. The ridges were far above, their steepness mesmerizing. The land had been carved out by water and storms over the centuries to create the current shape of the river bed.

"The fragile nature of the land makes it so easily eroded during heavy rains or when storms blow trees over as the water undermines them. It's almost as if nature is working against itself," observed Heather.

"Yes," agreed Janey. "But it has created such a lovely river bed for us to ride up, and I'm so thankful for that, I really love riding in here." "Brent told me that the river is very fast flowing in the headwaters and then became slower moving once leaving the higher ranges, flowing through wider valleys which eventually narrow up to create gorges and rapids. As the river flows around its many corners, it gouges out deep corner pools wherever it meets a turn in the river. They are 10 to 30 metres deep, even deeper in various places. Amazing, eh!" exclaimed Janey.

The river in between was shingly with bigger rocks jutting out and forming rapids. The water ran from one side to the other, finding its path, and leaving shingly gravel mounds against the side after storms. There were lots of logs, and in some places, especially where slipping and landslides had occurred, the big logs had created log jams in the corners of the river.

Heather replied, "Look at the deep pools over there. There are some really big logs in there that must have been too heavy to float." "The changes to the course of the river seem never ending. Look how the water gushes its way across the big flats in the corners of the river like it is searching to find a way to the sea," said Janey.

Because of the time of year, the river was well below its normal flow. It had been a very hot and dry summer ever since the big storm before Christmas.

"Sure is incredible," said Heather.

Heather and Janey wandered back to Sue and Roger; the fire was roaring, and it wasn't long before the billy was full of boiling water. The sun was warm on their backs, and Roger and the girls drank their cuppa while watching the progress on the log. After they had been hacking away for about half an hour Stevo stood with one arm straight out the side to where he rested against his now vertical axe.

"Which is meant to be the sharp side of this bloody axe?"

"It's like one of those Indians axes where both sides are sharp. If one side goes blunt you just have to turn it over and work harder," Brent laughed, also feeling the frustration along with the pain in his back and arms.

Roger was feeling refreshed after a rest, so he strolled up to where Stevo remained standing.

"Would you like me to have a turn?" he asked.

Stevo willingly handed him his axe and made his way towards the fire for a well-deserved break. "You're welcome to have a turn. It's not as easy as it looks," he laughingly told Roger. Within 10 minutes of Roger hacking furiously, sweat was starting to emerge from every pore on his body. Stevo and Brent exchanged a wry smile as they knew Roger would struggle.

Fantails had come to greet them. The little birds were happily flitting around and catching insects in mid air with their amazing aerobatics.

"Aren't they amazing little guys?" "Sure are, Sue!" Heather agreed.

Heather reached for Roger's bag and took out his book on native birds. She flicked through the pages until she found the paragraph about the fantail, then summarised the information for the others.

"Well, they are called Tiwakawaka in Māori. Apparently they have a long tail which makes up half of their length. They make a penetrating cheet call, and never stop moving."

"Yes," laughed Sue. "That cheet call definitely is penetrating my ear drums, very accurate description!"

"Oh, but they are really lovely, even with that cheet call!" Heather sighed contentedly.

Janey glanced towards a log where a movement beside her had caught her eye. She found a tiny bird sitting there and watching the ladies with great interest. She thought how the bird seemed as if it had the gentlest little eyes set amongst a very cute face. Janey quietly got the attention of the other girls to show them the bird.

"I think this one's a grey warbler," she whispered as she pointed. Heather thumbed through the pages to find the information,

"Yes, here it is. A grey warbler or, as it is known by the Māori people, Riroriro likes to be with other birds. Its song is a distinctive long, musical, wavering trill."

"Yes, it's definitely a warbler then," Janey whispered just as the riroriro called out and flew away to join the fantails.

"I hope we see lots more of these little guys on our trip."

"I am sure we will," reassured Heather. "They both feed mostly on insects and spiders and we know how there are plenty of them up here. "Yeah there are! And they are all a lot bigger than any of the ones
at home!" squealed Sue.

Heather stood up and brushed off her pants. She made her way over to where the boys were working. Janey and Sue followed behind her carrying their cups of tea.

"Come and take a photo of these cute birds, Roger," offered Heather. Stevo raised his eyebrow.

"I don't know about that. We are only half way, Rog. You had better keep going."

Roger sucked in a big breath and hacked away, even more furiously, for another five minutes before he finally dropped the axe in frustration.

"I'm getting blisters!"

"They will match the ones on your backside. Keep chopping," quipped Brent.

Roger rolled his eyes and moved away to take some photos of the birds. After enjoying the tea, Brent and Stevo finished off the log. They used a thick branch to help lever the butt off the log around so the horses would be able to make their way past it. Janey packed the cups and billy back into the bags on Bessie's back. Brent was still very concerned about the steepness the horses would have to negotiate.

"I will give it a go first and then let you all know how it goes okay?" Everyone nodded their heads in agreement - except Roger. "That is far too steep for any horse. We need to be riding mountain goats."

"These horses are station horses, Rog. Don't worry about a thing except staying in your saddle."

The girls joined the men by the log. Stevo led Brent's horse up as Brent dug out some of the steeper dirt, papa-rock, and shingle.

Brent mounted his horse at the bottom of the slip and pointed Big Red straight to where they had cut the big log. Brent knew Big Red was up to the challenge ahead and he nudged him firmly to give him as much momentum to go forward as possible. The horse seemed to sense Brent's urgency and surged forward towards the bank; its massive hind legs powering their way up the slip as Brent held on tightly. It was an awesome sight as the others watched Big Red manage the steep climb almost effortlessly. Dirt and papa-rock flew in all directions as Big Red made his way over the soft shingly slip to bring Brent safely down to the other side. Big Red was covered in the grey papa-rock which turned to slop once wet. It would dry and break up; turning into a sticky and gooey grey mess. Brent yelled out,

"I'll tie Big Red up and come back to get the pack horse."

Stevo approached Brent on his return. "What's it like?" he asked. "Worse than it looks," Brent warned.

"I'll go last and make sure the rest are OK then," offered Stevo. "I'll lead the pack horse up Stevo. Could you give it a whack from behind if it stops? Big Red has made it a smoother track, levelling out some of that papa."

Brent pulled the pack horse around to face the slip.

"You give it a whack when I say go, Stevo." Brent jerked on the lead. The horse looked reluctant but Stevo whacked it on the backside and it immediately jumped forward and started clawing its way up the slip with its heavy load. Brent looked back at the pack horse in admiration of the gutsy, powerful performance of such a great animal. The pack horse finally reached the top, sliding down the other side to stand beside Big Red. Stevo asked, "Do you girls want to ride your horses over or shall I lead them over?" Janey agreed she would be happy to ride her horse across, and so did Heather. Sue took Stevo up on the offer of having her horse led. Roger thought desperately about what he was going to do. The girls' horses had made it over safely so Roger mounted up and tried to swallow his nerves when he realised it was his turn.

His apprehension was apparent to Stevo.

"Make sure you give the horse plenty of reins, keep it straight up the slip, and hang on," Stevo reassured him.

Before Roger could say he had changed his mind and wanted the horse to be led up the slip, Stevo gave Roger's horse a big whack on the backside and it flew up the slip. Roger seemed to be doing okay until he hit the top where he somehow lost his balance. The horse lost its footing as it headed down the other side of the slip. Roger panicked and jumped straight off the horse, landing on the side of his foot. The horse regained itself, but Roger didn't. He rolled down the remaining few metres of the slip. Brent ran over to see if Roger was okay. Roger was spitting mud and dirt out of his mouth, spluttering,

"I've hurt my ankle and grazed my leg."

"We'll get you up on the bank and check out the damage."

Stevo appeared down the slip, his horse spraying dirt and shingle as he ploughed his way down. The girls had already moved up the river 100 metres to find a good place to stop, taking Roger's horse with them. Heather went back to check if Roger was okay. Stevo and Brent had managed to get Roger up; supporting him as they made their way over to where the girls had stopped. Janey, being a nurse, checked Roger's wounds.

"It's just a few grazes and a bit of a sprained ankle, by the look of it. No broken bones," she calmly reassured Roger.

Brent looked at Roger and then around at the rest of his friends. "We'll do another half an hour and see if we can find a good camp site."

The river had narrowed considerably due to being in such a gorgy part of the river but he knew it would open up more as they progressed further.

The papa and dirt that had splashed all over the horses, clinging to their manes and bodies as it dried.

"I'm going to give the horses a good clean and rub down when we reach our new campsite," said Janey.

They continued to trek further up the river. The dogs seemed to be pleased that they were on the move again. Roger was not pleased at all and the others had to endure some pretty serious moaning coming from his direction. Brent did his best to reassure Roger that a good camp site would not be too far away.

Sure enough, after a few more corners, Brent found the perfect spot for them to set up for the night. Stevo and Brent tied the horses on a patch of lush river grass and took their saddles off so that Janey and Sue could give the horses a clean. They used the crystal clear water from the river to gently wash them down. Heather began to get tea ready. Roger was complaining furiously about his throbbing ankle and the multitude of blisters on his backside and hands. Heather dug out a nice warm blanket and kissed him on the cheek as she wrapped it around him before rubbing some arnica cream into his wounds. After a nice hot cup of tea Roger seemed to have cheered up. Stevo prepared the nice juicy trout and stoked up the fire. Brent thoughtfully cleaned all of the gear, making sure there were no traces of papa and dirt remaining on Gabe's beautiful saddles.

Once the happy campers had their bellies full of freshly cooked trout, and the stars were starting to appear Brent tied the dogs up and checked on Buck's leg. He tended to the wound with some antibiotic cream. Stevo cracked open the rum and began to reminisce about the big trout Roger had caught. Stevo was doing his best to cheer Roger up as he explained it would be only another half a day's ride until they arrived at the bull ring where he would be able to rest up for a few days. "It's been quite a day, all things considered, and eating your giant

fish Roger was definitely the highlight!"

The girls each enjoyed a full glass of rum, congratulating themselves for getting their horses over that slip.

Roger looked down wistfully,

"I'd have got mine over too, if I hadn't jumped off. I think it was the blisters on my hands and backside that put me off, I got scared."

Stevo snorted,

"Yeah, the blister on your right cheek must be really big because that is the side you fell off on."

"It's easy for you to laugh, not all of us are natural born bush pigs," retorted Roger.

"Never mind dear, I'll rub it better for you," soothed Heather. Brent looked over at Heather and gave her a wink.

"You must have been rubbing them last night too, Heather. I could hear a lot of deep breathing coming from the direction of your sleeping bags."

Heather's mouth dropped open and her cheeks flushed a deep red. Janey glanced over at Brent with a smile,

"What's the going like tomorrow, Brent?"

"We've got about another hour of this gorgy stuff and then the river will open up and it will get a lot easier - and the scenery will get even more beautiful as you will be able to see the headwaters in the distance and some amazing landscapes."

The rum flowed freely as they relished finally having a chance to wind down and discuss the day that had been - and the one that lay ahead. Roger's eyes began to droop. "Come on," she said. "Bedtime." Stevo and Brent were the last to head for their tents as they had been reluctant to put the rum away for the night. They sipped eagerly at the glasses in their hands, discussing how it was a particularly good batch, and they then began to plan the finer points of the following day.

CHAPTER TWENTY

Can you drop us off us up there, mate?" asked Slade. "Sure thing." the truck driver replied. He dropped them off at the end of their road. Together, they walked slowly up the road towards the only family home they'd ever had. They barely said a word to each other as they pondered about the events of the night before and how they were going to explain things to their parents.

Shona had not been out of bed for long, rising soon after her 6.30 alarm pierced the morning silence and entered her dreams. She was sitting outside on the back door step, enjoying her first cup of tea for the day.

The boys continued to walk slowly up the driveway and as they rounded the final bend their mother jumped in surprise.

"Aue! What are you boys doing here?"

Shona had leapt up and rushed over to greet them. "Kia ora, my sons," she cried out. Slade kept back while Luke and Jake gave Shona huge hugs; he had not seen her since he was sent to jail and he wasn't sure how much she knew.

"Come over here, you," she called to him with the affectionate voice of a kind mother with a big heart.

He lumbered over to his mother and they wrapped their arms around each other in a large hug.

"Let me look at you," Shona demanded as she pushed her hands against his chest; holding him still with her hands clasped on each of his shoulders.

"Wow, you have grown really big. They must have good food up there. What are all those scars on your face from, Son?"

"Oh, don't worry about them Mum, it can be really tough work out in the bush," Slade deliberately said no more, but gave Luke and Jake a look which told them to keep quiet.

Shona just looked from one to the other, not knowing if Slade was telling the truth.

"It's been really wet and we haven't had much work on so we thought we would come home for a while. Might do a bit of hunting," Jake announced suddenly.

"It is great to be able to get some time off and be at home to catch up with you and Dad," Luke added. "It feels as if we have never been away when we come back here. You guys are the best parents anyone could wish for."

He grabbed Shona for another big hug.

"You boys just made my day. I've been missing you all so much!" Jake placed his arm around Shona and they all wandered inside where Shona immediately began cooking breakfast. She spoke to them over the noises of the kitchen, telling them how Hone would be on

his way home soon after checking his crayfish pots.

"He heard the sea is going to cut up and went out at day break to check them."

"Does Dad still have his old 303? Because we want to shoot some tia," Luke asked, cheering up at the thought of a hunting trip with his brothers.

"You boys like catching poaka, don't you? What is this about a deer?" said Shona.

"Of course we do! But we have also started hunting tia up in the bush where we have been working. We have shot some good ones too, but we know there are better ones down here. We borrow the bosses' gun," Jake explained.

"Have you boys got your gun licences yet?" Jake nodded proudly.

"Yeah, we've all got them."

Luke pulled his out of his wallet to show her. She smiled.

"Well done boys. I am so pleased."

"Yeah, the boss helped us get them. He wouldn't lend us his gun until we were over 18 and had our licences."

Slade went back outside once he heard Hone's van coming up the driveway.

"Boy, what on earth are you doing here?" shouted Hone excitedly as he jumped out of the van.

"We came to see you and Mum, of course! We've got a bit of time off work and I haven't seen Mum since I was released. It's really wet so there's not much work on. How was your catch this morning? Get many crays?"

"Yeah, there's a few in the van," Hone pointed over his shoulder, "Grab a couple and we'll have a boil up."

Slade fetched the bag out of the back of Hone's van and brought the crayfish out to the back of the house where Hone had a permanent boiling pot that ran off gas. Slade placed the crays beside the pot which his father was warming up.

"Should be ready in about 15 to 20 my boy," Hone said to Slade giving him a loving slap on the shoulder. He had a note of pride in his voice. "This new boiler doesn't take long to bring the water to the boil and we only need to drop the crays in for a minute or two. You know how much I don't like them overcooked!"

"Well, let's have a cuppa and a sing song while we wait!" Luke announced as he came out the back to join them, grabbing his father's ukulele on the way. When the music reached Jake and Shona inside, they made their way outside to join the others, and they all sat around talking and singing.

"How's work going? How's Jazz?" asked Hone.

"Work's slow at the moment," said Slade. Jazz is great, it's hard for him trying to find work to keep us all employed. He tells us great stories about the two of you."

"Hard case how he got his name for telling his men how to measure the jazz in the timber," said Luke.

Finally, the crayfish were ready and cooked to perfection. this reminded the boys of how much this was the taste of their home. Shona brought out the rest of the breakfast which they enjoyed with the fresh crayfish. Shona chattered away about their other brothers and sisters; how they all were and what they were each getting up to. "We might go up the river for a couple of nights to do some hunting," said Jake.

"Can we borrow the horses?" asked Luke.

"Sure!" Hone replied. "They need some work. They are in the horse paddock further down the coast. How did you boys get here? I didn't see a car or anything."

"Oh, we hitched 'cos I crashed my ute," Slade was quick to answer. "Hope you didn't hurt yourself when you crashed. You should have told us," Shona sounded worried by the idea of her sons in a car accident.

"It was nothing to worry about, Mum. Just made a bit of a mess of the ute sadly. We got a ride in a logging truck which was lucky."

"Will you need a dog? Sorry to say but old Boofy's had a sore foot for a while. Don't think you should take him."

"Nah, let him rest up," Luke paused. "We are just after a few deer.

They are roaring at this time of the year."

"Really? I *know,* I heard one roaring across the road there the other day!" Hone pointed to some scrub a few hundred metres away with a mock grin on his face.

"Awesome," said Luke. Hone just laughed.

"When do you want to go into the bush?"

"We thought maybe tomorrow or the day after, once we have had a chance to catch up with you two and the rest of the family. We need to buy some food and supplies for the trip," answered Jake.

"That suits me just fine boys. I will take you up to the horses tomorrow. I have got a couple of things I want to do today."

"You boys are looking rather tired," Shona noticed. "I suppose you have been burning the candle at both ends – working and partying."

"Oh well, Mum ..." Jake trailed off.

"You know what it's like. You are only young once," Luke continued. "Yea, life has been pretty full on," finished Slade. He looked over at his brothers.

"I don't know about you two, but I could do with a couple of hours kip, especially if we are going into the bush for a few days."

"Good idea," Luke said. The thought of a nice comfortable bed was very tempting. "We'll catch a few zzz's and then we had better get some supplies ready."

"Ok boys, the shop should be open for a while. But it doesn't stay open all day at this time of the year," Hone warned.

There were some little huts outside the main house, which Hone had made for the boys to use as bedrooms as the family grew. The boys each headed toward their old beds for some much needed sleep. Shona enthusiastically set about making some fresh scones and fried bread for lunch. "It's great having the boys home," she thought. She gave them a yell at about 1 o'clock, knowing that they wanted to catch the shop before it closed, and the three brothers drowsily

emerged from their sleeping huts.

"I just heard a story on the radio about a car chase up in the city over night. A police car got wrecked. Did you hear anything about it? I hope you boys were not involved."

"You know us better than that mum, we would never get involved in anything like that," Jake offered weakly.

"I hope not," cautioned Shona. "I hope you are telling me the truth son."

"You and Dad are the best parents, and if we did something like that we know it would really hurt you."

Shona looked at Jake suspiciously. This was the second time one of the boys had said they were the best parents within the very short time they had been home.

The boys had taken their jackets off when they had gone to sleep. They came into the house for lunch wearing only their tee-shirts. They had gotten used to their tattoos, but had forgotten that Hone and Shona hadn't seen them yet.

"What on earth is that on your forearm, Jake?" demanded Shona. "It's a tattoo of a koru, Mum. Do you like it?"

"No, you know I don't like tats," Shona grunted, with a really displeased look on her face. She turned to face Luke.

"Have you two got them as well? Oh, you have!" Shona exclaimed as she made her way over to see his arm more clearly, "What is your one, Luke?"

"It's an eagle, Mum." Shona gave another grunt. "And what have you got, Slade?"

Slade turned his shoulder to show her his snake and dagger tattoo. Shona gasped disgustedly.

"It's the sign of a soft head!"

Hone had shown up part way through the tattoo conversation and had been watching them all. He didn't say anything, keeping his face expressionless. Shona wasn't leaving it there.,

"What do you think of this, Hone? Our boys are all tatted up." "I don't know, love. Maybe they just had to express themselves." "Express themselves?! If I could still spank each of them I would!"

Slade had never seen their mother look so disappointed in the three of them.

"I guess you boys had better have your lunch now so you can make it to the shop in time," sighed Shona downheartedly.

Nobody said very much as they gratefully ate the lunch Shona had prepared.

"Thanks Mum, you are the salt of the earth. That was great," praised Luke.

"You're welcome. Just you boys remember all your father and I have taught you, and you will be fine."

"Yeah, Mum. Okay," reassured Slade, "We had better get going or we will miss the shop."

"Okay, boys," Shona waved them off. "See you later!"

Luke, Slade, and Jake wandered off up the old familiar road towards the shop.

"Mum's not happy about our tattoos." "Nah," Slade agreed with his twin.

"Hopefully she will come to love them just like we do."

"Yeah," agreed Jake. "Geez, I'm glad Mum didn't question us more about that car chase. Do you think she knows we were involved?"

Slade was first to reply,

"Nah, she is sweet. I know it was bad, but it was pretty exciting aye. It was one rush we never even had to pay for."

"We never want Mum to find out," Luke whispered before adding, "She'd be broken. Maybe we should lay off the marijuana for a while. It was pretty bad, what we did."

"Oh, get over it," snapped Slade. "It's all history now."

They carried on up the road towards the shop and got their supplies.

Slade looked at his brothers with a smile,

"Let's go to the pub, and get some rum and a few joints for up the river to keep us warm."

"Sounds good to me," smiled Jake. "We'll need something up there. Don't worry, boys. I'll take my little ghetto blaster and the ukulele. We'll be able to listen to some good music and chill out."

"I suppose we'll have to listen to that stuff you always play," quipped Luke.

"Best music on this planet," Jake threw back.

"The stags won't like it any more than we do. It could even stop them roaring," laughed Slade. He liked having Jake on about his music, and Jake never minded taking flack for it as he knew that they all really enjoyed his playing.

As they approached the door to the pub, Luke warned his twin, "No trouble, Slade. We are in enough crap now, even if we think we've got away with it."

"Yeah, yeah," mumbled Slade.

As evening drew in Slade said, "Let's head for home." Luke and Jake gave him a thumbs up. They grabbed some takeaways for dinner and bought a bottle of rum each and a bag of weed. Slade got talking to one of his old mates in the shady area at the back. Out of the corner of his eye Luke saw Slade pay him for something. He hoped with all his heart that it wasn't P, but he didn't ask Slade what he was doing as he knew better than to cause a scene. He decided to let it go and to see what happened next; thinking to himself how if his brother wanted to wreck himself, then that would be Slade's problem.

Luke suggested they head off after breakfast the following morning.

"It'll take at least two days to get up to the Bullring, depending on whether we stop for a hunt on the way up or not. And, of course, depending on how many slips in the river there are after all the rain they had just before Christmas. There should be some big stags around there."

The boys staggered home slowly, passing a bottle of rum between them as they made their way through the familiar streets of their youth. All of the main house lights were off when they arrived home because it was quite late. Shona had left the little outside light on for them, just like she had always done when they lived at home. They went into their sleeping huts and bunked down for the night.

CHAPTER TWENTY-ONE

Stevo had risen at first light and as dawn broke he decided that the others should be up by now too. He had already re-stoked the fire and saddled up the horses. Stevo let the dogs off their chain and Buck ran straight into Brent and Janey's tent and gave Brent a big wet lick on the face. Blue followed suit, and Brent sat up immediately looking confused and sleepy. He could hear the fire crackling and the horses stomping their feet, ready for action. He felt a pang of guilt at sleeping in and leaving his best friend to do all of the work.

As he climbed out of his tent Brent laughingly asked Stevo, "Did you wet the bed or something? Must have to have the horses all ready by now!" He scratched Blue and Buck a scratch behind their ears.

Quietly but efficiently, everybody climbed out of their beds, rolled up their sleeping bags, and helped to pile the rest of the gear onto the horses. Stevo had the bacon sizzling in a pan over the fire. Janey, walking towards Stevo, rubbed her eyes and asked what he thought the day would be like. They had camped under some big trees so the sky was hidden from view.

"It'll be a great one again. I was out getting wood a moment ago by the river and it was as clear as a bell."

Brent walked over to the fire and wrapped his arm around Janey.

He gave her a gentle good morning kiss.

Janey smiled up into his eyes.

"I hope you've wiped your lips, I saw you pashing those pig dogs." Brent laughed.

"Of course I've washed. Two days in the bush and you are still the sweetest thing I ever kissed."

Stevo had the breakfast ready to be eaten within no time and everybody was licking their lips in anticipation, including Roger who was limping and rubbing himself as he neared the campfire.

"You ready for those blisters to be popped, Rog?" Stevo quipped. "You won't be popping anything on me, Bud."

"Okay, then we will just leave it to the saddle." Heather piped up,

"Don't tease him, Stevo. He has had a hard night."

Brent looked at Heather with a beaming dirty smile on his face. "A hard night, aye?"

Janey dug Brent in the ribs to silence him, chuckling quietly. Stevo began handing the plates full of hot sizzling bacon, eggs, and bread around while Sue helped by passing out cups of freshly boiled billy tea. "We had better eat up and get moving. There should be some big trout to catch further up the river, Rog. By the way, you've done really

well riding that horse."

"Thanks, Brent," smiled Roger. Brent knew Roger was pleased with himself regardless of the throbbing pains in his backside and ankle. Stevo patiently waited another half hour while they finished their breakfast, packed up, and were all mounted and ready to set off for the Bullring. Getting Roger mounted on his horse had proven to be quite a task. Brent had never heard so many moans in his life, but he decided to cut Roger some slack for his gutsy effort to get over the slip the previous day. Sue looked really eager to get going and was the

first one to ride her horse out into the river.

"Gee, you're keen this morning, dear," laughed Stevo.

"Yeah, I just can't wait to get riding! It is just so beautiful up here.

What a great idea you guys had to come up here."

The riders moved off up the river, quickly catching up to Sue. Big Red was striding up the river heading for the Bullring. Brent was holding the reins firm as his horse was fresh and eager to get going after a full nights rest. The sun was just starting to brighten the day. The sun's warmth was enjoyable as it hit their backs while the river meandered beneath them. The horse's hooves hit the water and every splash created a different pattern in the water, the droplets slipping back into the river with the sun shining on them before they were reabsorbed into the smooth surface.

It was a great ride and the hours ticked by. Early in the afternoon, Big Red pricked his ears and snorted as he came around a large river bend.

"What's up boy?" Brent asked, before catching a sudden whiff of wood smoke. He immediately recognised the scent as rata smoke. Rata, a very hard NZ native timber, burns well and leaves good coals that give a constant heat throughout cooking time. Brent had always loved cooking on Rata coals as they were really great for baking bread in the camp oven, and for frying fresh venison back steaks in the frying pan. Brent loved a good fire. He would use woods such as Totara and other podocarps to get the initial fire burning and then put either the Rata, Manuka, or Kanuka on as they were all great timbers for producing coals. Usually he didn't have the luxury of being choosey as he often had to make do with whatever dry wood was around. But Brent wasn't wrong in knowing there would be at least one of these types of wood near the big river, especially after so much build up from the storms.

Brent immediately thought of an old possum hunter he and Stevo had spent time with on previous trips to the Bullring; their friend named Possum Jack who was an expert in knowing which timber was best to use for which stage of the cooking process. Brent had always really admired how Possum Jack could cook. Years of practice in the most difficult conditions had honed his endless skills.

As the horses continued to move along, Brent suddenly saw a puff of smoke coming up out of the trees. He realised it was somebody's camp rather than a passing hunter. He rode towards the camp; convinced he would find his friend sitting beside the fire at the base of the smoke stack. As Brent got nearer, he could see a little brown pony eating grass in a small clearing. He smiled to himself and waved an arm for his friends to follow behind; Brent would know that pony anywhere.

As they got closer, the pony lifted his head and snorted. "Who's that?" called a raspy voice.

A wiry, thin, long haired, and long whiskered man suddenly appeared from behind the bushes. He squinted towards the approaching group. He instantly recognised Brent and Stevo as the men he had met years ago, when they would regularly come hunting up in the Bullring area and the Green River country.

"Well what do you know!" the old man exclaimed. "Possum Jack!" Brent and Stevo excitedly called in unison. "Sure is," Possum Jack replied excitedly.

"I was just thinking of you when I smelt that Rata smoke, I had hoped it would be you here!"

Possum Jack eyed up their group as they approached.

"Man, the hunters are getting better looking these days - and I'm not talking about you and Brent either, Stevo!"

Brent and Stevo dismounted with a single movement, and strode over to shake Possum Jack's hand and slap him on the back. Brent wandered over towards the small pony to give Little Orphy a pat.

"It must be at least five years since we have seen you, Possum Jack. Orphy is still looking well, just like you." Possum Jack grinned.

"What do you want Brent? I suppose you want me to tell you where all the deer are or something, making nice remarks like that." Roger and the girls were watching from their horses. Brent introduced his wife and his friends to Possum Jack, explaining how he and Stevo had spent quite a bit of time with the possum hunter

on previous trips.

He was wearing short pants and short rubber boots. His legs looked like those of a 21-year-old; they were so muscular. Janey noticed how Possum Jack looked really fit, despite being at least 65. She thought to herself how he would have been quite a handsome man once, but the weather had masked all that.

He now looked as rough as a hardwood strainer on an exposed ridge. "Would you girls like a cup of tea? The billy has just boiled so you

are all in luck," Possum Jack looked around. "It's great to have some familiar company."

"That would be great," Janey graciously accepted.

Roger snapped a few photos of Orphy and tried to take some of Possum Jack who held up a weathered hand to block the lens from capturing his image.

"Oi! None of that fancy stuff up here paparazzi! You don't get my picture that easily."

They all dismounted and tethered their horses before gathering around Possum Jack's fire with their mugs of tea. He told them stories about his latest possuming adventures.

"You should see the size of the ones I've been catching lately. I've never seen anything like them."

As Possum Jack told his stories, Little Orphy wandered over and gently nudged in between Heather and Sue who immediately began doting on him.

"Don't you need to tie him up?" queried Sue.

"He's never been tied up in his life and, if I have anything to do with it, he never will be," Possum Jack paused to take a sip of his tea. "He's a free spirit, just like me."

As Little Orphy nudged Heather for more attention, she asked after the pony's name.

"Little Orphy," answered Jack. "Little – well that's obvious, and Orphy because when I was working on a sheep station in the off- season from possuming I found his mother giving birth to him. She died and the station owner said I could have the foal if I reared it. His mother was a little Welsh mountain pony. They used to use them for packing in posts on steep fence lines, wherever a bulldozer or vehicle couldn't get, because they are so sure footed. In those days they didn't have very good access. I mixed milk powder in the pan and taught him to drink out of it until he was old enough to eat grass. He became so tame he would follow me anywhere. He even sits beside me at night by the fire - he must think he is a dog."

"Does he really sit by the fire?" piped up Roger.

"Course, he does. Watch this." Possum Jack whistled and the horse wandered over and sat down next to Jack by the fire.

Roger snapped photos frantically, despite Possum Jack's dislike for the camera.

"Does he have any other tricks?" Roger asked excitedly. "Yeah, he will shake your hand."

On cue Orphy raised his hoof and placed it in Possum Jack's outreached hand.

"Wow!" Roger exclaimed. "That's too cool!"

He snapped even more photos. Possum Jack didn't make another comment on Roger taking more photos but gave him an odd sideways look instead.

"Orphy will even give you a smile, just like Mr Ed. He used to pucker his lips, with a mouth full of dry milk powder. It would stick to his lips and gums. His teeth looked really white. He would pinch milk powder out of the sack whenever he got the chance - Smile Orphy!"

The horse lifted his head and gave Roger and his awaiting camera a big smile. Everyone had a good laugh, fascinated by the little ponies domesticated behaviour. Obviously the bond between Orphy and Jack was very strong as they had lived together 24/7 for so many years.

"Speaking of dogs; those two look familiar. Are they Gabe's pig dogs?"

"Yeah, Blue and Buck," confirmed Stevo, "He lent them to us so we could give them some work."

Brent asked Possum Jack about the whereabouts of his dog; Tracker. Possum Jack didn't usually go hunting while he was away working, but he had been known to tell Tracker to chase a pig if he came across a nice big, juicy looking one.

Possum Jack replied with a really stony and sad look on his face, "We were after a half-grown pig, just something for the two of us

to eat, when he came across a big boar up in the Green River Country. Tracker got absolutely ripped up by the vicious pig in the river. So strange because Tracker had never got himself hurt by a pig. I mean, my Tracker knew how to hunt! I guess the pig must have been really hungry or something to get that aggressive. Tracker couldn't get out of its way in time, and so after he got ripped he was bleeding a lot. By the time I got to where he was baling the pig, a whole lot of these massive eels had come up and latched onto Tracker. It was so scary. The eels seemed to just go mad at the sign of blood. I ran down the side of the river. Tracker was getting washed away with the current and I tried my best to grab him, slashing some of the slimy bastards at the same time. But that just created even more blood and then my boy suddenly disappeared with the current. I just stood there shaking. It completely took me by surprise how things managed to turn so badly so quickly,

I could have screamed. It ripped my guts out watching Tracker being killed by these slimy buggers. He came up once more but by then it was too late and the eels were all over him. He just disappeared. Of course I was also keeping an eye on Orphy because he had rushed into the water and was stomping away on a few of the eels. I called him and he came out of the water just in time, when there were even more eels turning up."

Brent noticed the deep sadness in Possum Jack's eyes. He had always loved Tracker and Brent could see his friend clearly missed his beloved companion. Possum had raised Tracker from a six week old pup and sadly his death was cruelly slow and torturous; something that was even harder for his master to bear.

"There's something going on up this valley, Brent. I don't know what it is, but everything seems to be getting bigger and meaner. I've caught some huge possums in here, along the river catchment. It would take at least two skins in another area to equal just one, or even half of one of these skins."

"We have already seen a massive weta, some enormous eels, and giant blowflies. We just figured that was what all of the animals were like up here," Heather spoke quietly.

Possum Jack nodded his agreement.

"Yeah, they are mighty big. They weren't always like that though. I have noticed a drastic change over the last year. I've also noticed a different type of eel up here; they are meaner and bigger than our native ones. I'm pretty sure it was some of them that killed my Tracker." Heather's eyes looked like they were about to pop out of her head.

New Zealand had always been proud of being free of dangerous animals and insects, and she was worried maybe that wasn't quite the case deep in the bush.

Brent broke the silence.

"What do you mean by a different type of eel?"

Everybody had edged closer; wanting to be nearer to each other and also desiring to hear every single word that Possum was saying, especially the news about the killer eels.

"Well, I was over in the next catchment, let me see … It was on the trip before this one. I was doing possums and just having a quick look-see when I decided to go out to sell some skins. The possum skin buyer comes down the coast every fortnight to buy skins so I knew he was due that day. Of course I know him really well since I have been selling skins to him for years. He does eel fishing for a living, when he is not buying skins, and we got to talking about all sorts of things. He asked me if I had seen many eels up there. No more than normal, I told him. He asked me if I had seen any different looking eels. I said, what do you mean different? And he explained how he'd been catching some really different looking eels that were a lot bigger than our native eels; about four times bigger. He said he had done some research into them and found out they were Aussie longfinned eels of the Anguilla reinhardti species - but he called them Aussie invaders. Apparently, they come here as larvae on ocean currents, especially strong currents after the cyclones off Australia's eastern seaboard. They grow heaps faster than our eels but are hard to distinguish from our guys until they get bigger; over 500 mm. The bigger ones are usually easier to identify because they are a mottled green, have yellow fringes on their side markings, and a white underbelly. Turns out they have been found in many different rivers and in many different places. They have also got bigger teeth than our native eels which the Māori people call Kaiwharuwharu."

"Gosh, is that right?" piped up Roger. "Bigger teeth equal a bigger appetite?" Laughing, Stevo looked over at his friend.

"You had better just make sure you don't get bitten, Rog, or you will know all about it."

"Don't you worry about me mate, I will be staying well back from those trout pools when I am fishing just in case there is an Aussie invader in them."

"Puts a shiver up your spine," Sue whispered as she huddled into Stevo's side. Brent couldn't wait to go and have a look for the Aussie eels. He wanted to see if they had pools of their own or if they lived with the native longfinned silver bellied eels.

"So that's why you think it was them that killed Tracker, right? You recognised them as the invaders."

"Yeah, Brent," confirmed Possum. "Those eels were huge, I was really scared. When I tried to save Tracker they were coming at him from all directions out of the current of the river. He was bleeding from being ripped by the boar, and it's the blood that just made them go mad. They must have a really acute sense of smell, especially when it comes to blood because it seemed to attract them from miles down the river. I could see eels coming up the river before I even got near to where Tracker was. They were grabbing him and spinning around so they could tear him to pieces. I could see their big white underbellies so that's how I know they were the Aussie invader eels. Their eyesight is not that great according to my mate, but from what I noticed in these bigger eels their eyes are very large and seem to be becoming more useful to them. To be honest they reminded me of sharks on the hunt." "Oh no, that's awful," Janey spoke comfortingly as she placed her hand on Possum's shoulder. He was visibly upset; losing Tracker had obviously broken this man's heart.

"You know," Roger spoke up. "I suppose if you had spent your life living in a mud pool with a bunch of crocodiles like those eels would have done in Aussie, you would learn to be pretty mean and look as ferocious as you could."

The others turned to look at Roger in amazement. "What!!!" said Stevo. "What do you mean?" Heather gave Roger a look that told him to shut up. Roger was from the city and had never had a pet so he didn't understand the depth of the bond between Tracker and Possum Jack. "That was a very left field comment, Roger," Sue said sharply.

"Possum thought they probably came to NZ as larvae."

"Yeah, well they also could have swum here as adults while they were out spawning if they got caught in the strong currents from a cyclone," justified Roger. "Who knows?"

"Yeah, who knows?" Brent agreed. "But I surely would like to. We will have to be very careful. They must have to watch that their mates don't eat them. There's not much room in some of these pools for a dozen of these big sods. I think some of those eels we saw when we killed the pig were probably the Aussie invader breed rather than our native Kaiwharuwharu. They were massive."

Janey glanced over at the horses.

"I wonder if they would attack the horses while we are crossing the river?"

"Only if they are bleeding from a graze or something like that, I think. But we can't be too careful," Stevo warned grimly.

"When they're hunting or feeding on a carcass in the river they latch onto their prey and spin around as they tear pieces of meat off. They are really powerful for their size and if the prey is still alive they will drag it under the water. Fresh blood seems to make them act like they are on drugs or something. They just go insane," said Possum Jack."

"Man," sighed Roger. "This is getting scary." Heather looked at her husband.

"Don't worry, dear. They are in the river so just keep out of the water." "The only thing of mine that is going in that water is my fishing spinner and if any of those Aussies turn up I am just going to cut my line!" exclaimed Roger.

"Actually," Brent added, "We probably should fish in pairs, just in case. You girls be careful to only cross the river in wide, shallow crossings and to swim in clear, sandy bottomed pools. Make sure there are no logs or big boulders in them."

Roger's mind wandered to the beautiful scenery and the photos he had already taken and he smiled, deciding not to say anything more about his feelings of fear of the eels as he was already aware of how much of a city boy he was on such adventures.

Brent and Stevo were deep in conversation with Possum Jack as they had so much to catch up on. Possum Jack's hut was his base while he was possuming. It contained all his pieces of board for drying skins, hanging off a wire at the back of the hut, by an old makeshift fire place made from corrugated iron. The black ash had mixed with the tawa sap and stained it black, and the iron on the inside of the roof was the same colour from years of drying skins. There were lots of other pieces of equipment scattered around the walls of the old hut while the cobwebs in the corners would have made any spider proud. The webs had clearly never been touched since the day the spiders had moved in and spun their new home. A large black spider crawled out of a web, Janey spotted it first.

"Wow," she said. "That really is one huge spider! It is bigger than my hand." The other girls looked at the spider in amazement.

"Pleased that is not at my house!" said Sue.

CHAPTER TWENTY-TWO

The day drifted along. The horses enjoyed a nice meal of wild, lush, river grass, and Orphy was thrilled with their company; kicking up his heels and running around in delight. The girls were laughing at the horses' antics while they finished their cups of tea and enjoyed the warmth from the sun.

Heather nudged Janey.

"Doesn't look like we will be doing any more riding today. The boys are in for a big catch up session with Possum Jack."

"Yeah, I'll go check out what they are up to."

Janey walked up behind Brent and wrapped her arms around his neck from behind, pressing her face into his.

"What's happening, love? Are we staying the night?"

Brent looked over and raised an eyebrow at Stevo who simply shrugged.

"I'm easy."

Brent turned to Possum Jack who nodded.

"Well we've got a lot to talk about boys, and I haven't seen you for a few years. You and your lovely ladies are welcome to stay the night."

"That sounds like far too good an invitation to turn down." Janey kissed Brent's cheek and smiled.

"We'll take the saddles and gear off the horses and tether them up for the night."

Sue, who had wandered over and sat beside Stevo, was appearing relaxed as she was clearly enjoying the beautiful spot.

"Roger and Heather should be back soon. He got brave and went to try and catch a trout. We can go and see what he and Heather have got once we have finished the horses."

"Yeah, he'll want to fish that last half hour before dark. The fish seem to really start feeding about this time."

"Hope he keeps back from the edge of the pools with those big eels in there, especially those Aussie eels," Stevo mused as he pulled his wife towards him.

"Heather will make sure he does," replied Sue.

Brent, knowing his big chestnut could be a handful, offered if they would like any help with the horses.

"No thanks," replied Janey sweetly. "Just get some water boiling for the spuds, dear." Brent smiled; he knew how much the girls loved handling the horses.

Possum Jack whistled.

"Gee, you boys have got it sorted! You don't have to do nothing by the sounds of it! We may as well have another cuppa while we boil that water."

"Sounds good," Stevo agreed, kicking a few ashes together and throwing a few twigs in under the billy to stir the fire back into action. Possum Jack was leaning back in a very comfortable looking old chair he had crafted. He had made it by tying branches together before covering them with an old jute sack in which he had used to bring

gear to the hut over the years.

Brent moved to sit closer to Possum Jack.

"What do you really think is happening to the eels and the other wild life up here, Jack?"

"Well, I don't know. I've noticed big changes in everything up here. The insects are bigger and they really want to bite you. The big poaka and eels will attack you, especially if there's any blood around. They are getting bigger, hungrier, and meaner. The tia appear to be growing really massive heads of antlers too."

"Well, that's one good thing," piped up Stevo. He had always loved big stags, especially ones with large racks of antlers.

Brent told Possum Jack about the weta they had seen down the river, and how the eels had gone mad when they caught the boar.

Possum Jack shook his head.

"This has been happening over a long period of time, Brent. You notice little things, like the eels are more active in the day time when normally they would be resting under a log jam in the river or a rock, and they are getting really massive, especially up in the Green River country. I've seen insects and spiders ten times their normal size. I always check my sleeping bag carefully these days."

"You are really observant, Possum. If anyone is going to notice things that are different it will be you," said Brent.

"I've only been in this catchment for a week on this trip as Orphy and I were over in the other catchments catching possums. It would be about twelve months since we have been here and things have completely changed."

"Why do you think the insects and spiders are so big here?" asked Stevo.

"It seems like everything is just super desperate for food. Last time we were here, I felt like something was up because things seemed to be bigger in size, but I couldn't really put my finger on it. I thought the wildlife must have had a bountiful year or two with their food source being really good. But no, after coming back this time, I realise it's definitely not that. Everything is just unnaturally hungry, and the change in the size of everything in twelve months is unbelievable. Some of these spiders crawling around here are so large they give me the creeps."

Brent nodded, holding onto every single word his friend was saying. "Have you noticed anything strange happening in the other catchments?"

"Nah, not at all," Possum sighed. "It just seems to be in this catchment. I don't think there's been anybody up the river this far in the last twelve months or so because of the big slips. They would have just hunted the side creeks lower down, because they could catch a feed down there without coming way up here. There would have been the odd chopper flying around; shooting the odd deer. But even that's getting harder as the big slips from the storm about 15 years ago are starting to grow a lot of vegetation. Some of it is higher than your head and it's certainly not been as easy as it used to be for them to shoot tia, so it's pretty quiet up here. When I was last here there had been no horses up the river or any sign of man. That must be why no one has noticed anything different with the wildlife."

Stevo looked over at his best friend.

"We've got to get a handle on this, Brent. It's going to stuff up the wild life and the environment up here if we don't."

"Yes, the natural balance has been disrupted by something and they will just wipe themselves out with the way they have grown and their insatiable hunger."

Sue and Janey had met up with Roger and Heather when they were on their way back from the river, and the four friends approached the men sitting around the fire. Brent called out,

"Hey, nice job Rog! Looks like you have got us our tea! Wait, Are you okay? You look worried."

"Yes, it will feed all of us for sure! But you won't believe this, Brent. I have just been telling the girls about it. I'd just landed this trout out of a big pool on a corner of the river about a hundred metres upstream from here. There was another pool about 20 to 30 metres further upstream from me. It was full of boulders and there were rapids between the pools. I looked upstream because I thought I heard a loud splash, and I told Heather to listen and she heard it too. I could see water splashing into the air from the other pool so we walked up to have a look. I figured it must have been a massive trout jumping to catch insects for food. When we got closer we could see the water was frothing and that there was something really strange going down in this pool. Suddenly a massive tail appeared and I was standing well back so I moved a little closer to get a better look down into the pool. I could see these two huge eels," Roger paused, his eyes bulging and his face showing both fear and excitement. "They were definitely those eely Anguilas; I could see their mottled green colouring with yellow fringes just like Possum described. They had been after one of our long finned eels which was also huge. They had killed it and were feeding off it, just pulling it to bits and completely tearing it apart. They must be getting really hungry up here, Brent. The big trout must be too fast for them so they are picking on their kiwi cousins instead."

"Wow Rog, that would have been quite a shock to witness something like that," Brent empathised.

"We should go for a look," suggested Stevo.

"Yeah, I can show where they were in the river," offered Roger excitely. He was grateful for the rare opportunity to be helpful in the outdoors environment that he never truly felt he belonged within.

"Let's go!" Brent shouted, leaping to his feet.

The men all grabbed their torches and set off quickly towards the river with Roger leading the way. By the time they got upstream to where Roger had seen the eels it was too dark to see down into the water but they could still hear the odd splash.

"Just there is where I saw them," pointed Roger.

Shining their torches they could see the pool was murky where the eels had stirred up the sand and mud in the pool but it was too dark to see any of the eels. Brent was holding his 270 rifle in his left hand and was pointing the torch with his right. He knew it was pointless to keep searching in the dark.

"We'll have to come and have a look in the morning, first thing." "Yes," agreed Possum. "They'll still be around I'm sure."

"There are some really huge trout in the pool where I was fishing but I got one of the smaller ones, even still it's about four and a half kilos."

"I saw it when you brought it up," agreed Brent. "It looks tasty.

We'll have some nice steak and trout for tea."

They headed back to camp where the girls were waiting for them. Both billies were boiling; the one with the spuds and the other with the water for the tea. Stevo made a cuppa for everyone and they all sat down around the fire. Roger gutted his fish after Heather had taken some photos. He could not stop talking about what he had seen.

Brent smiled.

"When you said eely Anguilla I thought you were talking about some really strong drink that would just slide through your taste buds."

Stevo laughed.

"Yeah that has got a ring to it! Speaking of alcohol, I think we should all have a rum."

Stevo poured Roger a strong rum to help calm his nerves as he'd been quite shocked by what he had seen. Just being so deep into the mountains and wilderness was a really big effort for Roger. Brent could see the strange dangers were unsettling him. He tried to change the subject; not wanting to further upset their friend. Heather appeared to be calmer but she still eagerly accepted one of Stevo's large pourings of rum. As they drank their rum, the conversation slowly turned back to what was causing the problems up here.

"We still can't be 100% sure what species the eels Roger saw were, but they sure sound as if they were the Aussie Anguilas doing the damage to our long finned eels," Brent then turned to Possum Jack. "Do you know if there have been any poison drops in here? If there have been, maybe there's something reacting with it in the ground causing this."

Stevo, an adamant poison hater, slammed his fist.

"Well, if it is 1080 poison, they would have gone and stuffed everything because they have probably put it on our entire bush, and not just this catchment. Do you know how 1080 got its name?"

"No," Heather whispered, surprised at Stevo's angry outburst. "How?"

"Because it kills between 10 and 80 times. It begins with the herbivores who eat it and are then eaten by carnivores and so on, until the entire natural food chain is damaged."

Sue looked at Brent doubtfully. "Is that true?"

Brent replied,

"I am not so sure about the name thing, but yes Stevo is right with the rest of it."

"Yes, there have been drops, Brent," sighed Possum. "Couldn't tell you exactly when, but it would have been in the last two years. It really knocked out the possums, birds, and all the little pigs. The bigger poaka seemed to be able to handle it as they are the only animals that, like us, can vomit it up. It hammered the tia as well."

"I'm ok with them using 1080 when it is necessary but once the problem is under control they should bring in man power and a decent bounty system," said Brent. "I believe the overuse of it is a cheap and nasty way to treat the bush and animals."

"I hate it for what it did to my two really good pig dogs when they ate a possum that had been killed by the poison. They suffered a slow, painful death," said Stevo. "It kills everything, even the insects when they just drop it on the bush."

"Yeah, I really object to aerial dropping when they can't be sure where it will land. It should only be used to kill target animals, not just anything that is unlucky enough to eat it or to eat an animal that has eaten it," replied Brent.

Possum Jack said "If the right incentives are there to go out and kill possums, there would be no problem at all. I met one of those greenie people up the river a while back and he was telling me where they had been working. We got into some rather heated discussions about 1080. I am sure when he was talking to me I could smell it on his breath."

Janey laughed.

"Possum, you must be joking. It would have been on his clothes."

"Possibly," replied Possum with a smile on his face.

"Gee," quipped Roger. "I knew those guys took a few chemicals but I didn't know that 1080 was one of them."

Everybody laughed.

"We have the know-how and all the gear in the world as far as trapping, shooting, and bait stations for killing target pests. There are also some far less dangerous poisons, like cyanide, which only kills once. If a decent bounty system was brought in, where the possumer got a guaranteed price per possum, and he had to give a dry skin back to the tax payer so the tax payer could recoup some cost, everybody would be happy and there would be no pest problem. It would just have to be run and organised properly."

Heather looked over at Possum Jack, aware at how much thought he had put into it.

"Yes, I agree, you have clearly got it worked out. It's a shame you can't be in charge of that system Possum Jack."

The others raised their glasses, toasting as they agreed wholeheartedly Possum Jack would be the man for the job.

Sue looked up sadly.

"I just can't believe they would just keep putting on more 1080 with no end plan or backup system in place to try phase it out."

Roger added,

"It's just disappointing that this stuff is getting dropped all over our bush and waterways without anyone trying to get the hunters and everybody else who loves our bush to get involved. The real shame is the poor animals who are suffering from eating this stuff."

Brent had been deep in thought about what had been happening to the wildlife and turned suddenly to Possum Jack.

"If you believe it is only happening in this watershed, Possum, what else could be causing it?"

"The only thing foreign to this area, other than 1080, are these drums up in the head of the river that I came across a couple of years ago. Maybe they could have something to do with it," Possum replied thoughtfully.

"What kind of drums?" Brent asked interestedly.

Possum appeared not to have heard him as he was lost in his own thoughts. Brent asked again, and Possum continued,

"Yeah, I never gave them much thought when I was up there and came across the drums. I didn't even look closely at them. Orphy and I were running late and the weather was closing in. It was raining heavily and we wanted to get out of there in case the river came up and we weren't able to get back. I had a load of skins on so we just wanted to get back to camp. I guess there would have been about half a dozen or more barrels scattered around in this gully. I noticed some more 44 gallon drums further up in the bush. I didn't take much notice at the time. I remember thinking a chopper must have come up the valley to spray a pine plantation to the East and had been carrying the drums in a net under the chopper. I presumed they must have been jettisoned from the net in bad weather or wind at some stage or maybe the pilot dropped them knowing they were empty. Now I have to wonder what they could have been full of."

"God, who knows? It could be anything," Brent looked concerned,

"How many drums would you have seen?"

"At least six in the spot I was in. From memory I think some of them had burst open."

"Could you still find those drums?"

"It wouldn't be easy. I was in pretty rough country at the time but I know roughly the area they are in."

"What are you thinking, Brent?" asked Janey.

"Not sure yet, but I don't like the idea of some substance possibly leaking and affecting our beautiful native bush and the animals that live in it. I know none of us want our bush to be spoiled by any sort of chemical. We may have to do an expedition up there," Brent paused and turned his attention back to Possum Jack. "Would you be able to take us to the area if we got ourselves organised and came back here? That way we can all go and have a look to see if we can find out what is causing this problem. We might be able to get some samples from the drums."

"I would love to," assured Possum Jack. "I also like the idea of a trip up the river with you lot, tell some more yarns. Wonder if you could convince Gabe to come along? I haven't seen him for ages and it would be great to catch up. If we don't look after our wildlife and find out what is affecting them, pretty soon there won't be anything left. The eels will all eat each other, and the deer and pigs will all disappear - and that would be a disaster in itself."

"Do you really think you could find them again, Possum?" Stevo asked, trying to get a square answer out of his friend.

"Yeah, I would say so. They were off the end of the ridge system further up in the catchment."

The spuds which had been boiling quietly away were finally cooked so Brent put the frying pan on and threw the steak in. He'd hung Roger's trout in the smoke from the fire after cutting it open, so all of the flesh was exposed to the smoke.

"That'll be tasty," Stevo eyed the trout and licked his lips.

Brent put a small morsel of pork on the fork and passed it to Janey. It was straight out of the hot pan where it had been sizzling with the rest of the pork and venison which was just about ready.

"Yum!" exclaimed Janey. "That is definitely straight out of the wild. It is delicious. You were right, poaka and tia are very yummy." She smiled before adding, "Do you think we should go and look for those drums now, while we are up here? There could be something seeping into the water that is affecting the animals and fish."

Possum agreed with Janey.

"She's right, maybe we shouldn't delay. It seems pretty serious now we have discussed it and the possible implications. Checking it out sounds like a good idea, but it depends what your plans are. It's very steep up to the main ridge system and then it's not too bad. It would take at least a day and a half tramping just to get there."

Stevo said,

"All going well, that makes it at least a three day round trip, possibly four. Our whole trip is twelve days. We've got three hours riding to the Bullring, which we will finish tomorrow, and then three to four days up to the drums and back."

"And that would leave us with about two days at the Bullring before we head out," added Brent.

"That sounds about right," agreed Possum.

"I think it will work," remarked Brent. "Roger and the girls can stay at the Bullring and rest after that while Stevo and I go for a quick hunt up secret creek. We don't want to miss out hunting that big stag." "It will still depend on how long our trip to look for the drums takes, we would still need two or three days to ride out," Stevo reminded

Brent.

"Yeah, I reckon it will fit in all right. We will try to still have time to go hunting if we can, but this has to take priority."

Brent asked Possum if he could come with them to show them the way.

"Yeah of course! I wouldn't miss it for anything. If something in the drums is stuffing up our bush I want to do anything I can to fix it. The weather looks good for the next three to four days. It can be a world of hurt up there if the weather packs in, with the rugged going and the thickness of the bush, plus the the altitude up there is high and cold."

Little Orphy was giving Sue a nudge in demand for more pats. Sue squealed with delight.

"This is the loveliest little horse I have ever seen." Possum Jack smiled.

"Yeah, well I could tell you a lot of stories about Orphy, but one in particular I just have to tell you. You probably won't believe me, but it is as true as I am sitting here. Orphy and I were up on this steep ridge possuming one day, and I was walking out along this ridge that had just had a slip off it. The dirt gave out underneath me and I slipped down the slip, just managing to hang onto a branch. I would never have got out of there, but that little horse came down that slip on this narrow little deer track that was only wide enough for his feet to stand on. He backed down to where I was hanging so I could get hold of his tail, but his tail wasn't quite long enough for me to reach. I needed about another six inches. I said to Orphy, 'I need more tail' and without a word of a lie he squatted down on his hind haunches and I managed to get a hold of his tail and he dragged me up. I stood there giving him a cuddle for about 10 minutes. He saved my life."

Everyone looked mightily impressed, and Sue wrapped her arms around the little pony's neck and gave him a kiss on the side of his long nose.

CHAPTER TWENTY-THREE

The steak was cooked. Sue, Heather, and Janey got the plates out and were dishing the dinner. Possum Jack turned to the ladies. "Gosh, I am spoilt tonight having dinner cooked for me."

"Do you ever eat possum meat?" asked Janey curiously.

"Only if I really need to, Janey, and I can tell you, all animals are beautiful but some are tastier than others - and possum is definitely not one of the tastier ones!"

Stevo had gone to tie Blue and Buck up for the night and check on the horses before it got dark too dark. Brent examined Roger's trout to see how well it was smoking; it looked really good and the juices were just starting to appear, running down the flesh of the fish. It looked delicious.

Brent called over to Roger,

"Your trout will be ready later. We'll be able to have a bit before bed."

After they had eaten and cleaned up, Brent decided it would be a good time for another rum or two. While he was making everybody a drink, he could hear how the conversation had yet again turned to looking for the drums up in Green River country.

Possum Jack explained,

"I've got to check some of my possum lines in the morning. Orphy and I will come up to the Bullring tomorrow night and then we can head up to where the drums are the next day."

Joining the group again Brent admitted,

"That will be perfect actually. That will give us time to get our camp set up and sort out some gear for the three day trip."

Stevo asked Possum Jack which way they would go, whether they would go up the river or climb up and go around the big ridge system.

Possum Jack thought for a moment.

"I think the best way is to climb up a spur ridge that is not too far past Bullring. That will get us up onto the main ridge system. The country in there is so steep and dangerous, bluffs are everywhere and they are slippery and damp; we really don't want to get it wrong. It pays to keep to the main ridges. The river can be really hard going, with lots of waterfalls and gorgy bits. You are always getting wet; Orphy has trouble getting around the waterfalls. The golden rule in this country is to always come down the same way you have gone up as it is so bluffy. Where it looks like you may get down a spur, you can go all the way down and it can bluff out a hundred metres or more above the river, and then you have to go all the way back up because it's too steep and rocky to sidle it."

Roger was thinking about the opportunities to take some spectacular photos of the natural environment, and began telling Heather how much he was looking forward to finding the drums. Brent interrupted him and told him that his photography skills would be really helpful once they found what they were looking for as they may be needed to prove their find to people in official positions once they got out of the bush.

"Thanks Brent, I will do my best. When I caught that trout and saw those massive eels prowling around in that other pool, they reminded me of sharks hunting; the way they cruised around looking really hungry. I know exactly what Possum Jack meant when he was talking about them."

Brent shook his head in disbelief.

"The size of them, you just have to see them to believe them," Roger shuddered. "Hopefully we will see them in the morning, so we all know what we are dealing with," reassured Stevo.

Possum Jack just laughed.

"If you think they are big here Rog, wait 'til you get up into Green River country. They are twice as big."

"Those Anguilla Aussies are up there as well, marauding around those pools?" squeaked Roger.

"Well," surmised Possum. "I saw some up there with white on their underbellies so they surely will be the Aussie invaders."

Brent looked thoughtful.

"You know, it makes sense that those eels would be bigger up in the Green River country if our theory that something in those drums is affecting them is right."

Stevo agreed.

"Yeah, they would be closer and getting a bigger dose of whatever it is."

"Yeah," nodded Possum. "Makes sense all right."

The night was drifting on and the ladies were talking amongst themselves.

On the quiet, Stevo asked Possum Jack worriedly. "Do you think the ladies will get up there all right?"

"Yeah, no worries. We'll just take it quietly. They'll be fine. They all look pretty fit." Possum Jack grinned cheekily and raised his voice so the others could hear, "Our biggest problem of course will be getting around the Devil Bull."

Suddenly everybody's attention focussed on Possum Jack. Brent had a smile on his face, however Roger did not.

"What's this about a devil, Possum?"

"Well Rog, there's a really nasty bull that lives up there on that main ridge. He's the hairiest bull I have ever seen. He has a persona all of his own. I have only seen him a few times but he's scared the living daylights out of me. He's got a set of horns that look just like the devils which is why I gave him the nickname Devil Bull. He is truly a mountain bull. He's an Angus shorthorn cross," said Possum. Still smiling at Roger's fear, Brent said, "They used these cattle to break all the land that's in grass today and quite a few went wild and there are still a number of them in here. These cattle were the perfect animals for this job as they were very hardy and they could live on the barest amounts of food when times were tough. Stevo and I have

heard some bellowing in the distance on our earlier hunting trips."

Possum continued, "There were a lot of crosses like this bull but also they had the straight Angus and shorthorn cattle. The shorthorn cattle were a red white colour, while the Angus cattle were black. Also, there were a few Hereford cattle but they weren't as hardy, and they mainly used them to cross with the Angus to get a bit more size and a bit more milking ability into the Angus."

"My friesians wouldn't cope up here, they are not as hardy as the shorthorn cattle," said Brent.

Sue asked nervously,

"Do you think we will run into him up there?"

"I hope not. He's never charged me before, but I wouldn't trust him. He follows you, keeping out of sight. You can hear him snorting and blowing out his nose as if to say get off my patch. He bellows at night to cattle in the distance. It's very disconcerting."

Stevo laughed.

"He probably thought you were a possum, the way you guys smell, with all those possum skins hanging off Orphy and you skinning them."

"Yeah, maybe so," replied Possum. "Don't know what he'll think of you guys. Maybe the different smell will make him more aggressive. Or he may just stay away - hopefully. But if he doesn't, I think you should shoot him, Brent. He really does pose a big threat and when you are up in this country you can't afford to get hurt. I'd shoot him myself but I don't carry a gun."

Brent agreed,

"Well hopefully we can get around him on the tops of the ridges. In this country they aren't always very wide. They go from two metres to two hundred metres wide so it won't be easy to avoid him unless he's grazing down a spur. He must have an incredible sense of smell." The night had worn on and it was time to think about hitting the hay. Stevo made them all a brew before they headed for bed which they all enjoyed with a bit of Roger's trout; delicious from spending the evening in the smoke from the fire. It wasn't long before they were all ready to turn in for the night. Brent made sure everything was secure and the fire was safe. They all headed for their sleeping bags, which they checked over carefully in case of oversized creepy crawlies hiding within.

CHAPTER TWENTY-FOUR

Next morning Stevo woke early. He sat up and smiled to himself when he saw Orphy sitting tucked up next to the sleeping Possum Jack; he just couldn't believe how this little horse was just like a dog. When Stevo sat up it created a ripple effect; Orphy stood up, which then stirred Possum Jack.

Stevo got to his feet and kicked some life into the fire, nudging the hot ashes together with a thick branch before placing some twigs on top of the embers as the fire burst into life almost immediately. Stevo grabbed the billies and went down to the river for water, taking a towel with him so he could have a quick wash. As he was drying himself off with the towel he stared up at the sky, noticing it was absolutely crystal clear. The intensity of the blue sky was dazzling. It was going to be a glorious day with hardly a whisper of wind. Just perfect, he thought to himself. After having his wash and filling the billies, he headed back to camp with a slight skip to his step.

On his return, everybody was up and looking keen to get the day started. Janey, Heather, and Sue were checking the horses, and Brent had put some bacon and eggs into the pan for a fry up. Possum was in his little hut checking his skins and turning them towards the fire so they would dry evenly on both sides.

Stevo turned to Brent,

"Another beautiful day in God's own paradise. I'll help the girls get the horses ready while you cook the brekky, mate."

"Sure is a stunner! Ok, thanks. Brekky won't be too long now."

The fire was blazing and the billies were shaking in the flames as the cold water was rapidly beginning to boil.

They were finally going to make it to the Bullring today. It was amazing that the countryside had formed this way and how every corner they went around gave them something new to see. There were massive native trees towering wherever they could get a foot hold on a ridge or bit of flat by the river. Whenever they tried to look to the top of the ridge from their horses they would get a sore neck from looking straight up, especially in the gorgy bits. As they rode along, the landscape would change dramatically and the country seemed to rise up straight out of the ground. One moment they would be riding through open valleys, and the next thing the river closed in until there was nothing but sheer rock faces rising straight above. The water had carved its way through rock towards the sea over millions of years and during many violent storms, forming massive gorges and big river flats, where it had rushed out the other side or turned a sharp corner. After yet another delicious breakfast they decided to pack up camp before going to see Roger's fishing pool to check out the massive eels. They all headed towards the river with a nervously excited Roger in the lead. As they approached the riverbank they turned and headed upstream where Roger then pointed out the pool he had caught his trout in. As they approached the pool they could see two big Anguilla

eels lurking at the bottom of the pool.

"They are massive," Janey's whispered. "I am sure they are longer than my arm."

"Sure are," agreed Brent. "I never would have believed eels could get so big and ugly."

The eel's mouths were slightly open, displaying rows of sharp, pointy teeth.

"They are really fast, too," babbled Roger. "I couldn't believe how they could just spin around and go through the water like missiles." "Those trout wouldn't want to stop to sleep," observed Possum. "They have to keep moving. The trout seem to have found pools that have no camouflage for the eels so they can't sneak up on them. They know to keep away from the rocky pools and to stay in the sandy bottom pools."

The big anguillas were just cruising deep in the pool, every now and then they would disappear out of sight into the deeper dark parts.

The eels could be seen easily because the water had cleared from the night before. The water was no longer murky from when they had stirred up the bottom when they attacking and devouring the long finned eel.

"I reckon we will have to be super careful from now on," reiterated Brent, "They could kill a man no problem; hunting together in packs like that."

"They definitely could, Brent," Possum agreed with a stony look on his face, the same look he had when he was talking about his dog. "When they got Tracker they were everywhere and would have grabbed anything they could eat."

Concern showed on everybody's faces as they wondered what else they may encounter on their trip.

"Come on, let's go," decided Stevo, sensing that they needed to move away from the pool.

"Good idea, Stevo," agreed Brent. "The horses will be well rested and ready for the next stage of their journey."

They all headed quietly back to Possum's camp, deep in thought about the ginormous eels they had just seen lurking in the river.

After checking around the camp to make sure they hadn't left anything behind, Brent explained,

"See you tonight, Possum. We'll get camped up at the Bullring and be ready to go to check out the drums tomorrow."

"Yeah, sounds good Brent. I'm not sure how long I'll be. Depends on how many coons I get, 'cause I gotta skin them and hang 'em up on the drying boards today - seeing as I am going to be away a few days."

Roger queried,

"Coons? I thought you were hunting possums."

"Just another term for them," smiled Possum. "It must have come from the States and their raccoon hunters."

"Do you need a hand, Possum?"

"Nah," replied Possum. "Thanks for the offer Stevo, but me and Orphy will do it."

"Okay, see you tonight. Have a good day." Brent thought he could sense Possum Jack wanted to make the most of being on his own as he would be stuck with them for the next 3 or 4 days. After all the years being in the bush alone, Possum Jack enjoyed being in the company of others for short spells but he generally preferred to be on his own. The ladies were already on their horses, ready to go. Stevo mounted Stormy and held onto

Big Red. He passed Brent the reins. "Thanks mate," Brent called, as he mounted up.

Giving Possum a wave, Brent and Stevo moved off up the river with Sue and Janey following right behind. Roger seemed to be having trouble getting on his horse so Heather rode over to hold the reins for him. As the other riders moved off, Roger's horse wanted to move too so he stamped his feet in agitation at Roger being slow to get on.

Roger's face grimaced as he mounted his horse but together they set off after the others. As they rode up the river, Roger said, "I got some really nice photos of a tui feeding in a tree when I went for my walk before breakfast."

Heather loved his enthusiasm.

"I saw a couple of other birds there too but wasn't sure what they were. I'll check them out in my native bird book when we get to camp. I am pretty sure they were a saddleback and a bellbird."

"That was lucky, you must have been really quiet not to frighten them. They are two very different birds to the ones we saw further down the river," Heather replied as she looked over at her husband with a large smile plastered all over her face; she was so pleased to see Roger getting into the trip and enjoying himself in such a wonderful paradise.

They passed along a narrow path through the native bush and there seemed to be lots of spiders around.

"These critters are bigger than those ones we are always chasing away at home, Heather," Roger shuddered.

"Yeah, thank goodness the ones that want to live in the corners of our house aren't anywhere near as big as these ones. That one is as big as my hand," Heather pointed at a spider making its web in a tree beside the path. The sun was rising higher in the sky and the day was really warming up.

All morning, the dogs had been working right up the sides of the riverbank looking for any fresh sign but they hadn't managed to come onto any game. They had since drifted back to the group and fallen into line with the others and followed along behind the horses. If there had been any fresh sign around Blue and Buck would have taken off like a shot. The horses were working fairly hard through a particularly gorgy piece clambering over rocks and logs. It was especially tough on the old pack horse, Bessie. She had managed to get stuck in between rocks and logs a couple of times when her load jammed. She fell into a big water hole but was able to swim her way out. At one stage, while crossing the river, Stevo had thought the load was going to float off her back as she had to swim again. There was lots of crisscrossing the river because of big boulders, logs, and debris, and the load had to be retied on Bessie several times.

They emerged from the tricky part of the river. Stevo had been leading Bessie so that she would stay on the best track, and there had been a few small slips along the way that required careful navigation. Brent was leading the way for the whole party and Big Red had begun flicking his ears to let Brent know there was some wildlife about. Brent leaned forward and rubbed him on the shoulder to let Red know he got the message.

Coming around a corner in the river, Brent saw a massive slip running 500 metres straight up the side, with a grassy spot at the top. Brent could see two deer standing about three quarters of the way up the slip; a hind with a yearling. Brent smiled to himself, proud that his horse had managed to pick up the scent. Brent held his hand up for the party to stop; easily achieved as everybody was riding in single file and when Brent stopped the other horses followed suit. Brent decided to shoot the young tia as it looked the tastiest.

Brent smiled again as he heard Roger in the background as he whispered to Stevo, "He'll never hit that."

As Brent pulled the 270 from its scabbard and swung it towards the tia, he noticed they were looking very nervous and about to move off. He brought the 270 up, cranked a ballistic tip bullet into the chamber, and trained the Leopold Gold Ring scope onto the shoulder of the yearling. Brent knew it was a long shot so he aimed high on the shoulder as he fired the trigger. The yearling dropped like a stone and began to spin down the slip, bouncing all the way down towards Big Red. The horse stepped back and gave an undignified snort as the deer fell right into the river at its feet. Roger nearly fell off his horse in amazement, whereas Stevo just grinned with pride.

"Wow, Brent! What a shot!" exclaimed Roger, in amazement.

The ladies were looking around at each in other in delight, very impressed with Brent's shot.

Brent just smiled as he licked his lips. "It'll be tasty."

Stevo and Brent hopped off their horses without saying a word. Brent pulled the tia up out of the river so Stevo could get to work on it with his big bowie knife. Stevo removed the back steaks and the back legs. As Brent had shot it through the shoulder, there was quite a bit of damage in that area. Brent grabbed a bag off the pack horse as Stevo boned out the back legs. They put all of the meat into the bag which they then tied off and put into the saddle bags on Brent's horse, saving Bessie from carrying any more weight.

Stevo scratched the packhorse on the shoulder.

"Poor Bessie, this is hard going for her. Never mind, old girl, we are nearly there."

Brent and Stevo remounted and they were all getting ready to ride off when they saw some large black shapes gliding through the water.

"Look at that!" Janey squealed.

"Must be eels, just like when you killed that pig," whispered Heather. "The blood is attracting them."

"I'm glad we're moving," shuddered Roger. "They'll be up here in a minute."

The part of the river that the deer had fallen into was shallow, stony, and quite wide. When the slip had come down it had managed to push back the entire bush on the other side from where they were, and then the storms had helped the water to wash the slip away. The shallow water and stony bottom had slowed down the progress of the eels getting to the deer's blood.

As they moved off up the river, Stevo and Brent rode up the front engrossed in discussion. They were talking about what gear to take, and what to do with the horses for three days when they went on the trip to find the drums.

"Wow." Janey smiled to herself. She leant down to stroke her horse as she whispered half to herself and half to Lightning, "We are so lucky to have such experienced Bushmen with us. They are truly amazing, it's like nothing is an obstacle for them - it's so attractive! And their ability to get food surely means we will never starve!"

CHAPTER TWENTY-FIVE

The boys slept well until they heard Shona calling out to say that their breakfast was ready.

"Come on boys, time for some kai."

They dragged themselves out of bed and entered the main house for breakfast. Hone was sitting at the table with a smile on his face.

"A hard night aye boys?" Bleary eyed, Luke replied, "Yeah, a little bit aye Dad."

"Well those horses won't be easy to catch. They haven't been ridden for ages," Hone warned, rising from the table. "We will have to get going soon if you want to make the best of the day. It should be good hunting up the valley."

The boys wolfed down their breakfast and hugged Shona. "Ka kite," said Slade. "See you when we get back.

They organised their gear and headed off towards Hone's truck. Slade had Hone's old 303 slung over one shoulder and held a saddle in his other hand. Hone had also given him a dozen bullets; warning Slade that he may have to put a couple of bullets through the gun to check its accuracy because it hadn't been used in ages. Luke and Jake were carrying the rest of their gear and the saddles and they threw everything onto the back of the truck before climbing up themselves. Slade climbed into the cab of the truck with Hone.

"Thanks, Dad. We really appreciate you taking us up to the horse paddock. How long is it since you have seen them?"

"I was up here a couple of weeks ago and they were looking good; plenty of tucker and lots of fresh water for them. We had quite a good summer as far as rain goes," grinned Hone.

The truck followed the coastal road around to the mouth of the river where Hone's family had some land that the horses grazed on. The boys unloaded their gear and gave Hone a hug.

"Thanks again, Dad."

Hone was pleased that they were getting back to nature and hoped they would have a great hunt.

"Catch up with you when you get back. Fresh venison for dinner would be great!"

"We'll do our best, Dad!" chimed Jake.

After chasing the horses around for about half an hour they finally cornered them, got a bridle on, and managed to get them saddled up. Slade mounted and his horse just about bucked him straight off. Being an experienced horseman he quickly regained his composure and got the horse under control. Luke and Jake mounted easily and they moved off towards the river, the position of the sun told them that it was late morning.

The boys, being good riders, made good time up the river and were already about a third of the way to Bullring by mid-afternoon. Luckily they didn't have a pack horse to slow them down as they had already taken a while getting the day under way with the hassle of catching the horses. They decided to camp up, get a fire going, and tie the horses up for the night. Coming up the river they had already noticed horse marks.

Finally Luke pointed them out to the others. "Looks like there are other hunters in front of us."

"Yeah, and they're fresh marks, would've been only yesterday or the day before," Jake agreed. "There are heaps of hoof marks. At least four riders - could even be more."

"Bit stink that is," Slade sulked. "Hope they have gone right up to Green River and left the Bullring to us."

"Yeah, hope so," echoed Jake.

It wasn't long until darkness had set in and the boys were passing the rum bottle around after filling their bellies with dinner. They heard a stag roaring in the distance which got them quite excited. They had never really hunted deer, Jazz Jones had showed them how to but they had never hunted in the roar. The boys discussed what they expected to happen the following day, and where they might be able to get onto some tia. They realised the stag they had heard could be miles away because of the quietness of the bush at the night; sound always travels so much further in the darkness. Being pretty tired from the hard night before at the put they drifted off to sleep after no more than a few rums.

CHAPTER TWENTY-SIX

As the riders emerged from the last gorgy piece, they came out onto the big flats of the Bullring. Brent reined in his horse to let the others catch up and fan themselves out. They rode side by side facing upstream on the dry gravel riverbed. Sue exclaimed in amazement at the way the scenery kept getting better and better. "It's amazing how incredible New Zealand is. Nothing any man could ever make would equal the beauty of the natural environment.

This must truly be God's own paradise." She announced to the others as she continued to look around, taking it all in.

The others just nodded in amazement.

The sheer natural beauty of the sight before them was captivating; the wild rugged hills surrounding Bullring's big river flats that were home to dazzling wild river grasses blowing gently in the breeze. Both the grasses and the gravelly riverbed were truly inspiring, especially to a hunter and an animal. It had everything; lots of lush wild river grasses, lovely flats with plenty of sandy patches with dry pebble, gravelly river beds which only ran when it flooded, and it was all surrounded by majestic hills covered with native bush filled with wild animals. The upper reaches of the catchment lay in the hills behind the big flats of the Bullring. Brent, with a big smile on his face, pointed. "Look, there is the Bullring camp, just up the river on the right.

Let's go and take a look."

Janey turned to her husband. His smile mirrored the one on her own face.

"This is just amazing."

She felt as if she had been here before, with the way Brent had described it to her after his previous hunting trips. Everybody was both pleased and excited that they had finally arrived at the Bullring. Roger was shuffling in his saddle.

"Not long now, love, and we'll be at camp," Heather soothed. "Can't wait, my butt is killing me."

"No worries Roger, we'll move up to the camp now and then you can rest," said Brent.

They finally left the gorgy piece and could see the riverbed was about 40 metres wide with sheer rock cliffs on both sides. As they moved further up the river, they left the water as it flowed around to the left and opened up to the Bullring flats where at their widest points were about 500 metres wide. The river formed a large curve out towards the left and then meandered back to the right around the river flats before narrowing again further up the valley. The tremendous volumes of water which had poured down, especially during storms, and which were driven by gravity and their turbulence, had created the big flats with sandy patches, the lush grassy areas and gravelly river flats; The Bullring. The river looped around the flats, where the power of the water had carved its path into the bank on the left hand side, continually creating and maintaining the flats on its quest to race towards and through the 40metre gap where the riders had just emerged. In storms, many of the big logs had been brought down the river only to find new homes lying up in the sandy corners of the riverbed, or spread out over the braided flats. The land rose around each of the banks of the Bullring and had heavy native bush to its edges - except behind the Bullring camp which had a large pocket of big Kānuka which had most likely regrown after the storms had stripped away the native bush and created the Bullring camp. The camp consisted of an elevated area; two-and-a-half-metres above the Bullring flats on a big sandy corner. The elevation made it a very safe campsite, as the only way the river would ever reach them would be if it became dammed up in a terrible storm. The campsite was north facing and easily caught full sunshine all day long. The sand was pale, fine, and dry, and a spectacular rimu log lay along the topside of the camp. The river had carried it downstream in a severe storm and it had managed to wedge itself against the right hand riverbank. The root system had jammed against the true bank of the river curve and its majestic trunk faced out towards the river and angled slightly downstream. Each of its branches had long been stripped away and it seemed as if the giant rimu trees new role was to protect the camp from storms. It had been partly buried with up to half of its large 2metre girth covered with the powder like sand. On the topside of the rimu, the river descended from its source, while the other side was home to the raised campsite which had beautiful sand and a few other logs scattered by people as makeshift chairs. A large fireplace within a circle made of stones had been carefully created by hunters and trappers over time and was situated on the raised flat near the big rimu trunk. People approaching the Bullring from upstream would have to walk around the end of the trunk and climb up and over the bank to arrive at the campsite. Thankfully the bank up to the campsite was not particularly steep due to the gravel and sand having washed against it; making it an easy climb. The campsite boasted commanding views out over the Bullring flats and right down to where the river disappeared into the gorgy part. The raised flat area was approximately 100 metres long and 50 metres wide before the camp began to climb up into the heavier native. Kānuka trees grew in various places; their large trunks with their high foliage provided a clear space beneath for sitting in the shade upon wild native grasses. Not too far from the fireplace, one of the Kānuka stood beside an open grassy area; perfect for pitching the tents beneath the tall tree. There was also more than enough room to tether the horses at night, in the horse paddock that ran around behind the camp, where they would be safe if the river came up. The catchments were enormous and Brent and Stevo knew they always needed to be careful as it could be raining further up the river - which could make the river rise rapidly and unpredictably. Brent knew the power of nature and remembered that during a big cyclone there was once 900 millimetres of rain in just 5 days. He and Stevo were always aware of how quickly things could change in nature, and they always aimed to keep themselves safe - even when it required extra effort. The camp was very quiet due to being located far enough from the river noise. The quietness meant it was a great place to hear roaring stags and getting a lead on their position in the surrounding hills and valleys. Many of the animals; deer, pigs, and wild cattle, used the rivers as access to new feeding grounds because the country was so steep, rugged, and broken. They found it easier to use the river, and the Bullring was a big draw card with its large abundance of food and nice flats with wild grasses. The bush to the river's edge was also appealing as it made a quick escape route if they sensed danger.

As the group rode over the gravelly riverbeds towards the camp, Stevo was busily scanning the far edges of the Bullring flats for any sign of game. There was excitement at the thought of finally dismounting and being able to set up their camp. Roger was in excruciating pain from his blisters and his swollen ankle, which was hanging limply next to his stirrup.

After dismounting, Stevo got the fire going while the others unsaddled the horses - except for the pack horse which Stevo unsaddled. He had a good look at her and thought to himself how tired Bessie looked.

Brent came over to help Stevo.

"Bloody good horse, that one. She's a real stalwart. She has worked really hard. She will have a lighter trip home without all the food we will have eaten. Hopefully she'll be carrying lots of venison."

Stevo nodded with a smile.

"Yeah. Gabe reckons she is the best one he's ever had."

Brent had all the makings for a cup of tea in his saddle bag, which he hurriedly removed. The girls got the leads out of the pack saddle to tether the horses. Janey kissed Brent lightly on the cheek.

"We'll have a cuppa first, and then Heather, Sue, and I will go wash the horses down."

"Thanks love. Just stay in the shallow bits, remember what Possum Jack said. Stevo, Roger, and I will sort out the old horse paddock. It used to be on a flat part up the river a bit and it ran right back and around behind the camp. Hopefully it will hold the horses while we go to look for those drums."

Brent went off to explore, and easily stumbled across the old horse paddock that had been made many years ago. It was obvious that nobody used it anymore because branches and trees had blown over in storms, landing on the wires around the paddock.

'It will be a bit of work to make it secure again,' Brent thought to himself. 'But there is plenty of wild grass for the horses and there is lots of fresh water.'

The billy was boiling by the time Brent trekked back. They sat around in the sun enjoying both their brew and being in their final camping destination.

Brent looked over at the other men.

"We'd better get started sorting this horse paddock out. There's a lot of scrub to cut."

He ran his finger over what should have been the sharp edge of the axe. Deciding it was a bit blunt, he pulled his steel out of its sheath and gave the axe a rub while Stevo checked the big bush knife he always wore on his belt.

Roger looked over at his fully equipped friends. "What am I going to use, Brent?"

"Um, you can just throw the stuff over the fence as we cut it."

Roger's face formed a 'sounds like work' expression but he chose to say nothing.

The girls pulled a log closer to the fire and announced it was time for lunch. Heather had pulled out some of her famous triple chocolate cake that she had made for the trip, and Janey passed out freshly made sandwiches for each of them. Janey inspected Roger's leg. It was starting to look a bit better. It was the blisters causing him the most pain and problems but it was clear he still needed to use a stick to help him walk.

After lunch as they moved up towards the horse paddock and Brent, Stevo, and Roger looked back and could see the ladies out in the river washing the horses by a little grassy island.

Brent began cutting away the branches near the old boundary of the paddock. Roger followed close behind, clearing the debris. Every single branch and piece of fern Roger touched was handled with extra care. He had always passionately despised spiders and insects and he knew if they were anything like the size of the weta they had seen on their way up, he wanted nothing to do them!

After a few hours of hard work, the men managed to have a pretty good paddock sorted. Brent looked around and admired their handiwork, noticing the fresh water creek running through the far corner to provide plenty of water,

"The horses will be really happy in here for a few days." "Yeah, just ideal," whistled Stevo.

On arriving back to camp, they were excited to see the ladies had the fire going and a brew boiling away. The ladies had enjoyed their afternoon looking after the horses and relaxing in the sun on the grassy island. The men lay down next to them to soak up some rays, but after just 5 minutes of rest with his fresh cup of tea, Brent was ready to get back into action.

"We'd better get some gear sorted for tomorrow." Janey smiled,

"We've sorted the food dear. We used mostly the dried food and organised it into nine meals. We thought if we all carry some food each, and our sleeping bags and ground sheets, we should be about right." "Sounds good, Janey. You girls are onto it. Stevo and I will carry a fly for the tents each, just in case it rains. Your sleeping bags and food should fit into your day packs. Stevo and I will take our K-2 hunter packs. They are quite big so we will get all the stuff in them easily - and some meat too if we catch any!" Brent always tried his best to retrieve any meat he shot. He was convinced it tasted much better when it had been carried for a while; hard work always made people appreciate things more.

They worked together to organise dinner while Roger and Heather went off to fish for more trout. The sun was sinking rapidly and there was only another half an hour before dark would fall, yet there was still no sign of Possum Jack. Brent and Stevo were cleaning their rifles; preparing for the hunt ahead. They needed to be looked after even more carefully while out in the bush as, if they were left wet and dirty, they would soon rust. Somehow they always managed to collect some dirt and grime from leaves, dead ponga dust, and sand from the daily grind. The bolt of the rifle that puts the bullet into the chamber and ejects it could get built up with dirt; causing the firing pin to get stuck. After Brent had finished cleaning his rifle, he decided he would wander downstream and through the gorge to see if Possum Jack was on his way. He wandered off with his rifle slung over his shoulder.

He looked back to see Sue and Janey brushing each other's hair. The ladies had never been so long without a hot shower. Stevo wandered over and cheekily told them they looked lovely but he could really do with a hand putting the final touches on dinner. Sue's hair was very long and Janey was struggling with the very last knot in it.

"We'll be there in a minute!"

Janey's hair was far shorter and Sue had managed to comb it easily. The comforts of home quickly evaporated from their minds as they went to help Stevo. It was time to get back to business in the bush.

They were both smiling as they approached Stevo who was peeling the spuds.

"Gee, you Kiwi chicks look pretty good," Stevo winked. "Thanks, Stevo. More of those lovely comments would do you good."

Stevo looked up with a smirk. "Back to work you two."

Brent had not gone very far; he was walking slowly and admiring the way the bush had changed, yet again, due to dusk. He saw a dead looking clump of wild flowers and couldn't work out why they weren't growing well.

"That's weird," he thought to himself. He chose not to mention them to Janey.

He could see Roger fishing happily by a big pool with Heather sitting on the bank, watching on. Brent truly admired Roger's passion for fishing, and was impressed that he had carried on riding his horse even though he was covered in awful blisters and needed a crutch to walk; his enthusiasm never seemed to wane. He decided to walk over to Roger and ask him how the fishing was going. Roger kept his eyes on the water as he told Brent that he had not landed anything yet, but that he had seen one following his line which had him wondering if he needed to change his lure. He looked over at Brent.

"I think maybe they are eating something different."

Brent peered into the water, then stood back to survey the surrounding landscape. He kept glancing down the river, hoping to see Possum Jack approaching. Finally he made his way over towards a dry log and sat down to roll a cigarette and observe Roger's fantastic fishing skills.

Heather rose to her feet,

"Now you are here I will go back and help the girls with tea."

Minutes after she left, Stevo turned up carrying two mugs of tea in thermal mugs.

"Thanks mate," chuffed Brent as Roger put his finger to his lips, motioning them to talk quietly so as to not disturb the fish.

Stevo and Brent sat on the dry log and drank their tea and smoked a cigarette together. Stevo and Brent had always enjoyed each other's company, and having a cuppa and a smoke together was one of their favourite past times – especially out in the bush, when they could discuss the day that had passed and the one coming. Sometimes they would lie awake by the fire because they were so excited about the following day.

As they were finishing their tea, Brent spotted Possum coming up the river. Roger had a trout pretty interested in his lure. There were only mere minutes before the natural light would be gone for yet another day.

Brent laughed,

"Better hurry up and catch that fish. Here comes Possum Jack." "Yeah I reckon!" Roger paused. "Well technically, Brent, I should have hooked him by now. I've tried all my lures and nothing seems

to work. Do you want to try?"

Brent nodded and walked over to take the rod from Roger who then went to sit on the log next to Stevo.

Brent smirked,

"Don't go too far, Roger, and get the net ready."

Roger paled with a sick look on his face, fearing that Brent would have more luck than he had. While Brent had been clearing the horse paddock, he'd banged a rotten log and found a couple of huhu grubs which he'd put in his pocket without telling anyone. Slipping one onto Roger's lure he cast it down stream. Roger, not spotting that Brent had put the grub on his line, noticed Brent wasn't winding the lure in,

"Brent, you are meant to wind the lure in."

Brent turned around and gave Roger a full smile, just as the line took off down the river.

"Is that right, Rog?"

Brent brought the line up making sure to give the fish no slack. "I got one, Rog!"

Roger leapt up and moved quickly over to stand beside Brent. "You have too, Brent! You're tinny. How did you do that?" "Patience," Brent cooed.

He fought the fish up and down the pool. The fish was tiring, and it was getting really dark.

"Hey, Roger, Put your hand into my bullet bag and you will find a maglite."

Roger unzipped Brent's bullet pouch and retrieved the torch. He shone it towards where Brent had the fish right up near a sandy patch. It was lying on its side. Roger quietly walked over and put his net under the fish, scooping it up.

"Gee, Brent, it's a beauty," he remarked, shining the full beam of the torch directly onto it.

Brent licked his lips.

"Sure is. It will be as tasty as yours was last night. We'd better get back."

Possum Jack had just arrived to the pool where they were fishing. He admired the fish Brent had caught as they collected their gear together and headed back to camp. Roger could not stop talking about how Brent had managed to catch the fish without even winding his lure.

Stevo smirked and Possum Jack looked doubtful. "I thought you only used lead spinners, Brent." Brent winked.

"Nah. You know me; I do everything by the rules, Possum."

Roger insisted Brent hold up the fish while he took a photo. The trout weighed in at a hefty 7 and a half pound.

"A very nice river trout!" exclaimed Roger as he put away his scales. Brent opened the fish up and placed it in the smoke by the fire.

"We'll eat him later."

Brent asked Possum how many coons he had trapped. Possum sighed,

"Not that many, Brent. I was expecting more. It looked a very good ridge but we only picked up 20, very good skins though."

The horses had already been led up to the horse paddock; to save time in the morning. Heather was reading a book by the light of a little clip on reading lamp, and Sue was brushing her hair yet again.

Stevo called to her,

"I didn't think you would have to worry about that up here, dear." "I've got to keep myself looking good for you, Stevo," she cooed,

looking up at him with her lovely blue eyes and an easy smile.

Stevo whistled.

"You always look good to me, love."

After they had finished dinner Brent got one of the bottles of rum out of his bag. The boys sat back and enjoyed a drink while the girls tidied up the dinner plates and pots. Stevo and Brent had offered to help but the girls insisted they were ok doing them. When they had finished, they joined the boys for a drink around the fire to discuss the next day. They decided to get going at daybreak and Possum thought they should arrive at the main ridge by about 10.30am.

"It takes about 3 hours to get up there. It's pretty steep and slippery. There's a lot of shelf rock and it's really greasy. Doesn't get much sun and there's lots of moss."

They would have to hide the gear they were leaving behind, just in case somebody turned up.

"I haven't seen people up this way for a long time, but you can't be too careful. You wouldn't want to lose your gear up here in this wilderness," said Possum.

"Are we taking the dogs, Brent?"

"Yep of course we are, Janey. We can't really leave them here.

They'll be more than alright right tagging along." Possum Jack looked concerned.

"Hope they don't get onto the Devil Bull or all hell will break loose."
"We'll only worry about him if he sees us and charges," Brent decided. "I hope we don't have to shoot him," Sue's worried voice rang out.

Heather looked alarmed.

"No, we must do everything we can not to shoot him!" Possum Jack smiled at the girls responses.

"Well, it's a big ridge system. Hopefully he'll be somewhere that we aren't."

"But, I would like to see him - I'd love to get some photos," came one quiet voice.

Janey began chatting with Possum about his life as a trapper, "Do you ever get lonely here in the bush all on your own, Possum?" "Not very often to be honest, Janey. I have got Orphy for company and I can always find plenty to do to keep myself busy. I like writing poetry or short stories when I am sitting by the fire at night."

"Wow, that sounds cool. Where do you get all your ideas from?" "I carry a little notebook in my pocket and write down my ideas down as they come to me on my travels. They are usually about my experiences and the sights and sounds of this beautiful bush. My latest poem is about what life is like for a possum trapper." Heather had been listening to their conversation.

"I would love to hear your writing, Possum. Would you mind sharing a poem with us?"

"Aw, I don't know about that," blushed Possum. He was flattered that Heather would like to hear his work, "It is only the musings of an old man."

"Please, Possum. I am sure we would all love to hear a poem," chirped Janey.

"You girls are pretty persuasive," Possum sighed. "I guess it won't do any harm. Anyway, you might be able to give me some ideas on how to make it better."

Possum scrummaged around in his bag for his little poetry book. The whispers of 'hush hush' had gone around the circle, and all eyes were now on Possum Jack in anticipation as he began to read:

A Poem from Possum Jack

A trapper's life is not a troubled life But a double life.
His struggles are his own choice His trap lines are his own doing
His hair and whiskers may grow long and shaggy
He becomes fit and sleek doing his lines
During long months in the mountains so serene.
With rivers and streams busy in their pursuit to the sea Their currents, and the wind, adding life to the forests The birds making sounds and singing to help
Other life forms eating And listening
Quietly to the natural noises, Smells waft on the wind.
For the trapper the weather is his only master
And to become at one with these amazing sights and sounds Makes a trappers life a success.
Long days alone except for his companion A horse or a dog so he's not really alone And he has been blessed with both.
But alas it is a double life
For he has to leave the mountain's serenity For supplies and to sell his trapping
And to pay his taxes
To make his double life possible. But two lives are better than one He tells himself
And a trapper finds this no trouble at all As the mountains call

For he's a free spirit in an amazing place Why, it's no trouble at all.

⌒

Everyone clapped loudly when Possum finished reading his poem. "That was brilliant," applauded Janey.

"You have got hidden talents, Possum," Stevo called in awe. "Very creative, thank you for reading it for us," smiled Heather.

After they had all congratulated Possum on his writing, he looked around with a smile on his face.

"I've got heaps more back at my lifestyle block." He felt really chuffed with the positive response to his poem. He had never shared his writing with anyone before and had always been a bit nervous about doing so. "You can read them when you come to visit me, once we all get out of here. I'm sure I'll have had other experiences to write about by then." "We will certainly do that," Janey assured the grinning Possum.

"I'm looking forward to that visit already."

A loud swooping noise drew their attention to an old beech tree with long droopy, saggy horizontal branches growing not far from where they had lit the fire. They could make out a dark shape sitting on one of the branches of the beech tree.

Janey whispered, "What's that?" Possum Jack grinned.

"That's a morepork Janey. They normally come out at dusk to hunt - they are our birds of the night."

Roger smirked,

"I thought that the 'Birds of the Night' were on the dark streets in the big cities."

Heather rolled her eyes. "That's lame, Rog."

Possum just smiled; he liked a dry sense of humour and he had begun to really like Roger.

"You are showing your townie side with that urban wit," he laughed before explaining, "They are our native owl and have big yellow eyes."

As their eyes adjusted to the darkness, they discovered the morepork was quite visible, silhouetted against the night sky.

Possum continued,

"Māori associated the ruru or owl with the spirit world." Sue looked over at Possum wistfully.

"You have heaps of knowledge about the bush and the creatures that live in it, it is so interesting."

"Yeah, the Māori people see the morepork as a watchful guardian. As a bird of the night, moreporks like eating mice and anything else that is tasty and not too big for them to handle - even insects."

"Have you spent a lot of time with the Māori people, Possum?" "Yeah, quite a bit Heather," replied Possum. "I grew up on the coast

and went to school here. I was the only white guy. I lived and worked with mainly Māori people before I started doing the possums. They are great people; very proud, strong in their traditions, and always giving to others. And because of their influence, I have always tried to be just like them in many ways. And I guess that is how I got a lot of my knowledge about Te Ao Māori, or in English, The Māori World." "Wow!" Heather was impressed, "I can see how you would have learnt heaps about their culture and beliefs growing up as the only pakeha in school!"

"And that knowledge can be very handy to know out here in the bush," Brent smiled at Possum, "but it's a big day tomorrow so I think I'll hit the hay."

"Yeah, I'm coming too," followed Janey, "Goodnight everyone."

CHAPTER TWENTY-SEVEN

The following morning was cool and fresh when the boys woke up early.

Slade looked up at the sky and confirmed what they were all thinking.

"Looks like it will be a killer of a day boys!"

He kicked the fire back to life with his boots, nudging a few sticks from the edge toward the embers which still held some life as they had stoked the fire up before going to sleep. The three brothers used to love making fires down on the beach, where there was always plenty of driftwood and they would fry whitebait or fish on a plate of steel. They loved sitting on the beach and gazing up at the stars, or racing their horses up and down the beach with the other kids from the coast. Around sunset Luke would put his music on, or Jake would play either the ukulele or his guitar, and they would spend hours talking about what they thought their lives would turn out like.

After breakfast, they moved on up the river and found that it was still fairly easy. Slade suddenly reined his horse in as they rounded a sharp corner.

"Holy! Would you look at that?" He pointed towards the massive poaka strung up from a sturdy branch of a tree overhanging the river, "There must have been some keen hunters through here recently. That hasn't been dead many days."

Jake moved towards the boar for a closer inspection.

"In fact, it looks like it was only killed yesterday or the day before!" Slade was quite annoyed, frustrated that another hunter had beaten them to the poaka and had clearly been up the river before them - disturbing their stags.

"They'll be pleased with those huge tusks," Luke admired quietly. The boys continued up the river and arrived at the big slip. "Wow, this is huge! Luckily for us someone has already done all the hard work and cut through the log. It must have been those guys who got that boar."

After cautiously getting their horses to claw their way up the shingly papa-rock slip and down the other side, they slowly moved on up the river.

Jake looked around, trying to determine their location.

"I think we are still another day at this pace before we get to the Bullring."

They had finally broken free from the gorge when Slade recognised where they were.

"Your day is more like two days from what I remember." Jake sighed,

"I can't be right all the time, Sladey boy! Shall we get a bit closer before we stop, or go for a hunt from here today?"

They knew the area well, and that the area they had stopped in was home to at least three larger creeks and a lot of little side creeks that ran down to join up with the main river.

"Well, it is about one o'clock so I reckon we should set up camp and go for an afternoon hunt up a side creek - who gets the first shot?" Luke looked at his brothers, already knowing the answer.

"Me, Bro," claimed Slade as Jake called. "Me next!"

"How's that?" Luke asked indignantly. "Because I'm bigger than you, simple as that." "Is that right? Don't brains count, only brawn?"

Slade and Jake didn't answer but instead looked at each other and smiled.

After setting up camp and enjoying their lunch, they organised their gear to head off hunting up the creek. They made sure their camping gear was safely hidden before leaving the horses tethered securely to a nearby tree and heading up a nearby stream. They noticed some deer and pig sign as they made their way up the creek. The high sides at the entrance made the creek feel quite enclosed and as if they had re-entered the gorge. Slade was leading the way, scanning up the sides of the creek which had little grassy pieces where he was hoping to see a tia. The boys, being inexperienced deer hunters, were unaware big stags liked to be up high and that they would need to be high and away from the creek in order to find any fresh sign. Male tia liked to have a big high ridge where they could dominate their territory and where their roar would echo into the distance to attract as many hinds as possible.

Slade, Luke, and Jake trudged further on up the creek. It was very early afternoon and the sun was very high and warm. The bottom of the creek had turned from muddy sand to fine stones which was making it easier to hike.

The creek was leading them higher up into the valley and they had been climbing steadily for a couple of hours when Jake stopped dead in his tracks.

"It's time for a brew, boys." "Okay," agreed Slade nonchalantly.

They threw their day packs onto the ground near a sunny spot by a little creek and wordlessly began to make a fire on which to boil the billy. Hone had always insisted that the boys carry a day pack with food and a raincoat whenever they went hunting, something they were grateful for as it had been a heavy morning of trekking through the untouched environment.

Luke was lying on his back while Slade and Jake discussed the multitude of animal sign they could see.

"By the look of this sign up here, there must be plenty of tia in this valley which is good because it's closer to home - we won't have to carry it as far to get the meat back."

"Yeah, sure is Jake," agreed Slade.

Just as they leant back on their elbows to join Luke in the sunshine, they heard a stag roar on a ridge just above them. Slade leaped to his feet and grabbed at the 303 all in the same movement.

Jake shielded his eyes as he looked towards the ridge. "Shall I roar him to see if he will come towards us?" Slade scoffed,

"Nah, we'll try and stalk up on him because your roar will probably scare him. You haven't done any roaring before."

"I reckon I would be good at roaring," protested Jake.

"Yeah, whatever, but we will try the stalking first. He won't know we are here."

They packed their gear and quickly doused the fire before heading up in the direction of where the roar had come from. It was very steep and the going was not at all easy so they found it very difficult to stalk quietly. Because the boys were really fit from all the work in the bush, it didn't take them long to get to where they thought the tia should be. They got onto the end of a spur where there was heaps of fresh sign. They stopped there for a minute and looked hard at the bush around them to see if they could spot the stag. Slade checked the wind with his lighter and whispered to Jake,

"Wind seems ok. He can't have smelt us. He must be right here somewhere."

They stayed as still as possible, only their eyes flicked from side to side as they searched for movement. After a couple of minutes silently ticked by a stick cracked not too much further up the ridge. Luke pointed in the direction he had heard it. Slade readied himself with the 303 rifle and after a few seconds went by, the tia stepped into view where he was about to come down and give another roar from his favourite spot. Slade knew he had a great, safe view of the stag and so he fired. It reeled around and crashed straight down the side of the ridge. Slade rushed forward to see if he could get another shot at it but the stag had already disappeared.

Jake's voice was full of concern. "Do you think you hit him, Slade?"

"I should have," Slade said determinedly. "I had him dead in my sights."

He suddenly remembered how Hone had mentioned to check the sight when they were at home getting ready to go for their hunt. Slade cursed at himself, angry that he had forgotten to do something so simple.

Luke was looking around for some blood and he spotted a couple of drops on some leaves in the direction of where the stag had run.

"I think you did hit him, Slade." "You think so, Luke?" he perked up. "Yeah, bro. There's blood here."

"We'll try and track him then, come on boys!"

They tracked the stag by following its marks and the odd bit of blood on leaves. To Slade's delight they found the fat, 8 point tia was lying amongst some ponga.

"Not a bad head, Slade! And some nice meat. Hone will love this," prided Jake.

Slade looked really pleased with himself and the boys all high fived and slapped each other on the back to congratulate themselves. The afternoon was wearing on and they knew they had a fair walk back to camp, especially loaded further by all of the meat and the large stag head.

Luke looked at his brothers hopefully.

"I think I heard another stag further up the valley."

"That's for tomorrow, bro. We had better get going if we are going to get back to camp before dark," warned Slade.

They carried the tia in one piece, right back down the way they had come. It was a big load so they equally shared the carrying. The return was a lot easier being all downhill and it wasn't too long before they arrived back at camp.

Slade dropped the stag off his back and sat himself down on a log. "Man, it's good to get him off my back. That was an awesome hunt

and there are plenty more up there for you guys tomorrow."

"Sure is," smiled Luke. "We may as well camp up here for another day or so before we head to the Bullring."

"Sounds good to me!" Jake agreed, "I still want to get up to the Bullring, though. It will be nice to just see it again."

"Yeah man," Slade and Luke answered in unison.

Jake and Slade hung the stag up in a tree while Luke got the fire going before they all sat down together to have a few beers and share their success.

Jake threw another log on the fire.

"It's my turn with the 303 now, and I'm feeling lucky after hearing those other tia up there."

Luke looked up hopefully.

"Yeah, maybe we'll get one each tomorrow. That would be so cool. And we already know, it isn't far to home from here to carry all the meat, only a day or so."

Slade put his head back into his hands, elbows pointing out from behind his ears.

"I have got mine now. I might as well rest in camp until you boys get yours."

"Oh, come on Slade, don't be like that," Jake tried to persuade him. "I'll see how I feel tomorrow," Slade remarked as he took a big swig of his drink, holding it up high to see through the glass bottle if any of the contents remained. "But don't count on it!"

"We are going to need you, Slade," Luke scoffed. "To come and help us carry our stags because they'll be bigger than yours."

"Yeah right," scoffed Slade as he began to drift off to sleep, "We'll see."

It was getting late and the boys had finished tea and were thinking about settling in for the night. Luke had wandered off to check on the horses and Jake meandered his way down to the river. He was feeling a bit down with himself, his head was hung low, and he was kicking stones out into the river. He found his thoughts drifting back to the night that they had stolen the car, and how him and Slade had smoked some P together earlier that evening. Luke had been drinking beer with the rest of the boys and had not noticed when his brothers had gone to sit out the back of the bar and hit the pipe. Jake was really against the idea of Luke knowing he'd touched the stuff; he knew Luke's reaction would be full of disappointment. Jake wondered what was actually in the drug that had made everything they had done since then feel not quite real or normal.

Later that evening, the fire was stoked up and the brothers were settled by it, enjoying each other's company. They were having each other on about who was going to get the biggest stag, and Slade was joking about how Luke and Jake would miss theirs because they weren't as experienced as him. The conversation turned to stories of their early days on the Coast and the many adventures they had shared together.

They drank a lot of rum and shared a couple of joints which at some point must have caused Slade to drift off into a light sleep.

Cautious not to wake him or be overheard, Jake and Luke commented quietly to each other about how much better Slade's behaviour seemed after just a few days away from Rotorua.

"He must have been on P before we left. I hope he hasn't brought any with him," commented Jake.

Luke looked down. He knew Slade had brought something at the pub off one of his mates that Luke knew was on it but decided to say nothing about it to Jake. Luke was beginning to worry that Slade was becoming addicted. Jake had assumed that his brother was just a casual user, but had noticed recently how things were rapidly changing. The idea had already occurred to him that Slade may be wanting to use staying behind at camp to rest as an opportunity to get high. Jake didn't want to be too judgmental as he knew he was guilty of partaking in a few sessions and he had enjoyed the rush, the feeling of confidence, invincibility, and the high amount of energy that came with using P. But he was still making sure to be careful not to do it very often. Slade had been the same at first, but it seemed as if he didn't care as much since his release from prison. Jake kicked angrily at a stone, forcing it to skip noisily towards the river and causing Slade to wake up from his doze. He stretched dramatically, looking towards his brothers.

"Well, the pressures on you boys. I got my tia so I say you need to get to bed. You have got a big days hunting tomorrow. I'll look after the camp and our beers, aye."

"Yeah right, I told you Sladey boy. You are carrying my big tia out tomorrow."

"And mine too," agreed Jake, laughing. "It's the least you can do for us."

Slade kept quiet, and lay down by the fire again, drinking his beer. Jake turned back to Luke.

"From the amount of sign and stags we heard roar, I reckon there is plenty of action here for at least another two days."

"Yeah, sounds good. We'll just hunt this area and see how it goes," agreed Luke.

The effects of the alcohol and marijuana were now in full force and Slade was soon snoring, his bottle lay on its side after falling out of his hand. Jake and Luke headed off to bed so that they would be ready to get out and find their stag the following day. If they didn't get one they would never hear the end of it from Slade. They put a sleeping bag over Slade and left him snoring by the gently burning fire as they could not wake him. Luke looked worriedly at the sleeping face of his brother, hoping with all his heart that his brother would get his drug usage under control before something truly terrible happened.

CHAPTER TWENTY-EIGHT

The following morning came quickly and Brent was the first to rise. He let the dogs off and took the horses up to the paddock to graze. When he returned he found Stevo had also risen and was setting about getting the morning fire started. Stevo glanced over at Brent, knowing his best friend must have a lot on his mind to be up this early as daylight had only just broken.

"You right, mate?"

"Yeah, okay. Just want to get going in case the weather turns bad. Don't fancy being up there in bad weather." "Yeah, that's for sure."

Possum Jack got up and Orphy immediately ran off up the river to see the other horses. Possum Jack joined Brent and Stevo at the fire. "Do you think Orphy is getting fresh with one of those mares?"

"Yeah, could be. He's paying a lot of attention to Bessie."

"Well, if he does get too friendly, she won't have any trouble foaling!"

The men laughed, and Possum Jack called Orphy over so he could put the pack saddles on him, whistling and talking to Orphy all the while. The two small pack saddles were riveted to a belly strap with a chest strap and crop that went around and under his tail to stop everything from rubbing forward or backwards. When they were possum hunting, Orphy carried the traps while Possum would set them and skin the possums they had caught on their line.

The girls were out of bed and hurriedly eating the breakfast Brent had cooked.

"It looks like we are ready to go! Make sure your boots are all tight. We don't want any blisters," warned Stevo, looking directly at Roger.

Janey got up and walked towards her tent, "Actually, I'll take the first aid kit."

Everybody put their packs on; the girls and Roger had their day packs, and Brent and Stevo had their bigger K-2 packs with the waist straps clipped up to stop them moving on their back. Blue and Buck were racing all over the place with excitement as the group began to move up the river. Brent called out to the dogs, whistling for them to walk beside him, and as always they obediently did his bidding.

The group stopped at the horse paddock to check that everything was okay.

"Did you put the insect repellent in, Janey?" asked Brent. "Sure did," replied Janey.

"Great job honey, I think we are going to need it."

As they walked past the paddock, Possum Jack gave Orphy a whistle and the little horse quickly fell into line behind Possum who was leading as the group followed the main river into the bush.

Possum set an easy pace and Roger looked eagerly into every pool that they passed for trout. They passed a couple of big deep pools housing logs and big rocks, with some big black shapes lurking in them. Stevo commented on the lack of any smaller trout, and that there were only the big trout which were fast and cunning enough to keep away from the eels.

Possum agreed.

"The eels have eaten the smaller ones. No koura either. They have cleaned up everything they can catch. There's just a few of the big trout left."

Janey looked sadly towards the water.

"I hope we can get to the bottom of this and save them before they get wiped out."

They had been hiking for about 30 minutes when Possum pointed at a little creek.

"This is where we go up a spur to the main ridge. We'll go up this little side creek and cut up onto the spur. Not much water up top so best to fill your water bottles here. There's a good place well up on the main ridge where we can get fresh water so we will be able to have a brew there and refill again."

They filled their water bottles up and rested briefly before Possum Jack urged them back onto their feet, reminding them that it was still early and they had a long way to go.

The following hour of walking was treacherous – slippery and steep. There was no fresh pig sign where they were hiking as the pigs were down where there were more berry trees. Poaka were big fans of fresh berries and at this particular time of year the berries dropped on the ground to seed. Blue and Buck were somehow still full of endless energy and Brent was amazed at how easily Orphy managed to get around. Possum had made him special shoes with big grips welded to them and he coped well, even with the pack saddles on. The girls were doing well, helping each other. Orphy stayed near the girls' too - so he could help them if needed. He seemed to have a sixth sense about where he might be needed. Roger was really losing some sweat. His boots were not the right ones for the conditions and his pack was a bit loose, causing it to move on his back and put him off balance. Orphy stood to the side of the track chewing on some leaves. Orphy had learned to help Possum up some bad spots in the bush; he would get close by Possum and let him hold his mane or tail and pull him up as gently as he could. He moved around to find a position where Roger could grab hold of his mane.

Roger noticed Orphy moving closer beside him,

"What are you doing Orphy?" he asked as he gave him a little pat, all while trying to keep his balance on the steep slippery slope.

Heather was just in front and looked back at her husband with a smile on her face,

"He's trying to help you Roger. Hold onto his mane."

Roger did this, and Orphy with his great strength, slowly pulled Roger up the slippery slope. Roger was so amazed and grateful for Orphy's help that he immediately gave Orphy a big kiss on tip of his nose. He was indebted to the small horse as he felt well and truly out of his league, having never tramped in such wild conditions. It truly seemed like two steps forward and one back in a lot of places.

The others were struggling too. Every tree became useful for hanging onto. They grabbed supple jack to help stop them from slipping back down the track they had just climbed up. Possum had stopped a few times to give everybody a rest.

"Not far to the top now," he had said each time.

Yet another hour passed with a lot of red and sweaty faces making their way through the bush. Finally Possum cheered triumphantly.

"We are just about there. We'll have a rest on top of the ridge."

The dogs had finally slowed their pace. Brent said, "I think the walk is a lot longer than they had initially anticipated."

The game trail they had been following was hardly visible in places, but Possum knew exactly where they needed to go to find the best terrain to get up the spur. He brought them up to the top ridge and as they climbed up on to the flat of the main ridge; everybody looked relieved. Brent marked a tree, just in case they got separated from Possum Jack as the rest settled in to take a rest for a while.

"You wouldn't want to follow the wrong spur in this country."

Possum said, "I hope we will get to the end of the ridge before dropping down to the valley where I think the drums are by nightfall. We have made good time due to our early departure."

Janey replied, "Wow!! Look at the big trees with lichen growing and hanging off them. The thick dark undergrowth is full of supple jack and ponga. How high would we be?"

Possum hesitated for a moment and then replied, "About 1400 metres above the sea."

"It looks so primeval and prehistoric up here." "Yeah, Janey," agreed Roger. "It's creepy." Heather laughed at Roger.

"No, it's just ancient, love."

"No need to worry," Sue piped up, "The vegetation is probably a throw back to ancient times. I read a book all about it once. Apparently New Zealand was part of a great land mass; the southern super continent of Gondwanaland … and New Zealand broke away from it 60 to 80 million years ago."

"That's definitely in prehistoric times!" Stevo remarked.

"Yes, that's right dear," laughed Sue. "All the birds, reptiles and amphibians were already on board before it drifted away."

Brent got to his feet.

"That's very interesting Sue, but we had better get moving before I too drift away - to sleep! That walk was exhausting but there is still so much more to go."

They all rose to their feet, chattering about the idea of being descendants from Gondwanaland. They moved forward slowly, up and down all the dips and rises in the big ridge, sometimes losing 100 metres off the main ridge before having to climb back up again. The going was tough; there were vines, bush lawyer, and windfall on the ridge to get around. A lot of the windfall was old, caused by either snow building on the branches or strong winds. Possum Jack had a natural ability to get around, knowing to follow an animal trail. If the trail doubled back, he knew there would be a really difficult bit ahead. The animals would take their own detours when the going got too tough and they'd find themselves an easier track.

After what felt like an eternity, Possum Jack stopped and looked around.

"We'll be where we can get water for a brew soon – another 15 minutes or so."

"Sounds perfect, stopping for a cup of tea will be heaven," sighed Brent wistfully.

They arrived at the water; a little spring running straight out of the base of a bank. Animals had clearly been drinking from it as there were animal tracks in the soft sand around where the water had pooled. One set was cattle marks. Possum noticed them but didn't mention to the others as he didn't want to alarm the girls. He decided he would tell Brent and Stevo as soon as he got the chance but wasn't too worried as he knew they might not run into the Devil Bull.

There were a couple of good lookout points off big bits of rock sticking out of the bush which everybody climbed out onto with their mugs of hot tea.

"Look at that view," whispered Janey. "See how the cloud is hanging along the range."

"Yes," agreed Sue smiling. "Beautiful 'Aotearoa', Land of the long White Cloud."

"You will see plenty of that orographic type cloud form up here.

It forms because of the topography of the land," advised Stevo.

"Wow, you are a fountain of knowledge," laughed Brent. "Do you think you are a television weatherman or something?"

"Well you know what it's like, some of us just have it," replied Stevo casually.

They all soaked up the magnificent view of mountains, valleys, rivers, and of course, the Pacific Ocean. Possum roughly pointed to where he thought the barrels were located.

"I think they're over there in that second valley."

They all followed his lead, looking out over the vast headwaters, to where Possum Jack was pointing to one of the valleys that made up the headwaters. Brent could see exactly where they would have to tramp just by looking at the ridge as it curled around into the headwaters. It looked to be about another 5km, but he knew it was more likely to be 10km due to the rugged terrain.

"It's lunchtime now, so if all goes well, we should be there by about 4 o'clock?" suggested Brent.

"Yeah, that'll be about right. We've made pretty good time, Brent. You lot are doing well which is great 'cos it will give us a bit of time to set up camp before dark."

Everybody was refreshed from the break and the encouragement seemed to spur Roger's spirits. Brent coud see that the ladies looked like they were really enjoying their hike and the time out amongst the New Zealand wilderness. Every day they were getting fitter and it was starting to show in their enthusiasm - character building stuff.

CHAPTER TWENTY-NINE

They had their brew and a bite to eat and were getting ready to move on. Stevo had just pulled his pack onto his back and was watching the team do the same. He was ready to give a hand with buckles and straps if needed but stood back and watched, smiling, as he thought to himself how his friends looked like a happy bunch of hikers.

The group had made their way further up the ridge, about 200 metres past the water spring, when the dogs suddenly took off up the ridge. Brent knew there was something pretty close and he would have stopped them if he could - but they were on a mission as their enthusiasm had got the better of them. Possum waved out to Brent who went over to stand where Possum was. He pointed down to the ground where there was a fresh bull mark.

"Oh no! We've run into the Devil!"

Brent quickly told everyone to get behind a tree, and to be ready to climb up it if they had to. Possum called Orphy over to him and held tightly onto his mane. They all stood there waiting for a few moments, silently hoping the dogs would come back on their own.

Suddenly the silence was lost to loud barking coming from further up the ridge, quickly followed by the sound of a huge crash in the undergrowth. They all stood frozen behind the trees, listening to the bull forcing its way, flat stick, down the ridge.

Brent yelled out to Stevo,

"We'll try and grab the dogs when they come past!"

No sooner had he spoken, than what looked like a big, hairy, monster came charging past. Brent whistled to the dogs as they flew past on their race after the devil. To Brent's immediate relief they came to his side straight away as they were pig dogs and not really into cattle.

The Devil Bull spun himself around as soon as the dogs were no longer in pursuit. He stared back up the ridge, watching for any movement, and he gave a loud snort from his nostrils as they flared defiantly at the intruders. He was holding his head up, the long hair growing between his horns hung down, partially covering his eyes.

Where Brent and Roger stood was the closest to the bull and Roger's tree was only just big enough for him to hide behind. Stevo was with the girls safely behind some big rimu trees. Brent signalled that they needed to move even further up the ridge because they were in jeopardy if the bull focussed on them. Brent and Roger stayed where they were; Brent held his rifle trained on the bull's head. He knew the temperaments of these massive beasts and that if the devil decided to, he could be onto them in an instant. The bull was standing on the side of the ridge, shaking his head wildly from side to side, snorting constantly as if to call.

'Who are these creatures invading my territory? I'm the boss up here!'

Brent was able to get a really good look at him. He was quite a sight with his hairy, shaggy coat, and his sharp devil horns. The steam was coming out of his nostrils in big puffs; evidence that he was seriously unhappy about being disturbed. His foot pawed at the ground, throwing leaves, branches and dirt into the air as he shook his head with those deadly horns. The devil had been isolated on the ridge for so long that any visitors were seriously unwelcome.

Brent really didn't want to shoot the bull, and he stood there hoping that the devil would calm down and move off. After another minute or two of complete stillness the bull seemed to be calming.

Roger had taken his camera out, fiddling with the buttons as he knew a good photo would require the flash due to the heavy bush canopy. Without even thinking about what the bull's reaction to a flash would be, he squeezed off a shot.

The flash made the bull charge instantly, straight at Roger.

It all happened so quickly that Brent was unable to take his shot at it, and Stevo lost sight of the bull behind a tree. With a loud crash, the bull hit the tree Roger was hiding behind and its horns peeled the bark back like the peel of an orange. The bull recovered before careering on straight into the bush.

Roger dived sideways from behind the tree, bouncing onto the grass as he landed on his side. Brent rushed over to help Roger up as they both prayed the bull wouldn't come back.

The rest of the party remained huddled safely together; looking down on the unfolding events in dismay.

Brent had pulled Roger to his feet before immediately training his rifle to where he thought the bull might charge from. It felt like the entire bush held its breath in quiet anticipation, all Brent could hear was his heart thumping loudly in his ears. Roger and Brent's heads turned in unison as they heard a stick snap, just seconds before Brent saw a big black blur coming straight at him. He didn't hesitate and shot straight from the hip since the bull was so close. Reloading as he dived out of the way, he pulled Roger with him, feeling relief flush over him when he heard another gun roar from the ridge. The bull ploughed into the ground, skidding along on its side, peeling roots out of the earth as its horns dug deep. Brent climbed to his feet, still holding his rifle, and Roger quickly scrambled over to see if he could help in any way. The look of worry on Roger's face intensified when he saw the bull lying on the ground.

"You saved my life, Brent."

"We were lucky there, Rog. You know we can't afford to get hurt in here. We have got to be really careful," scolded Brent. "What a bloody stupid thing to do."

"I'm really sorry Brent. I didn't even think of the bull's reaction to the flash. I just wanted to get a good photo of the beast for us," Roger apologised remorsefully.

"You will have to curb your enthusiasm and put your brain into gear if we are all going to get home safely."

Roger looked over at the devil and then continued to thank Brent at least half a dozen times. Brent felt himself calming down and leaned over to Roger, putting his hand on his shoulder.

"It's okay, mate. Hope you did manage to get a good photo."

Everybody came down the hill to make sure Brent and Roger were okay, and to check out the bull. Stevo bounded down the hill and immediately took a very close look at the bull to make sure he was dead.

"That was a close call, mate!"

"Yeah, sure was," sighed Brent with relief.

"He's an ugly bugger, Brent. Are you sure you two are okay?" "Yeah, we're all right, mate. Although I think Roger will think

twice every time he ever wants to use his flash again!"

They examined the bull and noticed there were three bullets in him. Stevo told Brent how he had shot him twice and as Brent had only heard one other shot, they high fived when they realised they had taken their first shot at exactly the same time. All of the bullets had found their target, meaning the devil bull would have died instantly, and that it was the momentum that kept it going past Brent and Roger.

Janey ran up to Brent. "You okay, love?'"

"Yeah, no worries honey."

"I was so worried," Janey cooed as Brent wrapped his arms around her in a tight hug. "All I could see was that big, black, hairy animal careering down the track. I couldn't see where you were."

"Well, I wouldn't want to repeat the experience," assured Brent. They held each other tightly while the others gathered around, talking about all the action and how quickly it had unfolded.

Heather turned to Roger, after checking he was unharmed said, "That was a pretty stupid thing to do. I thought you had more

common sense than that."

"I just didn't think. I am so glad it all turned out okay." "Yeah, imagine having that on your conscience."

"I've certainly learned from it. Brent's right, I will think before I take photos of anything from now on," Roger paused, unsure of whether or not to continue. "But I do have a great photo of the devil while he was alive," he added sheepishly.

They all checked the bull out, both the body and the photo on Roger's camera. They were all amazed at the huge amount of hair the devil possessed. Roger asked Brent if it would be okay to take some more photos.

"Of course, he's not going to hurt anyone now!"

"This bull is primeval, just like this forest," exclaimed Heather. "Yeah, it's weird. It looks like a yak crossed with something," Sue observed.

Possum Jack slapped Brent on the back.

"I'm just glad he's dead now. He was a nasty bugger. I'll sleep better up here now. Thanks boys."

Brent looked down at the bull.

"We might as well not waste this meat. I'll get the back steaks."

The girls laughed, amused at Brent wanting the back steaks. They agreed he would be eating him all by himself as they wouldn't be lining up to sample the Devil.

"Stevo and Possum can chew on the steaks with him," Sue laughed. "Devil steaks don't appeal to me!"

"Hey, you can't be too fussy in the bush," replied Brent with a smirk.

The girls stared at him momentarily before moving off to get their packs on so they were ready to keep hiking.

They all started back up the ridge. The incident with the Devil Bull had held them up for about an hour and they knew they would have to make good to time to get to where they wanted to camp before darkness fell. It was a lovely afternoon. The views were breath taking. They could see right out to the Coast from a couple of points, and Roger eagerly took some great shots of the coastline. They were looking out over the unique native bush of New Zealand; its forests truly inspiring with a sub canopy of tawa dominated by totara, matai, rimu, miro, and kahikatea trees. As they walked along, Janey stopped by a rock outcrop. She held her hand up to block the sun from her eyes.

She said quietly, "This truly is paradise."

She could see out to the sea on the south side, right down to the headwaters of the nearby river, and quite a way up the coast. When she turned 90 degrees, she could see vast areas of the mountain range to the north. Towards the east she could see the tallest mountain in the range, standing proudly with a smattering of snow covering its peak.

"Absolutely gorgeous!" she exclaimed as Brent climbed up to stand beside her on the big, flat topped, rock. Brent wrapped his arms around her, pulling her right into him.

"I'm so glad we came up here to do this trip, Brent."

"Couldn't think of going anywhere ever again without you my love. It makes our struggles through life worthwhile to be here with you and to see you so happy."

"Ooh, Brent, you are going all soft on me," squealed Janey as she leant in and gave him a kiss.

Roger called out, "Brent!"

Brent and Janey both turned. Roger had the camera ready and snapped a few photos of them standing together on top of the world. They all set off hiking again and thankfully made good time around the ridge to where they were going to camp. When they finally arrived at the place that Possum Jack remembered to be a good campsite, everybody was well and truly ready for a rest after such an exhausting day. Brent got a fire going, the girls got dinner ready, and Stevo and Roger put the fly tents up ready for night fall.

Possum announced, "We are right at the headwaters of the river catchment now. The valley where the drums are is only about another half hour. It could take a while to find them as it has been a long time since I was up here and it's pretty steep in places … and I guess there will have been a lot of growth in the bush."

Roger and the three girls talked excitedly about the adventure they were on. They said how they each felt a great sense of achievement in being so deep in the wilderness. Brent was also really proud of them, feeling that they had all been far more successful than he previously imagined. Brent prayed that the weather would hold. He knew they were all committed to the trip now that they had come this far, but if it was to suddenly rain the going would become very treacherous up in such steep country. They were so high up that the temperature could drop very quickly and an icy breeze was usually prevalent. The tramp and adventures of the day had made everybody exhausted. Brent had set a lantern up in the area where they were going to sleep so that they would be able to find the way when it was time to go to bed. The fire was also giving them some much needed light and warmth. Roger and the girls headed straight to bed after dinner. They got into their sleeping bags and quickly drifted off to sleep.

Roger had just his nose and one eye visible out of the top of his sleeping bag when his sleep was disturbed by him hearing something repeatedly hitting the lantern. He let out a concerned squeak as he realised the loudness of the thump indicated whatever it was - was large. Heather woke at Roger's squeal.

"What's wrong, Roger?" she mumbled impatiently. "There's something hitting the lantern, Heather."

Brent had heard Roger's scared squeak and had come over to where he was huddled in his sleeping bag.

"What is it, Roger? Is there something wrong?"

"There's something hitting the lantern, Brent," he repeated groggily. Brent looked around trying to locate the sound,

"Ahh, don't worry, Rog. They are just some big puriri moths. They are NZs largest native moth and are nocturnal. They are attracted to the light. They are big green moths and they won't hurt you. They are good eating, Roger."

Roger pulled his sleeping bag right up over his face,

"Help yourself, Brent. But don't worry about cooking any for me." Brent walked back towards the fire with a smile on his face. He knew Roger wouldn't be impressed about eating moths. If he tried the Devil Bull steaks Brent would be really surprised. Roger certainly didn't seem to find the food from the wild very enticing, he was more of the type to pick his meat from the shelves of the supermarket.

CHAPTER THIRTY

Jake was up really early as the sun came quickly into camp. He hadn't slept very well as he was too excited about the hunting they were about to do. He knew it was his turn to hunt and shoot the stag, and that if his luck was good, he would proudly be able to show Hone.

Luke had also risen at the crack of dawn and was busy getting a brew going and their daypacks ready.

"We'll have some venison steaks for breakfast, aye Jake?"

The sun was well up on the ridge line where it could shine its warm rays down into the river, sending shimmers of light rippling across the surface.

"Yeah, sounds good to me, Bro. I'll go check on the horses." Jake came back from where the horses were tethered.

"I gave them a bit more grass, they seem fine."

"That's good. These steaks are nearly ready. Can you give Slade a nudge and get him up?"

Slade was snoring loudly, still sprawled out in the same position beside the fire; he hadn't moved an inch since the night before. Jake nudged him gently.

"Come on Slade, time for your brekky."

"Nah, I'll get some later," mumbled Slade. "I'm going to have a quiet day at camp. I'm stuffed."

"Come on, Slade. Get out of bed. We're going hunting man," whined Jake, annoyed that Slade wasn't getting up.

"Not coming," and with that, he pullled his sleeping bag over his head.

"Ok, fine then. Stay there," sighed Jake rudely, with a look of disappointment on his face.

Luke shrugged his shoulders.

"I guess just you and I will bring back the venison, Jake. Don't worry about Slade."

Jake smiled at his brother, knowing that he and Luke would have a good hunt, and that it could also be good to have some time on their own to discuss Slade and what could happen if he was to turn to the ways of his criminal mates. They finished their breakfast quickly, knowing it would take about two and a half to three hours to get up the valley to where they had heard the stags the previous day.

They pulled their day packs onto their backs and Jake got the 303 and some bullets out of Slade's pack. Luke walked over to Slade to double check.

"Are you sure you aren't coming, Slade?"

Slade mumbled grumpily that yes, he was sure, and that he hoped they had a good hunt.

"Sure will, bro." Luke too was really disappointed with Slade. Jake slapped his brother on the back.

"Let's go. See ya tonight, Slade," and then began to wander up the creek.

Luke dropped in behind and they tramped solidly for a couple of hours, hoping to get to where the stags were roaring while it was still early. The going was fairly easy at the start - despite the boys becoming quite damp from the water ferns which were dripping morning dew. They were keeping to the sides of the creek in an attempt to try and avoid getting their feet too wet – but were instead brushing against the ferns. As they got further up the creek, the type of undergrowth changed and the pongas and bigger ferns were hanging much closer to the water's edge.

Jake and Luke were making good time and had managed to keep their boots fairly dry.

"I'm glad I wore this Swazi coat," mentioned Jake. "Even though the dew has made it quite wet on the outside, I am still dry and warm inside. This Swazi gear is awesome."

"Shit yeah," agreed Luke. "We are lucky Hone taught us what to wear in the bush. He sure knows what he is talking about."

Jake and Luke kept moving quickly up the creek with the hope of having plenty of daylight in front of them to hunt a stag.

Arriving in the area where they had heard the tia the day before, Jake suggested,

"We may as well go up the creek another half an hour because that is where we heard one yesterday."

"Yep, I think that's a good plan too, bro."

They kept moving for another half an hour until they came to a fork in the creek.

"Shall we stop for a cuppa now, and then go up between the forks in the creek?" "Yeah, we better have a brew now because we might not see water for a while."

Jake turned excitedly to Luke.

"I reckon that stag we heard yesterday is up here somewhere. If we get high enough out of the creek, we should hear him if he roars. A guy at work was telling me how hata claim areas as their own during the roar. They call the areas pads and they pretty much stay in the same area."

They packed up their cups and made sure the fire was safely put out before continuing until they found a nice log-bench on the ridge where they stopped for their next rest.

"Do you think we should give a roar?" "Yeah, ok. Let's see what ya got Lukey!"

Luke looked a bit embarrassed as he had never roared a stag before and he was hoping he would sound convincing. He was just about to let his roar out when Jake, who was watching and waiting to hear what his brother's roar would sound like, suddenly burst out laughing.

"You should see the look on your face, Luke."

"Oh man, come on bro. That's not fair, you have a go then if you think you're so clever."

"Nahhhh, ok. Yeah, yeah, sorry you go ahead."

Jake composed himself and turned away so he and Luke couldn't make eye contact. Luke began to let out a bit of a roar - or some noise that slightly resembled one. It started quite deep before turning quite high-pitched and squeaky. Jake immediately cracked up with laughter; he could hardly contain himself.

Luke had gone bright red with embarrassment. "Ok, smart ass, your turn now."

But Jake could not stop laughing; tears were running down his face as he was laughing so hard. Luke just stood there glaring at his brother until Jake managed to get himself together.

"What on earth was that, Lukey? It sounded more like a pig squealing or something."

Luke replied sounding annoyed.

"Ok then, let's see if you can do any better."

Jake instantly became serious, composing himself with the hope of making a big, deep, convincing roar. Luke watched with interest, hoping something would make its way out of his brother's mouth before the sun set.

"Hurry up, we don't have all day."

Jake filled his lungs with a couple of deep breaths. "Here we go, Lukey …"

Jake let out something that resembled a cross between a donkey's bray and a cow's moo. Luke slapped his hand over his mouth so he would not burst out laughing.

Jake turned and looked the other way. "Better than your pig call."

"Yeah, right," laughed Luke. "I guess we had better get ready for the stag charge!"

And with that, both boys were in stitches, until Jake finally said, wiping the tears of laughter from his eyes,

"Ok, bro. We had better get serious here or we are never going to get a stag."

The brothers both smiled at each other, enjoying each other's company,

"Yeah, guess we had better be quiet," hushed Luke.

They sat around in silence for a while listening carefully to see if they could hear something.

Luke finally whispered,

"Do you think we should move further up the ridge, Jake?"

Jake nodded his head at the exact moment they heard the snap of a branch just up the ridge. Jake lifted the rifle and they motioned to each other silently that they would continue their wait. After a few more minutes of waiting silently they heard the sound of smashing and breaking leaves and twigs further up on the ridge.

Jake motioned.

"I'll go and have a look. You wait here."

Luke nodded his head and Jake moved off up the ridge and disappeared out of his brother's sight. All of a sudden an almighty boom rung through the air, followed by the sound of running footsteps as Jake rapidly made his way back down the ridge.

"I got him, Luke! Come up!"

Luke rushed to where his brother was standing over a big 10 point hata lying on the grassy patch on the ridge.

Luke congratulated Jake.

"Must have been my roar that made him come in!" Jake laughed.

"Nah bro, I snuck up on him while he was busy sharpening his antlers. I nailed him!"

"Bloody good shot, Jake. He's dead as. We'll take the back legs, the back steaks, the antlers – it'll be a heavy load!"

They took the meat and antlers down to the creek and began to hide them in a spot where they would easily be able to find them again; they knew they would have to go high onto another ridge to find Luke a stag.

"We'll head up this other creek to see if we can get onto another one for you, Luke."

"Actually," spoke Luke slowly. "We've got a load now, Jake. We may as well head back and show Slade this. It will take 3-4 hours to get back." "Yeah, maybe you're right. We should have fly-camped here. But

we can't really leave the horses on their own for too long. I know they will be okay but I doubt Slade will make sure they have got enough water and something to eat. Are you sure you don't want to try for one up this other creek, Luke?"

"Nah, like I said, it's going to take a while to get back. I will get one when we get up to the Bullring."

"Ok, bro. Let's get going then."

The boys found it to be a very hard trek back with the huge weight of the hind legs and antlers. The hata had been a big boy, and his hind quarters alone weighed about 60 kilograms. It was harder still because the antlers had such a good spread on them, they managed to catch on everything. They slowly slogged their way down the creek, finding themselves slipping in the parts that had not seen the sun in a while due to the overgrowth. Jake stopped, looked around and noticed where they were standing,

"I reckon another 15-20 minutes and we should be there, Luke."

Luke, who was carrying the hind legs on his back, was grateful for the stop in pace.

"We'll have a break here aye?" "Okay."

They stopped for a rest and relief washed over them as they offloaded the weight from their backs. They had found a nice little sunny patch on the bank of the stream and Jake was stretching; trying to get some of the numbness out of his muscles from where the stag had placed too much pressure on his shoulders. With a thoughtful look on his face Jake turned to his brother.

"What do you reckon about Slade, Luke?" Surprised by the question, Luke glanced at Jake. "What do you mean?"

"Well, I have been thinking about those prison mates of his turning up when we get back to the city. I am not looking forward to it. I reckon he didn't come out hunting with us today because he wanted to smoke that ice stuff he has been using. We'll soon be able to tell when we get back if he has been using P again."

"Yeah man, we have got to tell him we don't want his mates around our place. He can move out if he wants to hang out with them. But hopefully they will just move on and won't hang around because I don't want Slade to leave with them. It would mean another path downhill for him. All this trouble has happened since he started taking all those drugs," complained Luke.

"Yeah bro, that's right," agreed Jake. "He'd be alright if he stopped taking that stuff. I hate it. He just changes so quickly. He can be scary and unpredictable and it is as if he doesn't care about anyone, including himself."

"I don't know what is going to go down, Luke, but we have to be there for him," Jake looked over at his brother worriedly, "How can we get him some help if he doesn't think anything is wrong?"

Luke shook his head.

"We just have to make sure he leaves his criminal ways behind him, nothing more like nicking that car or beating up a cop and his girlfriend. We have to keep him away from the guys he met in prison. Hopefully being out here will be good for him. Even though I am sure he has brought some stuff with him."

"I hope you are wrong but as you say we will soon find out when we get back to camp," Jake looked away, unable to meet his brother's eye any longer.

"Yeah, I guess so," sighed Luke.

After about 10 minutes of resting they had regained their energy to make the final part of the trek. They followed the stream and it wasn't long until they found themselves arriving back at the camp. When they arrived, Slade was sitting by the fire methodically stirring at a cup of tea he held in his left hand. He looked over to see the boys stagger in with the venison and the antlers and he jumped up and yelled,

"Well, well boys, looks like you got a good hata. You must have had a good hunt."

"Yeah, we had some good luck and Jake nailed him. He did a dead eye dick shot," beamed Luke.

"My day has been great," Slade announced with a huge smile plastered across his face.

Jake and Luke were pleased to be back at camp but they glanced worriedly at each other as they wondered about Slade's exuberant greeting. Jake took the stag's head from Luke and placed it by the one Slade had shot the day before,

"Gee, Slade. You are missing a couple of points. Mine's a ten and yours is only an eight."

"Oh well, that's cool. Nice to know you can count. You're right though, but don't worry - I'll beat you next time. Good hunting boys," laughed Slade as he shook their hands and slapped them on their backs.

"You boys must need a brew. The billy has just boiled."

"Yeah, that sounds good, Slade. What have you been up to all day?" queried Luke.

"Just relaxing. Oh, and regaining my energy for tomorrow's hunt. You guys know it's important to relax right?" he laughed eerily.

Jake was convinced Slade had been smoking P again. He was far too upbeat and full of energy for someone who had just been relaxing at camp all day. Jake was worried about Slade being on it again and how out of control his behaviour always became after smoking. But he figured they would all be fine out in the wilderness; what could possibly go wrong when they were all so far away from civilisation? They sat around the fire and shared the story of the hunt and the terrible attempts at roaring. Slade seemed to be in great spirits; he laughed at everything and got super excited when they discussed the details of the hunt. The day was slowly turning into late evening, and Jake and Luke were exhausted. Slade was full of energy, almost restless. He cooked dinner for his brothers, cleaned up, and even sorted out the venison. When it came time to sit down and eat, Slade announced he wasn't hungry as he had eaten earlier in the day. Jake didn't believe it, he knew personally that the appetite is always one of the first things to go when someone smokes methamphetamines. Jake and Luke enjoyed the meal, and Slade sat with them and told funny stories while they ate. The three brothers climbed into their sleeping bags with smiles on their faces. They had had a great couple of days hunting and there was still more to come when they finally arrived at the Bullring.

No sooner had Slade got into his sleeping bag, he was promptly back out again.

"Too early for me to settle down for the night yet boys! You get some sleep. I am going to sit by the fire for a while."

Luke and Jake looked across at each other. "Okay, bro. Are you alright?"

"Yeah, I'm fine Luke, just not tired yet," replied Slade as he stirred up the fire again.

"See you in the morning," Jake mumbled as he pulled his sleeping bag down over his head in an attempt to shut the world out.

CHAPTER THIRTY-ONE

The following morning Brent woke up from a fitful sleep. He had been awake most of the night with flash backs to the near death experience with the charging devil bull. He was struggling with the strong sense of responsibility; having brought the girls and Roger up into the wilderness. Stevo passed a cuppa around to everyone at breakfast as Brent told him about the stags he had heard roaring last night while everyone was asleep.

"How far away were they, Brent?"

"Couldn't really tell, but they definitely aren't close. But they are the first I've heard so the red deer rut is definitely getting started in here." The girls rolled up their sleeping bags and sat by the fire enjoying their tea and the smells coming from the food Brent had put into the pan. Sue suddenly took a very keen interest in what was in the pan. She was determined not to eat even a single bite of meat; she didn't want the devil in her belly. As enticing as Brent had made them look with bacon on the top, its juices mingling with the steaks juices, she knew she wouldn't eat even a single bite. Brent noticed Sue taking a keen interest in what was frying in the pan and grinned. "The Devil steaks are ready, Sue. Just resting them for ya."

"No thanks," Sue pulled a face. "I will just have bacon and eggs please."

"But I saved the best bits for you, they'll be delicious!" "Nah, Brent. I'll have nightmares!"

Brent chuckled as he prepared the plates, loading the ladies ones with bacon and eggs instead of Devil steaks. They all enjoyed their breakfast, placed their things back into their packs, and got ready to head off for the day.

Possum Jack turned to everyone.

"Okay, we'll move on down to where I remember the drums to be. We'll have to be very careful as it's really slippery."

Moving slowly, they began trekking in the direction Possum Jack had pointed. The flora became denser as they followed the track down into the valley. There was lush prolific fern growth which, due to the large amount of it, had clearly been having a great growing season during the warmer months that had just passed. The ferns were nearly up to their knees and they found themselves having to take extra care to avoid slipping in the lush undergrowth. It was quite creepy having the fern completely surrounding their lower legs and their trek began very gradually as they made their way down the slippery sharp ridge. It improved as they moved down into the valley, and after about an hour and a half of trekking they were at the spot where Possum Jack thought the drums should be.

The flora in the valley had changed drastically from where they were up on the ridge and everyone could sense that the valley had a weird feeling about it. The mist was hanging low over everything and a still silence washed over the group as they experienced the eeriness of the valley. As they looked down into the valley they were following, they could see the headwaters of the river as they cautiously descended a sharp spur. Following close behind Brent, Janey put her hand out and touched him so as to get his attention. Brent turned his head to look at her as she whispered,

"I've a scary feeling about this place Brent." "Don't worry honey, we'll be all right."

Brent had noticed, as they descended into the valley, the spider webs were plentiful and there were some really big spiders in their depths. They had managed to catch small birds and insects in webs that looked like they were made from thick string rather than web. One particularly large web even had a tuatara lizard trapped inside it. The few spiders he had seen in their webs were at least three or four times as big as any he had ever seen before. They had the same markings as the poisonous katipo spiders, but were so much bigger it was hard to know if they were the same spider or not. He didn't mention to the others that there didn't seem to be as many spiders as there were numbers of webs.

Roger shuddered.

"I should have brought my 30 seconds spray with me to kill these spiders."

Stevo gave a weak smile.

"It would need to be pretty concentrated for it to deal to this number of spiders."

Possum Jack was in front, and he came to a very sudden halt forcing everybody to bang into each other as they immediately dropped their pace. He pointed up high in a tree, where a massive spider was sitting in the middle of its extraordinarily large web. The spider was as big as a frying pan and about six inches thick. It looked so creepy, especially with the way it was looking down at them.

Alongside the spider was a trapped bird.

"It looks like a fantail," whispered Heather, her eyes nearly popping out of her skull.

"Can I take a photo, Brent?" asked Roger tentatively, still nervous about snapping off with his camera after the bull incident.

Brent lifted the 270 up, just in case the spider made any sudden movements.

"Yeah, go for it Roger."

Roger took the photo and the oversized katipo spider didn't move a muscle, it remained in its web, with its big eyes looking straight at them.

"It mustn't be hungry. We may as well keep moving. Just move off slowly so as not to frighten it," warned Brent.

They tiptoed past the spider, which didn't even flinch. Possum commented, "I bet there are heaps of them, judging by all the spider webs. These webs are so big they are catching everything that flies into them."

Every single web had insects and birds hanging in them, anything that wasn't big or strong enough to make a bid for freedom.

Janey examined one of the webs,

"Poor birds. They seem to just hang in there until they die." Stevo voiced what Brent had been thinking all along,

"Yeah, but I wonder where all of the spiders are?" He pushed away a web, which a spider had industriously made right in his way.

"Maybe the big ones have eaten the smaller ones?" offered Janey thoughtfully.

"Possible, spiders as big as these would take a bit of feeding," agreed Possum Jack.

They kept moving slowly forward, careful not to bump into anything.

Finally Possum Jack announced, "The drums should be around here somewhere … I'm pretty sure this is where Orphy and I saw them."

The damp and dark landscape, amazing ferns and lichen and big trees and heavy undergrowth somehow made everything seem even more primeval and ancient looking than it had seemed up on the ridge. "How can you tell one valley from the next?" one of the girls asked. "Each has its own landmarks," replied Possum as he paused to look around again. "And, I'm pretty sure they were around here somewhere, right near this creek bed in this valley. If we spread out and make our

way up towards the top of the ridge we should find them." Brent nodded.

"Okay, but we'll stay close together, moving up in a line. We may have to do it more than once."

"Should we put our packs down to make it a bit easier going through the bush?" Janey asked. She was feeling tired and was desperate to rid herself of the extra weight.

"Sorry honey. Everyone must keep their packs on - but make sure to be very careful they don't catch in any webs, or on any trees or bushes. You never want to be separated from your gear in the bush," warned Brent.

Keeping his gun on his shoulder, Stevo moved out to the right. Brent had his gun handy too as he headed left, and Possum went up the middle with Orphy right behind him. The girls and Roger fanned out in between. They moved off up the valley, making sure they caught sight of each other every couple of steps. They had been going a while and had seen nothing but big spider webs and trapped insects. They could hear loud scratching up in the trees, coming from the big spiders that were hiding up there and catching the warmth from the sun. Brent stopped and looked up through the trees to what he figured was the top of the ridge, as all he could see was daylight. He guessed it must only be about 150 metres to the top. He began to move off again when he heard his wife yelling from about 30 metres away,

"I've found something!"

Her yell stopped everybody in their tracks momentarily before they all immediately began to rush over towards where Janey was standing.

Janey began shouting again.

"They are here! The drums are here!"

Brent got to where Janey was first. He could see at least a dozen drums scattered around the place. Everybody paused in their tracks, staring open mouthed at the drums, many which were very rusty and had burst open Brent moved closer to the drums to see if there was anything on them he could read, but any labelling had long moulded over. He looked around and saw a little creek where some of the drums had rolled down into strangley fluorescent blue water.

Stevo warned,

"There is a very strong smell. It is most definitely some type of chemical."

"You wouldn't think it would still smell after all this time if they were dropped from a helicopter," observed Heather.

"Yeah, I agree. But I think they had to have been dropped by a helicopter, can't think of another way they could have gotten here. Look at these drums, some are only just rusting through and starting to leak. But be careful, don't touch any of them. We don't know what the chemical is."

It looked as if some of the drums had burst on landing and others hadn't. The ones that were still intact had landed on big mounds of moss which cushioned their fall. Looking around at the surrounding bush, Stevo pointed and said,

"I think the drums have rolled down here from up there further. Look at the way those younger trees are growing. They look like they have been flattened and are growing on that funny angle as they try to reach the sunshine."

Stevo paused to look further up the valley.

"I think we should keep moving up the valley."

"Wait, Stevo. I can see something up there. In the overgrowth." Sue pointed.

Brent immediately moved in that direction. He let out a little yelp when he recognized the shiny object that had caught Sue's attention.

The tail end of a plane.

As Brent got closer he could see the main body of a plane; quite a big plane but both of the wings had been smashed off. There were massive holes in the undercarriage and severe damage along each side of the plane. The trees and bushes in its path had torn massive holes in the fuselage as it slid through the bush at speed when it crashed. The others had made their way over and were all completely blown away by what they were seeing.

None of them had expected they would find this when they had set out from the Bullring. The plane itself was covered in vines, ferns, and bush lawyer that had grown all over it - and there were enormous spider webs *everywhere*. They pushed their way through the undergrowth to try and get a closer look and as they approached the site of the crash they saw a clear little area of creek bed to their right. Pushing through the undergrowth, which was quite thick in parts but open in others, they made their way to the clearer area. There was enough space for them to put their packs down safely so Brent suggested taking them off and leaning them against a tree. Brent placed his gun beside his pack where he could grab it easily if he needed to. He was walking with an extra bounce in his step; anticipating what they would find now they had discovered the plane and the drums.

Stevo looked back up at the ridge line.

"Looks like it came over that ridge so low it went right in under the main canopy. I think I will go and have a closer look."

"Are you sure it is safe?" worried Sue. "Yeah, it looks okay. I won't be long."

He grabbed his gun and gave Sue a kiss before walking up towards the top of the ridge. He could see bits of debris from the plane all over the place. Both of the smashed off wings were not very far apart. One was jammed against a big rimu where the tree had smashed it off the fuselage, and the other wing had slid down the hill.

Stevo easily made it to the top of the sharp ridge which rose up both to the right and left, forming a saddle in the ridge which was where Stevo was standing. On its crest there was a lot of rock but no big trees. He could see broken off spars from damaged trees and accurately guessed they had came down in a cyclone. The bigger trees were all just off the top, out of the wind, and growing in the richer soil that lay just over the crown of the ridge. Stevo looked all around him; the view was spectacular and he could see right out to the coast.

He spoke aloud to himself,

"Looks like the plane must have been low and came in through the saddle, probably in heavy fog, clipped the top of this ridge and crashed down through these big trees in this valley."

He looked down and saw the path it had cut through the bush, taking everything out except the biggest trees. The way the plane had flown in under the main canopy was incredible - and very bad luck for whoever had been flying. The bush had regenerated and as the plane wasn't visible from the ridge it certainly couldn't have been visible from the air either.

Possum had already begun gathering some wood and sticks to start a fire. A fire would keep away some of the spiders, and he was also aching for a cup of tea. Because they were at the top of the valley, there was a little spring they could get some safe water from. When it rained, this water way would become a torrent as there was a wide catchment area feeding the valley. Roger and the ladies began to help Possum, but Brent was far too eager to examine the plane.

"Don't worry about a cuppa for me just yet. I want to have a closer look at that plane."

Taking his big machete, Brent headed toward the plane, cutting the vines and ferns to clear a pathway right up to the door of the plane. He was constantly looking around him as he was very aware there would most likely be big spiders or other creatures around. The door of the plane had been ripped off cleanly and there was old cargo scattered everywhere – more drums, clothes, and other miscellaneous items. Everything had clearly been thrown out of the plane through the doors and holes in the fuselage when it slid its way through the bush. Moss and ferns had already begun to grow through the old scattered cargo.

Janey, Heather, and Sue decided they weren't ready for a cup of tea yet either and made their way after Brent as he cut his way to the door.

Brent cautioned everyone seriously,

"Be careful around here. There are some pretty big looking cobwebs. Must be more massive spiders around here, probably oversized katipos like the ones we have already seen."

Sue shuddered.

"Ooh, these are huge spider webs. You know, I've read about giant venomous tarantula sized spiders in Australia. They are known to eat birds, and are bigger than the palm of your hand. But going on the size of these cobwebs, we have outdone the Aussies - yet again."

Heather looked at Sue in surprise. "Did you really read that?"

Sue nodded her head fervently.

"There might be a body or two in here. Girls, be prepared," warned Brent as he entered the main body of the plane.

Heather whispered,

"Oh man I hope not, poor buggers."

There were holes throughout the main fuselage but the cockpit area was still recognisable. Vines and ferns had even made their way inside and grown over everything within the plane. Brent was cutting through the vines and climbing over rotten logs and debris that had obviously been pushed up by the plane as it crashed. He was trying to get to the door of the cockpit but found it to be a very difficult task. He kept brushing cob webs aside with his arm, being very careful to not disturb the owners. Because the plane had landed on its side the job was extremely difficult and dangerous.

Stevo came back to where they had left the packs, and now that the fire was burning away nicely, he and Possum Jack followed the path Brent had cut. Stevo called to Brent,

"Possum and I will try to get round the front."

"Yeah, okay. Just be careful, there's a shitload of spider webs," cautioned Brent for the umpteenth time.

The plane had jammed itself up against a rocky outcrop and the front of the plane was completely covered in vines, ferns, and old broken branches. Brent got to the cockpit doorway, yanked it open, and tentatively looked inside. He drew in a sharp breath when he saw a clothed skeleton strapped into one of the seats, slumped forward over the controls. The plane had clearly been there for a long time and the body had completely decomposed; there was nothing left except bones and moth eaten clothing. The co-pilots seat was vacant but Brent imagined there would have been two people flying the plane. He wondered if someone had survived the original impact and had managed to get out. He called out to the girls to let them know of his discovery and to ask them to look around for signs of any other bodies. The girls drew closer together, clutching at each other's hands as they grew even more afraid of what any one of them could find next.

Brent saw a built in cupboard located just behind the pilot's seat. He carefully climbed into the cockpit, being very cautious in case the plane moved and he became trapped in the tightly enclosed space with the bones of the dead pilot. Luckily, he soon realised the plane was wedged so tightly against the rocky outcrop that it wasn't going to move at all. Edging his way towards the cupboard, he opened it and found a brown, leather brief case and a log book. Thankfully the cupboard was airtight so the contents remained in excellent condition. He removed everything that looked like it may give some information about the pilots and their plane - and what they were carrying.

He called to the others,

"We have got to tell the police about this as soon as we get out of here."

He shuddered as he glanced at the skeleton one last time before backing out of the cockpit and placing the briefcase and log book next to where the main entry to the plane once was, before making his way through the rest of the plane. He found two other drums in the rear end of the plane; one had been damaged badly and the contents had leaked long ago while the other drum remained in a very reasonable condition. He could see there was writing on the drum that was still decipherable as it had been protected from the weather. He wriggled it around to get a better look and to see if he could make out any of the words. As he knelt down to read the writing, he heard movement coming from behind the drum. He got up quickly, stepping backwards and crashing into the other drum in surprise. He looked down at the drum; waiting in anticipation to see what was going to appear. Suddenly it sounded as everything was being moved behind the drum. The dry leaves, sticks, and pieces of cargo that were trapped back there made quite a din as whatever was lurking made its move. Brent was still looking at the drum, watching to see what was going to appear when two very long spiny legs appeared over the top of the drum and grabbed onto the edge. The spider's main globular abdomen appeared as it hauled itself up onto the top of the drum using those same two big spiny legs. More legs began to protrude and Brent became aware of the bright red stripe running down its middle. The spider was easily the size of a domestic cat, and it was not impressed at having a human intruder in its home. The long spiny front legs were waving in fury at being disturbed, and Brent froze in shock. He regained his composure and slowly backed away to give some distance between him and the nasty looking thing. He turned his head slowly from right to left; looking for something in reach that he could use to protect himself with.

Stevo and Possum had cut their way through the vines and undergrowth and made it around to the front of the plane where the windows were completely smashed out. Inching their way up and over the nose of the plane, Stevo and Possum cautiously made their way into the cockpit. They had heard Brent's warning about the body in the cockpit, and they carefully avoided disturbing it as they too made their way into the plane. They looked towards the back where Brent was and as Stevo was standing in front of Possum he could see the spider.

"Will you look at that - Wow!"

Over his shoulder he mouthed to Possum,

"Can you see that? It looks like a katipo spider too, like the other one we saw, but I didn't think they lived in this area of the North Island?"

"Me neither, but you never know what you will find out here," marvelled Possum.

Stevo yelled,

"Stay still, Brent. I'll get the gun."

The big spider was waving its feelers around frantically, and as Brent didn't know how quick these things could move he wasn't taking any chances.

"Okay, Stevo. Hurry up and shoot the bastard."

Possum sat in the empty seat beside the pilot's and Stevo leapt back out of the window of the plane, raced back to where they had left the packs, and grabbed his rifle which was still leaning against his pack. He yelled to the girls and Roger so stay where they were as he needed to take a shot at a spider. He ran back to the plane, entering through the door Brent had discovered. The oversized katipo had already begun to move hungrily towards Brent. Out of the corner of his eye, Brent gratefully saw Stevo had come back.

"Be careful, I'm going to shoot. Brent."

Brent nodded and within an instant the gun roared and the spider disintegrated. Brent had covered his face with his arms and knelt down as quickly as he could; trying to avoid both a ricochet and spider parts splatting all over him. He looked relieved.

"Thank God you are an accurate shot, Stevo! I thought that thing was going to eat me!"

He shook his head and rubbed his fingers in his ears as the rifle shot had been deafening in the enclosed plane.

"Are you all right, Brent?" asked Stevo as he moved up to where Brent was getting slowly to his feet.

"Yeah just a bit slimy!"

Janey leapt into the plane to see if everyone was still in one piece but was then quickly motioned by Stevo to stop moving,

"Don't make any sudden movements. We don't know how sturdy this thing is."

"Oh right. Sorry. Are you guys all right? What a mess!"

There was rifle smoke, dust, leaves, cut vines, and spider legs floating all around the plane. Slimy pale green body fluid from the spider had coated everything it had splattered onto, including Brent's hair and arms. It was hanging like gooey glue from the ceiling of the plane.

"Yeah," replied Stevo who was also rubbing his ears. "I had to shoot him. God it was the biggest, scariest creature I have ever seen.

The stuff of nightmares! It had grown humungous. I have never seen a spider the size of it. It must have been really warm in this plane to enable something to grow that big."

Brent edged his way back towards Stevo, wiping the green slime onto anything he could find around him.

"Good shot mate. You got that arachnid smack bang in the middle of its head."

Possum had been watching all the drama from the cockpit and had a big smile plastered across his face.

Janey watched her husband carefully.

"I didn't know you knew spiders were called arachnids, Brent."

Brent just winked at her as he crawled carefully back over to check the drum out.

"There could be more in here. We need to be careful." Sue and Heather came up to the door.

"Are you all right in there?" Janey came to the door.

"Yes, they're ok. They had to kill the biggest spider ever - apparently it was the size of a cat."

"Oh my God!" squealed Heather. She looked in through the door to where she could see the head and parts of the spider's body splattered around.

"Oh my God, Oh my God. Sue come and take a look at this!" Sue poked her head in the door.

"Good God that thing is bloody hideous!" Being an ardent reader, Sue continued,

"In that article I was reading about some spiders in a town in Australia ..."

"I hope this is not going to be a creepy, crawlie story," interrupted an already frightened Heather. She hated spiders and she was already having a hard enough time coping with the giant spiders and the webs all around her. She hated how spider webs got caught on her clothing and the fibres of the web were so sticky and elastic that they were almost impossible to get off. Just the thought of it, made her skin crawl and feel itchy all over.

"I'm afraid it is Heather. Like I was telling you all before, the Aussies have got these spiders that are huge and can eat birds. They are definitely carnivores and they are venomous. They are called tarantula spiders. They are from a town in Queensland and they are awful looking creatures. Maybe that was one that came in on the cargo this plane was carrying?"

"Well, that's it," squealed Heather, who was feeling really afraid with the dense bush and lots of creepy crawlies. "I'm going home. You will be telling me there are crocodiles in here shortly. Those Aussies must be sending all their nasties over here."

"Settle down," calmed Brent. "You'll be fine, Heather. We'll just do what we have to and then head for home. No one is going home until we all go together."

Roger put his arm around Heather.

"It's ok honey. Remember this place is just like Jurassic Park – yes it's full of danger but it is also beautiful too. Let's go sit by the fire and start making the tea."

Sue picked up the briefcase and log book and wandered back to where the packs were so she could sit down and read through them.

Inside the plane, pointing to the drums Brent called out, "Let's have a look at this, guys."

Stevo and Janey moved closer to see what he had discovered. Just as they were about to try and read the writing Heather yelled from outside.

"There's something here!"

Stevo and Possum jumped out of the plane, clutching their guns, and rushed over to where Heather and Roger stood. Heather was upset and Roger was doing his best to reassure her they would be out of there soon.

Sue put the brief case and log book down and ran over to join her friends.

"What is it?" called Brent. Stevo called back tentatively,

"It looks like part of a skeleton."

Stevo dug around in the moss and twigs. He unearthed a weathered wallet and some human bones. Brent climbed out of the plane and walked down to where they were all gathered.

"He must have been alive and climbed out of the wreckage - or else he was thrown out on impact," Brent sighed.

Everyone looked sadly at the bones, at the plane, and around at the forest, each of them deep in thought about how awful the entire situation was. The only consolation was that perhaps due to their findings, the families would finally get their closure and the chemical would no longer be leaking through the bush.

"I took the briefcase and log book and put them out by our packs," whispered Sue, breaking the silence.

"Thank you," Brent looked around at his friends. "There's some writing on one of the drums that is still in the plane, but I haven't been able to read it yet."

Stevo coughed,

"I'll put these bones back, the ones we have disturbed."

"Yes," agreed Brent with a grim look on his face. "We won't disturb the skeleton. We have to be careful not to disturb anything too much actually. We'll go and see what is on this drum. You girls might like to look through those papers and see if you can find out who they are and what they were carrying."

Roger asked Brent if he thought now would be a good time to take some photos as proof for when they went to the police. Brent told him it would be perfect, but to remember to be careful when using the flash. After placing the bones carefully back where he had found them, Stevo looked over towards the plane. He could see a number and letters written along the side of the fuselage. He went up to the side of the plane and rubbed at the moss and slime. He could read the letters and numbers: ZT108 and he motioned for Roger to come and take some photos.

Stevo went to join Brent and Possum who were still in the plane reading the drum. They were struggling with it as it had lots of tiny printed writing which was proving very difficult to read. Brent could pick out a few words.

"What does it say, guys?" Stevo asked.

"Don't really know. It's something to do with fish, I think. We will have to get it out into the light and clean it so we can read it easier."

"Yeah, okay mate. The sooner we do what we've got to do here and get out, the happier I will be. I have already seen enough to know that whatever was in those drums has affected the wildlife in this catchment."

The girls had gone back to sit by the packs and were looking through the documents. A few minutes later they saw Possum, Brent, and Stevo rolling the heavy drum out of the plane. Janey went over to see if they had been able to read it,

"Any luck?"

"Nah," replied Stevo, "What about you guys, found anything?" Janey smiled grimly.

"Well it's all here – what it was carrying and who the pilots were. This plane is miles off course. It was on its way to Nelson from Auckland. It was carrying some drums of a growth promotant hormone which the aquaculture industry in the Marlborough Sounds uses in their salmon farming production programme."

"What did you say, Janey?" queried Roger who had just returned with his camera and caught the end of Janey's comment.

She repeated everything, to which he replied,

"Oh wow! This must be the plane I was reading about in a paper at Gabe Jacksons. Remember, Heather? I glanced through a few of the old newspapers I found on his coffee table. I remember it said they had searched all down the centre of the North Island which was its flight path but it was never found. It was presumed to have been lost at sea. The weather had been terrible and it must have got way off course. Is there a compass in the cockpit?"

"Yeah, I saw one," piped up Stevo. "I did notice it was stuck pointing south even though this plane is lying to the east. Maybe it got stuck while they were flying and they thought they were heading south."

"Well, something happened with their navigation anyway," Brent agreed with a grim look on his face.

Brent looked over at Roger.

"But 10 years! That would definitely explain the strange growth in the animals around here. This stuff has been seeping down into the waterways for as long as this plane has been here."

"According to the documents," Janey scanned her eyes over the book again, "it was just over ten years ago. That would definitely tie in with that newspaper article you read Rog."

Brent commented,

"Some of these drums are only just starting to rust now and are on the verge of leaking. Many have already leaked, and then the ones that burst on impact would have really primed the river. Does any of the information tell us how many drums there were originally, Janey?"

Janey looked back at the log book.

"Yes, it says there were 52 drums of pure undiluted double strength growth promoting hormone."

Stevo exclaimed,

"52 drums! Good god, no wonder! I reckon these spiders are addicted to the stuff judging by the size of them."

Brent shuddered at the memory of his close call.

"I've already counted 17 drums so there must be more around here."

Possum Jack had been looking around the area. He said, "I reckon they have rolled down further. Let's go and see what we can find."

"Have a cuppa first, Possum," suggested Sue.

"I suppose that is a good idea. They are not going anywhere now are they? Not after all this time!"

"I want to have another look at the plane," advised Brent.

"Me too, I will come with you," offered Janey as she slipped her hand into Brent's.

"But before we all go off again, let's finally sit and have a cuppa. I'll put a brew on," announced Roger. They all walked back to where the fire was still going, and they put some water on to boil.

Stevo said,

"I hope you were careful where you got the water from up here. I don't want to drink no growth promotant hormone infected water."

Possum smiled and told them he got it earlier from further up the creek, from higher above the crash site. They had their cuppa and discussed everything that had happened.

Possum rose to his feet and headed further down the valley to have a look for the extra drums. Sue, Stevo, and Roger decided to go as well,

"I'll bring my gun, just in case," Stevo reassured. "Rog, bring your camera."

Janey and Heather sat together looking through the documents a bit more closely.

Brent looked around.

"There's not much more we can do here. We'll report this to the police when we get home. Daniel might be able to come on the recovery mission since he is an experienced chopper pilot and knows this area. I'm going back to the plane. I'll take my gun with me just in case I see any more of those spiders."

"Okay, love. We'll be there soon, I still want to see the plane again. But now I just want to read more of these documents. Take care." Searching down through the undergrowth for the drums that had rolled further into the valley was hard going manoeuvring through all of the thick supple jack vines and heavy undergrowth. They had found themselves in a really thick patch and there were some really big spider webs in amongst all of the undergrowth. "Don't you hate

the way they stick to your face," said Roger.

"Yeah, glad I've got my gun," replied Stevo. He didn't want any of them to encounter another cat sized spider. Moving even further down, they broke out into an open patch that looked like an old creek bed where water would run down when it rained. They followed it down further and came across a creek with water trickling down it. Possum was leading and he glanced back over his shoulder telling Stevo, who was just behind him.

"I can see a drum."

As they got closer they could see there were many more drums than just one.

"They must have bounced their way down here from the plane crash site," observed Stevo.

Some had burst open and others were jammed up against big piles of moss and silt. The drums were spread right the way down the creek. It looked as if many had floated or been washed further down during big storms. They spent close to an hour searching around and as they had spread out, they had managed to locate 24 more drums between them.

Some had been buried in the creek as sand and debris had washed down around them during the floods, and every single one of them was leaking slowly as they had started rusting through. Stevo was standing on a little sandy corner in the creek and gave a call for everyone to come together. Possum and Roger made their way towards him. Once the men were altogether, they waited anxiously for

5 more minutes for Sue to appear. But she wasn't showing up.

Stevo turned to Possum and Roger. "Where and when did you see Sue last?"

"She was just back up the creek a way, not too long ago," reassured Possum.

"Maybe she went back up to Janey and the others?" offered Roger. Stevo doubted Sue would do that without letting him know first,

and gave another loud yell, "Sue, are you there?" There was real concern in Stevo's voice.

Stevo gave a few more yells but there was still no reply from Sue. Stevo turned to Roger and Possum.

"I really don't think Sue would go back without telling me, but maybe she could not see us and thought we had doubled back. It is really unlike her not to keep an eye on where I am. We'll go back up to the plane and see if she's there." Stevo wiped at a big spider web as he hurriedly moved off. Possum could see how Stevo was very worried; Possum too was growing concerned. He knew there could be some really nasty things living out in this dark, mossy, damp place - especially if they too had been getting a dose of the hormone. Sue was in a rocky gut behind a knoll. She was pushing her way through dense vines and undergrowth and had not heard Stevo calling because of the noise she was making — and because she was so far away from the others. Sue was moving down the creek with the rest of the party when she had noticed what looked like a piece of the plane further in under the undergrowth. She approached it to get a closer look only to find after checking it out that it was just a bit of driftwood sticking up. It had a shiny part to it that had attracted her attention, but she soon realised that it was just caused from water and sand blasting it during the many rough storms and floods.

As she started to go back in what she thought was the direction she had come from, she moved off in the wrong direction through the rocky gut and got completely disorientated. She started to panic but knew to hold herself together as Stevo had always told her to never panic in the bush. She knew how easy it would be to fall over and get hurt, to fall down a bank, or just become exhausted and even more lost. He had told her that the best thing to do once people know they are lost is to stay in the same place as it makes it easier for searchers. If a lost person goes charging off all over the bush then nobody knows where to look and it is very easy to cross paths without ever even knowing. Despite remembering this advice, Sue was adamant she could not be too far off from the original creek bed. She sat down for a few minutes to try and get her bearings before moving slowly forward in what she thought was the right direction. She found herself in a particularly bad patch, with a lot of vines and ferny undergrowth. Many of the tree roots were exposed from storms and flooding in the fragile environment. She was beginning to feel scared by all of the vines and dark shadowy patches in the bush. As she pushed forward through the vines, she noticed the spider webs were particularly thick and as she separated the densely tangled vines, she realised the webs were stuck to her on all sides. She tried desperately to brush them off but they were so large and so thick she realised she was fighting a losing battle. As she turned in circles around herself trying desperately to get them off, she only found herself becoming even more tangled in the string like webbing.

Sue was beyond scared, and she was yelling continuously for Stevo to help her. She heard a muffled noise from overhead and looked up to see a massive spider in the tree above her. She let out an almighty scream, louder than any of her previous yells for help, and scrambled forward. Watching the spider instead of where she was stepping, she placed her foot onto a log which moved with her weight, and she stumbled and fell heavily. As she fell, she banged her head on a tree root that was sticking out of the ground. The last thing she saw as she slipped into unconsciousness was the spider making its way down through the vines and the webs towards her.

CHAPTER THIRTY-TWO

Tearing through the bush and up the creek bed, the Stevo, Roger and Possum arrived back at the plane crash site. They were puffing profusely. They had gained a lot of height from where they had been down in the valley looking for the rest of the drums. Brent had come back from having a closer look at the plane to join Heather and Janey who were sitting on their packs by the fire, keeping warm as the climate was really damp and cold in the bush. "Have you seen Sue?" Stevo blurted with a very worried voice.

"No," Janey replied nonchalantly.

"You mean, she's not here with you," confirmed Stevo running his hands through his hair. "We couldn't find her and she didn't answer when I called out so we thought she must have come back up here to you guys. I wonder if she went back up to the crash site …"

"I don't know why she would do that without telling anyone," Janey said worriedly.

The minute the words had escaped Janey's lips, Stevo knew that Sue was still down in the creek. He immediately spun himself around to head straight back down to look for her. As he moved he heard a piercing scream from down in the valley.

"That's Sue," he yelled to the others.

"Why couldn't we hear her yells before?" asked Roger curiously. "She must have been in dense bush which muffled the sound," explained Possum. "We are higher up here than we were down there - which is why the sound has travelled up the valley to us."

Stevo grabbed his gun and took off through the bush like a man possessed. Brent grabbed his gun from the log it had been leaning on and he and Possum ran off right behind Stevo.

"One lost in the bush is enough," yelled Brent to the others. "You guys wait here with Orphy and the dogs – DO NOT MOVE!"

The men quickly arrived back to where they had found the scattered drums. Stevo stopped dead in his tracks, desperate to hear any sound from his wife.

"If she is okay she would still be screaming out for me, I know her."

Brent and Possum pulled up right behind their friend. Brent could see the very concerned, strained look on Stevo's face. They moved as quickly as they could through the ferny undergrowth which was making it very difficult for to work out where to place their feet at times. Their pace was really slowed by the tangled, dense vines and undergrowth.

"It's weird that we can't hear Sue," whispered Stevo. "It is so quiet down here. The bush must be muffling her yelling. I hope like hell she is not in any danger."

"Don't worry too much just yet, let's keep calm. We will find her soon, she can't have gone too far," reassured Brent who was holding his 270 rifle at the ready.

Stevo stopped again to listen. The three men were puffing profusely. Brent looked back up the valley through the light in the trees. "She must be right here somewhere. This is the direction the yell

came from. I hope she hasn't slipped and hurt herself."

"If that is what happened she may have knocked herself out."

Stevo was tense with worry and concern for Sue. They kept looking through the undergrowth but could find no trace of Sue anywhere. Stevo moved over to the left side of the creek as he had caught a glimpse of something shiny. He saw some footprints in the sand and realised they were Sue's size. He wasn't sure if any of the others had explored that side of the creek when they were searching earlier, but he decided to follow the footsteps in the hope he would find his wife. He wondered if Sue had seen the shiny thing too and gone to check it out, it did look like as if it could be part of the plane. He followed the footsteps for a while, noticing that they seemed to go in circles, before careering off in a completely different direction. There were spider webs everywhere, and some of the dark damp areas had large eyes glowing from their depths. He began to get very worried, especially when he saw the footsteps led to a particularly dense patch that had very thick strands of web running from branch to branch in every direction.

Suddenly, Stevo saw Sue lying in the undergrowth. He gave a yell to the others who came running over.

"She's over there!"

Stevo raced to where Sue lay sprawled out amongst the damp undergrowth, completely entwined in webbing. In the tree, not too far above Sue's head, Stevo could see an enormous spider.

"Brent, keep an eye on that spider. He is bigger than the one in the plane," yelled Stevo as he made a careful movement towards Sue. Brent aimed his rifle at the spider; "I'll be ready in case it starts to move towards you, Stevo." He really didn't want to shoot unnecessarily in case it triggered a bad reaction with the other spiders. Brent knew that some spiders were defensive and would come out to fight whenever they smelt the death of one of their own – and Brent was not prepared to take that chance unless there was no other option. As Stevo got closer to Sue he saw the root beside her head and her left foot trapped in the log. He was very grateful to realise she had fallen and banged her head, rather than a bite from a spider being the cause for her lying motionless on the ground. Stevo rushed in and began sweeping the cobwebs off her body. He pulled her close to him, checking her pulse, and stroking her face all while repeating her name in an attempt to bring her back to consciousness. After what felt like a life time, she finally began to come around.

"Oh thank God! Are you okay, honey? What happened?" fretted Stevo.

"I don't know. One minute I was walking along and now you are here," Sue looked very confused and stunned; it was clear she really had no idea where she was or what had happened.

"We thought you must have gone back to the plane crash site when we couldn't find you down here," Stevo shuddered at the memory. "Shit, I was so worried. Thank God you seem to be okay."

"My head hurts Stevo," Sue whispered.

"You must have knocked your head when you fell," Stevo tried to comfort her the best he could, searching with his hands through her hair to find any abrasions, lumps, or blood.

Brent knelt down beside them with his gun still aimed at the massive arachnid. The spider had not moved a single muscle but it was intently watching everything they were doing.

"Here, Sue. Have a drink of water," Brent passed her his water bottle.

"Thanks, Brent," Sue smiled as she sipped from the bottle. "That feels better. I don't seem to have hurt anything except my head." "That's good. Let's just sit quietly for a minute. There is no rush to move," reassured Stevo.

Possum had been standing a little way back from the others to keep watch and give Sue her space. He flinched as he heard a noise in trees.

"Did you hear that?"

"What?" Brent turned to face Possum.

"A crack, movement of some type," whispered Possum.

"No, I didn't hear anything," Brent replied as he got back on his feet, looking all around him to see if he could spot anything moving. He felt a little queasy as he looked at all of the webs. There seemed to be thousands and thousands of giant spiders surrounding their little group.

"This valley is absolutely infested with spiders living on that growth hormone, and it has changed both their behaviour and their appearance."

Stevo had finished checking Sue for wounds and had begun to make sure she would be okay to move. She had fully regained consciousness and appeared to be fine except for a nasty lump on her head. Brent asked Sue if she could walk her way back up to the plane to which she nodded meekly. Stevo brushed off as many of the cobwebs as he could that were still stuck to Sue's clothing,

"This is sticky, horrible stuff!" he cried as he yanked at it with his hands and a stick.

As Sue struggled to get to her feet everyone heard a loud crack from right above their heads. They all turned to stare up into the trees. There were numerous large spiders making their way down through the branches towards them. Their talking and movement had obviously attracted their attention.

Stevo warned,

"We had better get out of here right now. These things could be capable of anything. They don't look or act like normal spiders. Be careful."

The adrenalin from the search for Sue had kicked in, and Stevo was sweating profusely. Feeling very anxious and on edge due to the big, ugly spiders and the large number of webs around them, the three men readied themselves for anything. They had absolutely no idea of what the spiders were capable of.

Sue was absolutely terrified, her body was trembling uncontrollably. Stevo took his jacket off and wrapped it around Sue in an attempt to warm her up. It was both dark and cold in the dense native bush. Shock and low temperature could lead to her catching hypothermia. "They must think there's something in their web," observed Brent. "They look mean. Let's get out of here. Just walk away towards

the creek slowly. Keep an eye on the spiders."

Stevo kept his arm around Sue to support her, and they moved off together slowly. Brent had his gun aimed at the treetops where the spiders were appearing from.

"These things have got to be venemous," he whispered to Possum. "We need to stay calm and not upset them."

They backed away slowly, taking careful steps without taking their eyes off the spiders for even one second. When they were safe, Stevo and Sue turned and walked a little more quickly towards the creek. "Glad we don't have to hang around here any longer. Don't know how these creatures might react to strangers in their environment," Possum whispered to Brent as they continued walking backwards; watching the spiders who also seemed to be watching their every move. Stevo had a tight grip of Sue's hand and was helping her through the vines and undergrowth. She was traumatised, and still shaking, but was managing to move through the bush with the help of her husband. His desire was to get as far away from the spiders as soon as possible. They backed slowly away, and as soon as they realised they were all safe, they turned and walked as quickly as the undergrowth would let them towards the creek. When they got there, the 4 friends caught their breath, got their bearings, and headed back towards the crash site.

At the same time, up on the ridge above, Janey, Roger, and Heather couldn't sit still.

"Wonder if we should go and look for Sue as well," asked Janey worriedly.

"We should just wait here," said Roger. "It would be worse if we all got lost as well."

"I guess so," replied Janey. "I just feel so helpless sitting here when Sue may be hurt."

"I know how you feel, my sister is missing and there is nothing I can do," said Heather. "Hopefully they will come back here soon, with Sue. It must be really hard to see through the undergrowth."

Orphy was fidgeting and his ears were pricked right the way forward.

"Possum must be nearby," mentioned Heather.

Janey and Heather tried their best to calm the animals by talking kindly to them and scratching behind their ears. Roger was adamant that they shouldn't go down from the ridge, especially after the stern warning from Brent before he charged off into the bush. But Janey was really worried.

"If you are not going to come then you and Heather look after the animals while I go to see where they are."

Roger sighed defeatedly,

"No, I'll come. I've got my rifle." "Right, let's go!"

They had only gone a few steps when Janey saw Stevo helping Sue get to safety. She immediately ran straight over to them, calling back to Heather and Roger who arrived right behind her.

"What on earth happened down here? Where are Brent and Possum?" cried Janey.

"We are all fine, they're just behind us," reassured Stevo. "They won't be long and we'll all head back together towards the plane."

Stevo and Sue kept moving slowly up the ridge. Finally Janey could see Possum and Brent walking up the creek towards them, deep in conversation. Janey ran straight to Brent and threw her arms around his neck and he pulled her into a firm embrace. The look of terror on her face finally began to subside,

"Thank goodness you are all okay!"

"Yeah, I think it is safer out here than in the bush. Janey, there are so many spiders in there, as big as that one we saw in the plane." "Thought we might be dinner for a while," Possum laughed nervously as he headed back towards the plane crash site with a grin on his face.

The relief was tremendous as everyone was feeling safer to be back together and out of the bush.

"I couldn't bear it, not knowing if you were all right or not," Janey squeezed Brent tightly. "I had all sorts of possibilities running through my head."

"There were more spiders than I have ever seen in my life, and they were all banded together. They were huge and ugly. They had legs about 8 inches long and their body size was about the same as an average house cat. They looked as if they could get very mean. I don't like what is going on here Janey. We need to get far away from the crash site." Brent paused, seeing the look on Janey's face. "But for now, we had better catch up to Possum and the others."

Brent continued looking back and into the canopy. Moving quickly, they moved up the ridge to catch up to Possum who was walking with Stevo, Sue, Roger, and Heather. They all hugged each other. Sue had more colour in her face and Stevo could see she was much happier being out of the bush and back into the sunshine.

Heather voiced what was on everyone's mind,

"My God, we're so lucky we are all okay. If someone had been bitten, they could have died. We have no medication to fix anyone, and certainly not for an oversized dose of spider poison!"

Brent grimaced and nodded his head.

"Let's keep going out of here. The sooner we get back to our gear, the sooner we can pack up and get moving."

Nobody disagreed with Brent and they worked their way back through the bush to the crash site, taking extra care whenever they felt a spider web near their face. They all collapsed in a heap next to the wood Brent had begun gathering earlier to add to the fire.

"This bush is certainly full of surprises!" Possum mumbled with a filter in his mouth as he had begun to roll a cigarette.

"Not all of them are good ones, either," Sue trembled.

Reality had hit Sue hard. She was shaking with the shock of what had happened. Janey and Stevo hugged her tightly. Heather wrapped her coat around Sue, over the top of Stevo's and her own in an attempt to raise her body temperature.

"I am not surprised she is shaking," Brent began to put the fire together again to help warm Sue up. "I have never seen spiders like those ones before and I never want to see them again either."

"Why are some so much bigger than others?" Roger asked. Possum, his cigarette dangling from his lips, turned to Roger. "Well, I have actually given it some thought already. And I'm pretty sure it's because the hormones are affecting the spiders the most. Then the spiders climb up to the tops of the trees to get warmth from the sun, which also stimulates their growth. They also shelter under the big rimu branches or other big tree branches to stay dry and warm and this protects them. They need warmth and sunlight to live and only need to go down for their food source – the webs, which are lower down, where it is colder then preserves whatever is trapped. And then on top of that, the small birds and insects they catch and eat have also been drinking water contaminated by the growth hormone."

Brent sat back on his feet, and said,

"They are mainly giant katipos. But I noticed a few other types of spider have also done well on the hormone by the looks of them. There was more than one type of spider in those trees. They looked as if they would eat anything that came into their valley – birds, insects, game animals, and even humans if they were hungry enough and hunting in groups."

Possum looked around at the scared faces of his friends.

"Don't worry, we are safe here. It is more open so there won't be any big spiders, do you think you will be okay, Sue, to walk back?"

"Yeah, I'll be okay, as long as I can have a rest and a cup of tea first." Brent placed the billy over the fire and it wasn't long before it was boiling. Heather made a cuppa and handed one around to everyone while Brent and Stevo checked their rifles.

"I feel a lot safer with a full mag of bullets in this place," smiled Stevo.

Heather commented on how there were very few insects around them as they drank their tea and shared a box of cookies,

"The spiders are so big and hungry they must be devouring everything that flies into their webs."

Roger agreed,

"Yeah, and with the amount of cobwebs that are around here the insects wouldn't have a chance. They would all get tangled up!"

"By the way, how many more barrels did you find when you went down the valley?" asked Brent. "I saw some where we found Sue."

Possum nodded.

"Yeah, there are some there and even more down the creek further. Most of them have burst open or rusted through. They must have really got rolling to get down there."

"The impact of the plane crash would have thrown them for a way, I suppose. The heavy mossy patches and sandy creek would have saved the ones that never burst," Stevo guessed.

Brent looked around at everyone. Sue had stopped shaking.

"I hate to be pushy but we really need to get going as soon as possible. The day is getting on. We'll finish this cup of tea, have something a bit more substantial to eat, and then we really need to head off. We'll take the documents out and contact the police as soon as we get back. I imagine the families of the pilots will be very happy to know where they are so they can recover the bodies and bury them properly. It was real luck we bumped into you Possum, what with you having seen the drums and all. This plane may never have been found if it wasn't for you," said Brent.

"I never even gave it a thought, you guys were the ones to put the pieces together," Possum looked embarrassed by the praise. "I just assumed they were empty and had been dropped from a chopper or something."

After a hearty lunch beside the fire, Sue seemed to have fully recovered. Brent wiped the crumbs from his pants as he spoke,

"Well, we might as well head back to Bullring. We should be there by this time tomorrow. It's mostly downhill."

Sue reminded Brent,

"Hey don't forget, I've got the GPS in my bag."

"That's right," Stevo interjected, "I had forgotten all about that. You might as well get a reading of exactly where we are before we go." "That's a good idea," Janey paused. "Are you sure you are okay, Sue?"

The men put the fire out and had another quick look around to make sure they hadn't missed anything. Stevo went to check the back of the plane out one last time, taking his rifle with him. After a quick inspection he called to the others,

"Just big cobwebs and a few bits of cargo."

Once Sue had got the GPS reading, they were ready to make their way back down to the safety of the Bullring.

CHAPTER THIRTY-THREE

Orphy had been sitting down to rest with the dogs, but he leapt up as soon as Possum gave him a whistle. The group set off with Possum and Orphy leading the way. Blue and Buck had just as eagerly leapt up with full energy, and were bounding around ready for some more action.

"Settle down, boys," warned Possum, "We've got a long walk ahead of us."

Sue, Janey, Heather, and Roger were really struggling to keep up with Possum. He was walking quite quickly as he really wanted them to be far above the crash site before it got dark. It took a lot to make him afraid when he was alone, let alone with a large group of people, but he just couldn't calm himself when the ideas of what might be creeping around in the dark kept running through his mind. He was worried about the spiders becoming more active during the dark of night and he was determined that he and the others would not be around to find out.

Finally, the others reminded him that Sue was still recovering from her concussion and that they would need to take things a little bit easier for a while. They climbed steadily through the beautiful native bush and up the valley away from the crash site with Brent and Stevo bringing up the rear. Roger had to stop and rest his sore ankle every now and again. He used each rest stop as an opportunity to take some awesome photos of the bush.

"You'll be able to publish a book when we get back with all the great shots you have got," encouraged Heather.

"I don't know about that," replied Roger sadly. "I only got a few of those big spiders. I wish I had taken some more."

"Well, we are not going back!" protested Heather vehemently.

"I always really enjoy taking the shots but whether they are good enough to publish, I don't know. We could look into it though." Roger smiled at the thought of having his own book of photography published.

"The only shots I like taking are at pigs and deer," laughed Brent. "Yeah, those shots are pretty memorable!" winked Stevo.

"I know what you mean – well, now that I've seen you guys in action on the boar and then with the Devil Bull. That was pretty cool," admitted Roger.

"Surely there aren't any more massive katipo spiders like that other one around here, are there?" asked Sue.

"I don't think so, Sue. Pretty sure they are only around where that undiluted hormone is," reassured Stevo, doing his best to be honest and alleviate her fears at the same time.

The branches that were overhanging the track had vines curling around them and their thick stems and leaves were all really large. Thankfully there was no sign of the thick webbing as they had moved further up the ridge and away from the valley where the plane had crashed. They also noticed there was a normal amount of insect life buzzing around.

"The birds have got plenty of tucker here," Stevo noticed. "Although, the effects of that stuff are pretty far reaching and it

will probably affect these insects in time too," sighed Possum sadly. "We have no idea how much damage that chemical has done and how much change it has caused over the last ten years. Those big spiders are breeding up large and will be all over this area before too

long," said Stevo.

"Do you think there is any animal life up here that would not have been affected, Possum?" queried Roger as he looked around at the surrounding bush.

"I doubt it. The scientists who come in to check it out after we let them know will have a field day. Determining the amount of damage to the natural environment will keep a team of them busy for years," replied Possum.

They finally broke through the bush line and came out onto the top of the ridge.

"We'll follow this ridge back the way we came," decided Possum. "We might have to make a little detour."

"Why is that, Possum?" worried Sue.

"Oh, you never know what you might come across as you are walking along."

"Not another bloody Devil Bull, I hope," fretted Heather.

"No, don't worry about that," laughed Possum. "He was definitely one of a kind."

They filled their water bottles from the spring at the top of the ridge. Brent and Stevo carried extra water so they could stop a couple of times on their way back for a cup of tea. Sue was beginning to feel really tired. The lump on her head was giving her some trouble. Stevo got a damp cloth and held it up against Sue's bruise.

"I hope this will help, honey," he soothed as he placed one of his arms around her.

"Ahh, that is wonderful dear. It was feeling really hot and I have such a headache."

Janey found some Nurofen and Panadol in the emergency kit and gave two of each to Sue.

They were walking at a steady pace along the ridge when Janey asked, "Is it time for a cuppa yet?"

"Nearly. We've been going for about 3 hours. Another 30 minutes or so and we will be half way back to the top of the spur that leads down to the Bullring."

Stevo thought everyone seemed to have calmed down after their ordeal, possibly aided by the knowledge that they were nearly back to safety.

"Do you reckon we should camp at the top of the spur for the night, Possum?" asked Brent suddenly.

"Sounds like a plan. I had hoped to be back today but I can see we are going to run out of daylight," replied Possum. "I know there is a nice little spot just up here where we can boil the billy."

They tramped on and enjoyed listening to the amazing sounds of the native New Zealand birdlife. Roger had been keeping an eye out and spotted a kingfisher with a green gecko hanging from its beak. He was quick enough to get a good photo of it.

"That'll definitely be one for the book," squeaked Heather with excitement.

Roger just grinned back at her and didn't say anything. There were lots of tomtits fluttering around alongside the odd rifleman. The hike back was comparatively easy and despite their exhaustion they made good time, arriving at the spot where Possum announced it was finally time for that long desired cuppa.

Stevo got the fire going and Brent filled the billy with the water he had carried from the spring at the top of the valley.

"I hope you washed all that spider slime off you, Brent, and none got in the billy water," teased Roger.

Brent smiled,

"Not a drop, Rog. I hate those slimy buggers too." "Feels good to sit down and rest my ankle," said Roger.

"I'm proud of how well you and Sue have coped with the tramp down. You haven't let your injuries hold you back," said Heather.

Roger had untied his laces and was about to pull his boots off. "Might be better to leave them on," Janey suggested. "Just in case

your foot has swollen. You might never get them back on and it would be excruciatingly painful to walk back without them."

"Good thinking, Janey. Thanks," Roger winced as he tied his laces back up. "I will really look after it when we get to camp. We'll heat some water and give it a good soak with a warm rag."

They enjoyed their cuppa and break but weren't able to fully relax. They had to keep moving if they were going to make it to the top of the spur with plenty of daylight.

"Come on," encouraged Brent kindly. "The sooner we get going, the sooner we will be there."

He was trying his hardest to motivate them all and he knew they were feeling exhausted because he was also. Ever since they had left home they'd had nothing but long and exhausting days - with the horse ride into the Bullring, the tramp up to the crash site, and then the finding of the drums. Brent knew the others would be very pleased to finally be able to relax and enjoy nature once setting up properly at the Bullring for a couple of days, and he hoped nothing more would go wrong. Brent thought back to how he thought he has seen some eels with visible teeth. At the time he had thought it to be really strange and dismissed it as perhaps a trick of the light. However, it suddenly dawned on him how the growth promoting hormone may have also caused mutations and other strange side effects in the different animals. Brent stood to his feet after putting the fire out completely, and decided he would let the experts worry about the mutations. He knew there was nothing more to do than share their findings with the Department of Conservation who would then make the right decisions for the protection of the wildlife and their habitat. He looked around at his friends who were doing their best to power on with the huge hike through the untouched wilderness.

"Just keep on walking," Heather whispered quietly to Roger. "Enjoy the wildlife and have your camera ready. You never know what you might see. After some of the things we have seen in the last few days, anything is possible."

"Yeah, you're right, I suppose!" perked up Roger. Nothing made him happier than getting a good photo and telling Heather all about it. "I will try to forget about my stupid ankle and just enjoy the walk,

we must be nearly there."

Brent noticed Roger slowing and reached deep into his bag. He passed around some barley sugars.

"Have a few of these, Roger. They'll give you some energy." "Thanks, Brent. I'm feeling a bit stuffed and really sore." "You're doing really good, mate. Just have a little rest." Stevo called out to Roger,

"Hey Roger, why don't you walk up the front with Possum? That way you will see the birds and insects before we all disturb them. You might get some great photos."

"Thanks Stevo. Good idea," replied Roger happily. Brent knew what Stevo was really trying to do, thinking of Roger. Roger moved forward to walk alongside Possum, and the group carried on along the ridge. The going was fairly easy as they followed the track they had made the day before.

"Stop, shush!" whispered Possum suddenly. "Look!"

Everyone turned to where Possum was pointing to see three native wood pigeons feasting on a miro tree, just off to their left in a catchment - one of which was pure white.

Possum explained,

"This is the only place I have ever seen a pure white native wood pigeon. They would be the rarest bird to see - other than a moa. I've seen this pigeon feeding here before. They pretty much stay in the area where they hatch."

Roger busily clicked away with his camera. It was an awe inspiring sight with the three big birds, especially a rare white one, enjoying the fat berries of one of New Zealand's native trees.

"We will never forget the sights we have seen up here," sighed Janey contentedly. "It's amazing that there are thousands of people out there in the cities who will never see or appreciate sights like this. Those pigeons are so cool and the white wood pigeon is just spectacular."

"I'm so pleased you are enjoying this Janey," prided Brent. "This sort of thing is what makes Stevo and I enjoy hunting so much. You really just never know what you will see out here in the bush."

They walked for another 10 minutes when Possum stopped them again.

"We're going to make a little detour here. There's something I really want to show you. I know you are all very tired and want to get to camp … but I just can't miss showing you this. We may never come back up here again. We can leave our packs here and we will come back to them."

They all looked at each other and smiled, having no idea what it may be that Possum wanted to show them. They took their packs off and followed Possum who led the way to the new discovery. He led them down a small spur on the side of the ridge to where they had to make their own track through. Possum cut the track for them and as they made their way round a bend and over a small drop in the ridge they could suddenly see out. He stopped abruptly, stepping to the side and leaving everyone to stare out in utter amazement. Right in front of them were two of the most massive rimu trees they had ever seen. "Wow!" exclaimed Brent. "In all my time in the bush, I have never seen anything quite like this."

The trees made a perfect mirror images with their identical circumference around their trunks and each with a branch growing at a funny angle about three quarters of the way up on their eastern side. Both trees were exactly the same height and their massive heads towered above the natural podocarp canopy.

"Hey I know, let's all join arms around each tree and see if they are the same size or if my eyes are deceiving me," enticed Stevo.

They walked towards the trees as Possum cut back the undergrowth surrounding the trunks. They linked hands and tried to encircle the first tree. They found that the trunk was so wide they all had to drop hands, and were able to only just touch finger tips to be able to reach around it. Six members of their group of seven was linked around the tree as Roger was busy snapping photos of the amazing sight.

"Okay, let's try the other one," called Brent.

They broke their way through the undergrowth and encircled the trunk of the second tree. Sure enough it took the six of them, again with their arms outstretched and fingers only just touching, to get around it.

"It's as if these trees are twins," admired Possum.

They all looked up the tall trunk of the tree. It was at least 20 metres to where the first branches begun, and each trunk was as straight as an arrow.

"Look at the formation of the branches. I don't think anyone else would have ever seen these trees before, other than me and Orphy. We stumbled across them on one of our possum trips and I have never forgotten them. I am really pleased I could remember where they were. I wasn't one hundred percent sure which is why I didn't point them out on the way up yesterday."

As they looked around, they were amazed at the size of the beautiful matai and kahikatea trees standing alongside many other large rimu located in the stand.

"Our natives really are something incredible," admired Sue.

"Thanks, Possum, for bringing us here and sharing these trees with us." Stevo slapped his friend on his back.

"I am so glad you love it, I was concerned you mightn't think it was worth it since you are all so tired."

"It certainly was worth it, thank you Possum," Janey blew him a kiss and he blushed.

"Yeah, thank you," smiled Brent. "They are truly awesome. There's not many near where we live now and certainly none as big as these, aye Stevo?"

"No way, we have to protect them from too much logging. Who wants a country covered in bloody pines?"

"I can see why people get so involved in groups to save nature," grunted Roger. "When you see sights like this you really appreciate the natural environment."

"Yup!," nodded Stevo. "We'll turn you into a greenie yet Rog, don't you worry!"

They all laughed as they headed back up their freshly made track to where they had left their packs. Possum mused about how resilient they all were; they had just been through the most gruelling experience of their lives and yet they seemed to have already put it behind them and were feeling positive about New Zealand's beautiful native bush. He shook his head and smiled to himself, maybe being with other people wasn't so awful after all, especially people like this lot.

After pulling their packs back onto their backs, they wandered along the track at the top of the ridge and talked about the many natural sights they had seen. The discussion naturally returned to the plane crash and the consequences on the natural environment.

Possum Jack looked sadly around at the bush. "Things will never be quite the same again."

"No," agreed Brent. "But hopefully the damage can be stopped now that we have found what has caused the problem."

"Time will tell, Brent. Time will tell," echoed Possum. "But at least it is only confined to this one catchment."

They made good time as they walked for another two hours along the track to the spot they had found where the ridge met the spur when they had first climbed up from the Bullring.

Brent recognised the mark he had made earlier on a Totara tree just in case they'd gotten lost or couldn't remember where they had come up. They found the small natural clearing and collapsed happily onto the grass as Stevo declared,

"Right, we made it this far, well done guys! I think we should camp here for the night. It's about 4.30 now and we will never make the Bullring by dark. Remember how slippery it was in places? I think it would be asking for trouble."

"Yeah, I agree," confirmed Janey. "We need to be rested before we tackle that track again. I don't know about you guys but I am ready for a rest and a cuppa."

"Yep, I am too!" Brent agreed, stretching his arms high above his head after throwing his pack down. "It will be dark in the bush by about 5.30. It always gets dark earlier than out in the open because of the heavy bush canopy."

The others nodded in agreement and pulled themselves back to their feet and immediately set about sorting a fire and putting up the flies to provide shelter for the night. They organised their sleeping bags while the billy was boiling and managed to finish arranging everything so they could all sit down together around the fire and enjoy their well-earned cups of tea. Blue and Buck explored the area as they were somehow still full of energy, but they didn't come across any signs that excited them and soon returned to sit with the others beside the fire. Orphy seemed very content to stop for a while and he lay down beside Possum and looked up at his best friend as if to say,

"That's enough for today."

Possum scratched Orphy under the chin.

"It's okay old fella, don't worry. We will be staying here tonight and will head for home tomorrow."

The afternoon cooled down as evening approached and there was an icy feel to the breeze. They sat around talking quietly while Roger had a pre-dinner nap. Sue took a couple of panadol and lay down across Stevo's lap. Janey and Heather gathered up the food that was left in everyone's packs and sorted out what they could use for dinner and what they would need to keep for breakfast.

"It will be good to get some fresh fish or pork or venison when we get back to the Bullring," Janey scanned the ingredients hoping she had missed something.

"Yeah, this dried stuff is okay but you can't beat fresh food," agreed Heather with a smile on her face.

"I'd be a bit wary about eating any fish from up here now," worried Heather. "We don't know how those hormones might have contaminated the meat. Hopefully that one we ate on the way up was okay."

"God, we didn't even think about that! It probably will be best to give the fish a miss from now on, poor Roger!" Janey agreed.

Sue joined them and they worked together to pull a dinner together before it got too dark.

"It feels really late but must only be about 6.30," Sue tried to look up through the trees towards the sky.

"Yeah, the bush can trick you like that if you aren't careful. It has fooled Orphy and I a couple of times."

"I think it will be an early night all round," Brent guessed as he looked around at the tired faces of his friends.

As they knocked back a couple of glasses of rum the evening sounds of the bush started. The moreporks were calling to one another and they even heard a Kiwi calling out to its mate. Brent recognised its distinctive call and quietly whispered to the others what it was they were hearing. Once the other birds had all quietened down for the night, Stevo knew it was time to get some sleep.

"Time to hit the sack I reckon!"

"I'll just sit here for a while," stated Possum. "Orphy and I need to think about our next possuming trip – where we will go and for how long. I will see to the fire before I go to sleep."

"Okay, don't have any nightmares about those bloody spiders," laughed Stevo.

"I'm going to sleep with your shotgun," Possum grinned right back at his friend.

CHAPTER THIRTY-FOUR

Dawn broke and Stevo was, as usual, the first one to wake. He quietly climbed out of his sleeping bag and went for a walk a bit further along the ridge they had been following. The bush opened out about 500 metres from where they were camped, and he could see right down to the coast. He told himself he would have to get Roger to come and take a photo as he knew his kids would never believe it if he tried to describe it to them. He walked on a little further before turning back towards camp. He looked for any sign of pigs or deer but couldn't see any fresh marks. He realised Blue and Buck weren't just tired and that there really hadn't been anything around recently. As he approached camp he could tell from the sounds that the others had woken up. He could also smell the smoke from the fire where Brent had put the billy on for a cuppa. The water they had carried along the ridge was almost gone, but there would be enough for the morning. Brent wasn't particularly worried as he knew they would follow a stream down the spur and be able to get fresh water within an hour of walking.

"What have you been up to?" Brent called as Stevo arrived back to the campsite.

"Just letting you bloody sleepyheads get a bit more beauty sleep." Stevo looked around the others. He laughed, "Some of you certainly need it more than others!"

"Janey likes my early morning rugged look, don't you dear?" Brent laughed.

"Sure I do honey," replied Janey sleepily. "It hasn't changed much since I first met you."

"Just a little bit greyer now aye Janey?" quipped Stevo.

"Hey now, enough of that mate, shit what is this? Attack me day?" Brent held his hands up in defense laughing all the while.

Sue had made them each a cup of tea and they sat closely around the fire to drink it as there was still a cold sting to the morning breeze.

Stevo kissed Sue on the forehead. "That bruise looks a lot better, love." Sue held her hand up to touch it. "Yeah, Janey said it is healing okay."

They decided to set off for the Bullring as soon as they finished breakfast. It wouldn't be a long trip but they knew they would have to be a bit careful in places. Heather was massaging Roger's ankle with one hand as she held her cup of tea in the other. With a grimace on his face, Roger said, "My ankle is feeling better from resting it last night. I hope it will be fine for the rest of the tramp back to camp."

"It sure looks better than it did last night, not as swollen," said Heather.

Buck and Blue had been off exploring while the others ate breakfast but they came back as soon as Brent called for them.

"There can't have been any deer or poaka nearby recently or the dogs would have been onto them," Brent said to Stevo.

"No," sighed Stevo. "I didn't see any sign when I went for my walk this morning either. Hopefully we will have success up Secret Creek. Do you think we will still have time to go for a hunt? Or should we head straight back to talk to the Department of Conservation?"

Brent looked over at his friend and gave a cheeky grin,

"Well, it's not as if a couple more days are going to make a huge difference when it comes to those drums. I mean, they have been there for years. We'll be back at the Bullring well before lunch today and we will be able to get the girls and Roger set up. There would still be time for us to go hunting first thing in the morning tomorrow; I think Roger should rest his ankle for a bit before riding out anyway." Stevo grinned, loving the way his best friend looked at the situation.

"But do you think they will be okay on their own?"

"Of course they will," scoffed Brent. "We'll only be gone overnight.

They can't get into too much trouble in that time, can they?" Janey had come up to Brent and Stevo while they were talking.

"Who is not going to get into trouble?"

"You aren't. We were just talking about our Secret Creek hunt and whether or not we should still go ahead with it dear - we hope you can cope on your own without us."

"Of course, you should go. We will be happy to just sleep, eat, and swim for a couple of days. You guys are more than welcome to another day's tramping in the bush, I am not up for it and I know for a fact neither is Roger and that ankle of his."

"If we get the big stag it will all be worth it." Stevo licked his lips and grinned at his two best friends.

They packed their sleeping bags into their packs and made sure the fire was completely out. The group headed down the spur with Possum and Orphy leading the way again. They followed the exact same track they had come up and as the going was very steep in places, they had to be careful with every single step they took. The supple jack was useful as a hand hold. Roger was moving along very slowly as he was being extra careful; he really didn't want to go over on his already damaged ankle.

"I didn't notice on the way up how dense the bush is here," Sue pointed to her left. "Look at all those ponga trees. Their trunks are so close together you couldn't put a track between them even if you wanted to. The fern fronds at the top of the trunks have all grown together!"

"The rimu still towers above all the other trees," sighed Heather. "We really have seen some magnificent specimens on this …" Janey stopped speaking abruptly, losing her footing and slipping on the track. Brent reached an arm out to steady her, but was also very wary of his rifle being knocked. He had been extra careful with it throughout the hike as he didn't want it to accidentally get knocked and put the scope sights out - especially when he and Stevo were about to go on their quest for the big stag up Secret creek. As a result, they both ended up smacking hard down on their backsides in the bush.

"Are you okay?" Heather stifled a laugh.

"I think so," chuckled Brent. "What about you, dear?" Janey giggled.

"Yeah, I'm fine, luckily. I would hate for anyone to have to carry me down from here. All I hurt was my butt. It'll have a good bruise on it that's for sure!"

"Are you okay to keep going?" asked Possum nervously.

"Yeah of course, just give me a second to get up and find my feet again."

They had been going for about an hour when Possum and Orphy stopped all of a sudden and the others pulled up behind them.

"What's up?" panted Roger.

"Look for yourself," pointed Possum.

There was a magnificent tui sitting on a branch of a miro tree just off to their right. It was warbling so loudly it hadn't heard them approach. Roger got a few shots of it with his camera.

"That was good spotting, Possum," admired Stevo.

"You always have to have your eyes everywhere in the bush," shrugged Possum. "You know that, Stevo. A true bushman has his eyes and ears open at all times. He notices anything different or out of the ordinary."

"Yeah, you can miss so much by not being observant. But it all comes easily to a hardened bushman like you, Possum. I need to spend more time in the bush to hone my skills."

They moved on, being careful not to disturb the tui. The bush seemed to be alive with all kinds of bird song. As the day warmed up the sun's rays were shining through the trees yet the track was so slippery in places that they all wished they had shoes like Orphy. He didn't seem to be having any trouble with negotiating the track.

"Perhaps it's because he has four feet to steady him instead of just two," laughed Roger halfheartedly.

Blue and Buck, who had been staying close to Brent's heels for most of the trek, suddenly took off to the left of the track.

"Wonder what they are on to?" asked Possum excitedly. "Don't know, but hopefully they will chase it this way!"

"Look at those pig marks, Brent," Stevo pointed towards the side of the track; in the direction the dogs had disappeared into the bush. "They're huge," remarked Brent. "We had better be ready if they chase that poaka this way."

"Don't worry girls, you're safe with us. We'll be sweet, Devil Bull is well and truly dead," reassured Stevo. "Just take your packs off and be ready to move if you have to."

They suddenly heard the dogs crashing their way through the bush as the sounds of rustling leaves and breaking branches filled the air. The deep bark of one of the dogs was soon joined by the second dog, and Brent and Stevo followed their sound. They used their machetes to cut their way twenty metres through the bush. As Brent cleared some supple jack, Stevo caught sight of the massive black boar that the dogs had baled up against an old rata tree. The ferocious poaka was readying itself to charge at the dogs. Stevo took aim and fired, hitting the boar directly in the shoulder. Brent fired at the same moment and placed a clean shot right through the head.

"Wow," Stevo grinned.

"We didn't expect to get a pig on this trip up to see the drums! Mate, he's a beauty!" said Brent with pride.

Buck and Blue were looking really pleased with themselves and Stevo gave them lots of affection. Brent also gave them a scratch behind the ear and told them what good dogs they were. The men decided to take the head for Brent's trophy room because it really was a magnificent specimen.

"This pork will be tasty for dinner tonight," commented Brent as they cut off the back legs and hind steaks.

Once they had taken as much meat from the animal as they could, keeping a couple of large juicy bones for the dogs, the men made their way back to where the others were waiting on the track.

"Thank God you are okay," Janey's relief was evident in her voice. "We heard two shots and then silence." Sue squeaked. "We

wondered what was going on."

"I was just coming to check you out," added Possum. "But I didn't like to leave the girls and Roger on their own."

"Thanks for not leaving them," Brent smiled at Possum as he wrapped an arm around Janey and pulled her tightly towards him.

"We've got some nice fresh pork for dinner tonight." Stevo held up the meat to show everyone.

"Yum!" Roger licked his lips before turning to admire the head. "Man look at those tusks, they would tear you in two if he got a hold of you."

"That's for certain!" Brent laughed before adding, "hey, let's get going back to camp aye? How much further do you reckon we've got to go, Possum?"

"I think if we keep up this pace we should be at the Bullring in about an hour."

"Cool," sighed Heather with relief. "Let's just hurry up and go so we can get there!"

The group moved off eagerly down the track after sharing the load of the pork between each of their packs. "Hey Brent, look at Blue and Buck. They are almost smiling," Heather grinned.

"They know each other well," replied Brent. "They are best mates after all."

The going wasn't quite so steep as Possum had led them down a little side creek towards the main river. They stopped for a rest and to catch their breath.

"Half an hour and we'll be back down at the Bullring," Possum estimated. "I feel like I can sleep in peace tonight, now that I finally understand why the eels in this river are so big."

"Yeah, it all makes sense now we know what has been leaking from those drums," agreed Stevo.

"I hope the damage to the wildlife is not permanent," Janey looked grim. "I would hate to think these eels were so big they were eating everything they came across just to survive, especially since they would eventually deplete their food source."

"Yeah, we've already seen how quickly they can turn on each other. It would be a real shame if things became extinct or endangered because of that plane crash," Sue worried.

"We'll have to leave all of that to the experts, they will know what to do," reassured Brent. "We've done the best we possibly can by finding the crash site and the drums. Hopefully the GPS recording is right, cos that is what everything will rely on now."

Sue looked over at Brent with her eyes widening in fear,

"Oh God! I hope it's ok. I took the reading and I'm pretty sure I know what I am doing … But what if it isn't?"

"It's ok Sue, I know you did it perfectly. And anyway, they'd now find it regardless because we could always lead them in. I'm only having you on," replied Brent with a wink.

Orphy had perked up and seemed to have a completely new lease on life. He was trying to speed up the humans and Possum had to keep calling him back to join the group. His nostrils flared, he pricked up his ears, and he pointed his tail high in the air.

"What's up with Orphy?" Roger turned to Possum.

"I think he can smell the other horses," guessed Possum.

He had no sooner said this when Orphy took off with such an enthusiastic exuberance that there was absolutely no holding him back.

"He can smell that mare on heat," laughed Possum. "He is so excited he would beat us home and have the time to set up the camp

if he physically could!"

They all laughed as they carried on down the river to where the bush opened out into the horse paddock clearing.

"Sure enough, Orphy beat us here," winked Possum. "He looks as happy as a sand boy," teased Brent.

"I guess he is," smiled Possum.

"I hope Big Red doesn't take offence,' Brent suddenly thought aloud. Orphy had easily cleared the barbed wire with a brisk jump and landed inside the horse paddock where he was very happily sniffing around Lightning. Big Red paid no interest; most likely dismissing

him as no threat due to Orphy's tiny size.

Everyone was really happy to have finally made it back to the Bullring; it already felt like their home away from home.

"Thank goodness we are home, I will be glad to take off these tramping boots," said Janey.

"Sure feels good to be back here," said Heather.

They dropped their packs and slumped down onto the grass. With the warmth of the sun it really was a perfect spot.

"Our gear looks as if it hasn't been touched," Stevo announced as he came back from where he had stowed it.

"That's great," Possum nodded his head. "I thought it would be as safe as houses here. Bushmen usually tend to respect one another's property. They know how survival can depend on it."

"Yeah, we have learnt lots about survival during this trip," added Heather. "And I know I surely won't survive unless I go wash my hair and have a wash!"

"Me too," laughed Sue. Janey nodded in agreement.

"You boys are looking a bit different with all those whiskers. I think your bush look is really good. It makes you even more handsome."

"Is that right?" Brent chuckled as he wrapped his arm around Janey and gave her a whisker rub on the side of her face, followed by a big kiss.

The girls moved off to have their wash as Brent gathered some wood for a fire. It wasn't long before the billy was boiling for yet another much wanted cup of tea. Stevo congratulated them all on achieving such a big walk. He shook Roger's hand and pulled him in for a large manly hug.

"What's that for?" asked Roger with a grin. "It was just like a Sunday stroll. I didn't realise we were going to have so many stops."

Everyone laughed as Stevo slapped Roger on the back.

"It was a very successful mission and your photos are going to be a great help Rog."

"Yeah," agreed Brent. "We got to the bottom of the problem with the environment."

"There will be a lot of people who will be very interested in what we have to tell them," Stevo surmised. "Those government departments will be falling over themselves to get the information we've got."

"We could make a fortune with what we know – hey, we could even sell our story!" said Roger. "I can see the dollar signs!"

"I'm just happy our bush and wildlife is not going to suffer much more once it is all cleaned up and those drums are taken out," laughed Brent.

"Things will start to improve then," agreed Possum. "Once they get those growth hormones under control."

The girls had re-joined the others.

"It is such an amazing feeling knowing that we have been way up to the crash site and found the cause of the changes in the wild life," said Janey.

"It was a tough walk and some of those experiences won't be easily forgotten," cringed Sue.

"There were some hair raising moments but let's focus on the successes," said Stevo.

"It still feels really unreal, like we were in a movie," replied Sue. "Oh, it is real all right," said Brent. "We have really good info to

share with the authorities. Roger, hope your photos are all ok."

"I'll check them out, no reason they shouldn't be very clear," said Roger. "It was a gruelling hike in places but we are safe and sound now at Bullring."

CHAPTER THIRTY-FIVE

They removed their gear from where they had hidden it amongst the bushes. The girls got busy organising some food while the boys set about putting up the tents. They sat around the fire enjoying their lunch, and Brent and Stevo began discussing their hunting trip up Secret Creek.

"I wonder if there are any possums up there. There aren't many in this area. It's been pretty well cleaned out," mused Possum Jack.

"Do you want to come with us, Possum?" offered Stevo.

"No thanks, Orphy and I need to get back to the hut and check on those skins we left drying. My plan is to head out to my coastal block and check on everything. I haven't been home for so long and I do really enjoy the winter down there."

"Where's your block, Possum?" Sue piped up.

"About 30 minutes' drive from where you left the trucks. It's my little bit of paradise. I've got a few sheep and a pig wandering around there – oh, and a beefy ready for the freezer. My neighbour keeps an eye on things while I am away. I've got some great fishing spots down there. You can catch blue maumau right off the rock shelf on the high tide mark. It drops away in places to about 100 feet and you can catch kingfish if you burley them up. I drop a cray pot off the rock shelf and usually bring up a good one or two. You'll all have to come for a visit."

"Sounds like heaven Possum!" Janey enthused.

"I have got all sorts of native trees growing on my boundary – Ti tree, Kanuka, and Pohutukawa to name just a few."

"I think we will definitely have to come and check it out," agreed Heather.

Brent and Stevo explained to the girls and Roger how their plan was to head off at about 10 in the morning in order to get up their secret creek in time for an evening hunt. They planned to do a morning hunt the following day before returning to the main camp to meet up with everybody by lunchtime.

"Are you sure it will be all right to leave these injured soldiers here for a night?" worried Possum.

"They'll be sweet," smiled Stevo, rubbing Sue's back gently. "Maybe I could come with you, "Janey hinted. Looking around her

friends, she added, "No, on second thoughts that isn't a good idea. It would be good to keep an eye on Sue and Roger's injuries. I am sure we will be safe. I just hate being away from you, Brent."

"I know," replied Brent as he hugged her tightly. "You're right, though. This is the best place for you."

"I know how you feel," said Sue.

"We'll just hang out here and rest, we'll be fine," said Heather. "Just make sure you bring back the magnificent stag head," said

Janey. The more they discussed it, the safer they felt.

Possum reassured them,

"One of the very few things that could happen is the river could flood. But with such clear blue skies I wouldn't worry, there really isn't much possibility of that."

"And we haven't seen any of those giant spiders since we left the crash site …" Heather trailed off.

"Yes, I think it's safe to say they are only up where the chemical is so concentrated," Possum agreed.

Stevo quipped,

"The only other thing that could happen is a big hata or boar might come running into camp and Roger has to shoot it with his 303."

The gun, which had been a gift from Roger's grandfather, looked like it had gone to every war on the planet; it was covered with scratches and the wood was well worn from being held.

Roger replied indignantly,

"If a big stag or boar runs through here, you can guarantee it won't survive to run out the other side of the camp."

Everyone smiled at Roger's enthusiasm. Brent knew deep down that Roger would surely miss any shot he took. Stevo asked Roger if he had more bullets with him.

"Don't you worry mate. My gun will be more than ready when the big hata or poaka runs through here while you two are playing hunting games up your Secret Creek." He laughed as he spoke but reached into his pocket and pulled out a few bullets to reassure Stevo that he was well supplied with ammunition.

"Well, then you had better load up your mag and be ready for those boars and stags to run through in the night!" Brent picked up the old 303, took the bolt out and looked down the barrel.

The barrel looked spotless and Brent was impressed as he put the bolt back in and popped the mag out.

"Give us a feel of those bullets, Roger. I'll load her up for you." Roger handed Brent the bullets.

"Hey where did you buy these bullets from Roger? These are old solids!"

Roger replied meekly,

"They are out of one of the old boxes I got off Granddad when he gave me the gun."

"You need to get some better bullets than these if you want to shoot deer and pigs. These are just for target practice."

"Ahh, I am sure they'll do just fine for this trip. I'll leave the serious hunting up to you guys. However, I will deal to any deer or pig that comes into the camp and you will see the evidence hanging in the tree when you come back. We'll be well fed, if the wildlife comes near."

Everyone chuckled, including Roger.

"Hopefully Stevo and I will return with the 18 pointer stag head my chopper mate saw. It's right up in the headwaters of secret creek apparently," grinned Brent slyly.

"What's the secret of secret creek?" inquired Heather.

"If it wasn't secret, there would be no 18 pointers up there!"

Stevo explained that the mouth of their secret creek lay about 500 metres upriver from the Bullring.

"You don't notice the creek coming out into the main river because it goes underground about 100 metres inland up from the river before running down an old ryolite seam underground and coming out into the big pool up there. So we call it Secret Creek, because you wouldn't even know it was there!"

"I know what you mean," nodded Possum. "I've actually noticed one other creek do that. I've never possumed up in that area though because for a long time there was another trapper doing that piece of the country. You know how it is, we try to keep to our own areas. It's one of those unwritten rules."

The others looked intrigued by the idea of an underground creek. "We'll wander up after you have gone in the morning and check that out aye guys?" Sue turned to the others to see if they were interested in having a look too.

Stevo explained how they could dive down into the pool and feel the current hitting them in the face from where the creek exploded into the pool.

"That is the most natural spa you will ever get," added Brent with a wink as he saw the smiles grow on the girls' faces.

"A spa you say? That could be good for my ankle," piped up one keen voice.

"Yeah, but don't sit down on any rocks with that big septic blister on your butt Roger boy, you'll make it worse," warned Stevo. "And watch out for those eels!"

The afternoon slipped away and before they knew it, early evening was upon them.

"I'll sort out some more wood for the fire with the girls. Could you please check the horses are okay, Stevo? Hope they haven't got sore feet or any cuts," Brent worried. "Roger could please you start to get some dinner sorted? We've got that fresh pork."

"Sounds like a plan," replied Stevo.

"Suits me fine," said Roger. "My feet will appreciate not going too far."

"Where do you want to sleep, Possum?" asked Brent.

"Don't worry about me. Orphy and I will just kip down by the fire." Roger stoked up the fire and then grabbed the pork steaks, tossing them onto the steel barbecue plate to sizzle. Stevo was about to head for the horse paddock when he noticed Sue wasn't going on the search for wood.

"Are you ok, love?" he asked Sue.

"Yes, just feeling a bit woozy after the bang on my head," replied Sue. "Why don't you snuggle up in your sleeping bag for a while and rest?" Stevo asked.

"That would be lovely," said Sue.

He grabbed it for her and she willingly snuggled inside it and sat beside the fire.

Brent and Stevo led the horses' one at a time down to the river to give them a bit of exercise as Big Red was chomping at the bit to get moving.

"Easy boy," calmed Brent. "You'll need all of your energy for tomorrow."

"Do you think we should still do this hunt?" Stevo asked.

"I've been thinking the same thing, but we did come here for this. And Sue and Roger will be safe with Janey - she is a nurse after all. If anything, they are better off with her than they are with us. This is her field, not ours."

"Yeah, you're right. Just have a niggling feeling, that's all. But you're right, we are here for that 18 pointer. Maybe I'm just anxious to get out of here and get what's going wrong up here sorted."

"You're right, it's unfinished until we get out and get it sorted so things can improve in this catchment. But we still have time to have a quick look for that big stag and I'm sure there will be more than one." With the flames leaping high, the pork was soon cooked, and the delicious steaks were being eaten straight from the pan. The wood pile was stacked high, the beds were organised inside the tents, and Blue and Buck were tied up for the night. Orphy seemed to Possum to be more than happy to be in the horse paddock with the other horses until the morning. Possum laughed, "I guess I'll have to sleep on my own by the fire." The others were laughing as it really was quite a funny sight to see how Big Red and the other horses just ignored Orphy as he ran around the paddock with his chest puffed out. He seemed to be trying to impress the other horses. Brent pulled out the bottle of rum after they had cleaned up after dinner and poured everyone a straight shot or two. He apologised for not having any more coke, but assured everyone that Black Heart was okay straight; in fact quite tasty. They enjoyed a few rums but made sure not to empty the bottle so Brent and Stevo had some left to take up Secret Creek. Janey and Brent snuggled into each other's arms, Sue and Stevo cuddled up, and Heather and Roger wrapped their arms around each other.

Possum looked over at the loved up couples.

"I think it is time for me to catch 40 winks." With that, he promptly disappeared into his sleeping bag.

The evening was beautiful and calm and the moreporks were calling to each other with their unique sounds. Without warning, they heard a shrill screech far in the distance.

"What's that?" shrieked Heather, cuddling into Roger's arms even deeper.

"Don't worry, Heather. It's only a kiwi bird calling to its mate," Stevo informed them.

Janey turned to Stevo and Brent.

"Hey, you guys haven't packed your gear for tomorrow."

"We'll do it in the morning, first thing. Stevo is always up really early. We'll take Red and Stormy and leave Blue and Buck with you. We only need our sleeping bags and enough food for the night and the following morning," explained Brent.

It was starting to get late and there were a few yawns beginning to make their way around the group.

Stevo stood up.

"We had better get some sleep, Brent. It's going to be a long day tomorrow."

"OK you guys, no competitions tonight to see who can make the most noise," laughed Roger.

"We'll lose; Sue and I are far too tired," said Stevo.

"I'm just grateful we are all here safely," sighed Brent. "I really had my doubts for a while there."

"I know what you mean," agreed Stevo, hugging Sue more tightly and placing a kiss on her forehead.

"You never really know what surprises the bush has in store for you," Brent murmured as he checked the billy to see if the water he had put on was boiling yet. "Anyone want a quick cup of tea before we hit the sack?"

Janey and Brent always enjoyed a cup of tea together before going to bed. It was one of the little rituals they had enjoyed throughout their married life. Possum was already snoring as the six of them sat quietly and drank their cup of tea. The noises of the bush quietened as it settled down for the night. A peaceful calm had descended over the campers and the bush surrounding them.

"I am still so glad I came on this trip," smiled Roger. "This peace and quiet makes all the blisters and sore muscles worthwhile."

"How are those blisters, Rog?" enquired Stevo.

"They are all right. Heather has been putting some cream on them every night."

Everyone grinned as Roger quickly became embarrassed,

"Well you enjoy your butt rub Roger, it's definitely bed time for me," laughed Brent as he and Janey made their way into their tent.

CHAPTER THIRTY-SIX

The following morning the sparrows and the tuis were singing loudly. Stevo stoked up the fire and let the dogs off for a run, knowing they would probably run over and lick Brent on the face. Sure enough, within seconds, Stevo saw Brent sit bolt upright while trying to restrain two wet tongues from being his morning washcloth. The noise and motion woke Janey too.

"Ooo, Brent. I won't be kissing you for a week!"

Brent grinned, rolled over, and pulled Janey towards him and gave her a great big kiss. The dogs both began yelping and began to join in, licking both of their faces until all attention was given to scratching behind their ears.

Stevo moved off towards the horse paddock with a smile, he planned to saddle up the two horses before getting his hunting gear ready.

Possum and Orphy had woken with the commotion and were nearly organised and ready to go.

"What about breakfast?"

"No thanks, I want to get going. I'll get something down the track. I need to head up a spur to check some possum lines that I set there. That will take me a while and I want to be back at my camp well before dark."

Janey already had the billy boiling so there was time for Possum to join them for a quick cup of tea.

"Thanks for all your help, Possum." Brent shook his old friend's hand.

"No worries! I have no doubt we will be seeing each other again very soon."

"Yeah, thanks mate. We'll keep you informed about what happens with the plane and the drums," reassured Stevo.

"Well, it has certainly been an experience catching up with you guys again - and such a pleasure to meet the rest of you. Please say farewell to Roger and Heather for me when they wake up. Good luck with the hunting boys!"

Janey and Sue gave Possum a hug and wished him well; waving as he and Orphy headed off down the river. Before long they had put some distance between themselves and the campers and were just silhouettes against the blue sky of the early morning.

Janey then got stuck into making breakfast.

"You guys will need a decent feed. You have got a big day ahead of you."

As she fried up the fresh steaks in the pan, voices were heard from Heather and Roger's tent. Heather was agreeing with Roger that the blisters on his backside from their ride up appeared to have become slightly infected.

Janey walked right over to Roger and Heather's tent and called, "I think I need to check those blisters out Roger. You know I am a nurse. I am getting a little worried about them. They should have healed up by now."

The zip opened and Roger's face emerged. Janey noticed he had flushed bright red, but Heather looked at him kindly.

"Don't be embarrassed dear. Janey has seen it all before."

"Trust me Roger. I really have seen it all - and more. Turn yourself over and pull your pants down, *now please.*"

He sighed and gave in. Janey was the one who would know best about infection. He pulled his pants down reluctantly, just far enough for Janey to see the blisters.

"Just as I thought. One of the blisters has become infected," said Janey. She winced knowing how sore it would be for Roger.

"Hang on there for a minute okay. One is really red and I think there is an infection in the other large one. I'll just get the first aid kit out of Bessie's pack saddle."

When she returned, she said, "Don't worry, I'll be gentle. But you will have to keep off this, Roger. There will be no sitting down for you all day today or you'll be walking out of here instead of riding! We need to give it some time to heal."

Brent and Stevo had finished cooking the breakfast while Janey was administering to Roger's blisters. All except Roger sat around to enjoy it;

Roger leant against a tree so as to follow nurse's orders and keep weight off the blistered area.

Big Red and Stormy were all packed up and Brent and Stevo were ready to head off.

Stevo turned to the others.

"Let's have a last brew before we go! What are you guys going to do today?"

"I'm going to get into the book I brought with me," Janey said blissfully.

"With swimming and sunbathing, I think we will fill in our day, no worries," added Sue.

"Roger and I will be taking it very easy, lazing around camp," Heather smiled.

"Could you please make sure you chain the dogs up tonight? I have tied them up again for now, but if you give us about an hour head start then they can be let off and they won't come after us," advised Brent.

The horses were pawing the ground and looking like they wanted to get moving. "Have fun while we are away you lot. Hey, Roger, look out for those big eels if you go skinny-dipping or you might end up missing a few bits, especially with those blisters. They might attract the eels," laughed Stevo.

Sue and Janey gave their husbands one last cuddle before they mounted their horses.

"You be careful out there," whispered Janey. "I miss you already." Holding her tightly, Brent whispered into his wife's hair that he loved her. He knew exactly how she was feeling as he felt the same way.

Mounting his horse, Brent called,

"Hey, Stevo, are you ready yet? The big hata is waiting for us." "I was born ready," quipped Stevo.

And with that, the men kicked off and the horses eagerly moved forward. Janey, Sue, Heather, and Roger wandered out to the edge of the river to watch as Brent and Stevo headed up the river towards Secret Creek.

CHAPTER THIRTY-SEVEN

That same morning, three tired young brothers had not woken up early. Jake and Luke were tired after their two days of hunting, early rises, and late night drinking sprees. Slade had also slept in because he had been awake until well after the sun had begun to climb above the horizon.

By the time the boys got up, the sun was high above their heads and shining right down through the trees and into their camp. Jake woke first and stirred the fire to cook some venison back steaks for breakfast. He put the billy on to boil for a cup of tea. Luke and Slade stirred in their sleeping bags as Jake stirred the fire.

"Morning Jake," greeted Luke, shielding the sun from shining in his eyes. "Man, that sun's bright!"

"Considering it is nearly 9 o'clock I'm not surprised," laughed Jake. "We all slept in, but it'll be a great day by the look of it."

"Sounds like a good day for hunting aye boys?" piped up Slade cheerily.

Luke and Slade leaped out of bed and they all rolled their sleeping bags up and readied themselves for the next part of their trip. They enjoyed a hearty breakfast and discussed what they planned to do for the day. Jake looked over at Slade and noticed he was looking better than expected, considering he had been awake all night. He figured his brother had taken something this morning to take the edge off the comedown.

Luke laughed,

"Yeah, let's head up to the Bullring today. I reckon I'm gonna get the biggest stag of all up there."

"Yeah, well you might be lucky," laughed Slade. "Can't wait to get moving now aye!"

"To the Bullring it is then!" Jake cheered.

Jake took a quick look at the two tia they had hung in the tree, just to make sure the sun couldn't shine on them and make the meat go off. He got his cell phone out and took a couple of photos of the heads.

"Do you boys want to come and get a photo?" Slade was already mounted on his horse.

"Nah, let's do that on the way back when we have all three!"

Jake was holding the reins of his and Luke's horses and he led them both over to where Luke was standing. They made sure the fire was out safely and packed the last of the gear onto the horses so they were all ready to ride.

They wound their way up the river, looking for signs of life as they passed an old possumer's hut.

"Nobody home," called Luke. "But it looks like he has been here recently though."

'There's a lot of horse sign here. Those other riders must have stopped here," guessed Luke.

"Yea, bet it was those same hunters that got the big boar we saw down the river," offered Slade.

Jake grunted.

"Hope they haven't stopped at the Bullring and have gone on up to the Green River country. I will be pissed off if they did stop."

"I bet they have already shot everything that has been roaring around the Bullring!" Luke replied. He was really annoyed at the thought he might miss out on his stag.

Because the boys had lived on the Coast all of their lives, to them the river and hunting possie was theirs; anyone else was just an uninvited visitor.

"There's no point getting yourself worked up, boys. We'll just go and check it out," Slade advised.

As they continued to ride up the river they passed a big pool where a movement in the water caught Jake's eye. He turned his horse toward the pool to try to see what it could be.

Slade and Luke had stopped.

"What's up, Jake?"

"I saw something really big moving in the water. I want to try and see what it was," he paused as he tried to peer deeper into the water. "Holy shit! Come and look at this!"

Floating near the boulder towards the side of the pool was a three metre long eel. It was the biggest eel any of the boys had ever seen. Jake's jaw dropped open in amazement. The more they looked, the more they could make out others swimming in circles deeper down in the pool.

"I can't believe the size of these eels! They look funny too; different to the ones we catch," observed Luke.

"What do you mean, different?"

"They have got odd looking markings along their sides. The normal eels we catch are just black and slimy."

"Well, they must have been feeding on some good tucker because they are massive!"

Jake tried to get a photo.

"You would need a bloody strong fishing line to catch one of them.

Don't think I would like to go upsetting them that's for sure!"

They moved off up the river, Luke was riding in front with Hone's 303 just in case a hata or poaka was nearby.

"It's not that far to the Bullring now," Jake advised them. "We'll be there really soon."

As the boys emerged from the gorgy piece which lay before the Bullring part of the river, they talked eagerly about the best camp site and how it lay in the high corner on the opposite bank from the river. They knew it well and knew they would be safe there from any river floods. They hoped they wouldn't see any smoke from a fire, and that the other group of hunters had gone on further; leaving the Bullring for the three brothers to enjoy. As they got closer to the campsite, they began straining their eyes to see ahead of them to see if any one else was there. Disappointment soon washed over each of them as they saw smoke drifting lazily from a fire surrounded by a group of people. "Look at that," pointed Jake. "Must be the hunters who killed the boar we saw down the river. They have camped here at the Bullring after all, those bastards!"

They carried on towards the camp and were soon close enough to smell the smoke. As they rode up they saw three women and a man walk out to the bank of the river which lay further back from the main part of the river. The bank with the camp on it only ever saw water when the river flooded in major storms. As the boys pulled up an attractive woman in her very early forties approached them.

"Hi boys, have you had a good ride?"

Luke shuffled in his saddle, trying to lose his anger at being beaten to their favourite camping spot.

He said,

"Yeah, thanks. We have." "Have you come far today?" Jake responded,

"Yeah, we have come quite a way."

Slade flicked his eye lashes as he looked around at their camp. He didn't say anything. He noticed there were only four horses and four sleeping bags rolled up under a fly tent and that the fire remained in exactly the same place as he remembered.

"Just the perfect place for a fire at this campsite," he mumbled under his breath.

"Would you like a cuppa? My name's Janey."

Janey was feeling a bit nervous with the three strangers focusing their eyes on her and was at a loss for anything else to say.

Luke managed to say,

"No thanks. We just had a cuppa a bit further down the river." Janey continued trying to be friendly.

"Where are you heading?"

Jake thought how she asked a lot of questions but replied anyway, "We are not sure now. We were coming here but it looks a bit

crowded. Who said you could stay on our land?"

His brothers turned their heads to look at him with a smile. Their brother had seized the opportunity to have a bit of a wind up. They could see he was annoyed at not being able to stay at the Bullring.

Roger stepped forward. All he could think to say was,

"I thought this was Department of Conservation land, sir." Jake laughed with a sneer,

"Nobody has ever called me sir before."

Roger didn't quite know how to reply so kept his mouth shut to avoid further confrontation.

Heather was surprised and exclaimed,

"Is this private land? Because on the map we got with our hunting permits, it clearly shows this is public land."

"No, it's not really public land as our Māori family have the rights over it," lied Jake easily.

Slade finally spoke,

"Looks like you got it sussed with three women up here, *sir*. Big camera you got there."

Slade smiled dryly. He had noticed there was only one male with three females and was amused by the reasons he could think of for bringing such a big camera. Jake could easily see that Roger was out of place in the bush. He had very pale skin; indicating he worked inside, and his clothing was more what a fisherman would wear, not a hunter. He also knew fishermen didn't usually come this far up as they could easily catch trout miles down the river. Slade mused as to why Roger would be up here with three women and was confused by his very polite manner and general demeanour; either way they all knew he was out of place.

"That guy seems out of place up here," commented Slade quietly to Luke who had ridden up beside him.

"Takes all sorts," chuckled Luke in reply.

Janey was a bit concerned at the attitude of the boys, especially the one who hadn't said much; the one with the large nasty looking tattoo on his forearm. She felt herself wishing that Brent was still there; he would surely know how to talk to these guys. Heather and Sue were looking down the river and feigning interest in the scenery as the conversation had dried up. Slade's mannerisms, with his facial expressions and piercing eyes, were making her feel quite uneasy. No one quite seemed to know what to say or do next.

Janey was thinking about telling the boys about what they had found out about the drums and asking them if they had met Possum Jack on their way up the river. They had made her feel uncomfortable when they appeared antagonised by finding people camping in their spot so Janey decided she would get Brent to tell them about the drums when returned the following day. Despite the boy's hostility towards her and the others, she did not want them to get hurt or be in danger from the contaminated waterways. Jake asked if it was them who had caught the big poaka down the river.

"Yeah, it really made our day, getting that mighty boar," beamed Roger.

"My husband and his mate got it using the dogs. They worked really well," prided Janey.

"It sure is a beauty," admired Luke. "They must be good dogs." "Sure are," agreed Roger.

Jake looked at his brothers before turning back to face Janey.

"I don't think there is room here for all of us. We'll go and camp further up the river. There must be some other good spots."

"My husband and his friend are out hunting. You might see them because they headed off in that direction." Janey pointed further up the river. She did not know why she didn't want to say that they were going to be away for the night.

Slade rolled his eyes. "Sure they are lady."

He looked in the direction of the four horses and four sleeping bags. He raised his eyebrows indicating he presumed she was making up the story about the hunters.

"Come on you guys. Time to go." "Ka kite ano, see ya," scoffed Jake.

"See you later," called out Luke as they headed off up the river.

As they moved off Janey gave a little wave. She was quite shaken by the boys' behaviour and was relieved that they had left without too much trouble. As she turned to the others, she put on a brave face.

"Well, seeing as they don't want a cup of tea there is all the more for us."

She walked off towards the fire where she could hear the billy boiling happily. Looking up towards Secret Creek Janey she wished again that Brent would come back as she felt really uneasy.

Roger, Sue, and Heather joined Janey at the fire.

"They weren't a very friendly bunch, were they?" Roger stated. "In fact, those young men were very rude."

Heather nodded her head.

"I hope we don't see them again. They seemed upset we had taken their campsite and might be spoiling their hunting."

"Yeah, very rude fellas," agreed Sue.

She had been very quiet the whole time. Janey had a grim look on her face, she couldn't shake the feeling that the one boy with the awful snake tattoo had sent shivering through her veins.

CHAPTER THIRTY-EIGHT

The boys moved off up the river to find a different camping spot. They found a nice little clearing not too much further up the river and decided to set up camp and have some lunch before heading off on an afternoon hunt.

As they sat around cooking lunch, Jake blurted angrily,

"Who do they think they are? They are camping in the Bullring and we are up here in this stink spot."

"What's wrong with this camp?" Luke questioned as he was the one who had chosen the spot where they should stop for the night.

"Not much grass for the horses and the river is real noisy here!" Slade kicked at the ashes angrily. "Yeah who are they? That guy's got the best camp - and all the women." Slade already had a grudge against Roger despite only having met him briefly.

"Oi, stop it guys, chill. Where are we going for our next hunt?" Luke tried to distract his brothers. "I remember this next side creek up from here is not bad going. I have seen plenty of tia sign up there at other times when we were pig hunting it."

Slade sighed,

"Why don't we just rest up and go for a hunt in the morning tomorrow? My legs feel a bit stiff from the ride up the river. Might as well crack the rum open?"

"It's a bit early for rum isn't it?" queried Luke. "We should go and get my big stag. We have got a lot of day left yet."

"Nah, not going," Slade laid back on the grass. "I'm resting up." Luke looked over at Jake who just shrugged his shoulders lazily.

Luke gave up and instead set about making a cup of tea, it was still too early for him to have a drink.

CHAPTER THIRTY-NINE

Stevo and Brent arrived at the spot where Secret Creek met the main river. They had to get the horses up a 100 metre gut rising straight out of the river before the secret creek would level out. There was an old cattle track down the gut which had been worn down over the years and was no longer as steep as it used to be which would make it easier for the horses to get up. Brent rode towards the start of the gut and nudged Big Red in the ribs. He leapt up the bank and began climbing hard up the gut. It was really slippery and hard going for the horse, and Brent could hardly hold on as thick branches were hitting him from all directions. Stevo was following right behind on Stormy. By the time the horses made it to the top, the sweat was pouring profusely off both of them so they decided they would find a spot to stop and give them a bit of a rest. At the top of the gut lay a grassy area where they stopped and looked back over the river and the camp. Brent tried to see if he could make out what the girls were up to, knowing they wouldn't be able to see him because of the scrub. Because he was on his horse he was sitting a bit higher and could see over the trees and the shrubbery. As Brent looked out to see what the girls were doing, he noticed three riders emerging from the gorgy part of the river. He pointed them out to Stevo.

"Look, riders. They must be hunters."

"Yeah. We will just watch and see what they do."

From where Brent and Stevo sat perched upon Big Red and Stormy, everything appeared calm at the Bullring. The men watched their group talk for about ten minutes with the group of hunters. As they watched the riders headed off in the same direction Brent and Stevo had gone earlier.

"We'll just wait here to see where they are going and what they look like. They might be some of our old hunting mates," said Brent.

As the riders drew nearer, Stevo and Brent did not recognise any of the three boys and they could see they were all quite young.

"Couple of nice piebald horses they are riding, and that chestnut is not bad either. Proper coasty horses those," confirmed Stevo. "They must be locals by the look of those horses."

The riders came within 400 metres of the two men, and Brent had a good look at the boys through his scope.

"Three blokes; one blonde and two with dark hair. They look really young, and as if they only have the one gun."

"Yeah, and no dogs either. Not much of a hunting party," mocked Stevo.

The boys were moving off up the river at a good pace; it didn't look like they would be back down in a hurry.

"Probably going up to the green river country," guessed Brent. "That'll take them a couple of days and we will be back and long gone by then."

Stevo nodded his head, checking to see that Big Red and Stormy were rested enough to get going again. As they moved off up Secret Creek they knew they had a two hour ride ahead of them before they'd have to stop as the going would get too difficult for the horses to go any further. Secret Creek was laden with very heavy bush on both sides of the valley with the creek meandering down through the middle. There wasn't much chance of shooting a deer on either side of the creek they were riding up because of the dense foliage.

The creek itself had a stony bottom and the water was trickling busily downstream. The sun was shining through the trees and Brent thought to himself how it really was the most beautiful creek in the world. The valley floor was virtually flat with the pristine creek running straight down the middle as it followed a course that the water had shaped over millions of years. The banks were quite steep in places where the powerful water had eaten away at the land during torrential downpours.

After following the creek bed deeper into the lush native bush, they finally arrived at the place where they would stop with the horses and set up camp. There had been some slips to negotiate and the going had been quite hard as they made their way up and the horses were looking very tired.

"Wonder what the girls are up to? Do you think they are in that spa yet?" Brent asked Stevo as he passed him his cup of tea.

"I think they will be very relaxed and having a great time enjoying the sun and the water," grinned Stevo. "I hope Roger's ankle and those blisters come right so he can ride out."

"He'll be fine," answered Brent. "If he isn't I am sure Nurse Janey will come to the rescue and sort him out. There are more first aid items in her bag than anything else."

Stevo chuckled.

"Yea, I guess we all really need to rest and recuperate after the last couple of days. Especially for the others, they aren't used to life out in the bush. But God, it is bloody nice to be away from where those massive spiders are."

"Yeah, I agree mate. They sure were something else! It's good we can come here for a hunt and they can enjoy their time down at the Bullring. We are all here for a good time, not a long time so we do need to make the most if it. Wonder where those boys ended up camping." "They would have found a spot further up the river, there are plenty

of good spots to choose from. Hope they don't cause any trouble."

Brent and Stevo sipped at their cups of tea and looked up the valley. Secret Creek began to climb quite steeply from just beyond their campsite and the terrain was a mass of boulders; gutty in parts, which was why they couldn't take the horses any further. From where Brent was standing on the bank, at the side of the creek, he could see right up the valley into the headwaters of Secret Creek; maybe 3 or 4 kilometres in the distance. He could see the tussock tops at the top of the valley and he pointed them out to Stevo.

"I wonder if there any big hata roaring up there."

"Must be," grinned Stevo, "It's the first of April tomorrow, roar time!! We should walk straight up this ridge behind the camp for a couple of hours. I reckon it will take us high enough to hear up into the valley. If there are any stags roaring up there then we will know where they are in the morning and be able to get straight onto them."

"Sounds like a plan I would have thought of," Brent winked.

They tidied and secured their camp site after retrieving their daypacks and rifles before moving away from the camp further up the ridge. They found the first hour of tramping to be quite steep and hard going, but with just the two of them they were able to move along at a much better pace than when they had been with the others. They could climb quickly which was good as they had to be high if they were to hear anything in the distance. Stevo was leading the way and the sweat was dripping off him profusely. Brent was puffing hard behind him with each and every steep step through the raw nature. Stevo finally hit a nice little flat piece of land and instantly decided to have a break - and a bit of a roar to see if he could get any hata to answer him. Stevo looked over towards Brent who was still pulling his way up through the last boulders and onto the flat.

"Do you want to give a roar, Brent?"

"Hell no! I'm puffing way too hard! Besides, your roar sounds much more realistic than mine."

Stevo gave a big bellow up the valley, and they could hear the echo for ages. Brent sat down exhaustedly and decided to roll two cigarettes; one for him and one for Stevo. They sat in silence for a while and enjoyed the respite from their hike; the view, the nicotine, and each other's peaceful company. As they looked up the valley from their vantage point, they noticed a slip way up on the ridge near the head in Secret Creek.

"Look at that big broken spar sticking out of the side of the slip.

That's where we've got to head for tomorrow," exclaimed Brent.

They turned to face each other in excitement as they suddenly heard a roar right up in the head of the valley, at least one and a half to two hours walking distance from where they had set up their camp.

"That's not far from that slip you know," smiled Stevo.

Suddenly, a huge roar came from further up in the ridge right behind where they were sitting. It was Stevo's shot. They always took turns on hunting trips for safety reasons as well as fairness. Brent said, "Go get him, Stevo."

As they jumped up they heard another huge bellow coming from the ridge behind them. Stevo looked really excited as he moved off up the ridge with his Ruger 308 at the ready.

Brent waited another few minutes, hoping to hear either the stag or the sound of Stevo's rifle. After what felt like an eternity waiting in silence, the hata roared again. At virtually the same time Brent heard Stevo's shot ring through the air.

Brent moved off quickly, up towards where he had heard the shot come from. He could see it was a beautiful 14 pointer and the timber was very heavy. Stevo was looking very pleased with himself as Brent walked up to shake his hand. They were both smiling from ear to ear as they sat down and had another cigarette while ogling the magnificent beast.

Stevo turned to face Brent.

"He just came straight down the ridge at me when I accidently cracked a stick I had stood on. He must have thought I was the other stag, the one which he had been roaring at in the distance."

Brent looked like he couldn't believe their luck; he was so pleased for Stevo.

"God, a marlin, two boars, the devil bull, and now a massive hata - and all within the last couple of months. It is just unbelievable!" "That stag up the valley is yours tomorrow, Brent. It must be the 18 pointer."

Brent grinned over at his best friend's enthusiasm.

"Yeah! If that chopper mate of mine can count, he'll be a beauty. Let's hope what he thought he saw was right!"

Brent reached into his day pack and got his little camera out.

"I hope this takes photos as good as the ones Roger has been taking," Stevo grinned slyly.

"It sure does," replied Brent. "Get yourself over there by the stag. Put your best smile on."

"Just take photos of the head," Stevo laughed.

"No, I need you in the photo too. You are not too ugly to skip out on posing with your trophy stag."

The head was absolutely symmetrical, with 7 tines on each side. The top four tines at the head of the main beam were formed perfectly and each was 12 inches long.

Stevo pulled out his big bowie and cut off the back steaks. He boned out the rest of the animal as Brent held it on its back. He passed the meat to Brent who then put it into a ziplock bag before loading it into his day pack. They carefully skinned the big head out so it could be taxidermied. When they had salvaged what they could from the animal, and were loaded up as comfortably as possible, they headed back towards camp. It was quite a treacherous trek out through the bush with the big head, but they were grateful as it was all downhill. They had to be extremely careful not to catch the tines on the surrounding bush or to trip over a stray tree root and damage the head.

After following the ridge down for just over an hour, they arrived back at their camp site. The horses gave them a snort of a greeting. Stevo placed the head in a perfect spot for them to be able to sit and admire once their cup of tea was made. Darkness was beginning to fall, even though it was not late enough for sunset. Because they were in such heavy bush the sun went down over the horizon early and the day seemed shorter as the shadows lengthened.

"I wonder how the girls' day has gone. Sue's going to be very happy that you got your stag with the new rifle she bought you," Brent said as they settled by the fire with their cups.

Stevo beamed.

"You're right, she sure will be!"

"Do you think Roger would have gotten over his injuries by now and tried to catch a trout?" mused Brent.

"I reckon he would have. He loves trout fishing and will be doing everything to make the most of the opportunity while it is right there in front of him, even if he shouldn't really be eating it. I hope they had a spa in the big pool!"

"Ha, I bet the girls have been in that spa all day long Stevo! Thank goodness none of us have to worry about those giant god-awful spiders. They only seemed to be so huge up where the drums were. They must love the taste of it and be eating it in its undiluted form."

Stevo grinned as he pulled out two of the stag's finest cuts of meat for them to enjoy. While the steaks were sizzling on the fire, they fed and watered the horses before ensuring they were safely tethered for the night. As they sat down to enjoy the meal and sip on a few rums they chatted about the hunt and the plane; it was as if they had entered a whole different world on this trip. Hunting trips usually made the two of them feel this way but this was a completely different experience due to the oversized creatures. The night was clear and they knew there would be absolutely no dew so they decided to sleep out beside the fire under the stars. It was not long before they were both snoring away, dreaming of the 18 pointer stag they planned to catch the very next day.

CHAPTER FORTY

After the three brothers had moved off up the river, the day warmed up. It was a lovely autumn afternoon and the heat of the sun was making the temperature really pleasant. Roger limped his way out across the river as he gripped his fishing rod tightly in one hand. As the girls fed the horses Janey said, "We should go for a swim and wash our hair. We will be able to keep an eye on Roger fishing to make sure he doesn't slip on the wet rocks."

"Sounds good, we will stick to the shallows though. We don't want to tempt the eels!" replied Sue.

"Up to our knees or so should be ok," responded Heather.

"It will be a quick dip. The water will be cold as it flows fresh and cold straight out from the mountain," said Janey.

The girls dressed into their swim gear and waded out to a just by the entrance to Secret Creek. The clear and pristine water was sparkling in the sunlight. The bottom of the pool was covered with beautiful golden pebbly sand which they could easily see. They observed there were no eels in it so they felt comfortable enough to bathe freely. They washed their hair and scrubbed their skin free of four days of sweat, muck, pollen, leaves, and dirt.

By the time the girls were drying themselves off and readying themselves to lay on the river bank and tan, Roger had made his way a little further down the river to fish. He had hooked a good trout and was playing it beautifully, finding that he needed every trout fishing skill he had ever learnt to reel it in. The trout was at least 5kg and was swimming desperately from one end of the pool to the other, even leaping clean out of the water at times. He played the trout for what seemed like an eternity, all while trying to catch the girls' attention.

Noticing the fish Heather squealed in delight as she and the other girls made their way down to where Roger was. "Hope the line doesn't get caught around a log or a rock. It is thrashing about wildly."

"Could be because of the hook in its mouth," laughed Heather.

Roger finally managed to control the trout. As he reeled it closer to shore, he noticed a dark silhouette curling its way through the rocks and the logs, creating a three way current behind its huge tail. Roger's eyes were bulging out of his head as he wondered what the hell was going on. The girls could see the shape moving through the water; they stared down into the pool with both fear and amazement. Suddenly, from the depths of the pool the silhouette came straight for the trout on the end of Roger's line. It was one of the oversized Aussie invader eels. Roger yelped with surprise as he took a large step backwards.

"Not again!"

The eel had smelt the blood of the trout where the hook had pierced it. Roger continued to reel the line in as fast as he could, trying to beat the eel from getting his fish. As the fish jumped out of the water, the big eel leaped up behind it, opened its mouth, and attached itself to the body of the fish. The eel spun around as it prepared to re-submerge itself in the water, taking the body of the fish and leaving Roger with only a torn off head on his line. In absolute shock Roger reeled the remainder of the limp, lifeless fish into shore. He removed the head of the trout from his lure and threw it back into the pool.

"Might as well have the rest of it, you big fat bastard!"

Heather was really disappointed for Roger and completely gobsmacked by what she had seen. Roger was worried by the size and ferocity of the eel. He hadn't seen many eels in his life but he knew the trout thief had been huge. He couldn't wait to tell Brent and Stevo all about it. He felt as if a great camaraderie had developed between the three men on this trip. Sure, they had always been friends, but the depth of the friendship had grown the more he proved his capabilities in the wild.

"If that eel wasn't eight feet long and a foot wide at the head, then I'm a monkey's uncle!" Roger exclaimed excitedly.

The group headed back up the river to where the girls had left their packs and towels. They spread themselves out along the riverbank and lapped up the sunshine while discussing the big eel.

After an afternoon of napping and chatting in the sunshine as they evened out their end of summer tans and took quick dips into the sandy bottomed pool, they headed back towards camp together. Roger decided he would head off to check on the dogs.

"It's good to see you taking an interest in the animals, Roger," smiled Janey.

"You are developing into quite an outdoors man, Rog. Not quite the townie you were when we left home," laughed Heather with pride. "You can laugh," Roger grinned. "But I am really enjoying the trip actually. Especially Blue, Buck, and Orphy. I really miss that horse now he and Possum have gone. Anyway, I just want to make sure the dogs are safe and happy."

Roger checked on the dogs who were both safe and sound. They lapped up the human affection as Roger scratched behind their ears. He decided to go for a little walk with Buck and Blue a bit further into the bush. He spotted a big Rimu tree and thought to himself how it would be a beautiful tree to sit underneath and rest his ankle while the dogs ran about. He got himself comfortable at the base of the rimu and enjoyed the peace and tranquillity of the bush. He listened to the musical sounds coming from the birdlife of the native bush around him while thinking about the adventures of the previous few days. A rustling sound interrupted his thoughts, and he couldn't see the dogs so he knew it wasn't coming from them. He looked from side to side and couldn't see anything that could be causing the rustling sound.

Suddenly, he felt something touch his right leg and he froze, hoping it was just a twig he had brushed against. He leaned his upper body forward, trying not to move his right leg, so he could get a look at whatever it was that had touched him.

He peered down towards his shin. His heart began racing and his mouth went dry as he saw a spider that was the size of a dinner plate on his leg. Using its long, spiny legs it was crawling up his calf towards his stomach. Roger tried not to panic, and carefully picked up a stick, and leaned further down to try to flick the spider off his leg. The spider got a fright and bit Rogers' knee. Roger screamed in agony and half ran/half hobbled back towards camp as fast as he could. The dogs came running after him, barking like mad to alert the others.

Janey, who had been nearest to Roger, ran towards him. "What's wrong Roger?"

Roger's face was glowing bright red and he was desperately trying to talk through gritted teeth. His jaw was locked shut and Janey was pleading with Roger to tell her what had happened when Sue and Heather came running up to join them.

With concern in her voice Heather yelled, "What's wrong?"

Roger grabbed Heather with a hand on each of her shoulders. "Something bit my knee," he managed to mumble through his

clenched jaw.

"Let us have a look honey," calmed Heather as she quickly got Roger to sit down.

Looking at Roger's knee, Heather could see two red bite marks and one was bleeding quite badly. Janey ran to get the first aid kit and immediately washed and cleaned the area before treating it with anti- biotic ointment. Heather asked Roger what it was that had bit him. His face was starting to return to its normal colour and the shock had worn off so he was able to move his mouth properly again. "I tell you Heather, if I hadn't seen those other ones up by the plane

I would say it was the biggest spider in the whole world."

"Don't worry Roger," Janey soothed. "I'll go and have a look at where you were to make sure it hasn't followed you into camp. We need to stay safe up here."

"I was sitting by the big rimu just past where the dogs were tied up. Make sure you take the dogs and the gun with you. It's big Janey. Shoot as soon as you see it or it'll probably get you too. It's bigger than an oversized dinner plate. It has great big feelers with massive, big ugly, grotty, hairy legs."

Sue squealed, "Crikey!"

"I looked it straight in its humungous eyes," shivered Roger. Janey grabbed the gun and headed off up to the back of the camp.

The dogs led the way. She began having flashbacks to what she had seen the day before in the plane. Tracking where Roger had been wasn't a problem as the scuff marks through the leaves and debris where he had scrambled back to camp were really obvious. She arrived at the place where Roger had been seated on the rimu roots and she poked around with the barrel of the rifle. Janey had a bullet up the breach just in case - but she could not see anything,

'If I were a spider I wouldn't be hanging round here either. I hope it went a long way away,' she spoke softly to the trees.

Janey looked around a bit more but came up with nothing. There were plenty of big holes around the tree that something could easily have gone down. She wrapped her arms around herself and wished for the millionth time that Brent was still with her. She tried her best to comfort herself with the knowledge that he would be back in the morning as she walked back to where Roger, Heather, and Sue were gathered.

Roger was lying on his back with his eyes shut; it looked as if he had passed out, and Heather and Sue were examining his injuries.

"Is he alright?"

"Yeah," replied Heather. "He's just a bit embarrassed. Supposed to be the man of the camp and gets laid out by a spider bite. There appears to be no swelling but I'll keep an eye on him."

Roger opened his eyes halfway.

"I can't believe this trip. I hurt my ankle, got infected blisters on my backside, had my trout eaten by some monster eel, and now my knee has been chewed by a spider, probably an oversized white tail. Bloody great. When are we going home, Heather?"

"Please, Roger," pleaded Janey. "Just remember animals are not usually this big. It's the toxic stuff at the plane crash site that's done all this. It's not normal. Don't worry too much. Just think Roger, Brent and Stevo will be back tomorrow and then we will all head home and get this sorted out. Once those drums are removed and all this stuff is cleaned up, things around here will return to normal."

Janey was trying to calm herself as much as Roger with her words. She wanted him to enjoy the bush as much as he could. She knew there was still a long trip ahead of them once the hunters were back - and the last thing they needed was Roger panicking or being upset for the rest of their time in the bush.

CHAPTER FORTY-ONE

"Well it looks like this is going to be our camp. Not bad either, plenty of grass for the horses and a good spot here for us on this soft sandy patch, with a bit of grass on it too," said Luke.

"Yeah, this will be all good," grinned Jake.

"Rivers too close for my liking," sneered Slade rudely.

"Well, I reckon we should go for a hunt. It's far too early to waste the day sitting around here," suggested Luke, ignoring his twin's comment.

His brothers said nothing in response.

"Well, what do you reckon, then?" Luke prompted with a hint of a whine in his voice; he was becoming agitated by their lack of response and enthusiasm.

"Nah, we'll go tomorrow, Lukey. Rest up and chill out bro," patronised Jake.

"Fine, I am going for a hunt. If you two slack asses want to sit around here drinking that's up to you. I will be back before dark. I'm going up that little side creek up the river, the one on the right side." "Ok," Slade waved the rum bottle again. "See you later. Good luck."

Luke threw the billy onto the ground as he stormed off, grabbing the rifle on his way up the river. He tried to not think about his lazy brothers as best he could, and instead looked forward to hunting up the side creek. He had seen plenty of sign up there on previous hunts and hoped it would still be a good spot to find something. He was not averse to a bit of solitude as he used to spend hours walking along the beach on his own when he'd had the time. He had always found it quite refreshing. He knew he would have to walk quite far in order to be as high as all the deer they had heard up in the heads of the creeks, so he set his mind to thinking of returning to camp with a load that would be the envy of his two stoner brothers.

Luke had been walking for about an hour when he decided to climb up onto a spur so he could try and hear if any stags were roaring. A 15 minute climb straight up out of the creek had him sitting on the end of the wide spur. He listened for a while and enjoyed the noises of the native bush. Finally, he thought he heard a roar from a valley further ahead. He searched around for deer sign on the spur but couldn't see enough to make it worth hunting the ridge so he dropped back down into the creek. The afternoon was wearing on and he knew it was about an hour or so back to camp so he thought he'd make his way another half hour up the creek to try find the hata he thought he had heard. Arriving at a fork in the creek, he decided to get even more height to see if he could hear anything because there wasn't as much sign as Luke had hoped. He had desperately wanted to get a stag with Hones old 303 - just to be able to tell Hone about the hunt and show him the antlers. He was imagining it to be bigger than his brothers' ones. As soon as his brothers entered his mind, he felt the anger flush over him again. He couldn't believe Jake had sat there drinking with Slade when he should have been prepared to help on the hunt. He smugly thought to himself how if he snagged a deer, he would leave it in the bush and make his two lazy brothers come and help him carry it out.

As he climbed high, the sign didn't improve and he noticed how time was ticking on. He knew he should start heading back and he was immediately filled with a deep disappointment of how the day had turned out. He dropped back down to the creek and began to make his way back to join his brothers. His boots filled with water as he made his way through a gutty part in the creek. The cool water seeped through the fabric of his pants as he waded through pools where the banks were high on both sides and he didn't want to sidle them. Another half an hour went by and he broke out of the creek and back onto the main river. It was only another ten minutes down to their campsite and he could see by the remaining light that it was only another hour until darkness would fall.

Back at camp the alcohol was taking away Jake's sense of responsibility and he became morose as he felt the guilt about the stolen car wash over him. Slade was lying on his back and staring up at the sky as he dragged on a joint which they were sharing. They were lying on their padded sleeping bags and soon the effects of the alcohol and marijuana allowed them to drift them off into a light snooze.

Slade had been dozing dreamily for quite a while when he suddenly jumped up, slashed at the air in agitation and kicked a stone down the river loudly which caused Jake to wake up from his afternoon nap too. "What's wrong with you, Slade? Did something bite you or something?"

"Nothing bloody bit me bro. It's this terrible campsite," snorted Slade angrily.

"What do you mean?"

"I'm lying there and it feels like the river is running right through my head because we have had to camp so close to it. There are heaps of sandflies annoying me too."

Jake glanced over at his brother. It appeared as if Slade was experiencing withdrawal. He thought about making a joke that Slade's head had enough room for a river to run through it but quickly changed his mind; he knew Slade could be really unpredictable when he was like this.

"I'm going to check on the horses," grumbled Slade as he strolled off to where the horses were tied up on a grassy patch hidden amongst some totara trees.

Jake followed behind quietly, thinking how he would like to find out what was really bothering his brother. As he approached the area where the horses were tethered, he could see Slade searching for something in his saddle bags which were lying on the grass by where they had taken their saddles off. He finally grinned as he pulled something from the depths of his bag. Jake instantly recognised his brother's sly grin.

"Come on, Slade. You don't need that!"

"I guess not, but I want it …" grinned Slade wickedly; he seemed to have calmed down just with the reassurance of knowing he had some P for when he really needed it.

"Let's go back to the camp," suggested Jake.

They put their arms around each other's shoulders and walked back to the campsite. Slade put the drugs into his pocket instead of tucking them back into the saddle bag.

"Hey, I wonder how far away Luke is and if he has got anything?" asked Jake trying to distract his brother.

"He could be ages yet," Slade smirked, "Let's have a little smoke. I need something."

Jake looked at his brother wondering which type of smoke was being suggested; cigarettes, marijuana, or meth? Jake realised that if he was going to get high on P with his brother, then this was his only chance as he knew they wouldn't smoke ice while Luke was around. Something about the drug seemed to have a slight hold over him, it was tempting to take his brother up on the offer of a smoke – and he was pretty sure he knew which type his wayward brother was suggesting. "Ok, bro. Just this once …" caved Jake with a sly grin that matched

Slade's.

As he approached their little clearing, Luke could hear Slade and Jake laughing about something. He wandered into camp and saw his brothers with big smiles plastered all over their faces.

"Hey, where's all the venison, Luke?" teased Slade between snorts of laughter.

"Couldn't get onto anything, there was nothing roaring either," Luke replied defeatedly.

"Hope you never roared and scared them," Jake snorted with laughter.

This backhanded comment had Slade laughing even harder. "Ok, wise guys. Thought at least you might have put some tea or

the billy on, what have you been doing all day aye?" Luke could see that Slade and Jake had got themselves really drunk. He looked at each of his brothers slowly; they were both pumped and full of energy despite the empty bottles that lay scattered around the campsite. He realised they had been using the day without him as a chance to suck on the P pipe and Luke felt his anger returning.

"Want a rum, Lukey?" Slade asked as he passed over the bottle. Luke took a small swig before handing it straight back.

"I need a cuppa and something to eat first."

He stoked the fire and set about putting the billy on.

"It'll be dark soon and we haven't eaten," complained Luke. Slade called out,

"Nah, never mind about tea here. Let's go down and check out what the neighbours are cooking. We can get you a feed from them. I'm not hungry anyway."

"Yeah I reckon you're right Sladey-boy," chuckled Jake. "Dinner with them sounds good. They are much better looking than you, Luke."

Luke didn't reply and instead sat rolling a joint to smoke while he waited for the billy to boiled and his tea to be ready. Slade got up and wandered off to find a tree to use to relieve himself. Luke had finished rolling the joint when his brother returned,

"Where you been, took a while to take a leak aye? Hope you aren't sucking that shit again Slade."

"Shut up Luke. You are a real pain at times. Pass me that joint though bro."

"I know I go on about it … But that shit is so bad. You are a different person when you have been on it too."

Slade shrugged his shoulders in silent response as he toked on the joint he had been given. Slade and Jake were quite drunk, and the drugs were really beginning to take their toll. Slade exhaled and started to laugh for absolutely no reason at all. He was such a funny sight that his two brothers joined in, and they were all laughing like a group of school kids smoking pot for the first time. Luke noticed how Jake seemed to be laughing at Slade, rather than with him, because his laugh had become quite high pitched.

Slade suddenly stopped and jumped to his feet.

'Let's go and check out the neighbours and hopefully get some tea."
"Why don't we just cook our own? You can't go down there in

the state you are in. You'll cause trouble, Slade," Luke warned with a worried edge to his voice.

"We could … But they have probably got some ready to eat and there won't be any trouble, Lukey. You worry too much."

Jake jumped up and nearly fell over backwards before regaining his composure at the last minute.

Luke shrugged.

"Oh well, whatever. I'm bloody starving."

Slade and Jake began to move off impatiently down the river on foot.

"I have got to change my clothes. I am soaked and my boots are full of water. I'll catch you up in about 10-15 minutes," yelled Luke as he walked the opposite way towards where the horses and the bags were. Slade picked up the 303 from where Luke had left it leaning against a nearby tree. Luke yelled out to ask why he was taking the

gun with him.

"Who knows, there might be a deer in the river. Settle down bro.
I tell ya, nothings gonna happen!"

The brothers made their way down river with Slade in front and Jake tagging along behind. Slade and Jake had only gone about 20 metres when Luke called out to them again,

"You guys be polite to those people. We don't want any trouble."

Slade just waved his hand in the air and carried on without turning back.

"I hope the ladies' husbands are back and tell my loser brothers to bugger off," he spoke to himself as he quickly pulled on his dry shoes. He hoped he would make it quickly through the bush so he got to his brothers before they arrived at the neighbouring camp.

CHAPTER FORTY-TWO

"Wonder if that lady's husband and his mate have turned up like she said?" Slade wondered.

"They might tell us to bugger off and not give us anything to eat!" Jake laughed.

"Nah," scoffed Slade. "We'll be polite and it'll all be sweet. I don't reckon they will be there anyway. I think she was just saying that. I didn't see any other sleeping bags." "What do you reckon they are doing all the way up here anyway?"

"Don't know man," mused Slade. "Might be nudists or something!" Jake laughed at his brother.

"Get real, Slade. No way would you come all the way up here just to get your gear off."

"Well, must be here just for the nature then," Slade smirked as he took a swig of the rum.

The two brothers continued staggering along in their drugged, drunken state. They didn't even notice that nightfall was rapidly approaching. The sun was only just visible on the distant horizon.

Slade stopped and looked at Jake.

"You look a bit scruffy, better tidy yourself up and be polite like Lukey said!"

Slade broke into a dry laugh.

Jake cracked up at his brother and they both began to laugh hysterically as they drank some more rum from the bottle they had brought with them.

"Come on, Slade. You're right, we have got to pull ourselves together. We are visiting our neighbours for tea after all - we need to sober up. God, Lukey would have a fit if he knew we'd been smoking P."

"Yeah, you're right. Let's go."

Meanwhile, Luke had been hurrying to get ready. He had wanted to ask Slade to wait for him but he knew Slade's mind had been made up to go right then. Luke could see the mood his brother was in and decided it was better to let them go on ahead rather than have an argument and bring Slade's mood down. Luke had got his dry clothes on and swilled back his cup of tea. He was feeling quite hungry and cold from the water soaking him through. He regretted not taking much to eat or drink with him when he had set out hunting. He raced off down the river towards the Bullring camp as fast as he could.

Roger and the girls had been settled back at camp for a while. As the last of the day's sunshine leeched from the sky and disappeared behind the ridgeline they watched the colours of dusk began to fill the sky.

"Gosh," admired Janey. "That big anti-cyclone must be right over our camp. The sky is just beautiful."

Everybody agreed with her as they stared in wonder as the first stars began to appear amongst the twilight hues.

"Just takes your breath away," sighed Sue contentedly. Roger nodded.

"Yeah, its magic. We don't really notice the night sky at home."

They had been discussing what they would each do first when they got back from their trip, and how they needed to let the police know about the plane, the danger the eels posed, and about the changes to all of the wildlife. The fire was going really well and they were sitting having a relaxing drink as they dried off after their wash in the river. Sue and Heather were still wearing their swim suits as they warmed up by the fire in preparation to get changed into their pyjamas. Janey had already changed into warmer clothes at the back of the camp under the Kanuka trees by her tent. Roger was making tea and joining in the conversation whenever he could, especially when the conversation turned to the killer eels or the giant spiders. He stirred the fresh venison stew and leaned over the pot to taste a spoonful. Roger had always enjoyed cooking and he grinned as he swallowed down what tasted like the perfect stew. He had cooked just the right amount for the four of them and had used up the very last bit of venison from the deer that Brent had shot on the way up the river.

Blue and Buck were chained up at the back of the camp just behind Janey's tent. They were happy to sit there because they could keep an eye on everyone. They were sitting quietly as they had just been fed and tied up after a long day of playing around in the river. Janey noticed as they both suddenly stood up and pricked their ears forward and growled deeply.

"What can you smell, boys?"

She scanned the area out towards the river in the direction Blue and Buck were looking. It was still light enough to just make out the river flats. Buck's growl had caught the attention of the others in the camp. They too looked up to where Janey was.

Roger got up and came over to join her. "What is it, Janey?"

She pointed towards the entrance to the camp and Roger turned to look; someone coming and it sounded like they were making their way up the bank. Two figures appeared, one very tall and wide and the other shorter and stocky. For a few moments, the campers and the visitors all just stared at each other awkwardly. Janey was looking at the taller one who had an eerie smile on his face as he spoke, breaking the silence.

"Evening, people."

Roger exclaimed in surprise at seeing the boys back at the Bullring. "Hi there."

The two brothers made a greeting gesture but did not say anything else. Roger looked towards his stew and walked over to take it off the fire. Heather and Sue wished they had gotten dressed when Janey did so they grabbed at their towels and wrapped them hastily around their shoulders.

"Didn't think we would be getting any visitors," Heather announced abruptly with an edge to her voice.

Janey just stood where she was, wondering what the boys could possibly want. Nobody said anything for what seemed like an eternity – but was really only about 30 seconds.

Finally Janey composed herself and said,

"Hello boys. Are you going for an evening hunt?"

Janey remained standing by the dogs about 15 metres away from where Slade and Jake were and the light was fading fast. The flames were dancing up from the fire which was making it hard for Janey to see their faces. Roger hadn't said anything else but he was closest to the boys. He could smell the alcohol on their breath.

'Better be a bit careful here,' he warned himself.

Slade leaned the 303 on the end of a log as he stepped forward up the bank and entered into the camp.

"Hey that smells good." He paused and looked over at Janey and replied to her question with a big grin on his face. "Yeah, but we haven't been too successful, though. We hoped to scrounge some tea off you guys."

Roger knelt down to stir the stew; he didn't want it to stick to the bottom of the pot. He looked begrudgingly at Slade.

"Sorry boys, I've only put enough on for us."

Everything went awkwardly quiet again. Slade looked around the camp and could still see it was only the four of them there,

"Your husband's still out hunting ladies?" Janey winced.

"Yes, yes. But they should be back soon."

"Oh, really! They carry their sleeping bags around with them?" "Yes, if they are going a long way. Just in case they get caught in

the dark. They like to be prepared."

Jake's lips tugged at a smile. Janey was not being very convincing. Slade had thought they were having them on about having husbands and it appeared to Jake that his brother had been right – maybe they were nudists after all.

Roger continued to stir the venison stew wondering desperately how to change the subject. "Did you get any deer this afternoon?"

Jake quickly replied, slurring his words drunkenly as he spoke, "Me and Slade got one each on our way up here. Our brother has

been trying today but nahhh he ain't got none yet." "Where is he?" inquired Roger.

"Oh, he's following us down the river. He got back late from hunting and needed to change his clothes. That's why we came down to see you and hopefully scrounge some tea. Coz me and Slade were really tired from all the hunting we done and we fell asleep and never put any tea on."

Jake had handed the rum bottle to Slade who was nodding in agreement with his brother.

"Well, if you are really hungry I guess we could make something for you …" Heather trailed off unimpressed at this idea. Roger was feeling anxious with the boys intrusion into their camp. He could see from the boys' behaviour that they were really drunk and possibly on something else as well. They were swaying all over the place with grins wider than that of the cheshire cat. He had also noticed how the two men were constantly shuffling and moving around as if they had endless energy to burn.

Heather and Sue had caught Slade's attention as they were sitting on the log beside the fire wearing only their swimsuits with towels casually draped around their shoulders. Roger was still stirring the stew, even though it really didn't need anything more than to be served on to the four waiting plates. However, he was determined not to dish it up while the boys were there as he worried it may make them sit down and stay in their camp.

Janey looked at the boys carefully.

"How long will your brother be? Because if he is going to be a while we could have our tea and then cook you some."

"Oh yeah, sounds good," grinned Jake.

Slade smiled eerily as he watched Heather and Sue huddled together by the fire. He took a long swig at the rum bottle in his hand. Sue was sitting, leaning forward in an attempt to keep warm and to cover herself up, with her elbows on her knees and her hands holding the sides of her face. Her eyes were fixated on the fire. Heather looked over at Janey with a grim look on her face.

Nobody said anything for a while until Roger finally broke the silence.

"I'll dish ours and then I'll put some on for you guys."

"Yeah, that sounds good, bro," Slade slurred as he stepped up the bank.

Roger stood up to get the plates ready to serve. Slade was quite close behind him and it was making Roger feel very nervous as he muddled around getting the plates.

Janey kindly offered,

"I can make you boys a cuppa." Jake, standing at the back scoffed.

"No thanks, we brought our own drinks," and he proudly held up a second rum bottle that he had grabbed at the last moment. "Maybe you guys would you like some of this instead?"

Roger, smelling the alcohol and not liking the body language, declined.

"No thanks boys, we would like to have our dinner in peace." Roger calling them 'boys' annoyed Slade. "What do you mean,

boys?" he asked Roger rudely. He thought Roger was only pretending to be nice but actually wanted them to leave.

Jake spluttered,

"Wait, this is our land and you want us to go!"

Roger, quite shocked by the boys' demeanour and the way the conversation was going replied quickly.

"No, no, not at all. Of course not."

Slade grunted in Roger's direction as he moved over to stand in front of Heather and Sue. He eyed up Sue.

"You girls look pretty good," snarled Slade.

Roger got a really worried look on his face when he heard this comment. Jake, who had taken an instant dislike to Roger, was enjoying seeing this older man stressing out by his presence. The drugs and alcohol had really taken effect on both boys.

Slade continued to stare at Sue.

"Well, you couldn't give us tea. What about a cuddle instead?" That was the final straw for Roger who walked straight up to

Slade and interjected,

"Could you please leave our camp?"

Roger was not a small man. He stood at 6 foot tall, was quite solid, and had begun to carry a bit of weight over the last few years, but he was still looking up at the heavyset Slade. Slade kept his ground; he stood there with a look of absolute amusement on his face. Roger knew he was not a fighter but he had to do something to protect the three most important women in his life.

The three women were looking very worried. Janey was looking around nervously, wishing wholeheartedly that she could get to the dogs to untie them. They were making some pretty scary growling sounds and barking like mad.

"Please, boys, can you take a seat and we will make you some tea. Or maybe you want our stew and we will have something else?" Slade ignored Janey's offer and turned his attention back towards Sue. Her skin crawled as his piercing eyes wandered all over her body. Sue wished for the millionth time that she was properly dressed. The big tattoo on Slade's arm made him look even more menacing and intimidating.

"No, we are not hungry now - not for food anyway," Slade whispered as he licked his lips; never removing his eyes from Sue.

Roger, standing to the side of Slade, begged, "Come on. Can you please leave?"

Slade, who had already taken a big disliking to Roger telling him what to do, dragged his eyes off Sue's breasts.

"We will leave when we are ready. This isn't your land." Roger replied with as much staunch as he could muster, "This is our camp. Please go."

Slade turned his whole body so he could look down at Roger. "Are you going to make me?"

"Yes, if I have to," Roger was trembling, not really knowing what to do.

Slade pushed Roger backwards onto his bad ankle. Despite the pain, Roger came forward again as he shouted,

"PLEASE LEAVE."

The girls were all stunned, both by Slade's behaviour and Roger's anger. Roger needed some help. Heather stood up and went to step between Roger and Slade.

"You boys leave now," Heather spoke forcefully, her eyes darting angrily between the two young brothers.

Slade's anger at Roger had hit boiling point. He elbowed Heather out of the way and threw a punch at Roger, hitting him right in the middle of his chest. Roger flew backwards and as he crashed to the ground he brought the billy with the venison stew down with him. Jake remained quiet, taking swigs at his drink. Everything was getting out of control. He decided he should try to do something to control his brother. He had already stepped out of Roger's way as he tumbled past him and lazily kicked the billy in the opposite direction so as to save everyone from the scalding contents. Jake looked down at Roger on the ground.

"That's enough, Slade. We really don't need this."

Roger stood up from landing on his backside, glancing at his prize stew all over the grass and the violent man laughing down at him. He felt the unusual sensation of anger prickling at the back of his neck and without thinking he ran towards Slade with full force, as though he was going to rugby tackle him. Slade had plenty of time to react while waiting for Roger to come into range and he quickly grabbed a huge chunk of firewood from the heap by the fire. Roger saw him pick it up but couldn't stop his own momentum as he had launched himself full speed at Slade who slowly raised his arm and hit Roger as hard as he possibly could in the head with the wood. Roger's head snapped back as the momentum of the smack to his head sent him over a log by the edge of the camp to where he landed awkwardly; resting his full weight on his shoulders and neck with his legs splayed over the log.

Heather swore at Slade,

"You stupid bastard, look what you did to my husband!" as she rushed over to see if Roger was ok.

Sue screamed in fright. Janey marched up to Slade hoping to calm the situation. As Janey approached Slade, he let loose with his fists and gave her a heavy back hander which sent Janey flying backwards. Seeing Janey knocked out, Sue began to scream endlessly. Her shrill voice added to the horror unfolding around the Bullring campers. Heather gently held Roger's head off the ground. She choked back tears of gratitude that her husband was still breathing - despite his unconscious state. Jake stood staring, dumbfounded by everything that had happened, and by how quickly the situation had changed. He wished desperately Luke was with them. Jake had seen Slade in action many times before, but never quite like this - and certainly never against defenceless people. Slade yelled at Sue to shut up.

Resting Roger's head gently on the ground Heather moved beside Sue. She looked over to where Janey had fallen. She was desperately trying to think of a way to help her unconscious friend while trying to calm Sue. As Heather looked around a wave of despair and helplessness washed through her veins. Slade drunkenly swaggered over to where Sue and Heather were crouched together and pulled at the zipper of his jeans until it came undone.

Jake was not impressed with this turn of events and tried desperately to distract Slade. He yelled at his brother; trying to talk some sense into him.

"Knock it off. You have stuffed any chance we have of getting some tea. Let's get out of here."

Slade ignored him and continued to keep his eyes trained on Sue. As Sue saw him undo the fly on his jeans, she felt every muscle in her body go numb. Without any further warning, Slade grabbed Sue by the back of her head and wrapped her lovely blond hair around his hand like a limp rag. The blood rushed to Heather's brain and she thought she might faint from the fear, but she shook the dizziness away and desperately tried to get Slade to let go of Sue. Despite the drugs and alcohol coursing through his body, he was still able to shove Heather away effortlessly while never losing his grip on Sue. Heather looked towards the bush, hoping with all her heart to see Stevo and Brent riding back to save them in their moment of need.

Slade pulled Sue in really close, his lips brushed against the skin behind her neck. Sue screamed in terror and squirmed in an attempt to get away. It felt as if he was going to break her neck. Slade laughed as he bit hard on her ear.

"Hey Jake, you have that one, Bro," he sneered, referring to Heather. Heather got back to her feet and screamed at Slade,

"You disgusting bastard!" and went to make another run at the man about to rape her sister. While still holding Sue, Slade pulled his knife out of its sheath and held it up for Heather to see. Heather stopped dead in her tracks. She knew that Slade could and would kill if the moment came. He leaned over and slipped his knife under Sue's bikini strap and smirked as he cut the cord. Sue was shaking with fear as she too understood that Slade would think nothing of stabbing her. The bikini top fell down and her breasts were suddenly exposed for everyone to see. Slade looked over at Heather snarling,

"I'm warning both of you girls, any funny stuff and this bitch here will get this knife so deep she won't ever see another sunrise."

Jake was sobering up fast.

"Slade, stop!!" he yelled. The alcohol and drugs had completely numbed his brain but something still told Jake that what was happening was not right and that he must stop Slade.

Slade let out a blood curdling laugh. Jake knew he wouldn't be able to stop Slade doing whatever he wanted to.

Heather was cowering down, trying to cover herself. Jake knelt down beside her and tried to pass her a towel. When Jake knelt beside her Heather pulled away. Heather lashed out in self-defence; slapping him hard on the side of his face as she yelled at him to get out of their camp. She continued to scream as she was almost hysterical from feeling so helpless and frightened. The screaming and the sting on his face made Jake angry. He felt the egotistical pull of the methamphetamines surge through him again.

Slade looked over at his brother and laughed eerily. "What's wrong, bro? Can't handle a woman?"

"Just shut up, Slade! Let's get the fuck out of here now!"

Jake was getting more and more angry. He had been humiliated by his brother and by being attacked when he was trying to help. In a moment of madness he reached out and backhanded Heather hard, causing her nose to bleed.

"I'm not ready to leave yet," replied Slade with a sly grin, giving a hard slap to Sue's breasts. Sue was screaming as she wriggled and squirmed in a desperate attempt to get away from Slade. He tightened his hold on her and held up the knife to remind her who was in charge. He let go of her head and dropped his arm around her waist as he used the knife to cut the string to her bikini bottoms. He shoved her forward as he grasped her hair again, eyeing her nakedness up and down.

"You're not bad, bitch. We are going to have some fun." He licked his lips as he looked over towards where Janey lay. "That other one will be good too when she wakes up – or even if she doesn't."

Jake was feeling really unsure of what to think or do and was hoping Luke would hurry up. Heather held her face in an attempt to stop the blood flow. She got up to her feet and made her way around the log and over to where Roger was lying knocked out. Jake could see there was still no movement from the man.

"Keep an eye on her, Jake," Slade sneered as he kept his attention on the helpless woman in his grasp.

CHAPTER FORTY-THREE

Janey felt herself struggling to come out of an all-consuming darkness. She could hear voices and screams but she had no idea of where she was. She realised she must have hit her head because she was aware of pain coming from that region of her body. Something must be wrong because she couldn't feel Brent's hands or hear his comforting words. She decided to lie really still and open just one eye. As soon as she did, she was hit with the situation; of camping in the Bullring, and with what had happened with the intruders. She could see where Roger's rifle was leaning against a tree only a few metres away. She could see the mag was in place as Stevo had loaded it only the day before. She remembered him putting bullets in it and never thinking they would need to defend themselves against intruders of the human type. Janey opened her other eye and turned her head slowly to see where the screams were coming from. Her stomach dropped as she realised they were coming from Sue who was being raped by the largest of the two intruders.

Jake was continuing to yell at Slade to stop it. His cries were just adding to Slade's determination. Heather looked out from where she was crouched behind the log as she tried to make Roger more comfortable. Her nose was still bleeding. The reality of the situation fell hard upon Heather and she groaned in despair before screaming at Jake, "Stop him, that is my sister." She could still hear the death threat Slade had made towards Sue and she was terrified that anything she did would cause him to plunge that ugly knife deep. Jake continued to yell at his brother but found himself unable to have any effect on Slade. He was so intoxicated he couldn't quite believe everything unfolding was real.

Janey could see her one and only chance. She quietly crawled over and grabbed Roger's gun. She cranked a bullet into the chamber and pointed the barrel towards Slade who was panting as he lay motionless atop of Sue.

Janey screamed,

"Get off her, you dirty prick or I'll shoot!"

All other voices went quiet as Janey's words cut through the air. Slade pushed Sue's face into the dirt as he got up slowly with a deep- set snarl on his face and his eyes staring straight into Janey's.

As he pulled up his pants he sneered, "You're lucky. I was finished anyway."

Jake just looked at the woman threatening his brother. 'How did she get that gun?' he wondered.

Janey continued to point the gun at Slade who was doing up his belt without taking his eyes off of her face.

"Get out of our camp, now," Janey shouted.

Slade began moving towards her with his arms in the air. "One more step and I'll shoot," she growled in warning. "There's no need for this lady. Just put the gun down, aye."

The gun's barrel was going up and down with each of Janey's sharp breaths; she was shaking as she had never even pointed a gun at an animal let alone faced the possibly of having to shoot a human being. "You heard what I said. Get out of our camp, NOW!" screamed Janey.

"Put the gun down and there won't be any more trouble," Slade said as he ignored her warning and kept moving forward. The drugs had taken away the last of Slade's common sense. He was trying to get close enough to grab the barrel.

"I warned you," Janey whispered.

Janey knew what Slade was trying to do and she took a large step backward to prepare herself. She aimed the gun at his shoulder. Her mind was already made up and she pulled hard on the trigger. The gun exploded, causing a deafening sound to echo down the river. Slade went reeling backwards and began to roll around on the ground. He had lost his balance as the bullet hit his shoulder. He was screaming with rage and swearing every curse word he had ever heard all at once.

The bullet had got him in the muscle on his outer arm, and as it was an army solid bullet it had gone straight through the muscle to where it made an exit out the back of his arm. His own momentum had sent him rolling towards the entrance of the camp near to where they had entered from further upstream. He was really seething with anger, and he could see lots of blood flowing down his arm.

"That fucking bitch shot me!" Slade yelled at Jake.

Hone's old 303 was only about a metre away from where he was lying. Slade could see Janey was full of adrenalin. Her face was red with fury. She screamed, "Get out of our camp you raping, disgusting bastard. You deserved everything you got." Jake moved around towards the entrance of the camp where Slade was lying. With the drugs clouding his sanity, Slade's face had a vicious look on it. "I'll get her for what she has done to me," he sneered at Jake. Revenge was the only thing his mind could think of. Heather had rushed over to help Sue get to her feet. She kindly brushed the dirt from Sue's face and gave her the blood soaked towel she had been using to cover herself since Jake had thrown his backhander. The two sisters shared a glance of true fear and desperation as they pulled each other close.

Janey cranked a second bullet into the chamber and pointed the barrel towards Jake.

"Get out or I will shoot you too! Get out!!"

Slade could see his brother being threatened and he forced himself up and into a crouching position. The fire had died right down and the light throughout the camp was really dim. Jake's body was blocking Janey's view of Slade who remained in the crouched position as he held tightly to his injured shoulder. Slade inched forward as he slowly got to his feet and grabbed the rifle. He remained hidden by both Jake's body and the fading light. Janey screamed, "Get out, get out!" Slade was opening the bolt and slipping a bullet into the chamber. As Jake turned to make his exit from the camp, Slade managed to get a clear view of Janey. As he raised the 303 Jake caught his first glimpse of the rifle in Slade's hand. He tried in vain to grab it off his brother as he yelled,

"No! Slade, no!"

Slade ignored everything but the desire for revenge. He effortlessly aimed the 303 and fired it directly at Janey, smirking as the bullet hit her and caused her to fall backwards as blood began to gush from her mouth. The rifle she had been holding slipped from her grasp and fell to the ground with a thump. She slumped to the ground hard, only a couple of seconds after the rifle. The bullet had entered her chest and made a fist sized hole in her back where it had exited. The soft nosed hunting bullet had exploded on impact and fragmented as it was designed to do. Sue and Heather rushed over to their friend in absolute shock. They held onto Janey as they attempted to stop the flow of blood which soaked their own skin. Janey looked up at Sue who was gently holding her head. Tears were pouring down Sue's face and falling into Janey's lovely golden hair. Sue was trying to be strong for Janey but felt her body shaking with the shock of everything that had happened.

"Tell Brent I love him," Janey gasped.

"Hang in there, Janey. You will be ok. We will look after you," reassured Heather.

"Please look after Brent and the kids," she coughed as blood dripped from her mouth. "They are everything to me. Tell them all how much I love them," Janey whispered as she slipped in and out of consciousness.

"You can't die!" screamed Sue. A wave of despair washed over her.

Heather was overcome with grief and turned to face Slade who had dropped the gun.

"You murdering bastard!" Heather yelled as she grabbed a piece of wood and rushed towards Slade.

Heather got distracted as out of the corner of her eye she saw another person arrive at the entrance to the camp. When Luke had heard the first shot he was just leaving the camp and he knew it had come from down the river. He had imagined that Slade must have seen a deer and he had hurried down the river, driven by his desire to see what Slade had shot. His heart had begun to beat loudly in his ears as he ran towards the Bullring camp. By the time the second shot had rung through the air he was close enough to know the shot had come from the camp. He had let out a faint scream as he had sped up to run as fast as he could. He was worried sick from trying to imagine what could possibly have happened and what was going to confront him when he arrived at the camp.

Luke raced around the end of the log and jumped up the bank. He rushed straight over to Slade and grabbed the gun from his brother who had picked it up to defend himself against Heather and her stump of wood.

"What the hell has happened here?" Luke demanded.

Heather grabbed Roger's gun from where it had dropped beside Janey and pointed it towards the three of them.

"Ask your asshole mate what the hell has happened! Get out of here, all three of you!"

Luke could see terror and hatred written all over Heather's face as she yelled,

"Get out of here, I'm going to shoot you all, you raping, murdering bastards!"

Luke noticed an unaccompanied limp body at the back of the camp as he could see along the back of the log from where he stood. He looked around further and saw a naked woman cradling the body of another woman; both drenched with blood. Realising what must have happened, Luke felt tears stab at his eyes as the screams escaped his lips.

"You mad prick, you've killed her. You are the maddest prick on earth!"

Luke was hysterical, he felt himself shaking as he realised in that moment he could kill his own twin brother. Luke held tightly to the 303 and looked over at Jake who was also in shock - and sobering up fast. The three brothers backed out of the camp. Luke wasn't sure of who he could trust, he didn't know which brother had done what, but he could see by the eyes of Heather and Sue that Slade was the main perpetrator.

"I'm so sorry, I don't know what my brothers have done but I promise I will do all I can to help," mumbled Luke.

"Just get out of here and keep that mongrel away from us. We don't want your help," cried Sue as she pointed at Slade with hatred.

"Just leave us alone," shrieked Heather as she waved the gun at them.

Slade, continued to hold his shoulder as he staggered out towards the river.

"It was self-defence, bro," offered Slade. "Whatever," scoffed Jake. "I feel bloody sick."

"You will be sick when the cops catch up with you," scowled Luke. "And that is nothing to how you will feel when Mum and Dad find out what happened up here."

Slade stopped in his tracks and turned to head back towards the Bullring camp. The P had brought out the worst in Slade and hearing mention of the cops made him instantly determined to go back and shoot the others; to make sure they were all dead. Slade knew Luke was holding the gun. He was not pointing it directly at Slade but was in a position that he could if Slade started to head back towards the camp. Luke was distraught and Jake was sobbing hard.

Slade rolled his eyes at his brothers and muttered obnoxiously, "She shot first."

"You still shouldn't have shot her," Luke screamed at him.

Jake and Luke managed to convince Slade that they had better get moving, that the group of adults may have already made contact with the outside world and the police could already be on the way. Staggering back up the river in the black of the night, with only their small mag light torch, they made their way towards their own camp. Luke was swearing all the way back. Jake was looking utterly miserable, and Slade was holding tightly to the rum bottle as he drank heavily from the contents. Luke kept mentioning how he should go back and help the ladies back at camp.

"No, Luke, they'll shoot you," warned Jake defeatedly. "Come on, let's get back to camp and think about what to do now."

Meanwhile, Heather and Sue tried desperately to keep Janey alive. Any signs of consciousness had long left her and her breathing was jagged and laboured. They stroked her hair and spoke kind words to her in case she could hear them. The tears slipped down their cheeks as they looked down at the friend they loved so dearly. Janey took a small, sharp breath that was not followed by another, and life drained out of her. Heather and Sue sat with their friend, unable to believe the truth, as they stared blankly at Janey for several minutes with tears pouring down their faces. Heather grabbed Sue's wrist and whispered there was nothing more they could do, but that maybe there was something they could do for Roger. They rushed over to where he remained unconscious, but still breathing. Blood, which had been seeping out of a gash in the side of his head, was beginning to thicken. Heather grabbed some warm blankets and wrapped him up to make him as comfortable as she could. Sue ran to get their first aid kit so she could bandage Roger's head. When he seemed to be as comfortable as they could make him, they crossed over to Janey's body. Tears had not stopped pouring down either of their faces. They carefully picked Janey up and placed her gently into her sleeping bag which they had lain down near to the fire. Returning to Roger, Heather noticed his breathing had become a lot fainter. Heather was desperately trying to hold herself together as she sat with Roger's head on her knee. The girls were shaking and terrified as they feared they were still in danger. The women quickly dressed themselves in their warmest clothing.

Heather let the dogs off the chain and grabbed the gun as Sue stirred up the fire with shaking hands. Heather was petrified in case the three men made a return. She loaded a bullet into the breach,

"If anything moves out there, I'm going to shoot it."

Sue stoked up the fire as best as she could, grateful for the large supply of firewood that Brent and Stevo had left behind for them. They were determined to sit up all night beside Roger and keep an eye out for the mens return. Both were totally drained and their faces were ashen but there was no way either of them would be getting any sleep. They knew there was no cellphone reception and felt utterly helpless as there was no way they could think of to get help. They huddled together, praying and wishing for the return of Brent and Stevo from Secret Creek.

CHAPTER FORTY-FOUR

Slade, Jake, and Luke struggled their way back to their camp. They argued endlessly about the turn of the night's events. Slade and Jake continued to drink late into the night while trying to decide what to do. Jake turned angrily to Slade.

"You have really done it this time, bro. We are finished when we get out of here. You killed that nice lady."

"She might not be dead," mumbled Slade. Luke yelled at him, "She is dead, Slade! And I'm going back to see if I can help them." "No, please!" Jake insisted. "They'll shoot you, Luke. Please don't go, I know it feels like we should but it will honestly only make things worse."

"Oh my God!" groaned Luke in frustration. "Don't you realise what you have done? You shot her in the chest with Dad's 303." He felt the bile rise in his throat as he was hit with a wave of nausea and felt as if he was going to be sick.

"What about the other guy, Slade? I think you might have killed him too. I saw a lot of blood coming out of his head," admitted Luke. "I didn't mean to kill him. But he asked for it the way he kept going on at us to leave their camp. For fucks sake man, that Bullring camp is ours! It's all because of him that things have gone and bloody turned out the way they did." Luke knew Slade was trying his best to convince himself and the others that none of what had happened was his fault.

Jake just shook his head.

"You won't listen to anyone, Slade. You always think you know best but you have really messed up this time."

"We'll see," sneered Slade. "They might not tell the police or anyone." Luke looked over at his twin in disgust. He knew his brother must have taken P to behave the way that he had as everything had become totally out of control. Their fire had long gone out and Luke was shivering from both the cold and the events of the night. Luke left the two brothers drinking by the fire and climbed into his sleeping bag and eventually fell into a deep sleep filled with nightmares.

CHAPTER FORTY-FIVE

As day broke the following morning, Sue and Heather were exhausted with the tension of the night. The reality of their experience re-hit them as the sun began to climb over the horizon and send its rays down to warm the earth.

"Nothing will ever be the same again," sobbed Sue. She hadn't stopped shaking all night.

Heather whispered encouragingly,

"Please try to hold yourself together, Sue. I know everything is a mess right now but I really need you to be strong until the men get back."

Roger was miraculously clinging onto life and Heather wouldn't leave his side for even a minute.

"I think his breathing is a little easier than it was. I know he has improved a little."

They had managed to keep him well covered and it seemed as if his body temperature had warmed up to what felt somewhere near normal. Sue nodded meekly at Heather and wandered off to put the billy on to boil. Brent and Stevo wouldn't be back until at least midday. Sue knew they would be on their own until then, and she prayed that the hunters wouldn't be late. Heather had not let go of the rifle all night; she hadn't gone anywhere around camp without it. Sue and Heather were discussing the possibilities of where the three boys could have vanished to. They knew they had disappeared back up the river and hadn't come back down - which as far as they knew, was the only way out.

Heather grimaced.

"If I see them, I'm going to shoot first and ask questions later."

"Do you think we should let the dogs off for protection?" asked Sue.

"No," replied Heather. "They might take off on us. We have enough to worry about. They are better where they are."

Heather checked the mag and searched her husband's pockets for more bullets.

Sue appeared to be getting even more distraught as the daylight had sent her mind racing with the thoughts of Slade forcing himself inside her, and then Janey being killed. At the moment she didn't think her world could get any worse. She was filled with terror at the thought that the three boys may have to come back down the river. They huddled up with their two cups of tea beside Roger behind the log, keeping him warm with the sleeping bags and blankets, and with the gun constantly aimed towards the river. Heather had stretched her arm around Sue. The two women felt utterly traumatised; their faces were devoid of emotion and their bodies were exhausted after being on guard for nearly twelve hours.

Janey's blood had dried onto their skin and the warm clothing they had dressed in after the boys had left.

"I'm going to have a swim and scrub the physical reminders of last night away," said Sue.

"No," Heather almost shouted at her. "You can't do that. The police will need evidence and his DNA will be on you."

Sue hung her head and howled as she recalled the events of the night. Heather hugged her tightly.

It was about 7 a.m. and they faced at least another five hours alone together before Brent and Stevo were due back.

"Hang in there, Sue. It won't be long until Stevo is back," said Heather.

"I'm know, I can't wait. Poor Janey," whispered Sue.

"It is an unimaginable situation. Can you please hold the gun? I am going to check on Roger." Heather passed Sue the gun as she fussed over Roger to ensure he was comfortable. She could hear him finally starting to regain consciousness. She was able to get him to sit up against the log without too much trouble.

"How is your head, love?" Heather asked Roger. He could only moan a reply.

"Here, have a drink of water, we need to keep your fluids up." He managed to drink a small amount. The billy was still going so she was able to mix the hot water with some cold river water to wash his wounds tenderly.

Heather quickly checked back on Sue. "Are you okay, Sue?" fretted Heather. "Yes, I guess I'm okay."

"Would you like another cup of tea?" "Yes, that would be good."

Heather gave her a hug and then went off to make them each a fresh cuppa before returning to where they huddled together and drank the hot tea. They knew the dogs would alert them if there was any danger but Heather still placed the gun across Sue's knees as she drank her tea. There would be no hesitation in shooting if the three young men returned. Sue tried to think of other things to talk about, wondering out loud if Brent and Stevo may have had any luck up Secret Creek. Heather really didn't want to talk about Janey or Roger, or about Sue being so violently violated; they were both on the edge of a complete breakdown. Their only chance for survival was to remain strong for a few more hours; just in case the three intruders returned before their own two men.

The morning ticked slowly by, lunchtime was approaching and the girls began to feel pangs of hunger caused by not eating in nearly 24 hours. Roger was slowly improving and he opened his eyes again. He mumbled something that the girls couldn't make out before slipping back into unconsciousness. The girls felt their fears ebb a little at the relief of Stevo and Brent's approaching arrival.

CHAPTER FORTY-SIX

"Wake up sleepyhead. We have got to get out of here as fast as we can. Can you believe what went down last night?" Luke said as he dug Jake in the ribs with his boot.

Jake groaned painfully.

"I had hoped it was all a bloody nightmare!" "Shall we go back to see them?" asked Luke. "Nah, let's just get out of here," said Jake.

"I'm worried about the people at the Bullring," said Luke. "I still think we should go and help them. They must be terrified."

"I know, but our best option is to get out of this valley. We can head over into the neighbouring water shed and trek out that way," replied Jake.

"Let's wake Slade and get going. The police may be on their way by now for all we know." Luke kept looking towards Bullring.

"It's a plan. There's absolutely no way we can go back down the river," said Jake.

Slade was beginning to stir and he grabbed at his shoulder as he woke up.

"Shit, that is throbbing," groaned Slade.

"It is looking very swollen and red," said Luke. He got a rag and dipped it into some water before washing the wound. He wrapped the wet rag around it tightly, noticing that his brother was still very sluggish.

"Come on Slade, we've got to get going. You need to shake off the effects of all the drugs and alcohol you consumed last night so we can get the hell out of here," yelled Luke, trying to stir Slade into action. A chopper could be heard in the distance.

Panicking, Jake looked around with his eyes flashing.

"This could be the cops. Listen to that chopper. Let's get into the bush in case they can see us."

Moaning with pain Slade grabbed the 303 and they dived into the nearby bush. The chopper didn't seem to come any nearer but they could still hear it working overhead.

Luke spoke to his brothers,

"We can't move until we know what that chopper is doing. If it is the cops they will spot us easily."

Jake nodded in agreement.

"We'll have some grub and get going, making sure we stay in the bush on the side of the river. We're going to have to walk from here and stay in the bush. We'll tie the horses up in here where there is plenty of grass. When we get out, I will ring a mate and he can come up and get them. If you hear any choppers coming then we all have to get further into the bush quickly because they will spot us miles away."

∽

Slade began dishing out advice even though this mess they were in was all his fault.

"We'll go up into the head waters of Green River and get into the next catchment and walk back down to the coast. I reckon that will take us about two or three days and we'll worry about what to do about what happened up here when we get back to the coast."

Luke sighed,

"I guess we'll pinch another car and hightail it out of there." Jake scoffed,

"Now you are sounding like Slade. This is getting worse and worse." "Just relax, Jake," smirked Slade. "Things will all be okay."

"Are you kidding Slade? Things will never be okay again!" exclaimed Jake.

The boys headed off up the river and tried to stay hidden but the bush was making the going really slow with all the supple jack, bush lawyer, and logs from storms gone by. They had to do some river crossings. Slade looked around, his eyes were flashing angrily.

"Damn this. We're going back for the horses. This is way too slow. We'll get the horses and ride up in the dark. It will still be slow going, having to be careful with every step the horses make, but it will be quicker than this across all these river crossings and gorgy bits. We won't get as wet and cold on the horses."

They stopped to listen out for the sounds of the helicopter. "Mustn't have been the cops," Jake felt the relief nearly bring him

to his knees in gratitude.

"Cool," sighed Luke, half wishing it had been so the nightmare would be over.

They agreed with Slade's plan and they retraced their steps down the river back to where they had camped. The horses were well rested and had been chowing down on plenty of good food. They saddled up the horses and set out to move off up the river for the second time. After riding for two hours, the light was fading and the river had narrowed up to where it became full of large boulders. They had made some good progress, but the conditions were far too dangerous to carry on any further in the dark.

Jake said, "Let's call it a night, it's been a hell of a day." "Yeah, sure has been tough," said Luke.

Slade just nodded his head in silent agreement.

Dejectedly they decided to camp for the night and move on at first light.

CHAPTER FORTY-SEVEN

The sunrise had seen the moss draped trees allow rays of sunlight to shine through. Patches of fog were drifting in the gullies as it had been a cold night out in the bush. The secret creek which the two hunters had followed the day before had taken them high up into the ranges. Stevo was up first, as always, and had already set about stirring up the fire. He filled the billy from the creek and placed it on the fire to boil. Brent had woken to the sounds of the billy and had begun to sort out the breakfast. Looking up the valley, Brent could see the morning mist rising over the tops of the bush towards the blue sky which was like a beautiful painted backdrop. He was really keen to get going and found he had to drag Stevo away from admiring his big trophy.

"It will be safe here while we go up the valley hunting, I promise."

Stevo looked over at his best friend with a smile on his face, leaned down to grab his Ruger 308, and called with excitement,

"Let's go!"

Brent was already moving off up the creek at record pace. From where they were on the ridge, up behind the camp and looking up the valley to where they had heard the other stag the day before, they estimated they only needed to go about 2 kilometres up the creek - one and a half to two hours, depending on the going. The walking was easy for the first hour, and they stopped for a break which they knew they would need before they tackled the rest of the creek. Brent could see it was getting very steep and huge boulders were everywhere, making it harder to climb up and around in order to get where they wanted to be. He rolled a smoke as he leaned against the bank of the creek.

Stevo sat on a log nearby, did the same and commented,

"I think we will have to walk for about another half an hour. The going has been easier than I thought and we have made good time up until now."

After finishing their smokes they got to their feet and continued their way up the creek. The going was deteriorating rapidly as the boulders got bigger, and lots of log jams from big storms hindered their progress. The logs and rocks were very slippery and wet so they had to carefully negotiate their way gingerly up the creek for another half an hour. Finally they rounded a big sharp corner where Stevo looked up and saw the big slip that he had seen when first looking across from the ridge.

"That is the spar we could see from the ridge where I shot my stag yesterday."

The spar was the remains of a big tree where the top had broken out of in storms. "Great," whistled Brent grinning. "That big hata won't be too far from here. He'll have his pad out on a sharp ridge end I'm sure, one where he can see who is coming and so that his roar can be heard for miles."

They carefully picked their way around the slip and discovered a grassy area big enough for them to sit down on. They gathered up some firewood and hastily built a fire so they could boil the billy.

"Hopefully I will be lucky today," grinned Brent.

"Can't see any reason why not," answered Stevo reassuringly. "Just as well we have made good time coming up the creek. It's still only 7.30 in the morning! We'll go hard straight up for an hour because that stag we heard yesterday was really high."

"Okay," replied Brent. "Even if we make really good time we won't be back to camp by lunchtime. I hope Janey doesn't get too worried when we are late. She knows that our times are only approximate and is probably having a nice relaxing day, trying to finish her book before we get back."

Brent turned to Stevo.

"This is going to be a real haul. It looks pretty steep." Stevo nodded.

"Yeah but hopefully the rewards will be great!"

Brent smiled at Stevo's enthusiasm; even though he was in the lead because it was his shot, his best friend was always right there for support and giving energy. Brent found himself going really hard and fast up the ridge because he didn't want to be too late back to the Bullring and cause Janey unnecessary worry. He knew she wouldn't be too concerned if they were a couple of hours late, but Brent had always been a bit of a worrier. His main aim was still to have a go at getting the giant stag. Brent was on a bit of a mission. He did not like to be late when it came to meeting Janey.

"Don't worry, Brent. We'll be back on time," Stevo reassured his friend, knowing that he had to get Brent in his best frame of mind in order to hunt the prize hata.

As they reached three quarters of the way up the ridge, Brent and Stevo were puffing hard and sweating profusely.

Stevo paused with his hands supporting his back. "I think we should have a roar here, Brent." Brent, only too happy to have a break, nodded. "Yeah I'm keen! Give him a roar Stevo."

Stevo took a big breath before giving the biggest and loudest roar he had ever made through his favourite bullhorn roaring stick. It made the hairs on the back of Brent's neck stand up. They would have to wait quietly to see if anything answered, so they sat down and rolled themselves another smoke. They were about to move off when they heard the reply to Stevo's roar. It was the loudest and deepest roar they had ever heard, and it came out of a side creek just around to their right.

Stevo snapped his head to face Brents. "Brent, did you hear that?"

"Sure did." Brent leaped to his feet determinedly. "It doesn't seem to be far away either, like it is just over that next ridge! We'll have to go down this gut between us and that next ridge."

The deep roar was heard again, followed by another stag answering him from somewhere in the distance; obviously interested in trying to get the big stag's hinds off him. The men ignored the answering roar, left their ridge, and made a move knowing they had managed to get a really good bearing. Peeling down across the gully and up the other side, they approached the ridge that they believed the 18 pointer was on the other side of. They heard the second stag roar in the distance again and Brent could tell he wasn't anywhere near as big as the hata in the valley. Quietly they come up onto the ridge where they stood for a few moments to regain their breathing and get their adrenalin under control. They wanted to wait long enough to hear their stag roar again as they didn't want to roar and give away their position. Stevo was looking around at the ground while Brent tried to listen.

"Just look at the size of those marks," Stevo whispered.

Looking down, Brent saw the biggest stag marks he had ever seen. "They're as big as a poley bull mark," he whispered in reply.

The silence was shattered as they heard a lot of smashing and crashing down in the side gut off the side of the ridge where they stood. Brent checked the wind to find it was coming straight into their face.

"Wind feels okay, it is a straight southerly."

More smashing could be heard further down in the creek. The big hata was pushing his antlers into a ponga tree; absolutely tearing it apart. The more the ponga tree branches waved around, the more excited and wild the stag became.

Stevo offered,

"You go down and I'll stay here." Brent shook his head in refusal.

"No. I want you right here on this one. We either get him together or we don't get him at all."

Stevo grinned in agreement as Brent moved off, with the wind in his face, towards the big stag. The two hunting buddies walked really slowly and tried not to make any noise as they approached the smashing. They were within 50 metres of where the noise had come from when they found where the hata had been wallowing and pushing the ponga trees by thrashing his antlers up and down. Stevo pointed to a tree with marks where the stag had been rubbing. It had rubbed the bark off at least 3 metres or higher on the tree. Their attention turned immediately from the tree to a spot behind them when a massive roar came out of the gut just 50 metres away. The stag had not moved as he was obviously on his pad. The hairs stood up on the backs of both Brent and Steve's necks. The gully was full of thick supple jack which was making it really hard for them to sneak in without making too much noise. They had to get right down onto their bellies and crawl underneath it. It was a really slow process that, combined with the excitement, made the 50 metres feel more like 200. They were drawing really close to where the last roar had come from and they crouched back on their heels. Needing the stag to make a noise so they would know where to go next, they crouched for a few moments until they heard a stick snap just 20 metres ahead, in the thickest looking part of the gully. They both looked around, rifles at the ready. Nothing happened for a few long drawn out moments.

Because it was so thick, and two people made a lot more noise than one, Stevo nodded at his best friend.

"You got this mate. You go on, Brent."

Brent realised his oldest friend was right, and he crawled forward on his belly through even thicker supple jack. The hata let out another massive roar. It felt like the bush was shaking, as if they were in the midst of an earthquake. Brent sat up in a crouched position and stared towards where the roar had come from. He waited a few more moments and realised he could see movement in the supple jack. He was experienced enough to know it was the target he was after, but also knew enough to make sure he had a clear shot.

He knew he couldn't miss his shot or the stag could be really dangerous - there was nowhere for Brent to go to get out of his way quickly. Brent knew he had only one chance at the magnificent animal and he was not going to miss his opportunity. The big hata would have been tormented all night by the roar of other stags trying to come and steal his hinds away. It sounded as if he was infuriated and was determined to show he would not allow it. It was clear he had attracted a lot of hinds because of the amount of sign in the surrounding area - and no other stag was getting near them. The giant hata would stick one of his eighteen massive tines right through another if he tried getting too close. The other stag who constantly roared back at him was getting braver and nearer all of the time.

Another ponga branch moving in the wind got him wild and he started stripping it from its trunk with his mighty antlers, rasping up and down the trunk which was what Brent could see as he crawled along on his belly. Normally the big hata would be wary of any foreign smells in his valley; especially human ones. He would avoid them, knowing that humans were his only true predator. But he was so wild and his adrenalin was at its peak; he was ready to fight to the death with anything that threatened him and his position as top stag. In the natural cycle of life, the best stag gets to breed and keep the future generations strong. His natural wariness and divine sense of smell was momentarily put on hold as he stripped the ponga clean of its branches with one swipe of his massive antlers. His nostrils caught a foreign smell to his right and his massive head swung around instantly, looking straight to where the bizarre smell had come from. With the ponga branches hanging off his antlers, he looked so majestic despite his rage being at boiling point. He saw a movement and instantly let out a blood curdling roar as he charged. He tore supple and two inch thick jack vines into pieces as his huge body powered his antlers through it. Brent had been waiting for movement and was sweating with the anticipation of what was going to happen. He knew he had to be careful; an angry hata, wild and worked up with testosterone, was capable of killing anything in its way. Brent had just noticed the movement when the stag's huge head swung into sight. No sooner did he see it, did he realise it was coming at him at an unbelievable speed through the dense undergrowth. It was only metres away and there was no time to think, every skill with a weapon and every ounce of bravery was needed. He had to shoot and side step at the same time so the huge stag would not drill him with its antlers. Brent lifted the rifle and fired.

The big stag had lots of pieces of vine and ponga fern attached to his antlers because he had been coming through the bush like a bulldozer smashing everything in its path. Brent hadn't placed his shot as well as he would have liked and the big stag merely shook from the impact of the bullet as it thundered past Brent. A tine on his rack of antlers scraped Brent's shoulder as the momentum of the stag's body carried him past his target; Brent. The hata would have fully caught the scent of Brent as he roared past, and he spun around with all of the vines continuing to cling to his antlers as he stopped in his tracks.

He forcefully shook the vines off his antlers in one big shake of his majestic head. Sighting his human target again, he quickly came charging forward a second time. Brent hardly had time to reload. He could see that the big stag's adrenalin was at an extreme peak and the hata had felt no pain from the impact of the bullet; the loud noise and the odd sensation had just made him madder. Brent knew he had no choice but to take him down with a fatal shot or this stag was going to get him; there was nowhere to run. The bush was really thick and this stag could go through it like it wasn't there at all. The hata was almost on top of him and, as all the vines had come off his antlers, Brent could see his head more clearly.

He knew he had one more chance and he decided to hold his ground, aim the gun directly in front of him, and try to place the bullet exactly between his antlers. Brent focussed on the stag's head which was becoming entwined with vines again as he made his way through the shaking bush. As the vines got caught on the stag's antlers, they were being dragged out of the tree canopy above as the stag tore through the undergrowth to kill the human who had invaded his valley to torment him. The hata was a split second from being on top of his predator as the human finger squeezed the trigger; it was life or death for either warrior. If the stag won, Brent would have eighteen tines driven through his body.

Everything became a blur for Brent who felt something impact against his shoulder and send him f lying backwards into the undergrowth. His head hit something hard and he was momentarily stunned.

Stevo had moved in really close toward the commotion. He could just make out the hata charging at Brent. Stevo could not risk a shot as it was just too close to Brent. Brent's shot had hit the big hata in his heavily muscled neck. As the stag took the impact of Brent's bullet it had made him veer off from his line of charge and hit Brent with his shoulder causing him to go flinging backwards through the air like a feather. The hata was going down. Stevo could see a clear shot and finished him off. Brent was coming to as Stevo rushed over and helped him to his feet.

"Gee mate, that was close. Are you ok?"

"Sure was! Thanks mate, you always have my back!" Brent exclaimed gratefully.

As they moved over to admire the big stag they had nabbed together Brent was still looking a bit dazed but had a big smile on his face, seeing the eighteen tines and how even they were.

"That is some hata, mate. It was either you or him."

"That's for sure. Yeah, that was too close for comfort. Don't tell Janey, aye Stevo?"

"No, not that bit anyway," he slapped his mate on the back who had a big beaming smile on his face that mirrored his own.

It was a massive 18 pointer, with a perfectly symmetrical rack, just like Stevo's one. Stevo sighed contentedly,

"Man, that's a big deer, Brent. It must be the biggest we have ever got."

Brent wore a smile from ear to ear.

"Hunting is the biggest buzz you can have with your pants on." Stevo laughed.

"That's for real."

They sat down and enjoyed a cigarette as they admired the big stag. Brent looked down at his watch. Without saying anything, Stevo got to his feet and started skinning out the back legs and the back steaks while Brent worked on the trophy head.

Brent eventually piped up,

"Looks like we can go straight down this gut and out into the main creek, Stevo."

Stevo nodded.

"Yeah, should be easier and it will save us a lot of time."

The men headed off; Brent had the big stag head over his shoulders and Stevo was loaded down with meat. An hour and a half of hard slog later took them to back to their overnight camp where the horses were shuffling about on their leads. Brent greeted them as he dropped his pack, leaned over and picked up his saddle. An enormous spider scuttled out from under where his saddle had been sitting. It started backing up and away from Brent who was placing the saddle upon Big Red's back. The spider was the size of a dinner plate.

Stevo yelped,

"Oh no. Not again."

"What?" called Brent, spinning around to look for whatever Stevo was talking about.

"Look what was under your saddle," called Stevo.

The spider had a ferocious look about it as it backed away with its feelers high in the air. Brent called out in dismay,

"Oh God, not another big spider!"

Stevo examined the spider a little more closely.

"He's not anywhere as big as those ones we saw at the plane crash site. I didn't think those hormones would have got into this watershed." "It must have travelled from the other watershed, either with us

or maybe they are getting hungry and moving into new areas. Could also be that the big spiders are making the smaller ones move out or they will get eaten."

Stevo shuddered.

"I thought we had seen the last of those massive spiders. I'll be checking my sleeping bag carefully before I get into it if that is what the wildlife up here is like too."

The spider scampered down a root hole and disappeared from sight.

"I wouldn't want to be a rat living down a hole in the ground with that spider around," laughed Brent.

The men saddled up the horses and packed the meat on. Stevo tied his big deer head onto the saddle of his horse, but Brent decided to carry his because of the size; he didn't want it catching on any branches on their way back to camp and getting damaged.

"Looks like we are only going to be half an hour to an hour late, Brent," Stevo advised his friend.

"Great, that's not too bad," applauded Brent. "Let's go!"

Stevo and Brent made their way down Secret Creek, their horses were moving freely at a good pace but getting around the narrow, slippy bits, with the giant hata heads was causing quite a problem. They got tangled in the bush lawyer and would catch on trees and the undergrowth. They finally arrived after an hour and and a half of riding at the grassy clearing above the main river which looked out across the main camp. There was no sign of life and Brent figured that Roger and the girls must be by the fire or up at the big pool where Secret Creek joined the main river.

Brent pointed his horse down the gut which was so slippery and greasy that his horse was virtually sliding all the way down on its haunches. The deer head was catching on branches and almost pulling Brent off his horse. Stevo let his friend get a bit in front so Stormy wouldn't catch up with Big Red and slide into him. Brent's horse hit the main river in a shower of stones and mud as Stevo arrived abruptly behind him just seconds later.

CHAPTER FORTY-EIGHT

rent and Stevo were surprised to discover that despite their tardiness, Janey, Sue, and the others were not there to meet them - and were nowhere in sight. Brent sensed that things were not all as they should be and they two men urged their horses forward, nudging them in the side. Big Red reared up and took off at a gallop. Brent dropped the deer head so he could hold onto the reins for dear life. The impressive trophy landed in the soft sand at the side of the river.

"There must be something wrong," he yelled over to Stevo. "I hope no one has gotten hurt or anything while we have been away."

They reined their horses in and made their way directly towards the camp. Brent jumped his horse up the big bank and straight into camp. Reining Stormy in hard, Stevo was right behind him. Pulling up together in the camp they leapt off their horses and were confronted by Sue running towards them.

"Thank God you are back," Sue screamed through her sobs.

Brent, being in front, had a distraught Sue fall into his arms. He could see she was covered in blood, and the tears poured from her eyes. Stevo rushed up and Sue dove straight into his arms.

"What on earth is wrong?" Brent begged her to explain.

Sue could hardly speak, she was so choked up with emotion. Brent could only understand the odd word - Janey.

"I'm so, so sorry, Brent," she cried desperately. "Janey … dead … Roger may die too … three boys … one was evil … Janey's dead! … The evil one raped me …" And at those final words, Stevo pulled his wife closer to him as she sobbed uncontrollably.

"What are you talking about?" yelled Brent in disbelief at what he was hearing. He spun around and searched for a sign of his wife, knowing he could hardly understand the words coming from Sue let alone believe them. Surely there had been a terrible mistake. Heather gently lifted Roger's head from her knee and rushed over to wrap her arms around Sue and Stevo. Heather, crying profusely, looked sadly at Brent.

"It's true, it's all true."

Sue was hysterical. Stevo tried his best to calm her as every piece of strength she had mustered in his absence fell away. Heather slowly gathered her composure and went back to where Roger was lying. Brent took off at a run towards the camp site to see if he could make sense of what Sue and Heather were screaming about. He saw where Heather had settled herself, holding Roger's head on her knee and stroking the tuft of hair that poked out of a bloodstained bandage.

"What the hell has happened here, Heather?" yelled Brent, beginning to feel as though he couldn't hold himself together. "Sue said Janey is dead," he whispered in disbelief. He felt himself starting to panic as he realised everything else Sue had said was coming true before his eyes.

"Brent, these two young guys invaded us last night. It was really horrible. The big one with dark hair hit Roger with a lump of wood and knocked him senseless. He only regained consciousness at daylight this morning." Heather had tears pouring down her face and dribble coming out of her mouth. Brent knelt down and wrapped his arms around her. He needed to know what had happened.

Through her tears Heather recounted the events of the previous night.

"Then that same guy raped Sue. He threatened to kill us if we tried to stop it from happening; he was holding a knife the entire time. Then Janey woke up from where she had landed after they attacked her. She tried to stop him by pointing Roger's gun at him. The evil guy let go of Sue and went towards Janey to try and get the gun off her. She warned him but he wouldn't listen, and the bullet hit him in the shoulder. He fell backwards and grabbed his rifle before shooting Janey in the chest. She died trying to protect us. Sue and I tried to stop the bleeding and help Janey … But he killed her, Brent. I'm so sorry."

Brent was looking ashen faced in disbelief. He leaped to his feet as he looked around for Janey.

"Where is she? Where's my Janey?" he cried as he rushed over towards where he saw her sleeping bag beside the fire.

Stevo was trying to make some sense out of what Sue was mumbling. He was in shock at what he was hearing and when she described how the biggest intruder had raped her at knife point, he turned pale and almost fainted. He managed to pull himself together and thought how, despite what had happened, he was lucky to still have his wife whereas his best friend was not.

He ran over to where Brent had found Janey's body. Brent was trying to sit her up. As he placed his hand around behind her back to try and help her into a sitting position, he felt the huge hole in her back where the bullet had exited. Blood was soaking onto his hand from the blood drenched blanket. He softly let Janey back down and collapsed beside her in a heap of sobs. Stevo knelt down beside Brent and laid his hand gently on his best friend's shoulder. Brent didn't move as his grief was overwhelming him. Stevo stood up and joined Sue and Heather who were standing right behind them. He wrapped his arms around both of them.

"How is Roger?"

"Critical, but holding his own," replied Heather meekly.

"God, how the hell could something like this happen up here in paradise?" Stevo swore.

Brent was clinging to Janey's body and sobbing heavily.

"Let's give Brent some space and some time with Janey. I need a cuppa, and for you both to tell me exactly what the hell has been going on here." Stevo directed the ladies over towards the fire where he quickly put the billy on to boil. Heather made her way back to where Roger was sitting up against the log. He had been drifting in and out of consciousness since he got the whack on his head. The voices had woken him out of his coma again.

"There's been a bit of an improvement," Heather called to the others. "I can only hope and pray he is going to make it."

They did their best to explain to Stevo what had happened as the billy boiled. Stevo began trying to make a cup of tea but was shaking so much that Heather had to take over; grief and fury was gripping at his insides. Heather finished making the cups of tea and gave a cup to Stevo. She then picked up a second cup to take over to Brent. Stevo knew what he and Brent had been through while they were hunting and how they had hardly eaten or drunk much all day because they were hurrying back;

they had planned to have a feed when they arrived back to camp. Stevo's hand started shaking and he spilled the hot tea all over his hand. Heather quickly grabbed a towel and threw it to Sue. She grabbed for the bucket of cold water and quickly pushed his hand into it. Stevo just slumped down and put his head into his other hand.

Heather quietly approached Brent and knelt down beside him where he was lying next to Janey.

"There's a cup of tea here Brent. Please drink something."

Brent remained motionless and did not say a word. Heather lay down on the other side of Janey with her arm over them both, her hand gently resting on Brent's shoulder. Time was passing; Sue had told Stevo all of the details about their night of terror. Stevo had started to get himself back together. Anger was starting to replace grief and sadness. Sue went over to check on Roger and saw that he had completely come to.

"Thank God you are awake, Roger. It was touch and go for a while," murmured Sue. Roger looked blankly up at her.

"Stevo can you please help me to move Roger right around by the fire? He will be warmer and be closer to everyone," said Sue.

Stevo and Sue carefully helped Roger move. Heather re-joined the group by the fire. She forced a wee smile onto her face for Roger who warmly smiled back. She leaned forward and gave him a kiss and a hug.

"Here, try to drink some water my love."

Roger managed to drink a cup of water which pleased Heather enough that she let out a real smile.

"Thank you honey," Roger whispered quietly.

Heather kissed the back of Roger's hand. She was worried because she suspected Roger had received a fractured skull on top of his concussion as the wound was very deep from the impact of the wood hitting him on the head.

CHAPTER FORTY-NINE

Late afternoon was falling upon them and still Brent had not moved. Stevo got to his feet and sighed; his whole demeanour had changed. He had decided someone was going to pay, to do some serious dying for what had happened. He made his way slowly over to check on his best friend. He knelt down and placed one hand on Brent's shoulder and reached out with the other to gently stroke Janey's face. He could feel how cold her skin was and that she had clearly been gone for many hours. Stevo removed his hand from Janey's cheek and began to rub his friends back gruffly with both hands.

Finally, Brent began to move. He looked up at Stevo with tears running out of his eyes.

"What the hell am I going to tell the kids?"

A fat tear rolled it's way down Stevo's cheek, splashing on the ground as he looked sadly at his friend.

"God knows, mate. Please come and have something to eat and drink. You haven't eaten all day."

Brent forced himself up and into a sitting position while rubbing roughly at his eyes.

"Yeah, yeah I know mate, I guess I've got to eat. How are the girls coping and how's Roger?"

Brent knew he had to eat to keep himself strong enough to get his wife's body home. He also wanted to have enough strength to track down and kill the bastards who had stolen away the life of the person who had always meant the entire world to him.

"The girls are as good as can be I guess, and Roger is holding his own and seems to be improving a little. We're going to have to get him some help pretty soon though, Brent, or he won't make it out of here either," sighed Stevo.

Brent looked down helplessly at Janey's body, wringing his hands as the tears began to fall to his lap one after another.

"Please come and have a cup of tea by the fire, it will do you some good."

Stevo helped Brent to his feet and slapped him comfortingly across the back before moving off to brew yet another cup of tea. Brent felt close to passing out and his legs seemed as if they would never be able to work due to the shock and despair. He leaned back down and made sure Janey was lying comfortably and gave her a gentle kiss on the cheek. He moved slowly towards the fire where Heather approached him and wrapped a warm arm around his waist.

"I just don't know what I can say, Brent. It just doesn't feel real at all."

Brent looked at his friend and squeezed her tight. As devastated as he was for his own loss, he was livid at the thought of what his friends had gone through in his and Stevo's absence. He could think of nothing more than jumping onto Big Red and riding off into the bush until he found the scumbags and killed each one of them for what they had done. Somehow he managed to hold himself together and stay at the camp. He knew that no revenge would ever be enough; that Janey was completely irreplaceable and that living a full life without her would forever be impossible.

By the time the tea was poured into the cups, the sun was starting to slip away; causing darkness to spread across the sky. Stevo looked around at his friends.

"In the morning, I'll ride out first thing to get some help. I'll need to go down the river to get cell phone coverage and then I'll be back as soon as I can be."

Sue squealed in dismay,

"If you are going out I'm going out too. You're not leaving me here again."

"We can't move Roger," Stevo spoke softly. He wrapped an arm around his wife and spoke quietly to her.

"It'll be better if you wait here for me to get back with some help. It will be much quicker to get some help if I go alone. I will be a lot faster on my own." He drew her body towards him tightly as she reluctantly nodded her head in bitter agreement. Sue was terrified at being left alone, yet she was even more afraid of losing another one of her very best friends.

Heather was sitting at the fire beside Roger who was leaning against a large log and looking a little bit better. Brent made his way back to where Janey lay as he wondered how much worse everything could possibly get before they all got out of the bush and back to safety. Stevo followed closely behind him and placed an arm around his shoulder,

"We've got to get a plan together, mate."

Stevo was eyeing up his friend. A big change had come over Brent as the grief and despair rapidly began to turn into anger.

"I'm going to kill the lot of them, Stevo. You take the girls out to safety. It's too dark to move down the river tonight. You know as well as I do that it is too dangerous to negotiate the river at night; the going is just too rugged. So, we will move out at first light. I'm going up the river to find the men who did this to Janey. You get the girls out and ring the cops as soon as you can get some cell phone coverage. I don't want to have to ask you to tell Daniel, Eugene, and Ingrid what has happened - but there is no other choice."

"Hang on Brent, just wait a minute. I want to come with you to find the murdering pricks." Despair and disappointment wash over Stevo as he realised he couldn't go along with Brent to get his own revenge for what the young men had caused. He knew what had to be done and was forced to accept the circumstances; getting Roger to a medical facility was of most urgency.

"I wish you could be with me too Stevo, but you can't mate. Someone has to look after Roger, Sue, and Heather. Can you make sure they send a chopper to pick up Janey and …" Brent's voice waivered as he spoke, "and that they take really good care of her."

"Yeah, yeah mate. I'll sort it, don't you worry. We can sort the horses out later too." Stevo paused to catch his breath,

"I will leave Heather and Sue here with Roger and Janey. I know they won't like it but I'll be quicker if I go by myself. I'll ride down the river until I get to those twin peaks. I can climb up and I'm sure there will be cell phone coverage up there. I'll take all the phones to make sure I have at least one that works; they're useless here anyway. I'll let the cops and your boys know what has happened and then I will be right back to you here. Don't kill them until I get back, I want to be there."

"If you think that is best mate. I just can't think straight."

Brent walked over to Sue who had just got up from sitting beside the fire. He asked her gently, but with fury burning in his eyes,

"Was it a blonde haired guy and two black haired ones?" Sue shuddered.

"Yes that big black haired boy was the worst of them all, Brent. He was the one who raped me and then shot Janey. He was the biggest one and the instigator of everything. The other dark haired one's also very solid but he looked like he wanted to help. I heard him tell the bad one to stop at least twice. He hit Heather. To be honest, they both looked like they were drugged up to the eyeballs. The blonde one did nothing to hurt us. He only came just after everything happened."

"Did he help you at all, Sue?" Brent whispered, struggling to accept just how much the girls had been through.

"No, but I think he wanted to. We told him we would shoot him if he came near us and for them just to get out of our camp. The other boy did whatever the bigger one told him to. I think one of them said they were brothers but I can't remember. It all happened so fast. I know I definitely heard the others call the big one Slade."

Brent curled his hands into fists.

"Did they only have one rifle with them?"

"Yes," added Heather as she approached the duo. "Were they riding two piebalds and a chestnut?"

Sue nodded her head meekly as tears began to pour continuously down her cheeks.

"We saw them when we were leaving yesterday." Brent gritted his teeth, wishing with everything in him that they had turned back to check on everything instead of just watching the boys from a distance. "Did they head off up the river when they left last night?"

Sue stuttered,

"Yes, we were terrified they were going to come back this way."

Sue was really beginning to struggle with having to relive the events of the night before, but she knew Brent needed to know the facts. Brent wrapped an arm gently around her in an attempt to give her some comfort.

Brent dropped his arm and walked straight over to where his rifle lay on the ground. He picked it up and checked it over, making sure there was a bullet in the chamber.

Stevo rushed over to him.

"What the hell are you doing?" he yelled.

"It's ok Stevo. I'm not doing anything stupid. I just want us to be careful. These men are pretty bad, Stevo. They all deserve to die for what they did."

"I know Brent, I just can't believe what has happened. It is only just starting to sink in. I'm trying to keep myself together for Sue and Heather." Stevo looked carefully at Brent before continuing, "I don't want you to be a murderer. I know it's hard but we have got to be strong."

"Yeah, I know, I know. But someone's going to die for this, Stevo."

Stevo sighed in resignation, he wanted to get revenge as much as his best friend did – and he still had his wife.

"Come on mate, we need some food Stevo. We've got a big day ahead of us tomorrow. I want to write a note for you to give to Daniel, Eugene, and Ingrid," Brent spoke bravely. Stevo gave his friend a sharp look. Brent was determined to get revenge, regardless of the consequences.

"You wait for me to get back, you hear me? You have to stay here with Sue, Heather, Janey, and Roger. They are going to need you here for protection. I promise we will deal to the slimy pricks when I get back. I won't be long. The cops will come in with me and we will soon find them and deal to them. You don't want to kill them and wreck your own life for those slime balls, Brent. Let the court system deal the justice out to them."

Brent laughed drily,

"My life is wrecked and no one is going to sit in a warm cell watching TV while my wife lies dead in the cold earth."

Stevo felt his heart sink to the ground.

"You've still got your kids, Brent. Please don't do anything while I'm gone."

"Yeah, yeah, yeah. I guess you're right," mumbled Brent in an attempt to set Stevo's mind at rest. All the while he was thinking how as soon as Stevo had left in the morning he would be right off after the three men.

Stevo looked hard at his friend and saw the deeply set hatred glowing in Brent's eyes. He shook his head as he wandered over to join Sue. All emotion had disappeared from Brent's face. Brent walked back to Janey and briefly checked on her as if she was only sleeping. Buck and Blue were straining at their chains as they tried to get a pat. Brent walked over to the dogs and gave them a long scratch behind each ear. He just couldn't keep himself still and felt as if he were growing more and more restless by the minute. The adrenalin from the circumstances had repowered his body.

Stevo and Sue were serving up dinner and Brent walked over to where Heather kept vigil beside Roger at the fire. He wrapped an arm kindly around her.

"God, I'm so sorry, Heather." "It's not your fault, Brent."

"We should have never left you guys."

"Nobody could have ever dreamt this would happen to us up here in such a beautiful part of safe New Zealand!"

Brent reached his hand down and gently touched a sleeping Roger's face.

"Hang on in there mate. We'll soon have you out of here." Sue approached them with plates of food.

"Tea's ready, Brent and Heather."

During the meal, the girls repeated the story of the night before and added all of the small details they had forgotten on the first telling. Sue cuddled even closer to Stevo, who had pulled out the remnants of the last rum bottle.

"We need some stiff drinks here, mate," he grimaced as he passed the bottle to Brent. "Sure do," sighed Brent who still had the gun slung over his shoulder.

The two men told the girls of their plan. Sue began to get hysterical again; shouting that she wouldn't stay alone in the bush without Stevo. "I know you need me, Sue," Stevo said. "But you will have Brent and Heather here. My heart is breaking leaving you again, but Heather needs your support. It is still touch and go with Roger and she will be having to look after him. I don't want her to be worrying about

anything except Roger."

"But I can't be away from you. Those guys might come back," spluttered Sue between sobs.

"They had better not come anywhere near here," Brent growled as he slammed back some more rum. "Not if they value their lives. They won't survive another visit to the Bullring that's for sure!"

Heather piped up bravely,

"We will look after Sue, Stevo. She will be okay. I don't want to be left here either, but I won't go anywhere without my Roger."

"I will be as quick as I can, Sue. You have to be strong."

Taking a deep breath, Sue got to her feet and walked away from the group to be on her own. Heather started to get up to follow her but Stevo placed his hand on her shoulder.

"Wait, Heather. Just let her be."

After a few minutes, Sue came back with tears streaming down her face.

"Whatever you think is best, Stevo. Whatever will get us out of here as quickly as possible."

"I won't be long, love. I promise I will be going as fast as I can." He held her tightly to him as he tried to console her. "The worst is over, you will be okay here."

"I know that, but it is so hard to let you go again." "Be strong, Sue," Stevo encouraged kindly.

Brent had gone back to Janey and was holding her gently as he lay beside her. He was sure she still felt warm and he found himself thinking that she must still be here, there was no way she was really gone. He looked at her ashen face and realised he was hoping against hope. Brent had seen many dead things in his life and he knew the look of death; there was no way that he could continue to lie to himself. He felt his body heave as it gave way to the racking sobs once again.

Heather checked on Roger who was continuing to drift in and out of consciousness as he lay just to the side of the fire where Stevo had helped to move him. She held a glass of water to his lips and helped him to drink.

"He is still breathing and recognises me," she whispered to the rest of the group.

"That's great news, Heather. Let's all focus on the positive," pleaded Stevo.

The night dragged on and Brent came over to join the others. "Why don't you guys get some sleep and I'll keep watch." Stevo nodded.

"Yeah, wake me at two and I'll take over, Brent. You need some sleep too."

They decided to leave the gas lantern burning all night so to keep the camp bright, and Stevo helped to make sure the fire was going strong with plenty of wood ready to throw on as it simmered down. It wasn't long before the others drifted off to sleep and Brent was sitting alone by the fire thinking about all the things he and Janey and the kids used to do. Memories of their camping holidays came flooding back. He could hear the laughter of their children as they swam and played with their friends. They had such a joyful time bringing up their children. He and Janey were a strong, happy team. For the hundredth time that day, tears began pouring down his cheeks.

He spoke to Janey while staring at the fire.

"I should have been here to protect you, Janey. The one time in our lives when you most truly needed me - and I wasn't there … Away hunting a bloody deer when your life was at risk. I am so sorry, Janey. I let you down and I will never forgive myself for that. You are the most precious thing in my life and I should have been here to take care of you. I am so selfish, how could I leave you here while I hunted a stupid deer? I will never forgive myself."

He shook his head as if to pull himself together. He knew Janey wouldn't want him to be beating himself up in this way; she knew he loved the bush, and so did she. He stretched his legs and sat himself up a bit. He knew that he had to stay awake just in case the three guys came back down the river to try to get out - or finish what they had started. Two o'clock took forever to roll around, but when it did Stevo took over the watch. Brent snuggled up to Janey and managed to get some dreamless sleep while lying beside her on the hard ground. He awoke at around 5.30am to the sound of Stevo saddling his horse up. Brent yawned as he rose to his feet and gave his best friend a hand with the horse.

While they were standing close together and saddling the horse, Stevo looked over at Brent and said pleadingly,

"Please don't do anything while I am away, Brent."

Brent lifted his arm and dropped it down on Stevo's left shoulder. "Nah, I won't mate."

Stevo looked deep into Brent's face. Where Brent's eyes used to be full of life, they were replaced by a hollow dullness and a glimmer of danger. Stevo looked over at Janey and noticed that Brent had put even more blankets over her as if he was trying to make her warm.

Brent coughed.

"Take your sleeping bag with you and something to eat in case it takes longer than expected to get to the peaks. With any luck, if you get away soon you should be back here by dark - but who knows what could happen."

Stevo had the billy on and Brent walked over to let Buck and Blue off their chain. The girls began to stir in their sleeping bags. Stevo walked briskly over to Sue and squeezed her, kissing her cheek and patting her hair. Brent leaned down to check on Roger. He seemed to be lying comfortably and his breathing was far less laboured; it looked as if his condition was stable. Brent just crouched beside him, unable to think of the right thing to say. He wasn't sure how much his friend was aware of, or how much he could hear in his unconscious state. Finally he spoke,

"We'll get you to the hospital as soon as we can, and we'll make sure Heather and the kids are okay."

Heather slept fitfully during the night and kept waking to check on Roger. She had spent a great deal of time looking through the photos on his digital camera. She had smiled to herself as she looked through them; he really had taken photos of absolutely everything.

"Look at this Brent," she called softly, "Roger got a photo of our attackers when they first rode up the river on their piebalds and chestnut. I remember the horses had looked so pretty in the sunshine." "Let me see that." Brent grabbed at the camera. He immediately recognised the three hunters he and Stevo had seen; the photo confirmed what he had thought. He knew who the attackers were. Brent was looking so intently at the photo that it was as if his eyes were going to pierce right through the camera. Stevo walked over with a cup of tea for each of them and joined Brent in looking at the photo, "Those are the ones we saw all right, Brent." The hatred Brent felt was overwhelming. Stevo put his hand on Brent's shoulder. He didn't say anything, words could not express the emotion of the moment.

Shaking his head, Stevo turned to the girls. "I had better get going."

Sue was up and dressed and she sat perched on the large log with her cup of tea as tears ran down her face. She had resigned herself to the fact that the sooner Stevo left, the sooner he would be back.

"I will be back with the chopper as soon as possible," Stevo assured everyone.

Brent called out to the dogs which came immediately running over to where he stood with the awaiting chains,

"The dogs can stay here with us. You wouldn't want them going off down the river. They'll only hold you up."

Stevo mounted his horse and looked around at the others before determinedly moving off down the river waving his left hand in the air behind him. Stevo had his 308 Ruger resting across his knees as he rode off. He had cranked a round into his Ruger as he mounted up; leaving the bolt open. He knew he would kill them himself if he ran into the three delinquents. His horse was going as fast as it could for the terrain and the morning was only just light enough to proceed without difficulty through the first part of the gorge which came into the Bullring. Stevo knew within the next half an hour, the sun would rise and the sky would be a lot lighter.

Stevo was soon far out of Brent's sight. Throughout the night, Brent had become even more determined to track down the three men who had raped his friend and murdered his wife. He had packed some food into a day pack and checked out each and every single one of his bullets. He knew he had a full ammo belt in his big pack and he thought sadly to himself about his decision.

'I won't be coming out of here. So I will put one bullet in my left pocket just for myself.'

CHAPTER FIFTY

Brent placed four bullets in the mag of his 270 and another two in his right pocket for back up. He secured his full ammo belt inside the day pack. He knew the girls and Roger would be safe without him. There were only two ways in and out of the Bullring camp – one way was down where Stevo had headed, and the other was further upstream where he was going. They couldn't have turned and gone up Secret Creek either as they would have already crossed paths. Brent was on a mission; as far as he was concerned the murdering, raping pricks were riding on a ticket straight to hell.

'They have ruined our paradise and will pay for it big time. It will be a world of hurt for them!' he exclaimed angrily to himself.

Brent called Sue and Heather over.

"I know you need me here, but I just can't sit here while those pricks are out there. My Janey is dead and I won't rest until I have got justice for her. You will be okay here. Stevo will be back by nightfall and you have got Roger's gun to protect you."

Sue and Heather clung to each other as what Brent was saying began to sink in; they were going to be left alone with the body of their best friend and an injured Roger while their friend rode upstream to hunt three murderers and a rapist. A terrifying shiver came over Sue's body and she began to sob hysterically as Heather tried her best to comfort her. Although she was terrified at the idea of being alone again, she bravely nodded to Brent.

"You do what you need to."

"Is there any way they can come back down this way?" Sue asked with a trembling voice.

"No, I can guarantee they can't come anywhere near here. Stevo has downstream covered even though we know they haven't headed that way

- and I am heading up after them. I sure as hell won't let them get past me if they try to make their way down here. Also, I have checked Roger's rifle and it has got a full magazine, you both know how to use if if you need to." Brent's voice also trembled as he spoke.

They bid their farewells quickly as Brent wanted to get going, and the girls returned to sit and care for Roger as Brent mounted Big Red. They moved off up the river at as fast a pace as the river and terrain would allow; Big Red was riding fresh after a night's rest and was more than keen to get going.

As soon as Brent was out of their sight, the two sisters huddled together. They kept their eyes trained up the river. Sue was shaking. Heather knew Sue couldn't take much more of being in the bush. Knowing her baby sister had been raped was making Heather's skin crawl. She felt herself hoping that Brent would catch up to the three young men and find his revenge; one that would hurt them well and truly for what they had done to Janey, Sue, and Roger.

Sue leaned into Heather's shoulder, mumbling as her mouth struggled to form the words.

"Do you think Brent and Stevo will be ok? They have hardly eaten properly for two days and they look worn and ragged."

Heather rubbed Sue's back and spoke reassuringly. "They are tough men, Sue."

Both women knew Brent would never be the same again. He would need all the love in the world just to be able to make it through a single day. Tears began to pour down Heather's cheeks as she realised that things would never be what they were; not for any of them. Sue was shocked to see Heather crumbling as Heather had always been the pillar of strength. As Sue turned to wrap her arms around her elder sister she tried to gather her strength by quietly speaking harshly to herself,

'I've got to be my strongest. Stevo would want me to be strong now.' Heather could feel Sue getting really anxious and she too tried to pull herself together, brushing her cheeks dry as she reassured her sister,

"Sorry, Sue. I just lost it for a moment."

"Don't worry, Heather, we have been through a lot in the last 48 hours but it will be over soon."

Heather pulled Sue towards herself, hugging her closely and telling her how much she loved her.

"Stevo will be well on his way to get help by now and Brent assured us we are quite safe here now. I trust him."

Heather's hands were starting to shake. She had no idea whether it was from the cold or the stress. She had clung to the relief she had felt when Stevo and Brent had returned, and for them to leave again so soon was almost too much to handle. Heather kept telling herself to be strong and to not let Sue think that she wasn't handling things; she worried if Sue saw her crying then Sue would break down even further. Heather had always been the backbone of their family; organising and helping her mother and sisters. They had never had much money when they were growing up but they had always made do somehow. Heather had looked after Sue when they were younger, always giving her good advice, helping her with her school work, and making pretty clothes for her. Sue had been terrified to see Heather break down, for the first time in her life. Sue was watching her sister's hands shaking and the tears fall uncontrollably. Sue understood that they had to be strong for each other if they wanted to get out of the bush and she began mumbling to herself under her breath,

"I must be strong, I must be strong."

She continued to repeat the mantra to herself over and over, until she almost began to believe she might be strong enough to get through.

Heather stoked the fire before again huddling near the flames to warm up with Sue and Roger.

Sue had become very pale as all of her strength had drained away. Neither Sue nor Heather had slept properly in 48 hours and they had barely been able to stomach food after what had happened the night the boys invaded their camp. They had enjoyed a full and busy day of swimming and looking after the horses and were about to have a large dinner when everything had been interrupted by the three intruders. Sue's mind turned dark, and images of the big, tall, tattooed man flashed before her eyes and made her feel like vomiting. She felt her stomach retch but the contents were empty, there was nothing to come up.

Heather realised that they couldn't continue this way or they too would be being airlifted alongside Roger out of the bush on a stretcher. She immediately began to stir the fire and set about making some breakfast.

She had to stay strong for both her sister and her husband. After downing as much of the breakfast that the two sisters could manage, Heather looked over at Sue whose head was beginning to droop at an awkward angle. Heather reached out and gave Sue a gentle shake. They were both sitting beside Roger, who suddenly surprised

them both by saying,

"What's happening ladies?"

Heather smiled warmly at him and gave him a hug. "You are looking better."

"I feel like standing up," Roger announced with only a slight stutter to his speech.

Sue and Heather smiled as they helped Roger to his feet. He was very woozy but seemed to be much stronger than he had been before. Heather gave him a drink of water and Sue boiled the billy for yet another cup of tea. From across the fire, Sue looked mournfully at Heather who had propped Roger against the log into a sitting position with a camping pillow behind his head.

Heather winked. "Not long now, Sue."

Despite Heather's attempts to keep Sue's spirits up, the tears began pouring down her cheeks again.

"I just can't stop thinking about our poor Janey." Sue sobbed even harder. "I can't stop thinking of what that man did to me. I feel so dirty and used. I think I want to die."

"You can't die, Sue. I need you to give me strength so we can get through the next days. Stevo will be here soon, what would happen to him if you weren't here? Things will be better when he gets back, you will see," Heather said in a shaky voice.

Tears were pouring down both of their faces and Sue began repeating her mantra of strength to herself. Finally she sniffed and forced her eyes to meet Heather's.

"We have still got the kids, and Roger and Stevo, and of course there is Brent, as well. We will have to be strong for them, aye Heather?" "Of course we will. Please promise me you won't ever say anything like that again, Sue. Please promise me, will you?" begged Heather. "I promise. I'm sorry. I will be okay, we will get through this somehow," reassured Sue.

CHAPTER FIFTY-ONE

Brent had been envisaging the boys' movements all night. He knew they must have headed up the river to get over to the next watershed, otherwise they would most certainly have tried to come back down the river already. He had done that trip himself many years before and he remembered where there was an old cattle track that led up from the end of the river and into the neighbouring water shed. It always amazed Brent how the cattle could walk up a track that was so steep in search of food with only their knowledge of good grass in the next valley guiding them up the steep inclines.

Brent was moving as fast as he could up the river on Big Red and he could already see the horse marks in front of him; he was simply following the three men's trail. He saw where they had camped, and knew his suspicions were right; they had definitely moved up the river. He felt dizzy with relief as he immediately realised Roger, Sue, and Heather would be safe back at the Bullring camp until Stevo arrived with help. As Brent scoured the surrounding land for the any sign they had headed up river, he noticed there were three very clear sets of hoof marks. He knew the land well enough to know that from where he stood it would be another two hours ride until he got to the place where the boys would have to leave their horses and continue on foot. He knew he had no time to lose and he instantly spurred Big Red on and together they hit every river crossing at full pace.

The valley floor had widened from where it came out of the Bullring gorge above the camp. The river catchment was much wider from Bullring, and ran right up into Green River Country where the river begun to get more difficult due to the boulders and log jams.

The spray from the water was shooting 10 feet into the air as the big chestnut's hooves ploughed their way through.

It was 7.30 in the morning and Brent realised he had already been riding for nearly an hour and a half. Brent had covered the distance quickly, better than he had thought he would considering the half light when he had left camp. He had easily been riding at double the pace of what was normal for the type of terrain. The sweat was pouring off Big Red and it had begun to lather up. Brent knew he was really pushing Big Red too hard, but he also knew that they only had to last another hour or so until Big Red could rest while Brent continued on foot. Brent leaned forward and patted his horse encouragingly.

"Not far now, Red. We can do it. I couldn't do this without you boy." The big chestnut's ears pricked forward. It was as if he could smell other horses. The fury was building up in Brent as he thought about what the three boys had done. Brent was aware that the blonde one hadn't done anything - but Brent still wanted him to feel the same terror since he had done nothing to help. Brent couldn't stop thinking that there must have been something he could have done to help as Heather and Sue said he was the only one who did not appear to be intoxicated. God help all three of them when he finally caught up to

them; he knew it was only a matter of time.

As Brent rode on, he knew he had the element of surprise as the boys wouldn't be expecting any riders to arrive so quickly. Brent had decided he was not going to kill any of the boys outright; instead they were all going to suffer. He wanted to look straight into each of their eyes before inflicting physical pain and damage.

Brent rounded the next corner and spotted the culprits straight away. They were out on a big loop where the river opened out for only a very short time; a good spot for them to have camped overnight. As Brent came around the corner, they noticed him immediately. They were located about 300 metres further up the river and had just mounted their horses. They panicked when they saw Brent and they drove hard kicks into each of their horses which immediately caused them to gallop across the corner in the river. Two were riding in front with the third lagging a little behind as his horse was slower than the other two. The first two disappeared around the next corner leaving Brent to make the most of the opportunity to have a go at the rider who was being left behind. Because it was such a long shot, Brent rapidly dismounted, secured Big Red, aimed, and fired. The bullet flew true and hit the blonde boy's horse in the neck; killing it instantly. The shot echoed thunderously up the valley. Big Red just flicked his ears as the shot roared off; a sound he had heard many times before. The horse buckled at the knees, dropped its head, and ploughed straight down into the sand, somersaulting into the river, and finishing up partially on a sand bank. The front half of the horse's body remained submerged in water. As the horse had dropped, the momentum had catapulted the rider to where he crashed down about 10 metres in front of it.

Brent mounted back up and rode up the river at a slower place. He could see how the rider had landed in a sprawling mess beside the water. It appeared as if he was trying to sit up. Brent approached him slowly with his gun at the ready; just in case the others had stopped and turned back at the sound of the shot. As Brent neared he could see the fear shining brightly in the man's eyes which were as round as saucers. Brent kept looking up the river beyond the injured man to make sure the others hadn't stopped; he feared the other men may be getting into a position to shoot. He could see the sheer cliffs on both sides of the river and figured they must have gone up and around the next corner. Brent noticed that the injured man who lay in front of him did not have the gun; just a small bowie knife.

CHAPTER FIFTY-TWO

Slade and Jake pulled their horses to a halt around the following corner.
"HE SHOT LUKE!" screamed Jake.

"No. That's what I thought too, but when I looked back I saw that the shot had only got the horse. Lukey had landed funny but he was definitely still moving," reassured Slade.

"What do we do now?" fretted Jake hysterically.

"We will have to carry on and hope Luke is okay. We will wait for this dude further up the river and deal to him, and then we will go back and get Luke."

Jake just hung his head in silent agreement with his brother as he didn't have a better idea. He was shaken up really badly as he realised the guy who had been shooting at them, probably wanted to kill all three of them.

Brent's horse was standing two metres from Luke. He had finally managed to pull himself into a sitting position at the edge of the river. He was fearfully looking straight up at Brent who just stared right down at the whimpering man while keeping the gun aimed straight at him.

"What's your name?" scowled Brent.

"Luke," he yelled back at Brent. Luke was starting to push himself backwards with both hands, clambering for any type of leverage in the soft sand. One leg seemed to be dragging limply behind and it appeared to Brent as if it had broken in the fall. There was blood running down Luke's face from a deep gash above his left eye. Luke edged himself slowly and painfully backwards towards the river as Brent inched Big Red closer and closer towards him. Luke didn't take his eyes off Brent. Brent could see the fear and hysteria building in Luke's eyes. Brent's fury was burning; all he could think about was revenge; all he wanted was to make them suffer. The whole way up the river, riding Red hard out, Brent's mind had been absorbed by rage. Almost shaking with fury and hatred, Brent's eyes bored right down into Lukes.

"What are you doing shooting my horse?" Luke screamed at his attacker.

"You shot my wife and raped my friend, you bloody mongrel," scowled Brent in disgust.

Luke's eyes widened with the realisation that Brent was the husband of one of the women from the Bullring camp, one of the ones who had been out hunting. A look of terror crossed Luke's face.

"It wasn't me; it was my brother, Slade. You've got it all wrong," spluttered Luke cowardly.

Brent was struggling not fly into a fit of rage; he could feel his body and mind were at an extreme level of tension and he was on the brink of losing it. Unfortunately for Luke, Brent had caught him first and he was about to feel the force of Brent's rage.

Brent was in no mood for polite conversation and aimed his 270 straight at Luke's right temple. At the same time as he pulled the trigger, he swiftly moved the gun to the left and the bullet ploughed into the shingle, spraying rocks everywhere.

He growled at the young man cowering before him.

"You will never get your day in court. You are going to experience real justice. I want you to suffer, just like you made my Janey suffer." Luke threw himself backwards as the gun went off a second time.

He lay motionless, waiting for the pain. He wasn't even sure if the bullet had hit him due to the fear and adrenaline coursing through his veins. Brent dismounted, the water pouring out of his rubber hunting boots as his feet hit the river shingle. He was saturated from head to toe due to riding his horse hard up the river and through the big crossings. Dropping the reins, he kept the rifle trained on Luke with his finger firmly on the trigger. The big chestnut, dripping with sweat and water, just stood there looking on while pawing at the sand. Big Red could smell the blood of death, the same scent he had smelled at the camp. It was as if the horse also wanted his revenge on the people who had shot Janey.

Brent could sense the tenseness in his horse as he held the rifle with one hand and used the other to move a rock onto the horse's reins; securing him against the far side of the bank where he would be out of sight from the other two men on the loose. Big Red continuously pawed at the sand with his front foot while snorting loudly.

"Easy boy," calmed Brent. "I know you want your revenge too.

Don't you worry; I'll deal to him for you and Janey."

Brent pulled his hunting knife from the sheath slowly as Luke screamed.

"What are you doing? It wasn't me; it wasn't me. Slade was the one who killed her. Let me go. He is the one you want!"

As Brent approached Luke he slung his gun over his shoulder. "I want all of you," Brent snarled.

He was constantly casting his eyes up the river as he was sure the other two would come back to help their mate. He grabbed Luke by the hair and growled,

"I see your mates have left you on your own. Doesn't say much for the type of people they are does it? Gutless pricks just like you."

Brent swiftly jolted Luke's head back and held the knife to his throat menacingly. Every fibre in his body wanted to cut Luke's throat. Every muscle in Luke's body went tense with fear and he lost control of his bladder. Brent scoffed as he looked down at the scared man in front of him wetting his pants like a child. Luke was lucky that Brent knew he was telling the truth when he had said he didn't touch Janey, Heather, or Sue; and that it wasn't he who had hurt Roger either. Brent let Luke's head go.

"Please believe me, I didn't do anything," he begged through his tears. Luke was crying openly, and the tears fell limply onto his unclean shirt as he repeated over and over how sorry he was for what had happened at the camp. Brent ignored his cries, choosing to instead push the point of the knife into Luke's shoulder. The sharp point of the well-honed knife easily pierced his skin.

Brent growled, "Feel some pain."

Brent snarled," I'm going to leave you here while I go after your two cowardly mates."

Luke began to scream and kick around despite his injured leg. He pulled himself into the river in an attempt to get away from Brent. His blood quickly turned the water red.

Brent marched over to Big Red, grabbed a rope from his saddle bag, and made his way back to the river where he noticed the water was swarming with eels. The blood from the dead horse, and the blood from Luke's injuries, had attracted the eels and sent them into one of their frenzies. There were some absolutely huge eels appearing in the river.

Brent could see the look of terror on Luke's face when he saw what was coming towards him. Luke desperately began to scramble up the river bank - but he was too slow. The biggest eels were beginning to grab at him with their sharp teeth and powerful jaws. Brent was momentarily startled and took a step back from the water's edge to protect himself. He had always known the eels were dangerous and capable of hurting humans but seeing them in real life was something else. He realised instantly that he could not let Luke die at the mercy of the eels; he wasn't the one who had killed Janey.

"Here, grab this," Brent screamed as he threw him the rope. The eel's massive tails were thrashing around in the water as they attacked Luke who was screaming continuously as he struggled to reach for the rope. Brent shook his head in confusion at finding himself desperately trying to save Luke. Ten minutes earlier he had been happy enough to drive a knife through his shoulder and hope for his death; now he was saving him from the very same fate.

As Brent tugged at the rope, more and more oversized eels were turning up and in full ferocity. One particularly massive eel began to slither its way through the water. It was about five feet long with a head about 12 inches wide at the mouth. It was clearly intoxicated with the blood trail and looking for the blood source. It swam right past Luke in the water to where the river began to shallow out. As the eel spun around while thrashing its massive tail, it managed to launch itself high out of the water and onto the sand. Brent leaped backwards in fright and dropped the rope before reeling around with his 270 aiming at the eel. He instantly blew it in half with his 270 ballistic tipped bullets and watched as each piece of the big eel slithered off in opposite directions with their damaged nerves still twitching. The front half, with the head, was still trying to make its way towards Luke. Brent noticed the mouth of the eel was wide open and each tooth was at least one centimetre long and as sharp as razors. The teeth of an eel were usually very small, so to see such large and dangerous teeth showed Brent again how much they were affected by the growth hormone.

Luke was still holding on to the other end of the rope and Brent quickly leant down, picked up the rope at a tighter spot, and with a few strong heaves managed to pull Luke up onto the safety of the sand. Luke was screaming in pain. Brent kicked at a large eel that had come up out of the water with Luke when he had been dragged out. He noticed how the other eels were beginning to attack each other in the river; forgetting about the horse instantaneously. Brent watched as the front half of the dead eel was ravaged into pieces by the rest of its species. He realised that the blood from the dead eel had deepened their taste for blood and was turning them further into savagery.

Luke looked at Brent gratefully. "You saved me."

"The only reason you are alive, is because I know you never did anything to my Janey. But as you never helped either, you are also just as guilty."

"No, no!" protested Luke. "It was Slade, my brother. I wasn't there when it happened, I promise. I got to the camp just after he had fired the shot and there was nothing I could do. I wanted to help, I swear. But the two women screamed at us all to get out. They would have shot us."

Brent scoffed as he looked down at the pitiful sight before him; a young man with blood and urine all over him, a puncture in one shoulder from the knife wound, and a very broken looking leg from coming off the horse badly. On top of everything, Brent noticed that the young man's other shoulder looked swollen where his shirt had ripped from landing in the river when the horse had gone down. Brent walked over to where Luke's horse was being ravaged by the giant eels and he quickly pulled the bag off the saddle and threw it at Luke,

"I'm just going to leave you here."

Brent could see the eels had done no real damage to Luke as they had only been able to grab at his clothes before Brent had managed to pull him out of the water. The eels had stopped attacking each other and had since turned their attention back to the largest source of blood; they were ferociously chewing at the dead horse.

Brent asked, "How bad do you think your leg is?"

Luke said, "My knee is bloody sore but I think it has stopped bleeding."

"I'm going to find the other two murderers. If you're lucky I will come back to get you on my way out. Don't go anywhere till I get back or I'll track you down and then you will be dead," said Brent angrily. "I won't move. I promise." Luke shook his head fervently as he pulled himself up with the help of a nearby log, leaning against it.

Brent mounted up and looked down at Luke. Luke watched intently to see if Brent was going to change his mind and get back off his horse. Moments passed before Brent finally nudged Big Red to move. Brent knew Luke wasn't physically able to go anywhere as his knee had been smashed in the fall, and he decided that the young man could sit and suffer in his pain and self-pity. Brent also knew that once Stevo got in touch with the police, the helicopter would be able to pick up the young man as he and the dead horse – if there was anything left of the horse - would easily be seen from above.

Luke watched Brent disappear into the native bush, perched high upon his magnificent horse. His thoughts turned to Slade and Jake. "I hate to think what will happen to them once the hunter has caught up with them." The tears of terror were rolling steadily down his face and he lashed out at the sand with his fist.

"Bloody Slade and that P shit caused all of this!" he cursed to himself.

Brent had ridden quite a way up the sand on Luke's side of the river. He had not wanted to cross because he could still see the eels rushing to get at the dead horse and he knew that the deeper he got into Green River Country, the bigger the eels would be. The dead horse was distracting them but Brent knew there was no way he was going to underestimate their power and aggression.

Brent felt confident that his human prey had gone further ahead as the sheer drops on each side of the river would be impossible to climb within the gorge. As he rounded a large bend, he could see that it opened up a bit further on and he would need to remain vigilant and be on the lookout for any possible movement.

CHAPTER FIFTY-THREE

Slade and Jake had continued to ride their horses hard and fast up the river to put as much distance between them and the threat of the hunter. Upon rounding a large corner, they saw a huge log that had obviously been uprooted by a storm. It had fallen across the river and every single one of its massive roots were exposed from where it had been wrenched from the earth. It was lying straight across the river, forcing the water to change course and run around the far end of the log. They had reined their horses in as the second shot reverberated up and through the valley.

"What the hell was that? What could he possibly have been shooting at now?" yelled Jake hysterically.

"There's only one thing he could have shot up here," admitted Slade sadly.

"No! No way! He wouldn't. Would he? Who the hell could that rider have been anyway?"

"Well, those women reckoned there were two hunters with them.

Maybe they were telling the truth and he was one of them."

"Hell, if he was with those women then he of course he will be after us just to kill us!" There was fear and guilt in his Jake's words as they tumbled from his mouth.

"If he has shot Luke, he's obviously capable of anything," Slade grimaced. "He's not going to get away with that. It sounds like he is using a pretty big rifle. Must have a bloody good scope on it too, seeing as he shot Luke's horse from so far away. We will have to get in really close with our old 303 because it is off, remember. We want to make sure we get him. We'll lie in wait behind that log for him …" Slade paused as he weighed up the situation. "He's dangerous, Jake. We'll have to be extra careful."

Two more shots echoed their way up the valley causing Jake to shriek again,

"Holy shit Slade, that old guy means business! He must be mad with grief."

Slade gritted his teeth but said nothing as Jake continued to cry out. "What can he be doing? Shall we go back?"

"No," Slade waved his hand in dismissal. "I have a better idea.

We'll get him when he comes up here."

The brothers dismounted and led their horses 20 metres into the bush where they hid them by tethering them behind a large tree. Jake's fingers were trembling as he fastened the knots and Slade noticed he was about to cry.

"Harden up, Jake. We won't get out of here otherwise."

Brent had been continuing to move his way up the river. He had come out of the gorgy piece with the sheer walls and was no longer protected by nature as the river had widened significantly. He paused to survey the next piece of river; knowing very well the killers could be waiting for him. He dismounted with one swift movement and led Big Red quietly to where Brent could peer around the next corner. He leaned hard against a big rock wall on the corner of the river and turned his head ever so slightly so he could view what lay ahead of him up the next straight.

Brent turned to face Big Red before moving off and noticed his leg was bleeding quite badly by the fetlock. He wasn't limping on it so Brent felt it would be safe to take the horse around a few more corners before continuing to hunt on foot. Brent felt quite confident that the killers had moved on as he could see with the scope that there were hoof marks right up and around the next corner. Brent hopped back onto the chestnut with his gun at the ready, trying to stay quite close to the bank in case he had to leap into the bush if he came under fire. The river was deepening in places and as Brent looked ahead, he could see how the river twisted around to the right where there was a big log jam and lots of deep pools. In order to progress further, he would need to negotiate a big, deep pool. He knew Big Red was a competent swimmer and in his desperation to catch up with the two killers he forgot about his horse's injury. He was halfway across when he noticed a dark movement out of the corner of his left eye. A massive eel, at least 7 to 8 feet long and a foot wide, was coming out of the logs and straight towards Big Red.

The eel had smelt the blood! Brent kicked hard into Big Red to push him forward just as he saw another eel coming out from the logs after the first. Brent was trying to move his horse faster to get out of the water. The water was way up to the horse's chest and forcing Red to swim. They were in the deepest part of the pool. There was at least another 20 metres to go until the bank. The eels were swimming at top speed towards the horse, each competing to be the first to get at the blood supply.

With about 5 metres to go until they reached the bank, Brent realised that the eels were swimming a lot faster than the horse could move. He calmly urged the horse on. He didn't want to scare Big Red. The eels easily caught up to him. The biggest one latched onto the horse's front leg. Another eel clamped itself onto Big Red's rump. It was twisting violently and spun itself off as quickly as it had attached itself. Without warning, the horse reared violently and it took all of Brent's strength and skill to hang on. Brent was reassured by his knowledge that the horse was about to clear the pool. The eel was still hanging onto the Big Red's front leg and was trying to wrap its body around the leg of the horse.

As the horse leaped out of the pool, the eel was hanging on so hard that it was dragged up onto the sand by its teeth. Finally, it's own bodyweight was too much and the eel was forced to let go. Brent swung himself around and shot it with the 270 which sent it spinning back into the water. Another oversized eel lunged out of the water. Brent pointed the barrel at the eel and pulled the trigger, watching as its head was blown to pieces. The other eels were already attacking the first eel. They had been sent into yet another frenzy over their own blood. Brent's first priority was to get the the big chestnut over onto a grassy corner; away from the eels where he would also be safely hidden from view.

As he moved away from the river, yet another massive eel launched itself at the horse's back leg. Big Red kicked furiously with its back leg, catching the eel in the head. The impact of the kick sent the eel skyward and it somersaulted out and over the water. The ferocity of the kick must have killed or stunned the eel because it began floating down the river where the other eels started attacking it. Brent was worried the two men may have heard the last shot and be alerted to his presence, his location, and the distance between them. He was shaking his head, unable to comprehend the danger and the size of the overgrown eels lurking in the water. He checked Big Red's leg and rump, relieved to see that everything appeared to be all right. The eels had not had enough time to inflict more than a few gashes where they had bitten him; and thankfully were not too deep.

Brent decided not to risk Big Red being attacked by the eels again. As he tied him up in a spot hidden from the river but not from above, Brent gave the horse a pat and told him quietly that he or a helicopter could be a while. He tethered him to a small branch so that if he did not return, Big Red could break free easily.

"I've got a job to do, and I don't know how long I will be. I will avenge Janey's death for both of us."

The big chestnut seemed to understand and gave Brent a little nudge and a whinny as if to say,

"Get going. I will be all right here."

Brent loaded more bullets into the mag of his 270 to ensure it was full and he carried on up the river about another quarter of a mile. He was proceeding with extreme caution, trying to stay as near to the bush as possible, to ensure he was not going to get bushwhacked. He came out of the gorgy part, rounded a corner, and looked up a big long straight. He noticed a massive log that had been forced out of the gorgy piece of river bank and spewed into the river.

Brent continued to survey the river before looking up at the sky. The clouds were starting to roll over as if the weather could take a turn for the worse. He stopped and studied the path of the river for about 10 minutes as he knew that if they were going to bushwhack him, it would be the ideal place for an ambush. From where he stood, he could see a bush covered rock face with slips leading to a ridge above it that then wound its way up and away from the river. He rapidly formed a plan and whispered it to himself to bring him the strength he needed to continue, 'I will follow that ridge up so I can get above that big log to see if they are behind it.'

As Brent was leaving the river to climb up onto the ridge, he found himself having to get through some really thick scrub and undergrowth with bush lawyer laced throughout. Brent could feel it holding him back as he pushed through the undergrowth. He gave a big heave forward to free himself, and the vine tore away from his clothing. A piece pulled roughly across his throat as he launched forward, drawing blood and cutting a gash down his neck. Brent was sweating profusely and he could feel the sweat in the cut starting to sting. He moved forward to a clear patch and tried to get any remaining prickles out. He noticed his shirt had been torn by the vines and there was a cut to his shoulder as well. He reached his fingers up to the cut on his neck to see if there was much blood.

As he looked at his index finger, coated in a light crimson blood, he seemed to become mesmerised. It looked just like the blood that had covered his hand as he had lifted Janey after she had been shot at the camp. He could still feel the big hole in her back where the bullet had left her body. He could also still see Roger lying unconscious against the log. Brent's eyes brimmed with tears as the reality of the situation he was in hit home; hunting two humans who were responsible for the death of his wife. He felt real anguish and was sorry he was in the position of having to do it. Suddenly his eyes cleared, and he felt himself begin to shake as the trance left him dazed and with a heaving chest. The sweat on his body felt cold and a shiver ran down his spine as he realised, he was suddenly feeling and thinking like a killer himself.

He knew his heart was in the same way as his paradise; broken. He never dreamt he would ever lose Janey. The realisation that he wasn't living a dream hit him hard and he almost howled with rage and grief. He managed to get himself under control by thinking of the terror and revenge he was about to unleash on the two young men who were responsible for his nightmare. The loving memories of Janey and his family, mixed with the growing hatred he felt for the killers, were starting to consume him and he really did not know whether he would be able to carry on after everything was over. He placed a hand on the pocket where he had put the bullet he wanted to save for himself; just to check it was still there. It was. But before the time came to use it, he vowed to make the pricks wish they had never been born.

The valleys in Green River country where the rivers flowed down didn't often get the sun for very long during the day so it remained very wet, especially on the southern side where Brent was crawling through the bush. He gave a sly laugh as it dawned on him that he was like an oversized eel with legs, gliding and sliding his way through the bush. Brent was grateful for his bush skills as he knew they were going to make all the difference; one slip or crack would alert his foe and he would be in real danger of being shot. He had to cross some small guts which he negotiated carefully, down one side and up the other. He was constantly casting his eyes back down towards the river so as to keep an eye out for the killers. He crossed a second gut and spotted a slippy bit about 100 metres ahead of him. Looking down at the river, he knew that when he got to that slip he would have a clear view down behind the majestic log that was blocking the river.

The day was very still with a slight breeze, despite the clouds rolling casually in up above. All Brent could hear was the river noise as the water ran away and around the end of the big log. He wondered how Stevo was getting on. He figured he would be a fair way down the river but still with quite a way to go before reaching cell phone coverage. Brent crossed another gut and came up onto the slippy bit he had been aiming for. It protruded out from the ridge even further than he had hoped, and the extra height helped carve a clear view right down to the river below. His instincts had not let him astray and he found himself looking straight down at the other side of the massive log obstructing the river – where he could see two men. They had positioned themselves so they could see directly down the river and the two men were peering over the log with the rifle neatly hidden between the broken branches of the big log so it could not have been seen from downstream.

CHAPTER FIFTY-FOUR

Brent could clearly see one of the men holding the rifle. He was crouched behind the gun with one leg out behind the other so as to brace himself for when he had to shoot. Brent studied the scene for a moment before making a decision, again speaking aloud to calm and prepare himself,

"I will take out the one with the gun. I will shoot him in the knee which will immobilise him. I don't want to kill him outright. He has to suffer and I want to have a wee talk to him before I finish him off." He could tell that the two murderers had no idea where he was; they hadn't moved an inch during the entire time Brent had been surveying the situation. It was not a long shot for Brent but he wanted to be accurate with it and he took aim by balancing his rifle on the fork of a tree. The rifle shot echoed thunderously up and through the valley as the bullet hit the man he aimed at true in the back of his knee - exactly where Brent had aimed. He threw his arms into the air and away from the gun as the impact of the shot sent him flying backwards. Brent swung his rifle around onto the killers 303 and shot again with precision, the bullet impacting right at the spot where the barrel and the bolt chamber met. The timber butt sent splinters showering everywhere as the gun was torn in half. The barrel fell forward to the other side of the log and the butt toppled backwards and landed next to the man with a thud. The other man swiftly slunk around to the other side of the big root system and out of Brent's vision. "You might run but you can't hide, you gutless piece of shit," Brent yelled down from up on the ridge. The 150 grain ballistic tip bullet had torn the man's right knee to pieces and blood was spurting everywhere in all directions. A main artery just above the knee had been severed by a bit of flying shrapnel from the ballistic tip which had disintegrated on impact. Brent knew those particular bullets always took out their target instantly as he had killed many a deer with them. Brent watched for a minute through the scope on his rifle and saw the man rolling around on the ground, clutching his leg above the knee in an attempt to stop the flow of blood. He could hear the screams from below.

"Sladey, Sladey I've been hit. Help me! Help me!" A second voice yelled in reply,

"Try to crawl over here and I will tie something around your leg.

I can't come out there. I will be an easy target." "I think I am going to die, Slade."

"Just hang on, I will think of something," said Slade gruffly.

From his hiding spot behind the big tree root, Slade could see how badly his brother's knee was damaged. Where the kneecap had once been; nothing remained but a stain of blood in the sand where the bullet had driven itself into the ground. Slade knew there was nothing he could do to help and realised if he tried to help his brother, then he would die too. Slade, with no rifle and only his bowie knife to defend himself, decided to make a break to the other side of the river while he could - because he knew Brent would be making his way down from where he had taken the shot. Staying in line with the root of the tree, he hoped he would not be seen as he ran full pace towards the other side of the river. He was expecting to hear or feel a bullet at any second and threw himself headfirst into the scrub on the opposite bank where he was able to take cover. He regained his composure and peered out of his new hiding place to watch and see who turned up to where Jake was lying. He wanted to run back and help Jake but knew it was far too dangerous.

As Brent worked his way down the steep rocky ridge, with the big Matai and Rimu trees and very little new undergrowth, he had a clear view across the river. The ridge dropped sharply into the water and he only needed to drop down another steep, challenging 60 metres before he would be back at the river's edge. He caught a glimpse of Slade disappearing into the bush on the far side of the river and knew the young man was without a rifle so presented no real danger - yet.

Slade didn't have to wait for long, as a tall black haired figure soon came out of the bush with his rifle held at the ready. Slade had never seen this person before but he instinctively knew it was one of the people to do with the Bullring camp. He wished he had not gone down to the Bullring that night; it was bringing him a lot of grief he really didn't need. He knew that what had happened was because of the drugs and alcohol and he feared that because of his actions he and his two brothers would all die in the bush. Slade was filled with shame and guilt and he swore to himself that if he, Jake, and Luke got out of this, they would never touch drugs again. Slade felt himself thinking about Hone and Shona. He knew Hone would kill him if anything happened to Jake or Luke. He peered out from behind the ferns to where he could see the man was clearly standing beside Jake. The hunter was about 70 to 80 metres away, right across the river. He stood over 6 feet tall and looked to weigh about 100kg. He looked lean and fit with jet black hair and he was wearing a sleeveless oilskin coat. The way he held his rifle in one hand, like a pistol, made Slade think, 'This guy must be some amazing hunter. How could he know we were behind that log?'

For the first time in his life, Slade felt real fear course through his veins, it was a feeling that was almost overwhelming him. He had felt fear before, of course he had, but this was to an entirely new extent. His whole body was going numb and a lone teardrop made a dusty track down his face. Managing to pull himself together by thinking of the lads in prison and what they would do in this situation, he looked across the river and tried to think of what he could do to help Jake. Deep down Slade knew he was defeated, they all were. Surely the hunter had known it was not Jake or Luke who had done the killing, yet they were both about to be lifeless themselves.

As Brent reached the river, he stepped through a muddy little pool that was in against the bank and he walked towards where the young man was lying, holding tightly onto his injured knee. The man had turned into a blithering mess; crying and babbling to himself like a young child.

Brent had his rifle trained straight on the man.

"I heard you yell out. So, the other guy's name is Slade – the murderer!! What's your name?" sneered Brent.

Jake's face dropped in panic and he felt himself expecting the gun to go off again at any second. He was too stunned to answer Brent's question.

Brent was also constantly looking all around with anxiety as he continued to approach the injured man. He finally stopped moving when the man was within a metre of the end of the barrel. Brent just stood there looking down at the man who was partly responsible for the death of his wife. There was a cold look on Brent's face. Without warning the injured man screamed,

"You prick, you shot me. I could die."

"There is no could about it, buddy," Brent mocked. "I asked you a question, what's your name?" He crouched down with the gun still pointing straight at the man's head. He had a clear view across the river to where Slade had disappeared into the bush.

"I'm Jake, my brother is the one you want, Slade killed the lady," sobbed Jake. He was trying to push himself away from Brent but came up against a log and was unable to move any further. Brent just watched. He could see the blood pouring profusely from Jake's knee; he knew he had hit a main artery. Brent realised Jake hadn't got very long to live unless someone stopped the blood. The red liquid was rapidly trickling down through the sand like a tiny stream.

Brent growled,

"You killed my wife and raped my friend."

"I didn't kill your wife or rape your friend," reiterated Jake. "It was Slade."

"What would make him do a thing like that?"

"We just got drunk and had too many drugs. We didn't go to your camp meaning to hurt anyone. We only wanted some food for our tea. Things just got out of hand," swore Jake, his face distorted with pain and agony.

As Jake spoke, Brent had been watching his leg and noticed the blood flow was not slowing down at all.

"I'm going to put a bandage on your leg. If you move, I'll kill you."

"Yes! Please, please!" Jake begged.

Brent shrugged off his day pack from his back while never failing to watch the other side of the river at all times. He tugged at his small emergency kit of bandages and remembered how Janey always packed it for him before he went hunting. He hung his head as the grief hit him again.

"Hey, what's going on??" panicked Jake. "Hurry up, I'm dying man!"

His voice jolted Brent back to reality. Jake had his arms back behind the log as he held his body up and off the riverbed. Brent leaned down with the bandage and some antibiotic cream. Jake's legs were straight out in front of him.

"I'm going to cut your trousers back to have a look at your wound. Don't do anything," Brent warned Jake as he pulled his hunting knife from its sheath. He cut the trousers right back and examined the wound. The knee cap was completely gone and it had taken the meat out of the front of the right thigh, just up from the knee, which was causing the blood loss. The tendons looked ok as far as Brent could see, and he hastily covered it with antibiotic before wrapping the bandage around his leg.

He looked at Jake.

"I'm going to have to pull this very tight."

"Yes, yes," sighed Jake, closing his eyes and gritting his teeth.

Brent yanked on the bandage until it was tight enough that the blood stopped. He continued to bandage the wound and looked up to see that Jake appeared as if he was going to pass out. Brent knelt beside Jake and waited to see if the blood flow had really stopped for good. He kept looking around to make sure Slade wasn't sneaking around from across the river.

Jake regained himself and opened his eyes, "What did you shoot me in the knee for?"

"So that every step you take, for the rest of your life, you will remember what you have done," Brent spoke wildly through his teeth at Jake.

"I'm so sorry man," sighed Jake disheartedly. "I did try to stop Slade, I swear. Hey, is Lukey all right? I heard lots of shots from down there and saw him come off his horse."

Ignoring Jake, Brent suddenly stood up and grabbed at his rifle at the same time. He was looking around and across the river as he knew he could not drop his guard for even a second. Failure was not an option.

"I will get the bastard," he muttered severely.

Brent swung his rifle around and again pointed it at a terrified Jake. "Yes, he is alive and the only reason he is, is because I'm told he didn't do anything … But you, I'm not so sure about. That's why you and he are in one piece at the moment. But if I hear anything different, and you do make it out of here, I will come and take everything that matters to you apart."

Jake's face was becoming paler as his life flowed away with every drop of lost blood. The bandage had stemmed the blood loss and Brent sighed as he remembered the sight of Janey lying dead at the camp. Brent again felt the rush of determination to have his revenge. "You might not have killed my wife but you didn't stop that other guy from killing her either, or from raping my friend. You deserve to die."

The hatred built up in Brent as he became more and more agitated by the second. Brent suddenly growled at Jake to move towards the river and he poked the gun hard into his shoulder to get him to move. Brent had decided he would feed him to the eels.

Unsure what the hell was going on Jake looked at Brent in disbelief. He could not understand why he was being forced towards the river

- but he could see the look on Brent's face and knew it was not a joke. Brent shoved the barrel of the gun into Jake's mouth. "Get going!" The river was only two metres from the end of the log.

"Shit, I feel so weak I can hardly move," mumbled Jake.

"Should have thought about the consequences before you invaded our camp," yelled Brent. As Jake struggled towards the water, Brent remembered Heather saying that Jake hadn't done anything serious in comparison and had only slapped her in the face.

He placed his free hand on Jake's shoulder which halted Jake just short of the water. The young man looked up at him fearfully. "What are you going to do to me now? Are you going to drown me or torture me?" Jake asked. He felt his body give way as he began to drift in and out of consciousness, both from fear and blood loss.

Brent just stood there, scanning the far bank and up the river as he searched for any sign of Slade, while also keeping an eye on Jake. As he watched, he heard something coming from higher up in the bush, smashing and crashing its way down towards them through the undergrowth. Brent quickly stepped back into cover thinking it was Slade coming for him just as a massive boar broke cover 50 metres down the river.

It was the biggest poaka Brent had ever seen; black with a big white patch over its shoulder, abnormally large tusks stuck out from each side of its mouth. They each looked to be about six inches long and as sharp as razor blades; sharpened from wearing on its massive grinders which jutted out from the top jaw. It looked to be an easy 250 kgs and was physically huge and rippling with muscle. The big boar began running up the river with its nose high in the air.

Brent trained the rifle on the beast and followed it to see what it would do. He kept the gun trained on it as the big poaka ran up to the overturned log. It had not seen Jake nor Brent as it sniffed around the log. It looked like it was attempting to pick up the trail. There was a large amount of blood, but Brent could see that the boar seemed unable to pick up the source.

The big boar began to desperately try moving the blood-soaked log. Jake, who had been unaware of the poaka's presence, suddenly regained consciousness. The beast was sniffing for the source of the blood trail. Jake let out a loud scream and tried desperately to throw himself into the river in an attempt to get away. Brent knew he couldn't do anything about Jake as he had to give his full concentration to the wild animal. He knew how dangerous and unpredictable they could be - even when they had not been feeding on growth hormone! Jake's scream was followed by splashing. The big poaka spun its head around to where it heard the noise coming from. It saw Jake. The animal eyed up his target for a split second before charging straight for the injured young man. Jake was furiously pulling himself along with his hands, pushing as hard as he could with his good leg. Brent wordlessly fired a shot that hit the boar in a vital spot behind its left ear. The poaka dropped to the ground, kicking and squealing as it bounced heavily into the river. It was incapacitated, but not dead. Brent rushed over to Jake and dragged him further back from the river.

Jake was shaking with fear. He had come close to being mauled to death by the giant pig.

"You saved my life, thank you," he sputtered.

"Your life is not saved yet," growled Brent. "I will leave you here while I hunt down your murdering prick of a brother. I will see if you are still alive when I come back down the river."

Slade had been watching the dramatic turn of events, wanting to dash out and help but knowing the hunter was forever watching. He swore he was going to get himself and his brothers out of the bush and back home in one piece.

'I'm going to kill him in revenge for him hurting Jakey and Luke.'

Slade couldn't watch anymore and he silently moved off up the river as fast as his two legs would take him.

Brent noticed two big shapes moving swiftly up the river. They had come out of a deep pool on the far bank. He recognised the shapes of the eels approaching so rapidly their tails and backs were breaking the surface of the water. Brent didn't need to watch to know there were more eels coming in right behind them. Within seconds the boar was surrounded, one had grabbed his leg while several other eels took nips wherever they could. The poaka was squealing and thrashing around in the river as the eels began to drag him down the creek in the current. The animal was taken into deeper water where more and more eels were joining the attack as Brent watched in amazement. In just minutes, the oversized boar had disappeared under the water which continued to froth in the centre of the pool as the eels devoured the giant animal under the water.

CHAPTER FIFTY-FIVE

"**I**f you are lucky medical assistance will be here by nightfall. My mate has gone for help," said Brent. He moved Jake to a safe distance from the river.

Jake pleaded for Brent not to go, and for him not to kill Slade. "He's my brother! Please don't leave me. I don't want to die alone."

Brent looked at Jake, feeling only a slight pang of sadness for the young man before remembering why he was doing what he was doing. The anger within Brent returned with a vengeance as soon as Jake mentioned Slade's name. Without another glance back at the injured Jake, Brent stood up and began to move up the river again while encouraging himself forward.

'I've still got one to get. From what the others have said - this is the bastard who killed Janey.'

Brent moved over to the other side of the river where Slade had disappeared, hoping to pick up his tracks. Moving up the river he soon picked up his boot marks. Brent tracked him up the river for another hour, only having to double back a couple of times to pick up the tracks again. At the same time, Brent was being very careful about the possibility of Slade ambushing him, especially as the river was getting really narrow as it approached the headwaters. He reached down with his hand to touch his knife; reassuring himself it was there for if the gun got knocked out of his hand. Brent noticed a massive side river coming in to his left that he had never been up before. Slade's boot marks were heading straight up the big side river. He checked up the main river another 100 metres in case Slade had doubled back, but quickly decided Slade must have gone up the way the marks were heading. Looking up the sides of the big river, Brent could see they had sheer drops and there was no way up. Brent followed the boot marks up the side river and continued to look up both sides all of the time. He was scanning for any sign of movement, with his rifle at the ready, worrying to himself slightly that this would be a very bad place to get bushwhacked. The going was tough, and due to the large number of rocks he seemed to have lost Slade's trail. Brent was looking for any freshly turned over rocks but there was nothing to go by and he was becoming more and more concerned that Slade may have doubled back.

CHAPTER FIFTY-SIX

S lade knew he was up against a foe that he needed to have the ultimate respect for.

He knew the man who had shot at them was out for revenge and would stop at nothing. He hadn't heard any more shots and feared for what could be happening back at the river.

Slade had been trying to think of a way to outrun the hunter, when an idea came to him - one idea that seemed like it would work. He scarpered as fast as he could across the river and into the bush. He knew the area well, and how further up the river led into a big side river catchment.

The big side river was really gorgy with sheer sides for about one kilometre up. It led right up to the base of a massive waterfall where there was a huge pool underneath and a big flat sandy area of about an acre where the water, in storms, had carved away everything in its path to create such a picturesque piece of nature. On the opposite side of the pool, from where the waterfall cascaded down, the river ran out and the water churned as it forced its way down the narrow funnel at the start of the river.

Slade planned to lure Brent up the side river to where he would be lying in wait on the ridge above. The plan would only work if Brent didn't know about the waterfall, because it was the type of fall that would have him trapped; the only way to get out of there was to turn around and go right back down the side river. Slade knew it would give him plenty of time to get far into the next catchment if he just waited for Brent to pass him.

Slade moved off up the river, keeping in the bush but as close to the edge of the river as possible. When he neared the side river, he left heavy footprints that were clearly visible in the sand and led right up the side river. He made his way about 300 metres up while always checking to see he was leaving a clear trail. Once the side river began to get rocky and it was not obvious that the trail was a diversion, Slade stepped into the river so Brent would not see his boot marks as he doubled his way back to the mouth of the side river. He climbed up onto the ridge beside it, covered his tracks very carefully, and then made his way slowly around the top. He worked his way up and along the ridge toward the waterfall, all the while looking down into the side river to see if Brent was approaching.

He had reached the halfway mark to the waterfall, far further than where he had gone up the side river below, when he saw a big slip with a lot of loose material and debris clinging to the sides of it. It appeared to be waiting for something to give it reason to crash its way down into the water below. Slade laughed evilly as another idea occurred to him, one that would still give him plenty of time to get away if it didn't work. The side river at the bottom of the slip had become very narrow, and Slade knew Brent would come up through there if he was to continue following in the direction of his footprint trail.

Slade climbed and pushed his way through the bush for about an hour as he worked his way up to the top of the slip from the side river. It was incredibly steep, and the bush on the ridge was thick and scrubby from the topsoil being decayed by storms and heavy rain over the years. Slade decided to wait at the top of the slip to see if he could cause a landslide and bring some loose rocks showering down to maim his pursuer. There were three big rocks sitting on the very edge of the slip amongst the loose material. Slade knew he could easily push and get them to crash down and make a landslide. He retreated into the bush and continued to wait and see if Brent would continue to follow the tracks up the side river.

Slade tried to think of a plan b, whispering to himself for company and reassurance, 'Even if the old guy doesn't come, I will carry on up this side creek past the waterfall and up to the top of the main ridge. I think that is the same ridge system where the main river slowly breaks up into heaps of side creeks. Once over this ridge, I'll drop down into the next catchment and work my back down to the coast. Then I will go get a gun and come back after him. Either way, he's the dead one.'

CHAPTER FIFTY-SEVEN

Stevo had set off at a fast pace and was finding it to be a lot quicker than on the way in as he didn't have the pack horse with all the gear or the other riders to slow him down. He rode past the spot where Brent had shot the first deer on their way up the river. He couldn't believe how that hunt could already feel like a lifetime ago, how so much had changed, and how things would never be the same. The carcass had already rotted in the bush and he was greeted with a whiff as rotten as his circumstances as he rode past. After riding for just over three hours, he pulled up in a small clearing and dismounted. He had found his mind constantly wandering back to what could be happening back at the Bullring. He had 4 cellphones on him and he checked each of them to see if he had any coverage. He hadn't tried any of them yet because he wanted to save any remaining battery for when he knew there would be signal. As he had feared, there was no signal yet and two of the phones wouldn't even turn on due to such low battery. He whacked his hand on his knee; all he wanted to do was to get help for his mates as soon as possible. He looked up at the sky and ran his hands through his hair, spinning slowly in a circle and stretching his back as he did so.

His eyes focussed on a rock formation that he recognised as one he had climbed on an earlier trip. He grinned as he quickly did the sums in his head. If he carried on down the track it would be at least a four hour ride until he got to a place where the cell phone would definitely work. Yet the high point of the rock would be at maximum a two hour walk. Even though it was steep, Stevo knew for sure he would get coverage as it had clear visibility all the way to the coast.

"I reckon the chopper will only take 20-25 minutes to get up here once he gets my call. I will call them and they will be at the Bullring before me – or maybe they will even be able to get me from up there at the top," Stevo muttered to himself.

He paused as he thought about the three men responsible for causing so much destruction. "Shit, I want to be there when those little bastards are caught. Five minutes on my own with them and they'll truly feel the justice they deserve for breaking our paradise." He took a deep breath and focussed his eyes captivatingly on the cell phone with the most battery. He placed it in his chest pocket as he knew he must not damage or drop it – he had never been a man to embrace modern technology but he was fully aware that those cell phones were the only way to get the help his friends needed as soon as possible. He left the two phones that wouldn't turn on behind, and slipped the one with very low battery into his back pocket just in case.

Stevo loaded his rifle and checked that the mag was full of ammo before beginning his climb.

CHAPTER FIFTY-EIGHT

Brent had continued moving slowly up the side river towards a thundering of water he could hear in the distance ahead. He was feeling ready to turn around and head back to the main river to try and pick up Slade's trail again because there had been no sign for quite a distance – and Brent knew there should have been something.

Brent was amazed at how sheer the sides had stayed as they had narrowed until there was only just enough room for him to make his way up the left hand side of the river. The river was roaring down a channel it had carved through the rock and he just couldn't shake the feeling that he was going the wrong way. He had stopped his intent search for signs of Slade and had was starting to feel downhearted and desperate. He knew he needed to stop for a rest or he would run out of energy because, despite the circumstances, he hadn't completely lost his senses and he knew he needed to take care of himself in the bush – perhaps now more than ever before.

He decided he would continue moving around a couple more corners of the side river to where he could hear the waterfall roaring as it spewed water over the top and thundered down into the pool below. A waterfall would be a good place for him to sit and rest while thinking of a new action plan for revenge.

As Brent made his way around a second corner he looked about 200 metres up the river to where he could see only the top of the waterfall as the bush in front was obscuring his vision of the rest.

As Brent approached the falls, he noticed a big slip of 150 metres high that spilled into the river just in front of him. The slip had made the narrow river deep and swift below, but Brent figured there was enough room for him to get around.

Slade could see Brent making his way up towards the waterfall; just as he had been hoping. All he needed him to do was to keep going – because Slade was going to trigger a deadly landslide.

CHAPTER FIFTY-NINE

Stevo had to first cross the river in order to get to the side of the rocky mountain. He took a moment to stare straight up at the pinnacle. He powered his way up the ridge as fast as he could and it only took him about 40 minutes to reach halfway at the quick pace he was boosting up. He had found himself on a jutty bit of rock that protruded out of the bush and looked straight up at the pinnacle. He allowed himself to rest for 5 minutes before continuing to move as fast as he could go. He was sweating profusely and his mouth was parched and dry. He licked at his lips to moisten them, wishing desperately he hadn't left his water bottle with his horse below.

"It is mind over matter," Stevo told himself as he kept ploughing on. He patted his pocket to check on the cellphone as he really wanted to get his friends out of the bush before the clouds burst open.

Finally, as he pushed through a large patch of undergrowth, he came out onto a rocky piece where the pinnacle lay right before him. He knew it would be just five to ten minutes until he would be there. He had to climb like a mountain goat as there were big, jutty, bits of rock sticking out all over the place. There was only another 20 metres to the top and he decided to try the cell phone because it was just getting too steep. Stevo sat out on a little ledge and stared out over the bush, all the way to the coast. After what felt like an eternity, the cell phone sprung to life and his heart skipped a beat as he waited for the phone to pick up coverage.

As the tiny triangle of lines indicating service showed up thick and strong, Stevo sighed with both relief and trepidation of what would come next. He knew he needed to get help for his friends and Sue, but leaving the bush without Janey was going to make everything even more real. He didn't know how to face the future, and decided it was best to just deal with things as they came. He dialled 111.

"We need help fast, shit has happened and we need you to get here now!!" yelled Stevo into the phone. The guy on the other end of the phone couldn't hear Stevo clearly because of the wind at the pinnacle; what he could hear sounded so farfetched and bizarre.

"For God's sake, send the rescue chopper up to Bullring as fast as possible," Stevo repeated. He grew frustrated as he repeated the story for the third time.

Thankfully, his message was taken seriously and Stevo was told that the rescue chopper was on its way, and for him to stay where he was as the chopper would get him first.

He looked down at his phone and saw that a couple of battery bars still remained. He decided to call Daniel and tell him what had happened. He was nervous about making the call but knew he needed to. If Daniel was working and heard what had happened but didn't hear the news from Stevo, he would be even more devastated.

Stevo shared the basic story with Daniel, Brent and Janey's oldest son. Stevo had cracked as soon as had heard Daniel's voice, and both men held their phones to their ears with tears rolling down their cheeks.

Daniel and Eugene had just pulled in to shore from an early morning fish out on Brent's warrior. Eugene had gone up to the parking lot to get the vehicle to tow the boat out of the water and as he returned he took one look at Daniel and turned pale himself. Stevo heard Eugene's voice shake as he asked his brother,

"What's going on?"

Daniel hung up on Stevo and turned to his brother. "I've got something to tell you."

Daniel explained to him everything that Stevo had said happened at the Bullring.

Eugene stared bleakly at his brother.

"You can't be for real. No way could that have happened to our parents. They are too good to have anything like that happen to them."

Daniel's felt his stomach drop as he kicked at the stones on the road while continuing to tell the story to Eugene.

Stevo rang again; he was worried about Daniel. Stevo mentioned the need for someone to tell Ingrid.

"The news has to come from me. It'll be tough, what do I tell her?" asked Daniel.

Stevo heard Daniel's voice fade as his emotions took over and he tried his best to console his best friend's eldest son.

"Are you all right, Dan?"

"Yeah, yeah Stevo. I'm okay. I will do it."

Daniel's mind was whirling a thousand miles a minute and he began to think out loud.

"My mate has a small chopper that I can fly. I will ring him and borrow it. I need to see what has happened for myself. I will be up there with Dad and Mum as quickly as I can." Eugene nodded in agreement and Stevo could hear him saying that he would come up the river with Daniel.

"Hey Dan, I've got to go," shouted Stevo against the noise of the wind on the pinnacle. "My phone is about to go flat. You take care." "Yeah, Stevo. Thanks for letting me know, it can't have been easy."

Daniel called Ingrid. He explained what he knew of his parents hunting trip to the Bullring.

"I am sorry, I don't know much," Daniel replied sadly.

"Ok, don't worry. We will find out what has happened soon enough, I guess." Ingrid had always been a very capable girl and didn't often let her emotions take over. "I'm on my way now," she assured her brother. "I'll meet you at the hospital."

Reality hadn't hit Ingrid yet and Daniel was really worried about her and what may happen when she was struck with the severity of the situation. He called her again and she told him she had picked up a friend who was driving her. He could hear the tears in her voice and he was able to put his mind at rest a little with the knowledge she was not on her own.

"We won't come to the hospital just yet. I am going to borrow my mate's chopper and fly in to see what is going on. Eugene is coming with me. I will call you when we are all organised. You go to the hospital to wait for Mum to arrive."

"Oh, Dan," sobbed Ingrid, "What on earth could have happened up there? Dad called it his Paradise."

Daniel focussed on his next task, and tried not to let himself get swept away with his own emotions. He spoke to his friend with the helicopter, who promised to drop everything and fly with Daniel immediately,

"I've got a little Robinson that is available. It will get the two of us there really quickly."

Daniel asked if there was room for three because when he thought about what he may find; he really wanted his brother with him.

However, he was told it was just a two man chopper

"If it's ok with you can I fly the chopper? My brother really needs to come too."

"Sure, as long as you think you will be ok. It will be ready to go for ya in 20 minutes. I'll have it fuelled up and out of the hangar."

"We'll be there at the hangar in 15 minutes. I'll fly the chopper and we can be at the Bullring in no time. Those pricks had better hope that the cops get to them before Dad does. There's no telling what he might do," said Daniel.

Daniel had already radioed the police to let them know he was on his way up the valley. He had seen many a criminal get a light sentence and he decided that he would do whatever he could to make sure that the guys responsible for his mother's death would not get away lightly.

Daniel and Eugene arrived at the helicopter hangar after making a quick detour to Daniel's house. Daniel thought how his father had always taught him to be ready for anything. He grabbed his stainless steel Ruger 308 from his gun cabinet and strapped his ammo belt around his waist. He wore a look of death on his face; he was going to get those guys who had destroyed his family. Daniel knew there was no way he could forgive anyone who had taken any part in ending his mother's life prematurely. He had always believed in listening to all viewpoints before making a judgement about people or situations - but this strong sense of justice was being severely tested as he tried to make sense of what Stevo had told him.

CHAPTER SIXTY

Stevo was grateful the rescue chopper guys had told him they would come and get him first. He knew that as soon as he was on board, they would drop down the river and fly to the Bullring where Sue would be waiting for him. They needed to get Roger, Janey's body, and the girls to a hospital as quickly as possible.

"This nightmare will soon be over," he whispered to himself, scanning the sky for their salvation.

The rescue helicopter came up from the eastern side of the peak. Even though he could hear its familiar sound echoing throughout the valley, it arrived suddenly upon Stevo who was waving frantically from the rocky outcrop. The blades were vibrating with the turbulence from being up so high, and they were sending out a thunderous noise as the chopper hovered above, searching for the best place to pick up Stevo. The only choice for landing was the rocky outcrop that Stevo was standing on. After circling around a few times and assessing the wind to determine there was no way to land, the helicopter swerved and put one skid on the edge of the rock. Stevo bravely stepped onto the skid so he could quickly get pulled up and into the chopper. The wind and the height made it breath-taking, and under different circumstances he would have been having the time of his life.

Stevo looked blankly at his rescuers. "Hi."

With a grim look on his face the pilot turned to face him saying, "Sounds like you have had a terrible ordeal. Are you okay?"

Stevo was bleeding from where the bush lawyer and scrub had cut his face when he was pushing through the dense undergrowth.

"I'm holding together, mate. Thanks for coming so quickly."

He slipped the headphones over his ears so he could speak more easily with the pilot and the two paramedics, and he relayed the whole story. The pilot listened intently. He did not want to ask any questions, choosing to concentrate solely on the job he had come to do. He knew the Bullring area well and told Stevo the police helicopter was already on its way as the 111 operators had put the call through to both police and medical rescue.

"How will we all fit on board?" inquired Stevo.

"We'll get your mate who is hurt and the two ladies out first. We will deliver them straight to the nearest hospital. We'll leave one medic there with you and he will check you and your other mate out. I've radioed ahead for a police chopper to come and pick up you three and the body of the woman who was killed. I'm sure you need to rest and eat so we have some supplies for that too. I'm sure the police will want to have a look at the crime scene. I know where the Bullring is and can easily land there," assured the pilot. Stevo nodded his head in acknowledgement. His mouth was dry and he was beginning to feel sick to his stomach with worry for the others.

"Are you all right?" one of the medics asked him. "Nah, I really need a drink."

Handing him a bottle of glucose water the medic spoke kindly. "Try some of this, its magic. I think you are dehydrated."

Stevo drank the bottle dry and was handed another; he could feel himself improving almost immediately.

The rescue chopper, spiralling its way down into the river, hovered above the Bullring. As they were dropping in towards the camp, the pilot asked,

"Are those horses pretty quiet?"

"Yeah, they'll be okay." Stevo had tied them at a distance as he knew the chopper may spook them. The horses already had their heads up and were looking at the chopper nervously. The pilot safely managed to land on the sandy river piece right beside the camp. Sue had already stood up and was wringing her hands nervously as she glanced at the door. Stevo and the medics leaped out and ran over to the campsite. Stevo ran straight to Sue and swept her up into a giant bear hug and planted kisses all over her cheeks and forehead as he held her face in his hands. Glancing around, Stevo noticed he couldn't see Brent.

"Where is Brent?" Sue whispered,

"He went off up the River, Stevo. We tried to stop him but we couldn't." Sue and Stevo walked over to where Heather and Roger were huddled together by Janey. Stevo stared up the river with a sad look

on his face before telling the others of the plan.

"This chopper will take you three out. There is another one on its way and it will pick up Janey, the medic, and me. I imagine we will now have to go up the river to try and find Brent. Shit, I hope he is ok. I had enough battery on the phone to call Daniel who was with Eugene, and they have called Ingrid. He and Eugene are hopefully on their way up here in Daniel's mate's helicopter. Heather, after you call your kids, can you please let ours know before the media gets a hold of the story?" "Sure, Stevo. They need to hear the terrible news from us," sighed

Heather sadly.

Sue was becoming hysterical. Stevo held onto her tightly and reassured her that they both would be safe. Heather agreed to the plan and knew it was really important to find Brent as soon as possible. It only made sense that Stevo went searching for him; he was the one who best knew Brent out in the bush. Sue clung to Stevo, desperate not to let him go.

"It'll be ok, love. We'll be right behind you," reassured Stevo as he stroked her face and hair kindly.

The girls nervously looked towards the helicopter as they had never been in one before and were unsure of how to approach it. Stevo carried Sue to the door of the chopper and hugged her tightly.

"I'll be as quick as I can and then I won't need to leave you again. You are safe now honey."

Sue couldn't contain her fear and desperation, and she continued to sob hysterically as she shakily climbed into her seat. The medic helped her to get her seatbelt on and linked her straight up to an intravenous line that promptly delivered her painkillers and a strong medication to help calm her. The tears began to subside as the substances began pumping through her dehydrated system. She waved meekly at Stevo.

The ground was very uneven, and the chopper, with the motor still running, had just one skid on the ground. The other medic had already made a quick assessment of Roger and had reassured Heather he was going to be okay. Roger had a fractured skull, and there was concern about the amount of blood lost.

Stevo and the medic took a side each of Roger and assisted him safely aboard the chopper where Heather immediately jumped up to sat beside him. The on-board medic quickly took over and all three passengers were immediately wrapped in warm blankets. Stevo was concerned that Sue had begun to hallucinate mildly and it looked as if she was about to pass out. The extra pressure was almost too much for him. He could see the medic was doing everything he could for her as she drifted in and out of consciousness. He monitored her weak but steady vital signs as the pilot radioed ahead to inform them of a traumatised woman suffering from a lack of food and hypothermia. Stevo desperately wished he could jump on board and fly away with them, but he knew he needed to find his best friend. He also knew his best friend wouldn't want Janey to be left alone. He kissed Sue goodbye gently and whispered to her to stay strong and that he loved her. Heather kindly wrapped her arm around Stevo and promised that everything would be fine.

"Thanks for everything Stevo. I'll look after her. You look after Janey and take care of yourself. We will see you soon. I promise."

The pilot motioned to where he had seen another helicopter coming up the valley. They guessed it was the police helicopter, but when they looked back they realised it was a much smaller one.

"Daniel must have got his mate's chopper," commented Stevo. "Bloody brilliant!"

"I wonder who he brought with him," piped up Heather as she strained her eyes to see.

The helicopter came down close and hovered for a few minutes directly above the Bullring. Heather and Stevo could see Daniel was flying alongside a very worried and grim looking Eugene. Stevo waved out to them and signalled for Daniel to land in the clearing on the other side of the fire pit. As soon as the chopper touched down, Stevo rushed over to greet the boys.

"Daniel, Eugene, you got here so quickly! Things have changed since I talked to you. When I got back, the girls told me that Brent has gone up the river after all - to find the bastards."

Daniel had already shut the motor off and was carefully climbing out of the cockpit.

"Where's Mum?" yelled Eugene.

Stevo was torn. He realised that if they were to see their mother, it would be really distressing for them. He knew they wanted to see her but also knew that the most important thing was to find Brent before he did anything regrettable.

"Your mother is safe, she is tucked up in her sleeping bag just over there," Stevo said kindly as he pointed towards the mound of blankets that cradled Janey's body.

Stevo continued, "Look, right now the rescue chopper is about to leave for the hospital with Heather, Sue, and Rog. The police chopper is on its way to pick up Janey, Brent, and I – but Brent isn't here. It is urgent that we find Brent. I was going to go, since I know how he hunts – but now you boys are here, I think you will be much stronger out there than I will be; I haven't slept or eaten in days. I will stay here with Janey and the medic; we will wait for the police to get here. I promise you, your mother is cared for."

Stevo placed his hand on Daniel's shoulder and looked him in his eyes; eyes that mirrored the sadness of his own. "Can you boys please head up the river in the chopper to see if you can find Brent? I don't want him to be alone any longer than is necessary or to do anything he will regret to get revenge."

With heavy hearts, they climbed back into the chopper and Daniel started the motor up again. Stevo thanked the boys for coming so quickly and for going in search of Brent.

"No worries, Stevo. You look after yourself too mate, you have done a great job and we are so grateful for what you've done. Please tell the rescue chopper pilots that I will radio them as soon as we find Dad, just to let them know what is happening up there."

Stevo nodded and stepped back from the helicopter to give it space as Daniel revved the motor and lifted off from the Bullring as quickly as he had arrived.

CHAPTER SIXTY-ONE

Only minutes after Daniel and Eugene left, the rescue chopper closed the doors and prepared to lift off and out of the valley. Heather asked, "What's going to happen now?" The medic spoke kindly to her, "Well, pretty soon we will have you at the hospital where you will get a nice hot cup of tea and something to eat. We will get you warmed up and into a nice hot shower. I'm sure that sounds pretty good since Stevo said you have all been in there for over a week."

Heather attempted a small smile in reply as the medic continued. "We have notified the police and they will meet us at the hospital.

They will need statements from you all and will be gathering any evidence they need."

"My husband's camera has all the evidence they will need. It has a photo of the killers on it," grimaced Heather.

The pilot leaned back and spoke encouragingly.

"That is going to be a great help, you have done very well considering the circumstances. I just heard that the police chopper is well on its way. They will do a quick scene examination before they pick up Janey, Stevo, and the medic. Then if Brent hasn't been found yet, they will head off to help find Brent. But our job here, right now, is to get you three to safety first."

Heather sat up and turned worriedly to the medic.

"Do the press know already? I don't want our kids to hear from them first. They will know it was us even without using names."

"I don't think they would know yet," the medic reassured her honestly.

Heather snuggled into Roger underneath a warm and oversized blanket.

The chopper's massive blades slowly wound up, building the power needed to create enough momentum to lift it up and away from the river. The chopper manoeuvred its way down the valley at top speed, the big blades vibrating with the strain of the load and the turbulence of the wind up in the high country. Heather turned away from the window as they left behind the place that had been their paradise but was where they had felt such pain and torment.

CHAPTER SIXTY-TWO

About half way down the river valley, the rescue helicopter passed the police chopper flying in.

Heather was immensely reassured. "Sue, the police have arrived. It won't be long until Stevo is with us again." Heather was worried about Sue as she still had not gained full consciousness. A small smile crossed Sue's lips at the mention of Stevo. The rescue chopper pilot had already let the police know they had picked up Heather, Sue, and Roger, and how they had left Janey and Stevo at the campsite. There had been no word to either the police or the rescue team from Daniel and Eugene, so they knew Brent was still out in the bush.

After what felt like an eternity to Heather, the chopper began to descend as the hospital came into sight. The chopper landed swiftly and precisely, and the pilot shut off the engine so the helicopter would stop vibrating and shaking. The medical teams raced in quickly for Sue and Roger who were immediately carried out and placed onto the stretchers and covered with even more blankets. Heather refused to be carried out, choosing instead to hop out herself and follow them on foot into the building.

Heather looked around at the busy faces belonging to the white coats.

"Can someone please get me a phone? I need to ring our children." A doctor had already administered more fluids into Sue's IV and Heather saw she was beginning to come around.

Roger had been wheeled away for x-rays and scans, Heather was feeling lost without him at her side. She realised she still had not let the children know and began frantically asking again for a phone. Heather decided it would be best to call Ingrid first when a kind hearted nurse brought her a phone. Ingrid explained that she was on her way, and Heather could hear her friend who was driving say that they were about an hour away from the hospital. Heather called her own children before checking with Sue if she felt up to calling the boys. Sue asked if Heather could do it, as she didn't have the heart to explain to them what had happened. Not a single one of the children could believe what they were hearing yet they all knew it wasn't a lie. They all told Heather they would drop everything and be at the hospital as soon as they possibly could.

CHAPTER SIXTY-THREE

rent had crossed over to the left side of the river. The falls were roaring so loudly that he could hardly hear himself think. The water was gushing past at great speed on his right, and he was on the same level as the slip.

He felt a stone fall from above and land heavily as it hit the smattering of rocks beside him. Brent immediately looked up to see a shower of boulders racing and tumbling their way down the slip directly towards him. He panicked and threw himself into the scrub at the left side of the bank as the falling boulders bounced off the rocks around him. He jammed himself against the bank facing the slip as there was no time for him to get anywhere safer.

There was a 5-metre shelf of rock between him and the river and the boulders and debris splashed and crashed into the water. He looked up and saw three particularly big boulders racing directly towards him. They bounced off the bottom of the slip, flew over the river and landed on the shelf of rock where Brent was standing. Their momentum sent them skidding at him and he found himself trapped with nowhere to go. He managed to duck the first two, but the third came right toward him at full speed.

He stepped sideways to the right, mindful to keep his rifle out of harm's way. He hadn't been quick enough; as he moved, the boulder brushed up against his left side and came to an abrupt stop, catching his arm and jamming it hard against the rock bank. A sharp piece of rock broke off and caught Brent smack on the side of his head. He was instantly knocked out cold, his arm supporting the weight of his limp body as it was jammed so tightly between the rock and the river bank of solid rock.

Slade looked down at the scene from above, his heart racing from the adrenaline of what he had just done. He was ecstatic; from his position he could see Brent was hurt and in some serious bother. Slade kept watching and tried to think of his next moves. He could tell Brent was still alive but that he appeared to be unconscious and jammed by the boulder. He thought about going all the way back down the ridge and up the side river to finish him off - but knew it would take him at least an hour to get down there and then another hour or so up to Brent. And he still needed to go down over the next ridge before heading around and up the main river. He needed to get out of the bush before the police were called. And then there were his brothers to think about. Slade felt his mind racing in all directions but decided that the best thing for him would be to hightail himself far from the scene.

Brent slowly regained consciousness. As he became more aware of his surroundings he began to feel real panic at his arm being jammed. He was in excruciating pain and imagined his arm to be completely broken and smashed. Looking up the slip to the top he could see Slade standing there looking down on him with a sly grin. Luckily for Brent, he had managed to hold onto the rifle with his free hand. He moved the gun slowly and put the point of the rifle on his boot to rest it while he closed the bolt with his right hand. Swinging the rifle up quickly, all with the one arm, he squeezed the trigger just as Slade came into view through the scope. The bullet flew straight and true and only just missed Slade's head. Brent swore to himself as Slade hastily threw himself into the scrub for the second time that day.

Slade knew then that there was no way he could take the chance of going all the way around and up the side river to get Brent while Brent still had the gun – and was such good aim even with only one arm! Slade peeked out from the bush. He could hear a chopper working in the distance. He knew the only way to get himself out alive was to keep going; he needed to get over into the next watershed.

Slade scoffed as he looked back down towards the injured man below, "He'll keep!"

Brent was slumped against the rock in extraordinary pain. His arm had been shattered by the boulder and his head was pounding. He regained a level of consciousness and looked around at the sheer walls surrounding the waterfall. Brent could see that the only way in or out from the base of the waterfall was the way he had come up through the side river. He could also see that Slade could not get off the ridge and down to where he was without backtracking. From where Brent was trapped, he could see the entire waterfall cascading down into the big sandy patched area underneath. He could also see quite far back down where he had come from, and Brent knew he would be able to see Slade if the young man did decide to come down and finish him off.

As Brent's ears accustomed to the sound of the falls, he realised he could make out a faint sound in the distance. He concentrated hard through the fog of his pounding mind to distinguish that it was the sound of a helicopter.

"That'll be Stevo with help for my darling Janey," he realised gratefully.

He strained his ears over the thump in his head and the thundering of the waterfall so he could hear the helicopter more clearly. He listened to the sound changes as he wondered if the chopper had seen Jake or Luke and stopped to help them. Brent reassured himself that it was the helicopter for Janey as he drifted in and out of consciousness.

Brent woke from vivid dreams a small while later with a jolt. He remembered where he was due to a sharp pain in his left arm. He tried pulling his arm and pushing on the boulder at the same time but he couldn't move either one even an inch. There was no way he would be able to free himself as he wasn't strong enough on his own, with only one arm free and the other in excruciating pain.

"Shit, this is bad!" swore Brent as he closed his eyes and gritted his teeth to counter the pain. "What the hell am I going to do? I've got to kill that bastard for Janey." Brent's mind was filled with a thousand images of his wife; images of her caring for their children, running together through the fields as children, her grooming the animals with love and care, rubbing his back after a long day, making love down by the river of Rosenfee amongst their wildflowers. He thought of their luck at having three beautiful children, and how Janey would never get to see them marry or have their own babies. Janey did not deserve to have such a cruel and untimely death, Brent had always considered her as the backbone of his family and he thought how much he had loved every single moment of their lives together. He couldn't get his head around what had happened, or how he was going to explain this tragedy occurring in his paradise? Brent squeezed his eyes closed even tighter as the tears forced their way through his eyelashes and rolled steadily down his face.

He slumped forward and as he did, one of the bullets he had put into his pocket rolled out. He managed to reach out and grab it with his free hand. He brought it up to his face and stared intently at the tiny piece of metal that was capable of taking away life in an instant. He shook his head and told himself he needed to pull things together and concentrate on getting himself free. He was filled with a sense of anxiety from the desire to stay on his mission. He knew he had to keep his mind focussed because he was scared of falling into unconsciousness and letting Janey down.

"The kids will need me. I have to sort this." He spoke harshly to himself as he wriggled around a bit. He looked again at the bullet in his hand and as he spun it in his fingers he growled,

"This one will get your killer, Janey."

The rifle was lying by his leg on the rock and he steadied it with his knee as he pulled the bolt back with his free hand. He pushed the round into the chamber and cranked the bolt forward; he was ready to go.

CHAPTER SIXTY-FOUR

Daniel and Eugene flew carefully up the river. Eugene cried out and his voice came out strong over the headset, "There's a guy down there Dan. It's not Dad cos this guy's blonde - but he looks injured."

Daniel manoeuvred the helicopter quickly and landed on the sandy bank not too far from where Eugene had spotted the young man lying beside the river.

Eugene grabbed Daniel's rifle and jumped out and ran straight over to the guy on the ground.

"Where is my father?" he yelled as he pointed the gun at the man's head.

The man looked up. Eugene could see the terror in his eyes.

"He … um, he … he just left me here after he shot my horse and stabbed a knife into my shoulder! He knows I didn't have anything to do with what happened at the camp. He went on up the river to find my brothers, hours ago man, honest! It's Slade he wants 'cos he is the one who caused everything. I swear I didn't do anything, seriously!" Luke pleaded, not at all worried about throwing his brothers under the bus since they had just abandoned him.

"You had better not be lying to me you piece of shit, because we will meet again. Our father is far more important than you will ever be. We will be back, believe me!!" Eugene kicked forcefully at the stones sending a dust shower in a tearful Luke's direction as he ran back to the waiting chopper and climbed in. He told Daniel what the blonde man had told him and they discussed it for a minute before carrying on up the river. They figured their father had injured the man and then left him there to pursue the other two; obviously the londe man was not the one Brent was after. Their main goal was to find their father.

The helicopter had barely gone half a mile, when they rounded a corner and saw a second man lying alongside the river. Daniel flew right down close to the ground and Eugene quickly jumped out before it had even landed. He ran over to the man and it was clear that he was in a very bad way. The man was sweating profusely and had become very pale. Eugene shook him but he could only make out a strange delirious babbling about giant eels eating boars and attempting to climb out of the river to munch on his leg. Eugene scoffed at how pathetic the young man looked, and felt disappointed he could not get any information out of him. Eugene could see the wound on the leg had been well dressed, and he presumed it was his father who had done it as it was well applied. The bandage was saturated with dark red blood and he could see the man was not doing very well at all. He raced back to the chopper and told Daniel that there was no point trying to talk to the young man as he was very injured and delusional. Daniel radioed both the police and rescue choppers to let them know the locations of the two men needing help. They also explained that they were going to carry on working their way up the river to find their father.

CHAPTER SIXTY-FIVE

After the rescue chopper left Stevo and the medic at the Bullring, the medic stirred up the fire and put the billy on to boil. The medic checked Stevo's injuries and cleaned his cuts and grazes before covering them with antibiotic cream.

"Lucky you are fit and strong," the medic observed. "You have come off very lightly."

"Especially compared to my wife …" He paused sadly. "And my friend's wife." Stevo looked towards where Janey lay in her sleeping bag. Stevo wandered off to check on the dogs and horses to see if they had enough food. The bush was suddenly filled with the sound of another chopper roaring its way up the river.

"Thank God, they didn't take long," muttered Stevo as he ran back to the main camp area to greet the police helicopter. He needed to find his best friend and to make sure he was all right; he couldn't lose both of his best and oldest friends out in one of his most favourite parts of his own country. Stevo thought of the damage that had been done, and was filled with his own sense of revenge.

"As for the bastards that caused this, we'll have to do what needs to be done." He vowed silently as the police chopper landed in front of him.

A fully uniformed policeman jumped out and strode over to Stevo. "Boy, I am glad to see you," Stevo greeted him eagerly. "You would never in a million years think our paradise could be destroyed like this."

Two other policemen followed. Stevo filled them in with the events of their time in the bush. The officer in charge explained how he and the other policemen would need to take photos and samples of the crime scene.

"I knew you would say that, but can't we just get Janey on board and get out of here? I want to find Brent as quickly as possible, before anything else terrible happens!" panicked Stevo with frustration.

"I know, we do too," reassured the charge officer. "We will be as quick as we can."

One of the officers took some photos of the campsite and Janey's body, little plastic numbers were placed around in different areas, and one of the officers put Roger's gun and the bloodstained piece of wood into separate plastic bags as evidence.

The medic and Stevo carefully and respectfully carried Janey to the chopper. It was a really sobering experience for Stevo who felt sick as they slid the stretcher into the back of the chopper and strapped her in. They took their seats and the three policemen joined them a little while later as the pilot relayed to everyone that they had received a call from Daniel about two people needing immediate assistance in the river; the second one being described as an urgent case.

"Did he say if he had seen Brent yet?" fretted Stevo, not caring at all to hear of the injuries of the two men.

"No, sorry. No news of him yet," replied the pilot professionally as the chopper lifted off and headed steadily up the river.

Stevo looked down at the Bullring below him; unable to believe what had happened over the past 48 odd hours. He really didn't know how he would react when he saw the two guys in the river. He hoped he wouldn't lose it but he couldn't count on it as he was already feeling sick and angry to the core of his being. Stevo let out a deep breath. The pilot turned and spoke to him,

"Don't worry, Stevo. We will get this sorted." Stevo smiled weakly.

"Yeah, thanks mate."

Stevo scanned every bit of river as the chopper flew, searching desperately for any sign of Brent and Big Red. As they came around a corner, Stevo gave a small shout and pointed down to where he could see one of the people Daniel had told them about. The pilot explained that they would go further up to where Daniel had seen the severely injured man. "This guy will keep," said the pilot.

He radioed again through to another rescue chopper of their exact location and Stevo felt a wave of relief wash over him as he realised he wouldn't have to sit with the criminals for the ride to the hospital. Stevo shrieked out when he saw Big Red tied up on a grassy patch near to the river. He was instantly worried about Brent because he knew how

Brent wouldn't have liked leaving Big Red behind in a place where he was vulnerable.

"Hang in there mate, we are nearly with you," he telepathically sent the thoughts down to Big Red below.

It wasn't long before they spotted the second man lying sprawled against a log near to the river. The chopper landed swiftly and as they all got out to access the situation Stevo exclaimed,

"Shit, he looks like he is dead!"

Stevo climbed out of the chopper and walked over to where he could see the young man was in such a bad way that he was unable to sit up or talk coherently.

Two of the policemen ushered Stevo back into the helicopter while the third officer and the medic quickly assessed the injured man. They placed him on a stretcher that had been pulled out from under a seat, and they tried to make him comfortable enough to wait for the rescue chopper.

The helicopter then headed back to where they had seen the first man. They left one of the officers and a portable radio with Jake.

As they came in to land near Luke, Stevo could see it was the blonde one of the three men. He explained to the officers that from what he had been told, the blonde one did not enter the camp with the other two. Luke was in a bad way, his leg was swollen to twice its normal size and one of his arms looked as if it had been broken. Luke's shoulder had been pierced with a knife, the heavy blood flow had stopped but it would still require a stitch or two. The medic requested to be returned to stay with Jake whose medical situation was deemed as far more serious while one of the two remaining officers was required to stay with Luke.

The remaining police officer in charge, the medic, and Stevo flew back to drop the medic where the other man lay. On the way, Daniel radioed to say that they were on the left, up the first big branch in the river, after the second person in the river, and by the waterfall - and that they had found Brent.

"I know where that is, won't take us long to get there," said the pilot.

CHAPTER SIXTY-SIX

Brent had known it would take Slade at least 40 minutes to make his way down the ridge and another 40 minutes to get to where Brent was since the banks were so steep. He wasn't even sure if Slade would come back to finish him off – maybe he would go off to check on his brothers. Or maybe he would make a run for freedom. Brent mused over what he would have done in Slade's position.

Brent lay against the bank and closed his eyes every now and then to counteract the pain. He slipped in and out of consciousness as he thought about Janey and their three children; trying to understand how everything could have gone so wrong in such a short time.

'This area of Aoteoroa is paradise to me, to my friends, and to my family. How could these guys come up here and kill my wife, and rape my friend's wife? What the hell drove them to do something like that? They have broken paradise. They have no respect. I *will* teach them some.' Brent growled as he opened his eyes suddenly. He was disheartened to realise he could still hear the waterfall and see the bush surrounding him. His arm no longer throbbed viciously as it seemed to have gone completely numb. He pulled on his arm with his full body strength but knew there was no way it was coming free from under the boulder. He was trapped, and he had found himself well and truly living the nightmare.

Brent looked down at his numb, trapped arm and found himself feeling almost objective about the situation. He was determined to kill Slade and make him suffer for killing Janey, but in order to do so he needed to be free from the boulder. He realised that in order to be free to hunt Slade, he had no choice other than to take his own arm off. Brent could not believe what he was contemplating, but figured it couldn't be too different to taking the hind legs off a deer.

His thoughts turned to a future without Janey and he knew he had to revenge her death. He had no option but to try to cut his arm free from the rock. He looked down at his trusty knife and reached over with his right hand to feel his left arm. He could feel that it had been smashed right back to the elbow and guessed if he was really going to go through with it, the best place would be to take it off just below the elbow.

Brent closed his eyes; resting a moment as he cleared his mind to build up the strength he needed to go through with making the cut. His mind wandered back to the life he and Janey had shared. He reminisced about the good times as tears spiralled down his cheeks to land in amongst the dusty debris that was about to cause the loss of his arm. He remembered all their great times down at the river watching the wild flowers, with their magic powers, blowing in the breeze. He wished with all his heart that they had remembered to pick a bunch before this trip – they surely would have given them a warning. He thought fondly of the first time they climbed onto the rickety old school bus and a small smile tugged at his lips.

He opened his eyes and the reality of his situation hit him hard for the millionth time. He began to feel really angry as his mind cleared and he remembered what he was planning to do once he was free: he would go back down the river, up onto the ridge where he last saw Slade, find him, and kill him - slowly. It would be revenge for Janey. Brent shut everything out of his mind as sheer determination set upon him. He winced with pain as he unhooked his belt and wound it around his left arm and back through the buckle; using his teeth to hold the end of it as he positioned it with his right hand. He pulled the makeshift tourniquet as hard as he could before wrapping the belt back over itself to hold it tight; just in case his arm bled too badly. He picked up his knife again and held it firmly in his free hand. He was grateful it was sharp.

Brent took a deep breath and tried to stop himself from trembling. In his concentration, Brent had blocked out all sounds and had not heard the chopper approaching over the noise of the waterfall.

He slowly brought his right arm around and positioned the knife right at the centre of his left elbow. He was hoping to cut the top half of the meat down to the bone in one slice, and then lever up with his body to break the joint, before quickly cutting the rest. He dug the sharp knife in, almost effortlessly cutting quickly across the width of his arm. Blood began to spurt out and he pulled on the belt as he ground his teeth together and his eyes blurred with tears due to the pain. As far as Brent was concerned, it didn't matter if he had no arm; he was going to end his own life and join Janey as soon as he had gotten his revenge.

He took another big breath to steady himself, and just as he was about to force his body upwards to break the joint, he heard Janey's voice,

"Don't do it, Brent. You need that arm." Brent's weak and exhausted body was entering delirium and he passed out instantly as blood poured from the incision and began to stain the rocky ledge he was trapped on.

CHAPTER SIXTY-SEVEN

Brent was in a fog of unconsciousness when he awoke to a voice screaming.

"Dad! Dad!"

Brent presumed he was hallucinating; there was no way his children could be in the bush.

"It's a trick, it must be that bastard who killed my wife," swore Brent as he felt around for the gun next to him on the ledge. He swung it up onto his free shoulder and pointed it in the direction of the sound. Brent's looked towards the falls and shook his head in disbelief. Only metres away stood his eldest son Daniel. Moving the gun to point away from Daniel, but not wanting to take any chances, Brent called out tentatively,

"Dan? Is that really you, Dan?" "Yes Dad. It's me."

Brent remained convinced it was all a trick of his mind; his eyes were full of tears from the pain in his arm, and it was taking a long time for him to focus. As Dan got closer, calling out to his father the entire time, Brent finally realised it was indeed his son who had joined him in the bush.

"Don't sneak up on me like that," Brent scowled through his teeth. There was a massive quantity of blood pouring from Brent's arm. "What are you doing, Dad?"

"I'm a bit stuck, Dan. I'm just trying to get free."

Brent threw the gun down and wryly smiled as Eugene appeared beside Daniel. The boys quickly applied pressure to the wound and tried to stop the blood flow. They gave Brent an awkward hug as he gave both of them a pat on the back with his free arm.

"Alright, now get me out of here!"

The pain was immense as Brent tried to move again. "Hold on, Dad. We'll get you out."

"Where did you boys even come from?" "We came in on the chopper."

Brent winced with pain as he looked for the helicopter. "What chopper?"

"It's right there, at the bottom of the falls. It belongs to my mate Robbie. Shit Dad, we have been looking all over for you! We came up the side creek, saw the big slip and how fresh it was, did a loop around and spotted you. Thank God we did that loop."

"Yeah because the last thing I remember is making the cut, then you were here calling out to me." Brent stared in amazement at his two sons; grateful for how quickly they had managed to get into the bush, and for how they were now going to help release him.

Daniel quickly assessed what needed to be done to get Brent free, as Eugene continued to tend to Brent's arm.

"Dad, you made a really deep cut. You were close to getting it off, Dad," sighed Eugene.

Brent, with tears running down his face, nodded as he asked them, "Do you boys know about your mother yet?"

"Yes Dad. Stevo told me," whispered Daniel.

"I still feel it is not true. The happenings of the last 36 hours are a blur. I keep waiting for Janey to shake me and tell me it's not true. I know that is not going to happen, but I still hope and pray this is all a bad dream."

As Eugene injected some pain killer from the well-equipped medical kit into his father's arm, Brent told the boys about what he and Stevo had discovered when they'd arrived back to camp from their hunting trip.

"I feel so guilty. I should never have left your mother alone but this is our paradise – or it was. But it is a broken paradise now. Life will never be the same."

Brent remembered Luke and Jake, and he asked if the boys had seen the two injured men while flying up and over the river. Eugene nodded and explained how they had seen two guys in different places and had dropped down to question them. They smiled as they described leaving them there for the police chopper to pick up as they had only been concerned with finding their father. Brent asked if they were still alive, and Daniel described the seriousness of Jakes condition.

Brent laughed when he heard that Jake was terrified of the eels, and the two boys passed a worried look between each other when their father began to talk about the eels too.

"No, seriously boys! You wouldn't believe the huge ferocious eels up here. It's a long story why, but I had to pull those two boys away from the river to save them from those bloody eels. You two need to be really careful near the water."

Brent continued talking,

"I spoke to both of them and let them know what I thought of them, and about what they had done. But I don't want their deaths on my conscience. As for the mongrel that shot your mother - that is a completely different story. I am going to make him pay with his life when I get free from this rock. He is up on that ridge, probably watching us. If he has any sense in his mongrel body, he will have scarpered as fast as he can before I get free - especially since he has no gun." Brent paused and looked at his two boys. "Now, can you two try to move this boulder? I need to get out of here and get that bastard too."

Daniel glanced at Eugene.

"I think we can, Dad. Hang in there," said Daniel.

Daniel and Eugene wedged themselves behind the rock and with all their strength they managed to roll it forward and off Brent's partially severed arm. Brent sat forward, grateful there was little pain as his numb arm hung limply beside him. He was feeling dizzy and sick from the medicine. He wanted to stand up so the boys helped him to his feet. He was very unstable and teetered dangerously so they forced him to sit by the rock as they bandaged the rest of the arm that had been trapped and continued to apply pressure to stop the bleeding. It was smashed up pretty badly and Brent had lost a lot of blood. There was no way Brent was going to be able to go anywhere other than a hospital, but he was not going to admit it.

"I want you to fly me up onto the top of that ridge and drop me off. The prick who killed your mother is up there - and most likely heading up that ridge. I'm going to kill the bastard."

The boys were a bit stunned at hearing their father's words. He sounded really dangerous.

"If he has any brain cells at all, he will be trying to get into that next catchment." Brent reached out and picked his gun up, but had to steady himself as the movement had him close to passing out again.

Thinking quickly, and seeing the state their father was in, Daniel nodded.

"I will just go check the chopper, okay? Then we will help you get aboard and we will be off."

Brent nodded. Eugene stood beside Brent and helped to prop him up. Eugene stared in confusion at his brother, not understanding. Daniel simply winked in silent reply as he jogged over to the helicopter. Next thing the chopper had lifted off and was flying up out of the river gorge! Brent swore furiously as he realised what had happened. He knew Daniel had tricked him and decided to go after Slade on his own. He yelled out but it was too late; Daniel had gone to finish the job Brent had wanted to do. He hung his head as endless tears

poured down his face.

"Daniel is a policeman and he knows how to handle situations like this - and himself. He will be all right."

He wrapped his arm around Brent's shoulder and did his best to comfort him.

As Eugene embraced his father gently he was wishing desperately that Janey was there with him. Brent winced at Eugene's touch and instantly realised he wouldn't have been able to go very far. Eugene helped Brent to be more comfortable by laying him down on a nice sandy bank near to the base of the falls and away from the slip. He got the first aid kit and started to carefully dress the wounds on Brent's arm. He checked underneath his father's shirt and saw massive bruising up his left side.

"That boulder must have crushed your side and then slid a bit before crushing your arm against the bank, Dad," observed Eugene.

"Yeah, I know it's not good, mate. But I feel better now you boys are here." He winced with pain and looked up towards where Daniel had flown out.

"Any chance for some more of that pain killer son?"

"Ahh Dad, we are so glad we found you," replied Eugene, genuine relief evident in his voice. "We will have to just rest here and wait for Daniel first. Stevo will be here soon with the police and a medic and they will sort you out some stronger meds."

Brent's face instantly lit up at the thought of his best mate; Stevo was flying in.

CHAPTER SIXTY-EIGHT

Daniel knew he could land the chopper on top of the ridge line that divided the two catchments. He had been there before and knew the tops were covered in tussock. He could easily make out the path Slade would have to take to get into the next catchment as it was a dry gully that ran up and off from the main river. Daniel remembered Brent saying that Slade did not have a gun as Brent had destroyed it when he took out Jake earlier down the river. Never the less, an unarmed Slade was still a very large and powerful man. A man who was dangerous and most likely to be carrying another style of weapon. Daniel landed the chopper and pulled his Ruger 308 from behind the seat, slinging the rifle over his shoulder after making sure it was loaded and ready to go. He began working his way down the dry gully he believed Slade was making his way up. The native bush was thick and the vision was poor as Daniel moved down the gully very cautiously; he knew Slade would have heard the chopper and could be waiting for him anywhere.

CHAPTER SIXTY-NINE

Brent watched his son fly the chopper up to the top of the ridge and he felt his anger rise as he wasn't going to be the one to finish Slade off. Brent could not hear anything because of how close they had moved to the thundering falls. He was furious at Daniel for leaving him behind, and Eugene was doing his best to calm him down.

"You aren't strong enough to walk anywhere, Dad. Stevo will be here soon and he will take us up to the top," Eugene reassured his father kindly, hoping desperately that Stevo would be able to talk some sense into Brent. "Look at your arm Dad and just be sensible." "I don't want to be sensible, I want justice! Our paradise has been broken and I want to kill that bastard!" screamed Brent as he pointed to where he had last seen Slade. Brent felt a surge of adrenalin as he realised how close he had come to getting his revenge. He tried to stand up, but the pain in his ribs and the rush of his blood sent him crashing back to the ground. Eugene sighed with desperation as he pointed to Brent's arm that had started to bleed again.

Brent turned slightly so he could sit with his back to the river bank. "Dad, what did you mean about those giant eels?" asked Eugene, trying to distract Brent.

Brent turned his attention to Eugene with wide open eyes and told him briefly about what they had seen at the plane crash site.

"You would have to see the effects on the wildlife to believe it, son." Brent flinched as his damaged ribs sent shooting pain down his left side. "You sure don't want to get in the water if you are bleeding. It makes the eels go into a frenzy and they'll eat anything that moves."

Brent could not bring himself to talk to Eugene about Janey.

"Janey, my Janey," Brent whispered quietly to himself before coughing as he swore out loud, "That guy is going to pay dearly. He doesn't realise who he is dealing with!"

Eugene was shocked at the depth of Brent's despair and anger.

Reality struck that his mother had died.

Brent felt the anger turn to fear, as he realised the danger Daniel was facing.

"If anything happens to Daniel I'll never forgive myself," he whispered as a lone tear trailed down his dusty cheek. Brent saw that Eugene was also struggling to come to terms with everything and he reached out and placed a hand on his son's shoulder.

"Sorry son, are you ok?" Eugene nodded meekly.

"Don't worry about me, Dad. It is you who is in bad shape."

Brent slumped down as the worry for his eldest son threatened to consume him. Brent knew first-hand how Slade was a very dangerous person and that he would make the most of any opportunity Daniel gave him. He hoped Daniel would not try and take Slade alive but, at the same time, he did not want Daniel getting into a situation where he could be charged with a criminal offence. Brent thought glumly about how desperate he had been to bring revenge on Slade. One of the reasons that he had wanted to do it himself was because he knew he would not be able to carry on after everything was over.

'If I do want to live after all this, it will only be for the kids. Life without Janey isn't worth living and I sure as hell won't be going to any jail. I guess I'll just have to wait and see what happens,' Brent thought miserably.

Eugene could see the grim look on his father's face. "What about you, are you all right, Dad?"

Brent felt for his pocket and the bullet he had saved for himself. "Yeah, I'm ok son."

As he turned the bullet around with his fingers in his pocket, he looked towards his rifle, which Daniel had rested up against the big log - he wanted to be familiar with where it was in case he needed it.

"Are you sure, Dad? You look really pale."

Brent reached out and touched Eugene's hand; patting it gently, "Yeah, I'm as good as I can be in this situation. How about you, son? Are you sure you are okay?" "I'm coping, Dad."

"I know it is hard mate. I guess we'll talk more when this is all over. I thought you said Stevo was coming."

"He is Dad. He should be here by now."

Brent closed his eyes as the physical pain and emptiness of his heart continued to hit him in waves.

CHAPTER SEVENTY

Daniel had made his way down the dry gully which ran out just above the falls. It was steep with an old dry creek bed covered with big, mossy, boulders and the odd puddle of water in the once substantial pools. The bush was quite thick on the sides and Daniel knew how careful he had to be as he moved forward. He was taking a few steps and then looking and listening all around him as he made his way down to about 200 metres above the falls. He was starting to feel really concerned as he was sure he should have caught sight of Slade if he had come this way. There was absolutely no sign; no boot marks or anything that had shown him Slade was ahead of him.

A twig snapped to the right of Daniel, catching his full attention. He turned and was immediately confronted by Slade rushing at him in full force. Slade had been hiding under a bank with water ferns hanging out over it; it had been the perfect hiding place. When Daniel moved past, Slade had rushed out and knocked him over. Daniel was frightened so badly that he flew sideways and lost his grip on the rifle which crashed haphazardly onto the dry creek bed. Daniel scrambled around trying to grab it but Slade was too quick, and pounced on top of him as quickly as a cat. Daniel, being trained at combat, threw Slade off easily but Slade was not put off. He charged again at Daniel, and they fought like savages all the way down the dry creek bed to where the creek met the river just above the falls.

Slade thought, 'If I can kill this guy I have a real chance of getting into the next catchment and away free.' Daniel knew that he was in deep trouble as Slade was an experienced fighter and was physically a lot stronger. He was doing everything he could to contain Slade, but Slade knew how to fight really dirty. Daniel noticed that Slade had a knife sheath attached to his belt but could see that it was empty as it must have come out when they were fighting further up the gully.

CHAPTER SEVENTY-ONE

At the bottom of the waterfall, Brent and Eugene were straining to catch a glimpse of the top of the falls to see if they could see either Daniel or Slade. The spray from the falls was making it hard for them to see and they were feeling very apprehensive as they really had no idea what was happening or where either of the two men were. They were suddenly confronted by a loud mechanical noise coming from behind them, and they turned to see a large police helicopter hovering above the riverbank. They watched intently as it landed skillfully on the sand and Stevo jumped out, followed by a fully uniformed policeman.

"Mate, am I glad to see you," Stevo called to Brent as he ran over at full speed.

"Stevo!" called Brent, lifting his right hand to wave as the tears fell freely as he choked up with emotion at seeing his oldest and best friend. Stevo ran up to him and hugged him tightly, not noticing Brent's injuries through the excitement and relief of finding Brent.

"It'll be ok, we'll get through this," Stevo reassured Brent kindly. Eugene interrupted gently.

"Careful, Stevo. Dad is quite badly injured."

"Watch out mate," sobbed Brent. "I'm pretty beaten up."

His worry returned as he saw the severity of Brent's arm and ribs. "Shit, what happened to your arm?" asked Stevo.

"Survival!!" replied Brent. "Daniel is up on top with the murderer. Can you see him?"

"I had wondered where his chopper was, no can't see anything up there," interjected Stevo. "We stopped at the Bullring and have Janey on board. I knew you would want to have her with you when we fly out of here."

Brent looked up at Stevo with an amazing sense of gratitude; his best mate knew him so well.

"Thank you, Stevo. You are a real mate," Brent whispered with fresh tears forming in the corners of his eyes.

Stevo hugged him again, but gently, and they grasped each other for comfort. They both knew things would never be the same after everything they had been through.

Brent turned to Stevo.

"We've got to fly up there somehow and get that bastard."

CHAPTER SEVENTY-TWO

aniel and Slade each had a firm grip on the other's throat. They rolled and tumbled their way down the dry creek. They stumbled over a drop in the creek which threw them apart as they landed with a thump. They both jumped quickly to their feet and stood about 2 metres apart; staring at each other with contempt.

Daniel growled,

"I'm going to kill you, you prick, for killing my mother!"

Blood was leaking from his mouth and he had a nasty gash down his right cheek.

Slade was bleeding from his right ankle, and Daniel noticed he seemed to be having a bit of trouble swinging one of his arms properly.

Slade grinned wickedly at Daniel.

"The stroppy cow shot me!" Slade pointed at the wound on his shoulder from where Janey had shot him; it was bleeding badly from the struggle with Daniel.

"That stroppy cow was my mother!" Daniel screamed as he lunged at Slade, knocking him backwards. He had never known deep hatred like what he felt now as they punched each other furiously.

Slade grabbed Daniel as his right fist was coming to land a big punch. The blow landed on the side of Slade's face but Slade pulled him off balance and Daniel landed smack down on his back in the dry creek. As Slade jumped on top of him, Daniel lifted his legs and catapulted Slade backwards and down the creek to where it met the main river right on top of the falls. Daniel rushed down and jumped on top of Slade, struggling to punch him as hard as he could.

Desperately, Slade grabbed Daniel by the throat and rolled him over, somehow managing to get on top of him, jamming his shoulder hard against a boulder. Slade was pinning Daniel to a rock in the bottom of the creek. He pushed at Daniel's face, which was facing to the left at a very unnatural angle, and held him down with all his weight. Daniel's left arm was poking out awkwardly in front of him. He was struggling to get leverage to throw Slade off.

Something caught his eye as it moved within the moss underneath a rock to his left. He couldn't believe what it was; the largest spider he had ever seen in his life. It was looking furious too as it had been disturbed by the boys brawl, and it appeared to have taken refuge in the moss. If Slade had not been on top of him, Daniel would have certainly leapt backwards and away from the oversized arachnid.

His mind raced as he felt Slade trying desperately to crush his skull into the rock below. Daniel looked up towards Slade where he could see the front of Slade's shirt hanging half open after the some of the buttons had been ripped off earlier.

Without thinking, Daniel grabbed the spider and flicked it into the front of Slade's shirt. Daniel felt the pressure come off his face immediately as Slade looked inside his shirt to see what had been thrown inside.

"What the hell was that?" Slade glanced at what he had presumed was a piece of dirt and moss. The large dark mass began to move angrily. when he saw the spider Slade leaped up and shrieked. The spider laid oversized fangs deeply into the skin on his chest. Slade began thrashing at his chest through his shirt, staggering backwards out of the creek and into the river. The spider was fighting for his life within the shirt as Slade tried to kill it. Daniel couldn't believe his luck and as he followed Slade, he could see that he was staggering to the precipice right on top of the falls. Daniel smiled slyly as he grabbed at a nearby piece of solid driftwood and moved forward towards a struggling Slade.

CHAPTER SEVENTY-THREE

Slade had always harnessed a deep hatred for spiders. His phobia was temporarily consuming him as he fought to get the spider out of his shirt. This caused him to momentarily forget about the fight with Daniel. He suddenly looked up to see Daniel moving forward with a large lump of wood in his hand. Slade desperately grabbed at the spider through his shirt, but the 8 legged creature was much quicker and shot up out of his shirt and landed on his face. Slade was so frightened he took yet another step backwards, blinded by the spider. The falls were roaring and the current of the river was very strong below where they stood.

Slade grabbed at his face with both hands. Daniel had side stepped to the right.

Daniel scoffed as he realised how a grown man's fear of spiders may mean Daniel didn't have to do anything further to cause the young murderer's death.

'One more step and he's over,' he laughed to himself.

The spider laid a second bite into an almost hysterical Slade's nose. Daniel had followed Slade right out onto the shelf of rock but had kept a safe distance. Slade, with his back to the falls, stared straight at Daniel and hissed,

"I'll kill you for this."

Slade tore the spider from his face and threw its body onto the rock in front of him. It was still well and truly alive much to Slade's dismay. It began crawling towards Slade's boot. In an effort to get away from it Slade stepped backwards at the same time as Daniel took a step closer. Daniel was ready to bash him with the piece of wood if he tried to come forward.

Daniel laughed aloud when he saw where Slade was standing - and that there was no more rock left behind him.

Slade's eyes looked as if they were about to pop out of his head. He realised he was going to fall. He knew there was nothing he could do to prevent falling. He used the leg that was still on the rock to push out as far as he could to hopefully miss the rocks below when he landed. It appeared to Daniel that Slade balanced in mid-air for a moment before disappearing completely out of Daniel's sight and right down over the falls. Daniel rushed to the edge of the rock ledge, just in time to see Slade hit the water of the big pool below through the mist and spray.

CHAPTER SEVENTY-FOUR

At the bottom of the falls, a loud and piercing scream filled the air causing Brent, Eugene, Stevo, the policeman, and the pilot to immediately turn their attention to the top of the falls. They all watched in disbelief at what was happening. Someone had fallen over the waterfall and they watched in unison as he hit the water at an immense speed. Daniel could see the group below and waved down to them. Brent looked up to the top of the waterfall and breathed a huge sigh of relief as he realised it was Daniel standing at the top – and he was not the one who had fallen over. He could tell the way Daniel waved anywhere; it had always been exactly the same as Janey's wave. She had always motioned her hand from side to side in a very unique way whenever she waved at anyone, one of the little things that Brent had always loved about her.

Brent was overcome with emotion when he realised his eldest son was safe from Slade. He tried again to get onto his feet but the lack of food, the blood loss, and the stress of everything had well and truly taken its toll. He had been running purely on adrenalin. The medic had already given him some electrolytes with glucose and had been about to put him in the chopper for some intravenous fluids when they had heard the scream. He felt his head rush with dizziness and he stumbled on his feet. Brent was woozy and Eugene immediately helped him to lean back against the bank to regain his strength. The medic was right there checking on him and making sure he was ok. It seemed as if the electrolytes were starting to take effect and restore some of his energy levels. Brent placed his hand in his pocket again; to make sure his bullet was still there. He turned it around with his fingers, contemplating whether or not he would still use it. He felt in his heart that he could not do it; he could not be so selfish as to leave his kids alone. They would need him more than ever now that Janey had gone.

It might stop his own suffering, but he knew he needed to be strong for his kids and his good friends who were also suffering. Brent knew that if anything was to happen to him, his friends and family would suffer even more – and it would be all Brent's own doing. He watched the policeman and Stevo as they made their way over to the pool at the bottom of the pools. He felt a sense of urgency to follow them. He wanted to be at the edge of the pool for when Slade surfaced; Brent was going to make sure that it was the end for Slade.

CHAPTER SEVENTY-FIVE

Slade hit the water feet first and sank 10 feet down into the dark, churning water before he was able to swim his way back up. As he surfaced, he began to tread water while looking around and thinking how lucky he was that he hadn't hit a single rock. Thinking fast, he decided to swim for the far bank as he could see a helicopter surrounded by people on the sand in front of the falls; and he didn't want to go anywhere near them. He reached to hold onto his shoulder which was bleeding badly where Janey had shot him. He refused to take any responsibility and instead cursed her and the others.

"If they had never been in that bloody Bullring camp, none of this would have happened and my brothers and I could be out hunting and enjoying the fucking bush!"

He began to swim in the direction of the scrub on the far bank when he felt something hit his body. He looked down into the water, scanning the depths but could not see anything. He thought he was going mad when he got hit a second time, but then he saw a large and slimy tail glide eerily out of the water before submerging again. Slade panicked as he already knew the size of the eels in Green River Country after seeing some of the big ones further down the river. He started swimming as fast as he could, but there were more and more eels turning up every second. One latched onto his left leg, pulling Slade right down into the water. He kicked so hard with both feet that as he propelled himself away from the eel, he almost cleared the water. As he came back down, he could see that the water was alive with eel monsters. The nearest bank was where the people were. He changed direction and began swimming towards them as fast as he could while screaming at them for help. He was 20 metres out from the bank where they stood, and the eels were all over him. He was fighting them off the best he could but there were too many - and they were slowly overpowering him. The more he bled, the more they began to go into their feverish feeding frenzy. He reached for his knife but found only an empty sheath and he filled the air with yet another blood curdling scream.

Brent had never heard a scream like it; sheer panic and terror. Everybody on the edge was standing dumbstruck on the bank, unable to do anything other than stare in amazement.

The policeman and Eugene raced to the water's edge and tried desperately to reach Slade. They held out a big stick for him to grab onto while Slade thrashed at the water as he tried to reach the stick that would pull him to safety.

Brent had regained enough strength to move slowly over to stand beside Stevo at the edge of the pool. He felt better as he watched Slade swimming towards the edge of the pool, Brent knew it would be his chance for revenge soon. Stevo, glanced at Brent standing beside him.

"If the prick makes it to the edge, I'll finish him off for you." Brent looked at Stevo with a determined look in his eye. "You keep the cop distracted and I'll do it myself."

He felt for his knife, wrapping his hand around the antler handle. Brent and Stevo moved over to where Slade was approaching the edge. Eugene and the policeman took no notice of them as they were too busy concentrating on Slade and the eels.

"If he makes it to shore, you rush over and try to help the cop. Knock him over and I'll stick the bastard then push him back into the water for the eels," Brent spoke with a wry smile on his face. "I want to watch him bleed out!"

The eels were hanging off both of Slade's arms and were slowly pulling him under. The river had turned red from the blood of Slade's shoulder and the many nips across his body from the eels. The water was frothing with movement and his head was bobbing up and down. He disappeared for a few moments before coming back up gasping for air. The policeman yelled at Slade to grab hold of the stick but as he reached out the hand of his non injured arm, an eel lunged out of the water and bit off Slade's hand effortlessly before sinking back down into the water. Eugene and the policeman took a small step back from the water's edge. They had done all they could to try and save Slade, and the sheer terror on Slade's face was a sight they would never forget. Slade was looking straight at them. There was nothing more that could be done to save him. Slade disappeared down into the deep darkness of the big pool for about 30 seconds. He suddenly reappeared, giving everybody a fright as his head broke the water. The eels were eating him alive; chunks of flesh were missing off the left side of his face. Sickened by what they were witnessing, unable to move or do anything the group just stood in stunned silence. The policeman rushed further around the edge of the pool, but all he could see was pinky-red, frothy water, and an occasional eel slithering towards the surface. Slade had been taken underwater again by the eels, and he was not resurfacing.

"Oh my God, that is the most awful thing I have ever experienced," complained the pilot.

"I feel like vomiting, even though he was the man who killed my mother," Eugene admitted as he ran his hands awkwardly through his hair.

Brent and Stevo turned to each other and shared a look that said simply: he got his just desserts. Brent felt slightly cheated by the eels, but knowing that Janey's death had been avenged filled him with a sense of calm. Brent could see how affected Eugene was by what he had seen, and he gave him a big hug.

The policeman returned to the group and with a grim look on his face he began to make plans.

"We've got to get you some medical help, Brent." Brent just nodded.

"What about the other two boys? Did you see them on your way up? Have you picked them up?"

"Yes, we spotted them when we were coming up the river, don't you worry about them. The rescue chopper crew will have taken them out by now. They were in pretty bad shape, but I think they will live." "Yeah, well I let them live because they said it was this guy who killed Janey and raped Sue. The girls had said the same thing - otherwise those two would be dead by now," growled Brent.

"Ok, Brent. You seem to be in a bad way yourself after all that *self-defence*. Let's get you out of here to where we can help you; after all, hunting to *protect* those you love can be mighty exhausting ..." The policeman spoke with a wry look on his face.

Eugene wrapped an arm around Brent's shoulders and told him everything would be ok as he helped him to walk towards the chopper. Brent felt his heart drop as he realised from the cops twisted warning that he may get into trouble for hurting those other two young men. He briefly wished he had chosen to feed them to the eels after all. He looked again to where his rifle was lying against the log; he always knew where his rifle was in the bush. Noticing what he was looking at Stevo caught up and wrapped himself around the other

side of Brent to help steady him.

"Don't worry about a thing, Brent. We are all safe now and you need to look after Daniel and Eugene. We'll also get Big Red out for you; Sue will hate me doing it but I can help if the chopper drops me off on the way down the river."

The policeman overheard Stevo and interjected,

"No way, we'll get another chopper to drop a policeman in to where the horse is tethered down the river. We will get a whole crew into the Bullring and they will tidy up, grab the horses and the dogs, and then ride the rest of the way out. Stevo, you need to get medical help, too."

Brent stopped for a break and sat on a log to rest as he couldn't walk the whole way back to the chopper in one go.

Stevo moved Eugene out of Brent's earshot.

"Can you please drop into the Bullring and pick up our trophy stag heads for him and me, too?"

"I am sure that will be fine. I will ask Daniel and we will sort that out."

"Maybe not in the near future, but one day Brent will be pleased you got them for us," Stevo assured Eugene.

Brent had regained a little energy and continued to move towards the chopper. He was feeling really weak and sick but was determined to get to the chopper to be with Janey. Stevo was walking at his side, discussing their plans.

"We'll fly to the top of the falls to get Daniel and then take him back to his chopper. He and Eugene will fly out together, and then we'll all meet up at the hospital."

"Thanks mate couldn't have done this without you," Brent smiled gratefully at his friend. Brent turned and looked back at the top of the falls to where Daniel had been standing; but he was no longer there. The warm afternoon sun was shining through the mist from the water going over the falls, and Brent noticed a bunch of wild flowers growing out of the side of the falls. They were waving sideways in the breeze created by the momentum of the water. Brent watched them and walked towards them slightly, entranced by their beauty. He cried out to Stevo, "That's Janey waving to me! Look the flowers are waving, the same way she always waved!" Brent felt a deep desire to be with her in that very moment and he felt again for the bullet in his pocket.

Eugene and Stevo looked to where Brent was staring and smiled when they too saw the wild flowers waving back at them. Stevo, Sue, and Janey and Brent's children were the only ones Brent had ever told about the magic of the wildflowers and what had happened when they had lost their little girl. Stevo stepped forward and put a hand on Brent's good shoulder.

"We need you mate."

Stevo had noticed Brent fumbling in his pocket and knew he would have one bullet in there as a good hunter always made sure he didn't run out of bullets. He knew Brent so well, that he also knew how deeply he would desire to be with Janey.

"Come on mate. Be strong. You are at rock bottom now. Janey would want you to be strong for your children."

Stevo turned to Eugene and whispered quietly,

"You boys will need to take really good care of your father over the next little while." Eugene nodded and wrapped an arm around Brent and told his father that he loved him.

Moments later, Daniel's chopper landed beside them and Daniel leaped out and ran over. He looked a real mess, beaten and covered in blood; but he was alive. No one spoke a word; they all just wrapped their arms around one another and pointed to the wildflowers waving prettily on the falls. A lone tear slowly rolled its way down each man's cheek.

EPILOGUE

After getting to the hospital for medical care from the waterfall, the afternoon had been long for Stevo. Roger has had a brain scan and Sue has a fractured vertebrae in her neck. She is under heavy sedation. Stevo always knew Sue was fragile in a lot of ways. Brent's arm was just ugly. He had nearly cut it right off. Dirt had rolled into the wound from the bank behind. Stevo had to look away as the doctors worked on it. Cut tendons and muscles were on lots of angles that they were not meant to be. He was also under sedation. Sue and Roger were in a ward together because of the circumstances. Heather was comfortable by their sides.

Feeling overwhelmed, Stevo just needed some fresh air.

He went to see Heather and told her he is going for some fresh air. As he's walking down the corridor to go outside, he sees there are so many people. Stevo's not in a good frame of mind. He's never felt so angry, he felt he could kill those boys right now. His chest starts heaving, tears well up and his stomach is churning. People are trying to talk to him, but he felt desperation to get outside. He made it out the big doors at the front of the hospital and got to the nearest garden because he thought he was going to be sick. As he leaned over the garden, he felt calmer, and the sick feeling dissipated. Stevo didn't want to feel sick. He had made plans to go back to get the horses and gear sorted with the police and they had some station staff to come ride the horses out the next morning.

He was still fighting his anger, he felt cheated. He had no closure; he would have loved to have had his chance to inflict some pain on the mongrels who killed Janey, hurt and raped Sue and hurt Roger.

He started breathing hard and felt sick again. He leant over the garden until the feeling passed.

Stevo thinks, as it is daylight saving there will be daylight for a few hours yet. That is enough time to go to Brent's place and get some wild flowers to take into Bullring tomorrow. He would take them to the spot where Janey died.

He spun on his heel and walked back down the long corridor to where Heather was with Sue and Roger.

Heather gave him a grim smile. Stevo leaned over towards Heather and asked if she has heard anything about Brent as he went into surgery immediately when they arrived. "No," says Heather. "They think it will take hours to try to fix his arm."

Stevo says to Heather, "I'm going back to the farm. I'll be back tonight. I'm going to get some wild flowers for Janey to take tomorrow." Heather bursts into tears. Stevo did too as he kneels holding Heather's hand.

After a moment or two Heather nods to Stevo. His eyes had turned red with tears. Heather leans forward and gives him a hug. "Yes, that's a great idea, Stevo. Be careful, you are so tired already."

"I'll be good. All Janey's children are coming tonight, and ours and yours. I'll be back."

Daniel had gone and got Stevo's truck for him in case he needed it. It was parked outside.

The journey back to the farm was long. Stevo knew he was overtired, and he wanted to make it before it got dark as he wanted to see the wild flowers in the daylight and check the farm for Brent as he knew he would ask.

As he drove into the farm his well trained eye could see that everything looked ok. He pulled up by Brent's cowshed and got a 20 litre bucket. He drove down to the creek where the flowers are, at the back of Brent's farm. He had half an hour before it would get dark.

He could not wait to see the wild flowers. It was as if something was telling him to get there quick and get them to Janey. He pulled up and walked over to the wild flowers. He is just astonished looking around at the flower patch and all the flowers Janey loved so much. The pinks, crimson and light yellows had all wilted but some had one or two petals still alive. The big Rosenfree rose had wilted down it's left side.

Stevo went down on one knee, tears running down his face. 'This means Brent is going to lose his arm!' he thought as he pounded the ground.

Quickly he got himself together. He picked some wild flowers that Janey loved and were still a bit alive, as many as he could get, and some roses off Rosenfree rose. The bucket was full. He had put water in the bucket and said to the wild flowers, "Please don't die, Janey needs you."

Quickly thinking about how he is going to carry them on the chopper, he gets a big wool bag from the shed and puts it around the bucket. He puts it carefully on the passenger side in his truck.

He stops off at his place for a quick coffee or two before he hits the road back to the hospital. He feels like something has reenergised him.

He's thinking, these wild flowers are just unbelievable. They are definitely magic.

He's feeling desperate to get them to Janey's place of death. He's feeling a real sense of urgency.

Arriving back at the hospital at 6am, Stevo knows it will be an hour before daylight when the chopper will leave.

He goes to see how everyone is. Heather spots him coming, "You've been so long, Stevo. Everybody was worried about you."

"I'm sorry, Heather. I know I missed meeting the kids and all. It's just such a long way."

"I know, I told them what you were doing."

Heather and Stevo move over to where Sue is. Stevo holds her hand and gives her a kiss. She is still sedated.

"How are Brent and Roger, Heather?" he asks.

"Roger good, Brent not so good. They think he will lose his arm." Stevo feels sick again and his chest start to heave. He feels like he wants to kill those boys again. Heather says, "Are you all right, Stevo?"

Stevo looks away. Heather says to him, "You're not all right, are you?" and puts her arms around him.

"Just seeing Sue lying there and Brent losing his arm just got to me. I'm good."

Stevo's looking at his watch. "I've got to go, Heather. The chopper will be leaving very soon. See you later."

And with that Stevo was gone.

He drove down to the chopper pad. Everybody was getting ready to go. Stevo pulled up and got his bucket of flowers with the wool pack around them.

He walked over and hopped onto the chopper. Nobody said a word. Everyone knew what had gone down and Stevo didn't want to look or even sit close to anybody.

All he cared about was getting these flowers to Janey. He felt like he had had a calling to do this, but he wanted to and would have done it anyway.

As the chopper lands outside Bullring Stevo hops out, holding the bucket inside the wool pack so that nobody could see the contents. After clearing the rotor blades, he stands erect. His 6 foot 4, 110kgs frame straightens up. His blonde hair is blowing in the wind.

He takes a really deep breath. He doesn't trust himself; he could really break down here. As he looks up at Bullring, camp he can see a person standing there. He takes a really hard look and sees it is Possum Jack. Stevo walks up to camp as Possum comes down to greet him. They come close; sadness is all over Possum's face. He says, "The police told me what happened, Stevo. You don't have to say anything."

Stevo puts his hand on Possum's shoulder. "Thanks, mate. Let's go and say a prayer for Janey."

Possum was looking at what Stevo was carrying as they walked up and into the camp. Stevo walked to where Janey had died and knelt down. So did Possum Jack. Stevo took the flowers out of the woolpack and put them by Janey's death place.

Possum looks at the flowers. Stevo is thinking 'Possum doesn't think they are the best flowers on the planet.'

He says to Possum, "They may not look the best flowers you have ever seen, Possum, but I assure you they are."

Possum says, "I'm sure they are. They are lovely, I love all flowers, Stevo."

Stevo takes some out and places them on the ground around the spot. He puts his hand on Possum's shoulder and says to Possum, "Shall we say a prayer?"

Possum nods and says, "I want to start. Stevo, is that all right?" "Please do," says Stevo.

Possum's prayer was the most beautiful thing Stevo had ever heard, and tears were flowing from both men. When he was finished, they just sat there for ages.

Possum says, "Would you like to say something, Stevo?"

Stevo says, "Nah, you pretty well covered it, Possum, but I would like some time here on my own."

Possum put his hand on Stevo's shoulder and went out by the river and up to the horse paddock where Orphy was.

Stevo started talking to Janey, telling her how Brent was and how they thought he may lose his arm. He was having really terrible thoughts about how he wants to kill the two boys who are left and that he hates them for ruining our lives and our Paradise, for raping Sue and for killing Janey. He told her how Sue, Roger and Heather were and about all the children constantly breaking down. He was feeling sick again and breathing really hard.

Stevo was just kneeling there looking at the ground for ages, not saying anything, almost feeling a bit of peace. He starts taking all the flowers out and putting them around the spot, telling Janey she is the most loving friend he could ever have dreamt of knowing and having. "You are like a sister to me." As Stevo put the flowers around he noticed a piece of grass on the inside of the clump he had brushed with his arm as he was placing the flowers. He saw it had blood on it. He knew it was Janey's.

He got a bunch of the flowers together that she loved so much, even though they were looking worse for wear. He picked up the leaf of grass with her blood and touched the flowers with it. Instantly Stevo got a feeling in his chest. He thought he was having a heart attack. It wasn't painful, just a rush of warmth. He fell back on his back, still holding the flowers tightly. His eyes were closed. He started seeing angels, beautiful white angels dancing all around and then he had a vision of Janey with her warm loving smile. She was looking down at Stevo.

With his hand that was free he wanted to touch her face. He heard Janey's voice, "Stevo. I will be leaving soon, so glad you got here. I wanted to tell you that your heart will be healed, Brent's arm will be good again, Sue will be fine and lovely Heather and Roger will grow old together. Tell my darling, Brent, I want his heart to be warm again and yours too. I will make this happen. I love you so much, Stevo." And the vision of Janey was gone.

Stevo's eyes opened, his mind felt clear, his body was warm. He sat up almost in a daze. He'd heard a noise; Possum was coming back.

Stevo could not wait to get back to tell Brent and the rest of the crew. He was on cloud 9 just hearing Janey. He felt transformed.

He wanted to keep an eye on Brent's arm because if his vision came true Brent's arm would heal. Only time would tell.

Suddenly all the flowers bloomed the brightest colours they had ever bloomed. Stevo sat there in amazement as Possum Jack walked up and he said, "Those flowers you brought with you are just amazing. They didn't look like that before."

"These are magic flowers, Possum. "I will tell you all about them one day soon when I come to visit."

"I hope it's soon, I can't wait," says Possum, astonished.

The two men sat by Janey's wild flowers watching them as they faded and Stevo knew Janey was gone. Tears rolled down his face.

www.ingramcontent.com/pod-product-compliance
Lightning Source LLC
Chambersburg PA
CBHW062109290726
48975CB00001B/162